CONFESSION

On their wedding night, Charles' heart was a lump in his throat when he saw her nude beauty. Her slender, gently curved body was so lovely it transcended even the beauty of her face and hair. Naked, they kissed, naked they sank to the bed and experienced all of glory. . . .

They lay welded and Marie-Louise, awash with love and fear, whispered, "I wasn't a virgin, darling." She held her breath, heartbeats shaking her body.

"I . . . found out," he said tonelessly. "Is that what you had to tell?"

"That and more, my darling." Charles waited, and she drove herself to continue. "It was as much my fault as his. I was sixteen; he was seventeen."

"Girls marry at sixteen."

A great throb jolted through her. This wasn't going well, not at all. Even so, she plunged on. "There was . . . a baby."

His arms loosened from her. He reared up in bed, swung his feet to the floor. "I'll kill Riel Rivard!"

Bantam Books by Saliee O'Brien
Ask your bookseller for the books you have missed

BAYOU
BLACK IVORY
CAJUN

CAJUN

Saliee O'Brien

BANTAM BOOKS
TORONTO · NEW YORK · LONDON · SYDNEY

CAJUN
A Bantam Book / November 1982

ISBN 0-553-20821-7

Published simultaneously in the United States and Canada

Bantam Books are published by Bantam Books, Inc. Its trademark, consisting of the words "Bantam Books" and the portrayal of a rooster, is Registered in U.S. Patent and Trademark Office and in other countries. Marca Registrada. Bantam Books, Inc., 666 Fifth Avenue, New York, New York 10103.

PRINTED IN THE UNITED STATES OF AMERICA

O 0 9 8 7 6 5 4 3 2 1

In memory of Thurlow Benjamin Weed, my son.

This is a novel. All characters, with the exception of Adolphe Thiers and a fellow patriot, are imaginary as are all events, except for the wars.

Family Tree

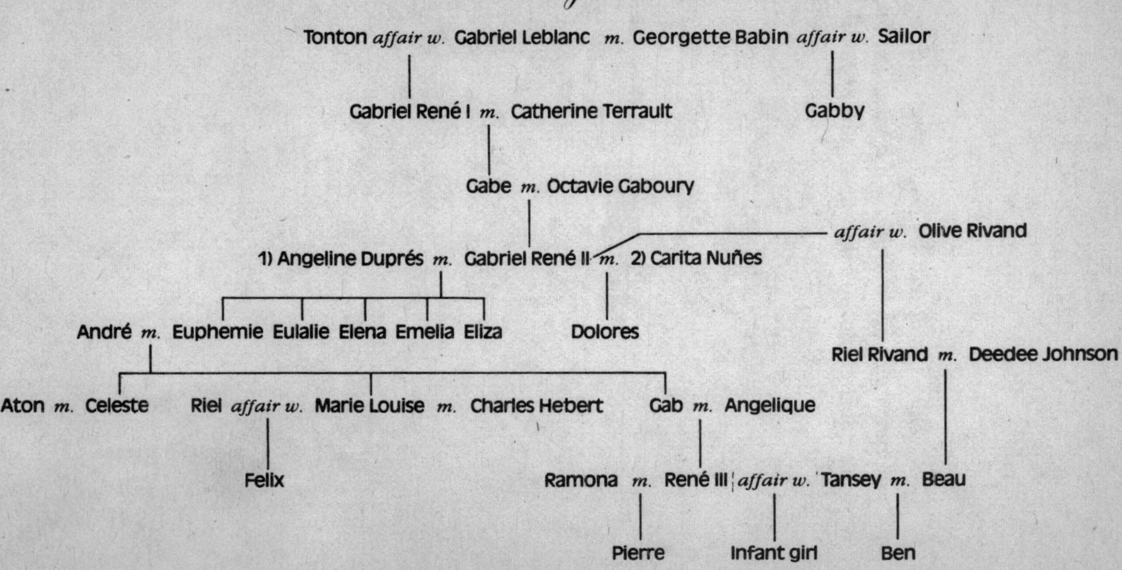
Tonton affair w. Gabriel Leblanc m. Georgette Babin affair w. Sailor
Gabriel René I m. Catherine Terrault
Gabby
Gabe m. Octavie Gaboury
affair w. Olive Rivand
1) Angeline Duprés m. Gabriel René II m. 2) Carita Nuñes
André m. Euphemie Eulalie Elena Emelia Eliza
Dolores
Riel Rivand m. Deedee Johnson
Aton m. Celeste
Riel affair w. Marie Louise m. Charles Hebert
Gab m. Angelique
Felix
Ramona m. René III affair w. Tansey m. Beau
Pierre
Infant girl
Ben

PROLOGUE

1856

Chapter I

She was running. Wild, reckless running. Skirts wrapping around her legs, untwisting, wrapping again. Crashing headlong down the rows of sugar cane, so tall above her. Heart fluttering in her neck, leaping in her throat, great, pulsing leaps, trying to get out. Breath an agony, slicing and cutting into her, a thing to be gulped, a quivering agony to push out again. Behind her, Consuela, her wench, panting and striving to keep up.

There were sounds far off, but she could hear them even while running, even with her gasping, noisy breath filling the world, and even with Consuela's feet running so loudly behind. Above all that, she could hear those others in the distance. Out from St. Martinville sounds came, not so clearly, but tinged with the thin baying of bloodhounds. Posses. Two of them. Both after her, pursuing her, and she had to get away from them. Consuela too, for there was a thing, a great, important thing, to accomplish, and she needed the wench. Her throat was as dry as winter leaves. Fear, terror, panic—they were winter leaves, too.

In spite of the posses and their bloodhounds, she must do this. And when she succeeded, when she was the winner, they would pursue no more but stand back humbly and treat her like the lady she was.

Faster she plunged through endless sugar cane, racing toward the sunset, toward the little bayou at the back of the plantation. She took comfort in the velvet bag of emeralds which made a great, wonderful lump between her breasts, striking her according to the rhythm of her running steps. She'd had to bring them, they were her comfort and joy, and she protected them as they protected her. She leaned her body toward the sunset glow, forcing herself to more speed, cane whipping above her head, striking her back, skirts winding tighter, faster, binding her legs.

"Fastah!" she gasped to Consuela, a step, only a step, behind her. "Fastah . . . you . . . black . . . baggage . . ." She kept running, running, filled with terror.

She heard Consuela moan, a moan loud enough to rise above the sound of their passage, too loud. She heard the gasping words, caught the breathless plea.

"We oughtn't . . . run away . . . Missy! We need . . . to go back. They is still . . . time."

"Hush! Just . . . run!"

"Please . . . Missy . . . go back!"

"Hush . . . oh, hush . . . befoah I . . . strangle you! . . . Fastah!"

She'd never go back, not until she found the emerald dagger which was hers . . . hers . . . the dagger she used on feckless, betraying René. When she found it, then, and not before, she'd go back to the plantation house, because with the dagger she would be in charge again, respected and loved and bowed down to.

Now came thin shouts from behind. She ran faster, despite the winding, unwinding skirts. That was the L'Acadie posse, sent by Old René, led by Hebert men, backed up by the best slave trackers of three plantations. All after her, to lock her and the wench in the master suite and keep her from finding the emerald dagger, ever.

Oh, she knew. Even as she fled through the cane, stricken by fear, overflowing with it, knowing how the dogs would rip her flesh, she was aware. They thought she didn't know anything, but she knew everything, for she had read the journals. The damnable, secret Leblanc journals.

She knew who she was—frightened and running—she knew. She was Carita Leblanc, Mrs. René Leblanc, twenty-four years old and the greatest beauty in all the Louisiana bayou country. She had pale red hair, fiercely blue eyes, chiseled features and skin as white as marble. She had lovely, maddening lips. And her garments were always turquoise blue; she'd never worn anything but turquoise and emeralds.

Yes, she was Carita, whom all men called exquisite and charming, whom all men desired; she was mistress of this vast plantation on which, somewhere, her enemies had hidden her most precious possession, the dagger. But now she was loose, broken out of the master suite, out of the great house, and Consuela was with her, to help or be sorely punished. Carita had to find the dagger before the posses caught up, because otherwise she'd be locked up again. An errant thought struck her; she stopped running in mid-step. Consuela crashed into her.

Carita spun, grabbed the wench by the arms, gave her a vicious shake. She glared at the dark creamy face so like her own, at the shapely breasts moving in gasps as deep as her own.

She stabbed her blue look at Consuela's green, pleading eyes, at the dark blond hair laced with gold, at the features so like her own, though not as finely sculpted. She knifed her look at lips exactly like her own lips, and rage that her daddy had got this wench on a slave burned through her.

"You did it!" Carita screamed. "You hid my daggah!"

"No, Missy. Nevah, Missy!"

"You want it to make people think we're sistahs! Well, we nevah could be! You're only my daddy's git on a black nigra animal! That makes you an animal, do you undahstand?" Carita finished in a scream.

"Please, Missy, don't scream. They hear you, they catch you!"

Carita sucked in her labored breath, held it, listened. The fields were quiet as death. Then, from the L'Acadie direction came a faint shout. At the same time, from the St. Martinville direction rose the baying of hounds, still thin from distance, but a sound that sent the fact of danger and chill to the heart of Carita's bones.

"That's the bad posse, Missy!" whispered Consuela. "With bloodhounds. The kind of posse that hunts runaways for money!"

"I'm not a runaway wench! I escaped people who had no

right to lock me up or to hide my daggah! I'm going back the instant I find it!"

"The posses think of you as a runaway, Missy! Because of what you did with the daggah, because—"

"I know that, you stupid wench! What ails you? Have you lost what little brain you used to have?"

"It just be bettah, Missy, for us to go back now. Even to meet the L'Acadie posse and do what they say. Then we won't be sent to the madhouse, like the bloodhound posse will do!"

She touched Carita's arm to start her moving back in the direction from which they had come, but Carita gave her a stinging slap across the face. "You did steal my daggah, and you hid it, and now you're tryin' to lead me away from it!"

"No, Missy, I sweah!"

"You hid it. Or lost it!" Another slap.

"No, Missy, please, no!"

"You swear you don't know where it is? Swear you didn't hide it? Swear you'll help me find it, no mattah what the posses do, no mattah how many bloodhounds they put on our trail?"

Weeping, tears streaming down her cheeks, Consuela choked out words. "I sweah, Missy! If I knew wheah the daggah was, I'd—I'd find it for you! But I beg you on my knees not to use it!"

"Get up, you black fool! Of course I won't use it, unless I have to. But I won't have to, because when they see I have it back, everything will be like it used to be. I'll be mistress again and everybody in the bayou country will worship me. All I need is the daggah! Without it, I'm in dangah—with it, I'm mistress!"

They gazed into each other's eyes. The world of sugar cane was quiet again. Then sounds of the L'Acadie posse drifted to them, and on its heels the fainter yelping of hounds.

Carita listened deeply. Was the bad posse following Bayou Teche, which passed L'Acadie, or was it heading cross-country? And was the L'Acadie posse coming straight for this spot, or angling to the north? Or would it be to the south? Directions were so deceitful, changing places all the time, and Consuela was too stupid to ask, for she'd never know, being a nigra.

They had to run, go someplace, keep away from both posses. This knowledge swept panic through her, and she gave Consuela another ringing slap, so hard the wench held her hand to her ear, dumb and bewildered.

"Why have you got us just standing here?" Carita hissed. "Why aren't we running? Always, every time things go wrong, it's your fault!"

"We run if you want, Missy. I—it seemed like you wanted to talk, decide what to do. That why we quit running."

Still another slap. Then Carita, instead of breaking into a run, grappled with her own raging mind, delving beneath fear and panic for facts. She sensed that Consuela was right about the intent of the posses—the one from L'Acadie would lock them in the master suite again, and the bad one would put them in the madhouse. And for no reason at all except that someone had stolen her emerald dagger. She sensed, too, that she had only a little time, so very little, to find it and be mistress again so nobody, no matter who, could tell her what to say or how to act or where to be.

Abruptly what she'd meant to do all along—her original plan—flashed into her mind. "The little bayou!" she gasped. "That's where they hid the daggah! They thought I'd nevah dream of going to the very end of L'Acadie to look, but I am! Come on, you nigra fool, don't waste time!"

She went into a plunging run, heard the wench run behind her. At first she was going fast, but when she tried to push on faster, those other feelings began again—her heart going here, going there; the pain of breath; the skirts wrapping faster and tighter; the great, velvet lump of emeralds a third, heavily bumping breast; her own breasts surging to their exquisite limits.

Bolting thus, Carita didn't hear the posses, but she knew they were there, tracking, pursuing, relentless, both of them. Each a danger beyond danger. Again she filled with panic, overflowed with panic, ran harder, on and on. She couldn't abide rough hands catching her, gripping, hurting, holding her prisoner, couldn't live if it happened. Horror spread; her throat went dry again.

With one final burst of speed, she fled for that small, hidden bayou where the dagger had to be, the bayou which would save her, for all she needed to do was show it, just show the dagger to any posse and they would melt away, never to return.

On they ran. They broke out of the cane into a wooded

area. Sunset was fading, but Carita hardly noticed. They'd find the dagger, even in the dark, she and Consuela, for they were in the right and the right always wins.

They reached the head of the bayou. Carita knew how it cut across the boundary line, somehow she knew, because once in the confused past, she'd been here, had seen.

Magnolias, graceful even in this moment of flight and danger, followed the bayou. Farther along, cypress trees, looking like women kneeling in the water, trailed their long moss hair downward. There was timber on each side of the bayou, a lush growth of bush and sapling and vine. She saw the flicker of squirrels, the jerk of their bushy tails, and these things, too, Carita remembered from the past. The tall reeds still grew alongside the banks and now, with the sudden fall of dusk, she heard the croak of frogs and the cry of a night bird.

For the moment there were only swamp sounds, no hint of posses. Feeling less panic, Carita fell into a trot, going away from this spot where the bayou rose, following it as it began to meander, growing wider, curling through fresh water marshes.

Suddenly she turned to the very edge of the bayou, fell to her knees, and began to dig in the soft, damp soil with her fingers. Consuela knelt beside her and dug a spot of her own.

"This is the place," Carita declared. "Near the head of the bayou, past the first magnolias on the way to the first cypresses. They nevah dreamed I'd be able to reason out where they hid it. All we have to do is dig."

"But it's getting dark, Missy. And the posses . . ."

"L'Acadie people can't see us in the dark. And we'll have the daggah before the bloodhounds get heah."

As they dug, finding nothing, the posse sounds grew louder. Carita was no longer terrified. Any moment, and she'd have the dagger. No more running ever again.

Consuela, however, had no such misconception. Her only wish was to save her mistress, to get her back to L'Acadie and safety.

"Missy, let's go back!" she pleaded when darkness enveloped them. "Slip to one side of the L'Acadie posse—they beating back and forth from the sounds—get to youah rooms, be safe!"

"Oh, hush! Or I'll use the daggah on you!"

"You need youah bed, Missy. Youah not strong yet. It ain't been but a month since—"

"Hush! Oh, hush! Where's that bayou?"

"We beside it, Missy. We diggin'." Consuela's voice shook. She didn't know what to do. She was terrified of the hounds, the evil men, knew it would be the end of her Missy if they caught her. The baying of the hounds wound faintly through the trees and up the bayou, entered her blood and shredded her heart so it bled. Her Missy was still digging here, digging there, searching for the dagger that Old René himself must have hidden safely away. Or got rid of. Into her panic speared a way to help her Missy, maybe save her from the bloodhounds.

The baying was stronger. Consuela shook the damp soil off her hands, grasped her mistress's arms, propelled her knee-deep into the bayou water.

Carita, words spitting, pulled back. "Let me go! I was just about to—"

"It's the hounds, Missy. We got to be careful a while, then hunt. You don't want the hounds to get here first."

"This watah will ruin my dress!"

"We may have to swim, Missy."

"Swim! And ruin my velvet bag? Get my emeralds wet?"

"We got to, Missy. The hounds have got ouah scent, and they can follow it if we stay on dirt. But if we walk in watah, they'll lose it! And we can get away and hunt for the daggah!"

Carita, suddenly and inexplicably convinced, let Consuela take the lead. They waded, Consuela moving them swiftly downriver toward the coming hounds, to confuse the hounds. Once when Carita insisted and could not be swayed, they stopped to dig, scooping their fingers into the muddy bed of the bayou, coming up with stones and shells.

On they floundered, the baying now far off, now nearer, as if the posse wasn't being well led. Every frog in the bayou was booming and trilling and tinkling out a chorus.

The runaways swam, skirts wet and strangling their legs. When they surfaced, the bayou was moonstruck in places, black velvet elsewhere, especially where the cypresses knelt. The hounds were closer; the L'Acadie posse was very near.

Again they swam. Carita stroked in desperation, felt her legs hampered by the skirt, felt the weight of the emeralds pulling her downward. She swam in panic in the watery darkness, lost in burning fear, but still she wanted the dagger.

They heard the L'Acadie posse, heard men talk, but voices only, not words. "They just downstream, Missy," Consuela whispered, arm around her sister, only their heads above water. "Let's go with them! Let's keep you safe!"

"I'll nevah be safe without my daggah!" Carita whispered fiercely. "You've spent lots of time along both bayous, the Teche and this one. You know ways to hide, so hide us now!"

Bested, as she always was when her mistress got that hard tone in her voice, driven by a lifetime of angry love and loyalty, Consuela gave in. "Come along with me," she whispered. "Real quiet, Missy."

The wench moved them to a spot where two great cypresses knelt. Leaving her mistress there, Consuela crawled on her knees to the bank where moonlight shimmered on a thicket of reeds. Not touching the bank, she broke off two long reeds, blew through them, one after the other, to see if they were hollow, then, holding them out of the water, she returned to Carita.

Now they heard the L'Acadie posse following the bayou. Consuela glimpsed the yellow eye of a lantern.

She put one of the reeds into Carita's hand. "When they come, Missy, put one end of this in youah mouth, sink youahself undah watah, leaving the othah end above watah. That's the way we got to breathe till they gone."

Chapter II

Bert Simpson kept his hard, red-knuckled hands clamped on his bloodhounds' leads. There were five of them, lean, bloodthirsty brutes, and they were vicious as sin. But he, broad and burly, with tangled light hair and hard slash of mouth, kept them under control as Bawley Grant, thin and dark, with a face like a rat, let them smell the thin blue scarf, over and over.

They yelped as they smelled, and they yapped in a growl, and their tails moved slowly, menacingly. They laid their ears back, brought them erect, laid them back again, and growls and whines came into their throats and they strained at the leads, but Bert kept his fist on them and admired his hounds, some dirt-colored, one or two spotted, white with black.

The other slave hunters laughed at the hounds. Crowder, strong as a bull himself, chortled, "Them hounds act like they the ones that'll git the re-ward when we catch them two!" Bull-faced and cold-eyed, he gave the bellow that was his laugh. "Joke may be on us! We ain't heard 'bout no re-ward. Don't know one'll be offered!"

As if they understood his doubts, the hounds stood on their hind legs and lunged, fighting to get free, to be on the chase for what they'd scented. Their howls and yips made a rise and fall like the beat of music.

Furious, Bert bawled their names, yanked mercilessly on the leads, choking them down. "Boomer!" he roared. "Tenor, Droopy, Stalker, Treer, down! Down, damn ye to hell an' gone!"

When he'd fought them to a sitting, yelping mass quivering with eagerness, he said, "There'll be a re-ward, Crowder, bet on that! Old René Leblanc ain't goin' ter let a woman bearin' his name be put in the madhouse! An' the law, once they find out she's loose, they'll give us a re-ward, we bring in mass killer like her!"

"Yer smarter'n a monkey's ass, Bert," said Crowder. "Workin' that Myrtie-wench like ye done."

Bert grunted, but inside he was grinning, ear to ear. He recalled just this morning out in the wilds with Myrtie, color of chocolate. Young and soft and rounded and all his, best he ever had. He'd put the deal to her, straight out.

"You still tote them grub trays to Crazy Carita and her wench?" he asked.

"Yas, I does."

"Good. And ye like me a heap, don't ye?"

She rolled her eyes, smiled a dimple into the corner of her mouth. She looked plain-out beautiful. "Of course, I likes you, Mastah Bert, awful much!"

"Well, if ye do me a lil' favor, I'll git ye a yaller ring with a red set. An' ye'll be my wench steadier'n ever."

She waited, her luscious red lips parted.

"Here's what ye got to do," he said. "Git a door key to Crazy Carita so she kin unlock the rooms an' run. Don't let her wench see ye do it. Where are the extry keys kept?"

"The housekeepah, she wear 'em on a ring at her belt."

"Pantry keys, sure," Bert said impatiently. "But not bedroom keys!"

Myrtie pondered. "They on a board in the pantry."

"Ye know which one goes to Crazy Carita's room?"

She nodded, eyes wide. "It on a blue ribbon. Why you ax?"

"So's ye kin slip it to her, an' she'll run. An' I kin catch her with my hounds an' git a re-ward. That's how I make my livin', remember."

"Is they a re-ward, Mastah Bert?"

"They will be, when she runs. Ye git the key. Today. An' somethin' she wears, somethin' with her smell on it."

"I don' know whut to git."

"Ye said she ties them scarves on her neck an' sets at the lookin' glass. One of them scarves. Scoop it up when they busy with grub. Hide it in yer clothes."

"Myrtie can't do that!"

"Ye got to, if ye want that ring. An' if ye want me. If ye don't, I'll drop ye hard, never see ye agin."

So Myrtie had tried and succeeded, and when she put the key and the scarf into his hands that same afternoon, saying she had the right key, he gave final orders. "Give her the key an' the split second she runs, git into a pirogue an' come let me know. That way, I'll be first on her trail. Smart plan, ain't it? See to it she runs, then catch her an' collect the re-ward from the one that'll pay most—Old René or the law!"

While Myrtie was doing her part, Bert had called in Bawley and the others—they were his regular posse—and he'd told them the plan and they'd shouted and laughed and pounded him on the back.

"My way," Bert told them, "we'll be first ones with

hounds after her. We're ready an' waitin', and they'll have to make up a posse even at L'Acadie an' other plantations!"

Myrtie brought the word. She was scared, teeth chattering, and Bert had to quiet her before she scuttled back to her pirogue. "Stop that!" he ordered. "Stay back from what goes on. They got their hands full with Crazy Carita on the run."

"And C-Consuela! She run too!"

"Their minds is on catchin' 'em, not on you. So stay quiet like most of the slaves will, and ye won't give yerself away."

"But my smell's on the scarf, too!"

"That don't matter." He yanked the hounds to Myrtie, and they gave tongue and tried to leap upon her, but Bert kicked them away. "No!" he thundered. "This! This's what's got the strong smell!" And they nosed the scarf again, whined at Myrtie but let her go without yelping again, and gathered round the scarf.

"They got the idee now," Bert said. "They smart."

They crossed the Teche in pirogues, the hounds whining, but otherwise quiet, and then they set out afoot for L'Acadie. The hounds would pick up the scent no telling where—wherever Crazy Carita and the wench had run—and they'd go straight for the catch.

The posse men talked as they moved along. "That crazy woman," said rat-faced Bawley, "ain't no woman's heart in her, even before. To smother her baby girl!"

"No good in her at all to stab her husband in the back and kill him!" added Crowder.

"Then to run that dagger up her own innards an' abort herself!" snorted Johnson.

"We ought ter let the dogs rip 'er ter pieces," snarled Bawley. "I vote fer that! Crazy er not, she hadn't ought ter be let live! Not after what she done!"

All four of the posse agreed, as they hurried through the fast-falling dusk, hounds yelping, that Carita Leblanc should be killed by the hounds.

Bert reasoned them out of this reluctantly. "On'y way we git paid," he reminded them, "is if we bring 'er back to St. Martinville alive. An' not all chawed up. Don't fergit we're doin' this on our own—they ain't no re-ward offered yet because the law gave in to Old René an' let him keep 'er at

L'Acadie, an' the law don't know she's loose yet, but they sure to give us a re-ward, we bring 'er in. I lean to the law myse'f; it'd do our reputation good. I say we bring 'er in alive."

The men grumbled, but admitted that Bert was right.

"We don't have to treat 'er like she's no lady," Bert continued. "We kin let 'er know we know she's no good, but we got to pre-sent her to the law in reasonable good shape. Make our de-mand fer doin' the bayou country a favor, catchin' a runaway crazy killer, an' hold out fer a rightful amount."

The others rumbled assent.

"Kin we let 'er be bit up some?" asked Bawley.

Bert paused, then grunted yes. "We got that much extry satisfaction comin' to us, besides the money," he said. "The hounds, too. They de-serve some fun. An' it won't hurt us none as slave-catchers. It'll show we never give up, that we bring in the runner."

"The wench—whut 'bout her?" asked Crowder.

"Let her be chawed some, too. Myrtie said she ran, so she ought ter git some of what 'er mistress gits."

They walked on with long, easy strides. Bert Simpson never used horses unless the runners were already at some distance, or had a boat and were trying to get to New Orleans. He figured to stay afoot like the runners was best, because a slower pace gave the hounds a chance at every inch of ground.

He reckoned the L'Acadie posse would be gathering now. But they didn't have no hounds. Even if they got a lead on Bert, he wasn't worried. He'd offset any lead with his hounds.

"Whut if we have to kill 'er to git 'er?" Bawley asked suddenly. "Whut'll the law do if we ask fer a re-ward fer catchin' a dead murderess?"

Bert laughed. "Hell, that's right! We'll still git the reward. Whut was I thinkin' of before? She's a mass killer an' the bayous is better off with her dead! So let the hounds have their fun fer once!"

He halted, held the scarf while the hounds nosed and whined, then strained at their leads, slavering. The posse started on again, every man as alert as every hound.

"I think," Bert told them, "they've run for the little bayou at the back of L'Acadie. I bin thinkin' an' figger now we'll go up-bayou, ketch them mebbe halfway as they run down-bayou. The hounds'll git their scent on the air, an' we'll know I'm right."

"Won't the Leblancs go fer the bayou?" asked Crowder.

"They'll beat back and forth across the fields on their way to the bayou."

"I don't see why we oughtn't to make straight fer L'Acadie, let the hounds pick up the scent," grumbled Bawley.

"Then we'd lead the other posse to the runners," snapped Bert. "An' at the very least, they'd be a fight over which posse gits control. My way is roundabout, but it'll fool the Leblancs, mix'em all up when they hear the dawgs."

The men laughed at that, chortled. And they hustled along behind the whining, snuffling, yelping bloodhounds. Once or twice the hounds bayed, then moved on, noses to the ground, tails slashing.

Ramsey, the overseer, reported to Old René the instant his wife told him that Carita and her wench had run. Old René and Hippolyte, his body-servant, exchanged despairing glances, and then the ancient white man rapped out orders as swiftly as if he were decades younger.

"Send across to Rob Hebert," he said. "Ask him to head up a posse and to bring Jason, among other trusties. And send up-bayou and ask Horace Hebert to bring Gill—he's visiting—and his trusty. You stay here and keep the blacks under control."

"What about dogs, sir?"

"I'd not want hounds after Carita, even if we could get them. Her state is bad enough without that. When the posse leaves, keep the slaves occupied, ward off hysteria. Keep close watch on them until Carita is back."

"Understood, sir," Ramsey said, and was gone.

The posse was soon ready. All the men, even the trusties, were mounted. Rob Hebert looked them over quickly before he gave the word to start. "I wish we had our own pack of dogs," he said. "They'd scare Carita, make her worse, but we could overtake her faster and bring her home where she belongs."

"Let's hope we find her before Bert Simpson gets on it with his hounds," Horace Hebert said.

"How would he find out?" Rob asked. "None of the

people at L'Acadie or at our places would tell. I say we beat the fields between here and the little bayou, then follow it south."

"Carita may run hither and yon," suggested Horace, "and not even think of the bayou."

"If she does reach it," Rob said, "she may try to follow it, thinking she'll get to New Orleans."

"Impossible!" ejaculated Horace.

"She has her emeralds," reminded Rob. "Mrs. Ramsey says they're gone. She could pay for a boat. I favor my plan—do some beating between here and the bayou, then ride for the stream and follow it south."

Agreed on this, they moved out, away from the house, past the Quarters and on. They were a party of eight, three white and five black, bound on a mission of mercy. They criss-crossed the fields, calling out Carita's name, calling Consuela, pleading with them to show themselves. And hoped the fugitives were not so far ahead that voices would be only a dim shout.

Sitting in the bayou, Consuela heard the L'Acadie posse call her name, recognized the hearty shout of Master Rob, that good and kind gentleman considered an enemy now by her mistress.

"Missy," she pleaded, "let me answah! L'Acadie folks, Heberts, they all good folks. Please, Missy, we need to go back before the hounds—" She stopped, trembling. She heard the steady, far-off voices of hounds winding through night, through frog-song and lap of water. She felt terror.

"Please, Missy, please!"

"No!" hissed Carita. "Nevah!"

"The L'Acadie posse's just up-bayou, Missy. If we stay hid from them, then the hounds'll be here latah, and we'll be in awful dangah then!"

"I'm not going back till I find my daggah!"

A shiver fled down the nape of Consuela's neck. She had to do what Missy said. Had to stay with her, hide her, protect her, while her Missy tried forever to find that dagger which was not to be found.

Now the posse was only yards away. The horses' hooves snapped undergrowth; one horse whinnied.

Quickly, Consuela put the end of one reed into Missy's mouth, one end of the other reed into her own mouth. "Remembah, breathe through the reed," she whispered, as she gently pushed Missy's head below water, then herself sat on the bayou bed so that the top ends of their reeds stood above water. She was glad that in the darkness the posse couldn't see their loosened hair floating on the surface, yet she was sorry they could not.

Carita, excited by this game of hiding, felt wildly triumphant as she breathed through the reed, the sound of water stroking her ears. Now she heard the voices of men, heard the noises of horses walking, all sounds muted by the water. Glorying in fooling them, she heard the sounds grow loud, then gradually diminish and fade. And then, they were gone.

Consuela pulled Carita to the surface. Water ran off their hair and down their faces, making whispery sounds as it entered the water of the bayou. Carita needed to cough, but she wouldn't. They might hear and come back. She took the reed out of her mouth, held it, drew a quivering breath.

"Missy," Consuela whispered, "let's go back to the house. Let's be safe. If we run fast, we can get theah befoah the hounds come! And if we're in the house, that bad posse can't touch us, because we're not running, we're at home wheah we belong!"

But Carita insisted on staying where they were, and Consuela knew that her mistress was right. Because now came the tramp of boots and the yelp of dogs headed up-bayou, apparently not meeting the mounted posse. Closer they tramped. Even closer. Carita's heart stood on edge, Consuela's breath stopped and she had to work to get it back. This was the danger, the peril—these men with dogs.

She glimpsed the party by moonlight as they rounded the bend. "Duck!" she whispered, and caught the faint sound of Missy's head going under as she herself ducked, holding onto her reed.

The baying stopped, and Consuela knew the dogs had found no scent, for they hadn't reached the spot where she and Missy had entered the bayou. They yelped, the wavering sound muffled by the water covering and filling her ears. She knew the dogs were snuffling the bank and the men would be arguing whether the runners went up-bayou or down-bayou.

The sounds lessened, faded, but still the mistress and her wench remained submerged, hearts bursting with fear. Carita was getting sick of this. It wasn't fun any more. She didn't like having dogs wanting to tear her to bits. Terror filled her bones the way water filled her ears, and she began to have trouble breathing through the reed, but she dared not lift her head, not yet.

The men and dogs came back, passed again, and the women could hear voices, but not words. Because of this, they didn't know that Bawley wanted to search in the water itself and that Bert consented, and the posse, all but Johnson who held the dogs, did enter the water and search, but downstream far enough so the sounds didn't reach them. Nor did they hear when Bert decided the runners were farther south, bound to be, and clambered out of the bayou, cursing. But they could tell when the posse moved south, away from those they sought.

The fugitives surfaced. They clawed water off their faces, choked back their coughs, breathed sweet air shakily. "They gone down-bayou, Missy," Consuela whispered. "Because upstream, wheah the bayou starts, is only trees. They must think we trying to get to New Orleans."

Thus, for the moment, both posses were gone. Again, fiercely, Carita refused to go home.

If only the L'Acadie posse would come back, Consuela thought desperately. I'd make some sound, I would! I'd get my Missy safe. They sat listening. Nothing. As they sat, tremendous fear took Consuela, filled every cell.

The bad posse, with the hounds, might come back. If they stopped on the bank yonder, and the breeze blew a certain way—the way it was blowing now—the hounds would scent Missy! And the men would come into the bayou and capture them and drag them before the law. And her Missy would be lost to the world.

Her heart stopped, then roared. Stark with fear, she knew that she had to get Missy to safety before the bloodhounds came back.

Chapter III

Consuela, on one of the rare occasions her mistress had given her free time, had made an intriguing discovery of which she had never spoken. Consequently, she knew of a place beyond L'Acadie in the forest. With this place in mind, she now led her mistress farther down-bayou, keeping to the water, then helped her to the bank, water streaming from hair and clothes, and hurried into the forest, her mistress protesting every step.

"You said we had to keep to the watah. The hounds, the scent . . ."

The wench tugged her frightened, trembling Missy on through the darkness, into tree growth so thick it was hard to find passage. "We got to risk it, Missy, got to!"

"Risk what?"

"That the hounds don't come back far enough to pick up youah scent wheah we left the bayou. Fastah, Missy. Oh, please, fastah!"

"The daggah—it's in the bayou!"

"It ain't in the bayou, Missy. Theah's anothah place to look! Hurry!"

Consuela peered around anxiously as they went, vaguely making out trees she knew to be hardwoods. The cypresses everywhere and the black gum laced and tangled with bush and vine underfoot hid her destination. She knew where it nestled, but it was so hidden, so tree-grown that she might never find it in the enveloping darkness. But she pressed on, drawing her stumbling, falling mistress along.

Low branches, some of them thorny, tore her dress and cut her flesh. Her Missy cried out suddenly, and Consuela knew she had been cut. She cried out again and again, but

Consuela would not let go of her wrist, and kept on the way she believed was right.

"Don't scream, Missy," she whispered. "They hear you and catch us! Only whispah. Or bettah, be quiet!"

Then Missy began to rave in frantic whispers, the sound shaking from fright and rage. "I don't want to go in heah. The thorns, they hurt, and I know I'm bleedin'! Why are you so mean to me?"

"I ain't mean, Missy. I know a hiding place. We got to reach it!" whispered Consuela, never slowing, but pulling her mistress on, ever on. It would be so easy, oh, so easy for those hounds to backtrack, to pick up the trail! She began to run, yanking her protesting Missy along, her Missy who had begun to cry and weep that the hounds were going to catch them because they'd left the bayou, demanding to return to the water.

"Just wait!" wept the mistress, trying to turn back and failing because Consuela jerked her along, slower now, but still deeper into the forest. "Just you wait. Aftah I get my daggah, aftah I get home, I'll use my emerald hairbrush, smash youah face!"

Closing her ears to all protest, Consuela dragged her mistress through the forest, through thorns and trailing, tangling Spanish moss which hung down and caught them at head or neck until they tore free. Now there was only Missy's sobbing and Consuela's terrified panting and their combined panic which seemed almost to have a scent of its own.

When the wench made out the form of the place which was her destination, she began to sob. She stopped for a moment and put her arms around her trembling mistress to comfort her. But as she comforted, she peered mightily at the spot to make sure it was the right one.

They were at the edge of a miniscule clearing lit by a faint scatter of moonlight. By peering closely, the wench saw the crude wilderness shelter hollowed out of a mammoth tree with a timbered portion at the front. Inside, there was candle glow.

"What place is this?" quavered the mistress, and her trembling increased.

"It's a safe place," whispered Consuela. "Unless the dogs come back." She drew her mistress to the rough wooden door of the tree-shack, knocked on it, and called out softly, "We're friends. We're in trouble. We need you!"

The door opened and an ancient slave stared at them with frightened black eyes through a network of wrinkles, his wooly head as white as magnolia blossoms. Behind him, inside, there was a crude table and chairs, and a couch of moss covered with a blanket.

Carita, the shock of finding him here banishing her terror, demanded, "Who are you? Why are you at L'Acadie?"

"I'se Pete, Missy. I'se gardner at L'Adacie all my life." He looked at Consuela. "You 'membah, I tol' yo' dat day." When she nodded, he spoke again to Carita. "Dis forest lan', Missy, it not L'Acadie."

"You're a runnah!" Carita spat.

"Mastah Ol' René, he say Pete free now. I foun' dis house—it old—an' settle in. Pete do no harm. Nobody want dis lil' place but Pete."

"We do!" Consuela cried, voice low. "Miss Carita got away—they keep her locked up—and theah's two posses aftah us! If we could hide heah, if you would let us, if it's safe—"

"Yo kin stay. It allus safe. It so hid."

Carita pierced him with a look, slowly lifted one hand to her brow, swayed. Before Consuela could catch her, she wilted.

"She's swooned!" Consuela whispered. "Close the door and bar it! And help me with her!"

As they worked over the unconscious woman, Consuela whispered on. "Missy wasn't always like this! She used to be so kind to me, gave me ribbons for my hair, kissed me goodnight. She fixed me up a room in my mammy's cabin, so pretty. It wasn't until latah that she got mad so easy, and now it's bad, so bad, and she's pitiful. But undah all the things, she still my good little Missy, no mattah what she does, and she loves me, like always!"

Chapter IV

When Carita opened her eyes, it was to Consuela's anxious face above her, to Consuela's hand smoothing back her damp hair. "You all right, Missy," Consuela breathed. "You safe. The hounds ain't come back. You all dry but your hair, and my clothes is dryin'. Youah's can't be wore."

Accepting Consuela's comfort, Carita breathed easily. There was no need to run, to swim. She was dry, a coarse material against her skin. She glanced down and saw it was a long shirt. It was then that alarm took her.

"My emeralds!"

Consuela opened a clean, red handkerchief on the edge of the moss bed. Emeralds by the dozen, set in gold, shone green in the candlelight.

"The bag, Missy. I washed it. It dryin'."

Consuela, who was also wearing a coarse shirt, fetched a wooden bowl of stew and spooned it into Carita's mouth. Carita ate it, mind flashing and darting, settling on the emeralds for an instant, flashing on.

Vaguely she heard Consuela say, "Both posses are gone. Pete went through the woods some. They ain't eithah one neah. We safe for now."

"The daggah. We can go back to the bayou and find it."

She started to get off the couch, gathering up the handkerchief into a bag, handing it to Consuela. "Tie them. Fix them on me."

"It's still black night, Missy. We need to wait till day."

"No, let's go now while the posses are gone."

"They must think we're running for New Orleans," Consuela reasoned. "They bound to think that. You need to rest. You need to talk to Pete. We got to thank him."

Carita's fierce blue eyes stabbed at Pete. "You know who I am!" she accused.

"Yes, Miss Carita. Pete know."

"Did you read the Leblanc journals?"

He shook his head. "Can't read, Miss Carita."

"So you don't know what that first Leblanc—Gabriel—had the gall to put on papah! Or the awful thing he did!"

"No'm, Miss Carita."

"Missy," pleaded Consuela, "don't talk 'bout that!"

"You hush, or I'll slap youah face!" She asked Pete again, "Do you know?"

"No'm, Miss Carita."

She felt a glory of wildness rise up through her veins and pool and sparkle in her eyes. She felt again the awesome power of what she knew and the world did not. But the world needed to know, had a right. Her facts were true, and truth must be freed, so she cried it out to Pete, ignoring the weeping and pleas of Consuela.

"Long, long ago off in Nova Scotia," she began, "a country far to the north, the people were French, they were Acadians, and they settled the country though England held the powah."

She paused, glared at the ancient slave. "Do you undahstand that much?"

His wrinkled face showed new wrinkles, some shaped like twigs, a few like leaves. Slowly, he nodded. "England de mastah, de French Acadians de slaves."

"Yes, but in a different way than here."

"How diff'runt, Miss Carita?"

"England let the Acadians think they were free since they owned their farms and herds, and the Acadians were happy and worked hard, and asked only that they nevah have to go to war."

Pete nodded his understanding.

"Finally, England tried to make the Acadians sign a papah saying they would fight for England. And they refused!" She waited, watching Pete.

"Whut England do, Miss Carita? Put de Acadians to de lash?"

"No, nothing so easy! England wanted all that fine land, all the herds and the fine houses. So they locked all the men and young boys in the church and told them what was going to happen!"

"Whut dat, Miss Carita?"

"They loaded every Acadian onto ships, separating families. They passed out smallpox-infested blankets that people had died on, and many Acadians got smallpox and died, too!"

"England a cruel, cruel mastah!"

"Those who didn't die were taken by ship far, far from Acadia, some to England, most to the American colonies, wheah they weren't wanted! And wheah they were treated mean! When they landed, they searched for their wives, their husbands, their children, and mostly nevah finding."

Pete was weeping. Tears filled his wrinkles, dripped off his withered chin.

Carita heard her voice grow thin as she continued. "That first Leblanc, that Gabriel, was Acadian. He and his friend, a Hebert, got here to the bayou country. New Orleans gave them vast grants of land and they worked and grew rich. But Gabriel's fiancée Georgette traced him, and found him right here on Bayou Teche!"

"Glory be to God!"

Throat raw, she screamed the rest, Consuela helplessly trying to quiet her lest the searchers hear. "And what did Georgette find?" Carita shrieked. "Gabriel had betrayed her with some loose doxy, and this scum had borne a child! And Georgette had also borne a child—Gabriel had despoiled her in Acadia and had not married her! Now he did marry Georgette, but made her promise to take his by-blow and pass him off as her own flesh!"

Weeping, Pete shook his head constantly.

"You see how the Leblancs are! It's bred in them! I know bettah than anyone in that journal knew! Because my own husband René betrayed me! Betrayed me, his wife, his bride, with a wicked, beautiful widow!"

Pete's head bowed.

"He got the widow enciente," Carita raved, "and theah was a baby! He had me, his bride, mothah of his daughtah, and a new baby beginnin'! A son, it would have been, and he wanted a son! But when the Journals told me about the Leblancs, all of them, I punished them! I had my daggah, and I'll have it again."

She paused, then suddenly leaned close to Pete. "You've got it! I know you have!"

And now as she tore into the moss bed, searching, ripping the soft, thick couch, shredding it, Consuela tried to stop her.

Twice, once before Carita swept everything off the food shelf and once before she began to throw the chairs on the floor to look under their seats, she slapped Consuela.

Finally, when she lifted the table to look under it, Consuela helped her. And there was no dagger, anywhere.

And then, completely beaten, Carita swooned again.

Chapter V

At L'Acadie, the great plantation house and the slave quarters were in an uproar. The slaves, despite the fact that Myrtie had kept her secret, all knew that Miss Carita had run, Consuela with her. They stared at one another with frightened eyes; they didn't talk.

Up in the big house, Old René, the family patriarch, and Hippolyte, his black, crippled, lifelong body-servant and dear friend, sat in the library, waiting.

"She'd rather die than be caught," said Old René.

Hippolyte nodded, made a steeple of his fingers. He and Old René gazed at each other in despair.

"She might be better off if she died," Old René reflected, tears in his eyes.

"Died?"

"You know her condition, her situation. If the bloodhound posse catches her, there can be no ease for her, no joy. That beauty—wasted. There is no way, after what she has done, for her to recover. And some day, living here, she'll manage to tell the family secret and ruin the Leblancs, pull down Euphemie and her future children and all Leblancs thereafter to disgrace and ridicule."

"Suppose Simpson and his bloodhounds catch her?"

"We both know she'd be put in a madhouse, a living death. What she said about the Leblancs wouldn't matter there, but her own agony would. She'd be held like an animal on the chance she might recover and be tried for murder, held all her life if she remains . . . as she is."

"And you've exhausted your influence?"

"Every drop. As long as we keep her locked away so she's a danger to no one, she stays at L'Acadie until and if she recovers and can stand trial."

"So," Hippolyte said sadly, "it rests on our own posse. If they bring her back and we lock her away again, we can keep her."

Thus did the two ancient men sit, and thus they spoke throughout the night.

By predawn, Consuela had argued her mistress into a new line of thought. "You've been tricked about the daggah," she insisted. "They've hidden it in youah own rooms, Missy. All we need do is search again."

"Go back to L'Acadie without the daggah?"

"If you want it, and it's in youah rooms, you'll have to go back, Missy. It's safe now, if we go befoah day. We can get theah, you'll see! Pete's been out again, and theah's no sound of eithah posse."

"Where are they, then?"

"Maybe going toward New Orleans, Missy."

Thus, Carita still wearing the shirt and carrying her emeralds, Consuela in her own torn, damp dress, they went through the forest to the little bayou. Consuela led to where the stream grew shallow, and they crossed to dry land and slipped across the L'Acadie fields, hidden by the sugar cane, hurried through the silent quarters where slaves stopped and stared.

At last they were inside the house. Mrs. Ramsey and the black housemen were in the lower hallway and saw them.

Carita stopped, head up, eyes ablaze.

"Youah the housekeepah?" she demanded of Mrs. Ramsey, with whom, in the past, she had spent hours planning meals and parties.

"Yes, ma'am, I'm the housekeeper," the woman said, face impassive.

"Then youah the one I'm going to tell the Leblanc story to! All that's in the Journals! Youah white, and you have a respected position in a fine house, and people will know you tell the truth! And when you've told what I'm goin' to tell you, all the bayou country will know about the Leblancs!"

"Missy! Missy, don't!" cried Consuela. She threw an imploring look at the housekeeper. "Help me, please! We've got to get her to her rooms, give her medicine!"

They struggled, the beauty with pale red hair, the wench who resembled her so closely, the housekeeper, the housemen. They got her under control and started up the stairway, passing Old René and Hippolyte in the open doorway of the library, watching sadly.

They got her into the spacious sitting room, into the bedchamber, onto the bed. Consuela brought the laudanum drops and they forced the drops past her lips.

Within moments, she was asleep.

Old René sent a trusty to call in the family posse, to tell them the chase was over. It wasn't until hours after the L'Acadie posse had gone home that Bert Simpson found out the Leblanc bitch had made it home. He cursed. He kicked Boomer, the leader of his pack. And then he kicked each of the other hounds.

Myrtie he punished by getting himself a new wench.

PART I

1856—1874

Chapter VI

Euphemie Leblanc, long black hair touching her hips, the skirt of her white cotton dress falling in soft folds, wandered the great hallway of L'Acadie. She gazed at the glistening white, painted stairway curving upward, its treads glowing with deep red carpeting. The drawing room behind her, which she had just left, was spacious, red-carpeted. The mahogany furniture was covered in pale rose and tan; crystal vases holding elegant arrangements of white roses were on the mantel and every table. And there was no one to look at them save herself, lonely and bereft.

She filled with a sense of remoteness, a feeling which came to her often and which she loved, for it bespoke the beauty and quiet of the country around her, but today the feeling was streaked with an aching sense of trouble. She turned, slowly moved toward the drawing room, then back along the hall, her sad black eyes seeking some little touch she might give the rooms, but every place she looked was perfect.

Mrs. Ramsey had seen to it that the house slaves missed nothing, and she herself had adjusted the turn of every rose petal. Forlorn, Euphemie wandered back into the drawing room, and tears welled deep inside for her adored, murdered father, but she crushed them back. What good were tears?

Papa had been a smiling, laughing man. Already she had wept too much. He'd not want her to mope and sob and grieve this long. For him, she must return to her old quiet and smiling self, even if she had to do it alone, which she must, for her mother and sister had been dead for many years. And she had no brothers.

She reflected on her situation. She was fourteen years old and mature, the grownups said, for her age. Since Papa's death, she was now mistress of twelve thousand acres of sugar cane land and all the slaves and cattle and, despite knowing she had to grow brave, she was at this moment bereft and bewildered. She was also unexpectedly angry and ready to fight back, not knowing how to do it.

How can you bring your murdered father back to life, your murdered baby sister? How do you deal with a bright, beautiful stepmother gone mad, truly mad, one who had escaped from her locked rooms only yesterday and had returned wild-eyed and raving?

Curiously, she didn't hate Carita. Actually, she was angry at God, a God who would allow such a terrible, multiple tragedy slip past His notice. Or, perhaps, in His all-encompassing power, He'd willed the tragedies to happen. Her fingers went into fists; her nails dented her flesh. But then she let them relax, fought away tears again. Angry at God she was, but she didn't hate Him; yet she did hold Him responsible for the unfair, undeserved tragedy in her life.

Lips firm, she went to stand at a window and gazed out. In her line of vision lay a grassy driveway lined on each side by a double row of giant oak trees laden with Spanish moss. The driveway covered the quarter mile from the house with its three stories to the levee on Bayou Teche where the pirogues were tied up.

The next window gave full view of an identical driveway leading from the big, older house of unpainted cypress, behind which stood the original kitchen. North of the kitchen, barely visible from here was the Grape House of one room. Walls and roof were made of rippling vines studded now with great, juicy purple grapes in season. There were openings for a door and windows, and wooden chairs were placed inside.

Beyond lay Honeymoon House, the cottage built for the marriage of a long-dead Leblanc. It was charming and spacious though it had only six rooms, and Euphemie had always loved it and had wished she could have it for a playhouse.

Out from the ends of both great houses, were twin octagonal towers. Each had two rooms, one over the other. They were garçonniéres, or boys' quarters, built for the sons of Euphemie's ancestors. Doves cooed in the cotes built near them.

All the grounds were embraced by rose gardens. Hooded warblers spread their music on the soft air, cardinals flashed amid the forest trees beyond the gardens, and woodpeckers hammered every day in the wooded sections which spread to the sides and back of the grounds.

Bewildered that L'Acadie could look so beautiful when such evil had invaded its heart, Euphemie thought of what Old René, her ancient great-grandfather had said to her in the library after breakfast.

Old René said to her, "I know your mind is full of questions, dear. Do you care to talk?"

"Why did she kill them?" Euphemie cried.

"She went mad, little dear. She lost her mind."

"I know that, Grandfather. But why did she go mad? Why did she scream about some journals?"

"Child. Simply accept that Carita Leblanc lost her mind."

"But she kept screaming! What was in the journals? Where are they?"

"Gone. Forget her ravings, Euphemie. She is mad, and we must go on from there. Your task is to build your future around L'Acadie."

"Why?"

"Because you own it. Because you are the last Leblanc."

"How do I do that, build my future?"

"Hippolyte and I are devising a plan, little darling. If it goes well, you'll have no worries. Your grief will pass, L'Acadie will prosper, and you will find happiness again."

She gazed at him, at Hippolyte, their faces so sober, so kind. They were very old—ninety-eight—and very wise. Even Hippolyte was filled with wisdom. He had studied Old René's college books long ago when both men were young, so he was educated, too.

"I'll do whatever you say," Euphemie murmured to them.

"You must think carefully when you know the plan," Old

René warned. "You must agree thoughtfully, for it will involve your whole future. Hold that in mind, little dear."

Now, going from window to window, she grew a bit angry with the two ancient, wise men. They were treating her as half-woman, half-child. But because they loved her, she would listen to their plan and, if she could, agree to it and carry it out the way it should be done.

Turning from the windows, the conviction rose in her that today was important, that its importance overshadowed even getting Missy back safely last night. It seemed there was an extra polish to everything, an unusual perfection of the flower arrangement. The very air of the great house was filled with a subdued excitement not connected with Missy, but with something more.

She rang for Mrs. Ramsey. The woman appeared, starched and pleasant.

"Why are things different today?" Euphemie asked. "Everything seems nicer than usual."

"Thank you, Miss Euphemie," said the housekeeper with pride. "It's that the old master is to have a caller."

"What caller . . . why?"

"I don't know, Miss Euphemie. If you feel lonely, my dear, Zeb and Sindy are polishing silver in the pantry. You've always liked to help with that."

Euphemie made a smile for the housekeeper. "That's what I'll do!" she exclaimed. "And after the silver's polished, maybe Grandfather's caller will be here, and I can meet whomever it is! Will the guest be here for noon dinner?"

"Yes, I believe so, Miss Euphemie. They're preparing for a guest in the kitchen. The old master ordered a fine meal, one that Miranda excels in."

Still smiling, Euphemie hurried to the pantry where Zeb and Sindy were rubbing silver vigorously. They were solemn on first seeing her, but when she smiled again, they dropped their sobriety and greeted her warmly and teased her about liking to polish silver.

She chose a fat teapot, took the cloths they gave her, and the new polish Papa had found in New Orleans and set to work. She didn't let the thought of Papa banish her smile, but held it in place and teased gently back, declaring that she was as good a silver polisher as they.

"And as fast!" she ended, and they laughed together.

Both slaves were excited that there was to be a caller. "It make the house like it ought to be," Zeb rejoiced. "Someone comin' and goin', takin' a meal with the old mastah and Miss Euphemie. And stay a few days, mebbe. It make L'Acadie like home again!"

They worked on, bantering. The slaves spoke with loving respect despite the banter, yet in spite of the lightness and the air of expectancy, the very atmosphere of the pantry seemed to have an underlay of sadness. Euphemie sensed this, and recognized that all the black house slaves were looking forward to this mysterious caller as an event to sun away, for a time, the aura of tragedy.

Her own mood lightened as she worked and smiled and teased, and when the silver was finished, she was content to sit in the drawing room alone. She wouldn't ask Grandfather a thing; she'd just sit here with her darning and watch. From this chair she could see anyone who came in at the front door.

Thus, she spied the arrival of a handsome, blackhaired young man. She moved to a hidden spot from which she could see. From it, she watched as Zeb, correct in his black suit, respectfully admitted the young man and showed him into the library where Old René and Hippolyte spent their days.

Euphemie returned to her darning, her heart, for some reason, aglow. While she stitched, she wondered who the handsome man was, whether he was here in connection with her grandfather's plan for herself. And she hoped with every throbbing cell that he was.

Chapter VII

André Guerra entered the library with its walls of leather-bound books, and saw two ancient men, twins in opposite colors—one white and one black—get to their feet.

The white one advanced.

"André Guerra?" he asked, voice firm.

"That's right, sir. And you are—?"

"Old René Leblanc, the only male Leblanc. This is Hippolyte, my dearest friend," he added, introducing the black man.

André released Old René's firm hand, took Hippolyte's equally firm, bony claw. "I'm honored," he murmured.

"Please," Old René said, "be seated."

They sat, the old men in high-backed, brown leather chairs, André on the brown divan between them. He saw the gleam of polish on tables, smelled the roses in silver vases on either end of the mantel, felt the thickness of the brown carpet, noted the rich dark orange of draperies. A solid room, he thought, a room for the mind.

As he absorbed the room, André was aware that the two old men were absorbing him slowly, carefully, and with purpose, though what that purpose might be, he could not imagine.

Old René spoke, quietly. "For so young a man—twenty-six—you have the look of maturity evidenced in your letters. You are handsome as well. You remind me strongly of your father, whom I knew well when I was younger. A fine good man he was. You've inherited his good looks."

André's face went hot. Though he was of a strong, smooth build and not homely, he believed himself to be an ordinary man. His late father had assured him that he was intelligent and compassionate and brave. "Other men on the Delta look up to you. And with good reason, my son."

"You redden at praise," Old René said into this memory. "I like that."

"Thank you, sir. Whatever I may be that is good, is the result of my father's training and example."

Old René nodded approval. "I recall that you quelled a slave uprising almost single-handedly two years back," he said. "If it's not an imposition, would you relate the incident to us? We've heard several stories about it, but would appreciate knowing from you exactly what happened."

Reluctantly, yet not wanting to refuse these ancient, kindly men, André asked for a moment in which to get his facts in order, and was granted it. He closed his eyes and let his mind flash back, and when he began to speak, the two old men leaned forward in their chairs.

It was Daniel Guerra, André's father, who first noticed a change in his slaves. Puzzled, he called both his sons, David, the elder, and André, the younger, into his study to discuss the matter. He looked at the brothers, so alike, studied their waiting faces, began to speak.

"I'm afraid there's something afoot," he said. "Our slaves no longer sing as they work in the fields. I see them watch me from the corners of their eyes."

"Oh, Pa!" David exclaimed. "Blacks always look at whites that way. They've got the idea a slave dare not look a white man in the eye, you know that!"

"This is different. They slant their glances. And they look sullen. Even the trusties. Haven't you noticed at all?"

"I have," André said, "and I've wondered. Maybe they feel neglected."

"In what manner, son?"

"Could it be they want more dances in the quarters?"

"They have only to ask," said the father. "I've never forbidden a dance. They have one every two months."

"Maybe they want it once a month," said David.

Guerra frowned. "Christopher Duncan has the same situation at Belle Glade. He's of the opinion we'd best take care or another Nat Turner may emerge, stir up the blacks and kill the masters."

"Duncan's a fine man," David said. "But he gets excited about things."

"Does he think his slaves and ours are plotting an insurrection?" asked André.

"Not really. What reason could they have? I suggest the three of us go to Belle Glade tomorrow, talk to Duncan."

Christopher Duncan was pacing the gallery of his plantation house when they arrived, his graying beard trimmed to its usual neat point, but his white hair standing in peaks where he'd run his fingers through it. He greeted them eagerly, shaking hands with each. André noted that Duncan's hand was quivering. "Just the people I need to see!" he exclaimed.

"Now, Christopher," said Guerra, "be calm. Don't get so upset. That's how men our age bring on apoplexy. We're here now, and surely there's nothing so bad we can't talk it out."

"Of course!" exclaimed Duncan. "Come inside, come inside! Rachel's spending a week with her sister. What am I thinking of, keeping guests standing? We'll close ourselves in my study and have a go at what I fear is going to be a real problem! But first, we'll have something to drink—whiskey, tea—whatever you prefer."

The Guerra men declined refreshment, but followed their host inside and they sat together. "All my nigras," Duncan said bluntly, "have gone sullen. My best workers have gone thick-lipped. Also, I believe that without your knowledge or my permission two of my trusties have been to Guerra talking to your trusties in the field."

"All our people seem sullen," Guerra said. "This looks as if our blacks are disturbed and it's something they won't come to us about, or are afraid to."

"Or they're plotting to murder us in our beds," said Duncan.

"Surely not, sir," André said. "These slaves have always been obedient and pleasant. Mr. Duncan, sir, have any of your slaves come to you with even a slight grievance?"

Duncan looked thoughtful. "Mine did want a bigger ration of salt pork," Duncan said. "I gave it to them without question."

"Our bucks wanted work pants," said Guerra. "They're wearing them now."

"No unreasonable request, Mr. Duncan, sir?"

"We-ll, one. Laughable, and I'm afraid I did laugh. But it couldn't be that!"

"What was it, sir?"

"They wanted me to buy that preacher stud who comes to Belle Glade—the one your blacks come to sit under—wanted me to set him free and ask folks on the Delta to pay him to go from plantation to plantation to preach."

The Guerras were astounded.

"I probably shouldn't have laughed."

Silence.

"They've asked unreasonable things before, and I've said no. But they never acted this way. Just in case this is what's turned them, I aim to send word downriver that the preacher isn't to come to Belle Glade this next Sunday." He slapped his leg. "There's bound to be a Nat Turner behind the whole scheme!"

André sat frowning, some of Duncan's alarm rousing his

own apprehension. "There could be trouble if you don't let the preacher come Sunday, sir," he ventured. "If there is a troublemaker, and our blacks join yours, things could get bad."

"The more the nigra gets, the more he wants," Duncan grumbled. "The only course I can see is let them remember who is master and who is slave."

They talked on, the Guerra men in favor, not of buying the preacher, but arguing that he should be permitted to preach at Belle Glade as planned. When they started home, they parted as friends, but in disagreement.

"I'm still sending word for the preacher not to come," was the last thing Duncan said.

"He's going to cause trouble!" David exploded as they rowed home. "That takes gall, to send his trusties with such a message! He's leading right into the trouble he's afraid of!"

"I'll have another talk with him tomorrow," Guerra said, "after he's slept on it. He'll cool off; he's a reasonable man. He's just got himself worked up."

That evening after supper, when Guerra and David had gone downstream to play cards, André settled down in the study to read. He hadn't turned a page before a wench tapped at the door and said that Sammy and Leander, from Belle Glade, wanted to see him.

She looked nervous, and André decided it was because even trusties never came to the big house and asked to see one of the masters. He laid aside his book, told the wench to bring in the slaves and stood, waiting.

They were both enormous, with legs like sturdy young trees and arms to match. They had huge, powerful hands and thick, strong necks. Both were very black, Sammy with a long face, Leander's square and with a gold tooth of which he was inordinately proud, but the tooth didn't show now because he didn't smile. Sammy was fully as sullen.

"There's trouble?" André asked. They nodded.

"Tell me what it is. Leander, please speak."

"It dat de mastah won' let de preachah come, one thing," Leander rumbled in his deep voice.

"And what else?"

"He laugh when us ax him to buy de preachah an' give

him freedom papahs so he kin preach up an' down de Delta an' be paid."

André was dumbfounded that Delta slaves were actually making such a serious demand, for a serious demand it was. He felt, suddenly, that perhaps Duncan wasn't wrong in thinking this was a plot.

"Whose idea was it to buy the preacher?" he asked.

"Mine, suh," said Sammy. "I tol' Leandah, an' he like it, an' all de people. God free. Us want a preachah, an' us want him to be free, like God."

Though Sammy spoke with sullen respect, André felt enmity flowing from both him and Leander. In a flash, he realized that it was possible, given the backing of all the slaves on both plantations, they might kill if denied what they wanted so deeply. Not that killing would get them their preacher, but they hadn't thought that far.

"Why is it you want your own preacher?" he asked.

"So he kin tell us whut is right. So we kin sing."

"Your master tells you what is right, and you sing in the fields and in the quarters and on the Sunday the preacher comes. You sing at your dances."

"Ain't de same," Leander rumbled. "An' wif a preachah, a buck don' have to jump de broomstick wif his wench. De preachah marry'em de white folks way, de preachin' way."

"None of you have ever objected to jumping the broomstick before."

The trusties stood tight-lipped and silent.

"The wrong preacher," André reasoned firmly, "can lead you wrong, the way Nat Turner did."

"Nat Turner brave man," Sammy said.

"Us wan' de preachah Sunday," Leander put in. "I got a wench. She don' wan' to jump no broomstick. I even got her a ring fum de peddlah."

André shook his head regretfully. "I have no authority over Belle Glade and the preacher's coming," he explained. "Master Duncan is the one to say. Belle Glade is his plantation, and you are his chattels. You'll have to talk to him."

"He won' lissen," Leander said. "Mebbe he lissen if yo' talk to him, Mastah André."

"He won't buy a preacher and give him freedom papers," André told them. "I'd never be able to talk him into that." He gazed, disturbed, at the two enormous blacks. Some masters allowed preaching services, even marriage, but he doubted that even his own father would approve marriage. He was kind and humane to his slaves, but would do nothing which smacked of pampering them.

Finally, though they were more tight-lipped now than when they arrived, André dismissed them. When they kept standing, reluctant to leave, yet disinclined to obey, he asked, "Does your master know you came here?"

They shook their heads.

"Then go back before you're missed. I'll try to get the preacher to you Sunday. I'll keep still about your visit, and suggest that you get the other slaves to drop this preacher matter. Later, more masters are bound to let their people have preachers come to hold services, and I promise to do all I can to influence my father and your master to do the same."

They departed, every line of their great bodies set in anger. Uneasily, André hoped there was, indeed, no Nat Turner to turn that anger into blood lust.

The next day Guerra persuaded Duncan not to forbid the Sunday services.

"But there'll be no white folks' marriage," Duncan decreed. "If the preaching nigra wants to preside over a broom-jumping, I'll permit that much. Nothing more."

At Duncan's request, the Guerra men and four other plantation owners gathered at Belle Glade on Sunday. They brought trusties each to help deal with possible trouble. All agreed that the slaves were in no position to make demands.

"Why damn it all," said one gentleman, "it's as if a stud and a filly wanted to get married in church. This demand of the nigras is just as ridiculous! Why, I've got horses with more brains than these nigras!"

The church service was held in the clearing of the Belle Glade quarters. The slaves, dressed in their best and brightest, sat on the ground in rows facing the gray-haired old preacher behind the makeshift pulpit. The congregation was large, for all the Guerra blacks were there, as well as Duncan's people.

The white men stood in the back, eight of them, and beyond, ten trusties. André stood behind his father. There was an aura of expectancy about the scene which made him uneasy. This was no mere religious service. It was a silent shout for white man's marriage, a united cry that the preacher be bought and freed. The demand lay on all the faces, unspoken on all the pursed lips. Glancing at his companions, André saw that they, too, were uneasy. Even the trusties shuffled their feet, and André wondered which side they'd be on should trouble come.

But there should be no trouble, André thought. The slaves will sing. The preacher will pray. Hands on the Bible, he will exhort, speak, and shout to his congregation and it will shout back with many an amen and hallelujah! Then the preacher will hold the broomstick, Leander and his wench will jump over it, and the slaves will feast and rejoice. They'd return to work tomorrow, not mollified perhaps, but no longer sullen, knowing there would be more frequent services in the future.

André quietly watched the service. At the end, the preacher lifted his hands and intoned, "We got two that wants to entah holy matrimony. Leandah and Mercy, stand befoah me."

André went stiff as the huge trusty and his light-skinned bride stepped before the preacher. He opened his Bible, lifted his hands.

Christopher Duncan stepped forward and stood before the pulpit. "Where's the broomstick?" he demanded. "I made it clear you could jump the broomstick. Nothing more."

"Suh," responded the preacher gently, "latah, at the dance I'll hold the broomstick. But not now, not in God's outdoah temple. Heah, I can only join them in holy matrimony, if you please, suh."

"No!" snapped Duncan. "It isn't my aim to be unreasonable, but I set the standards at Belle Glade. You can hold the broomstick here in your church and let them jump it. That's the same for them as being married."

"Suh. Beggin' youah pardon, but it ain't the same. Leandah and Mercy want to take the vows, need to take the vows. Please let me marry them propah, suh."

Duncan shook his head. The preacher looked at his Bible and it seemed he was going to begin the marriage ceremony despite the master.

Duncan, face fiery, gestured violently. "Throw him off the place!" he shouted. "He's the one behind the trouble, nobody else! Get rid of him, break up this meeting! All Guerra blacks go home! All Belle Glade blacks go into the field, Sunday or not!"

The white men and their trusties moved to take the preacher into custody. André didn't stir. He stared about at the strong, angry black faces, and knew with awful certainty that all present were on the verge of bloodshed.

"Run for the house!" he shouted as the blacks turned slowly and purposefully on the white men. Every black face was filled with hatred; they moved, a black tide, against the handful of whites and trusties.

The whites retreated into the house, their trusties with them. Duncan, who kept a small arsenal, passed out weapons and ammunition.

"Arm the trusties!" shouted Guerra.

"What for?" cried Duncan. "So they can turn on us?"

André, who had refused a weapon, peered out a window. The slow-moving, muttering black army was at the back steps, ready to mount, to invade the house. Someone inside fired a shot. A wiry buck grabbed his leg and fell, blood streaming. The blacks let out a roar.

"Stop shooting!" André shouted. "They're not armed! It'd be murder!"

"If we don't best them now," yelled Duncan, "they'll kill us in our beds! Listen to them roar! They're animals, beasts!"

He was scarlet-faced and his hands were shaking. André feared Duncan would have a heart seizure, took his gun from him, forcibly guided him to a chair, sat him in it. The others watched the slaves outside, watched the men in the room. Nobody fired a shot.

"We've got a full-scale insurrection in the making!" André cried. "Let me come to terms with them, all of you, whether you like the terms or not! It's the only way!"

Reluctantly, Duncan agreed, as did the others. Unarmed, André burst out onto the back gallery, and as he did, the black mob swayed at him threateningly. Some carried hoes; others gripped clubs; there were scythes, axes. One wench brandished the besom she used for sweeping.

André took another step forward; the blacks, a mutter swelling from them, moved closer. André lifted both arms to show them he carried no weapon. The great bloc of slaves halted, waited in awful, threatening suspense. How easily they could kill all of us now, André thought. If they only knew it, we're at their mercy. But the blacks quieted, watching André, and when he began to speak, their muttering fell away. His throat was so dry his voice sounded unnatural.

"Master Duncan has said I speak for him," he told them. "I speak also for my father, master of Guerra, and for the other masters inside. No master here will buy the preacher and give him freedom papers. But any qualified preacher can hold services at any plantation.

"There'll be no more jumping the broomstick. From now on, all bucks and wenches will be married by the preacher. It will be a real wedding according to the Bible. Go back now and sit in your church. Leander and Mercy, take your places before the preacher. Speak your vows and be man and wife. And know that your masters will never take this from you or from your children, that church and marriage go together from now on."

Wenches young and old began to weep. Older bucks patted their wenches on the shoulder. Seeing this, André added, "Let it be a mass marriage! All of you who jumped the broomstick can today take the Bible vows!"

A moan went up from the people. They dropped their scythes and clubs. They turned, making their way back to their outdoor temple. Wenches bound the wound of the buck who had been shot; he and his wench were among the dozens who stood before the preacher. In files they stood, and were married, each buck to his wench. The white men watched and afterward moved among the slaves, congratulating couple after couple. And the blacks were all smiles, radiating happiness; the white masters present told one another they, too, might adopt this custom.

André finished relating the account, then fell silent.

"And the outcome?" asked Old René.

"Peace. And that preacher is a good influence on his people. I wish it had been possible to free him."

"You were wise beyond your years. If you hadn't given the slaves marriage, you could all be dead now, all you whites. Even though you gave them what they'd demanded—gave in to them—you only granted what is their right as human beings. And now, having marriage, they are satisfied."

André smiled, disclaiming any virtue on his part. But Old René persisted, relating another incident he knew of André's diplomacy. In this case, slaves had been stealing from masters and the masters had scheduled a mass whipping, but André, persuading them to postpone it, got the preacher to hold a revival meeting and the thieves then became devout church members.

He added, "Your fine Creole blood is evident in your deeds. I presume that because you are the second son, thus not inheriting Guerra, you have your own way to make?"

"Correct, sir. I mean to buy a small farm."

"Hmm. My knowing your father, plus the letters you and I have exchanged, make me bold. Being in desperate straits, I asked you to come here."

"And gave no reason, sir, except that agreement between us could be of mutual benefit."

There was silence. Old René broke it. "With your permission, I'll speak bluntly."

André nodded.

"You've heard the Leblanc scandal?"

"Yes, sir, I have."

"Carita, my grandson's wife, went mad. She smothered her little daughter, stabbed my grandson to death. Then she turned the dagger on herself and aborted her unborn baby."

"I've heard, sir. I've also heard that you keep her locked up."

"In this house. The best suite. She escaped yesterday and her wench prevailed on her to return for reasons of her own. She is to remain in her rooms until she regains sanity and can be tried by law, or until she dies."

"I understand, sir."

"Most of the time, she sits and stares or plays with her emeralds. If she sees any of us, she rages, relives that murder night, tries to relate the story of the Leblancs, searches for the dagger, which I have in safekeeping. There's gossip, of course, that we keep a madwoman locked in L'Acadie."

"Madhouses are hellholes. You're to be commended, sir."

"The Leblancs caused her madness. She read the journals of the family, the Leblanc history. This you must know."

André sat motionless as Old René told of the long, tragic

years of events begun deep in history, which had led to Carita's madness. He withheld nothing, gave no reasons, made no excuses, and André listened in impassive shock. He found the story repelling and tragic even as he admired those who had lived it.

"My great-granddaughter Euphemie," Old René concluded, "knows nothing of the Journals' contents."

"I'll tell no one, sir."

"Unless in the future you must."

"Sir? I don't understand."

"Being ninety-eight, I have no time for negotiations. My judgment has come to serve me well, and I trust you. I have a proposition."

"I'm listening, sir."

"I want you for master of L'Acadie. Marry Euphemie, who is beautiful and fourteen, and beget sons. Change your name to Leblanc."

André got up, paced. The others waited.

"It's a tremendous challenge," Old René said.

"That it is, sir. If I may see the girl? And if she may see me?"

When the shy, beautiful girl entered, André's breath snagged. The qualms he'd had about her from the Leblanc story vanished. She was perfect: innocent, pure, devoid of any fault. Goodness and sweetness and spirit emanated from her.

As for Euphemie, when she put her hand in that of this handsome man, her knees trembled. She murmured when he spoke her name. She felt as if she had three hearts, all of them racing.

"Euphemie," André said, "it is a delight to meet you."

Euphemie felt a smile tremble briefly on her lips. But she remembered nothing she said for she could only look and look at André. When Old René dismissed her, somehow she managed to leave with dignity. She was certain now that André was part of Old René's plan and hoped that she would see him again. All her hearts merged back into one and trembled, and she wondered if being in love made a girl feel this way.

When Euphemie was gone, Old René said, "If you need time. . . ."

André gestured. His quick mind evaluated. He thought through the proposition again.

"Is it the Journals?" Old René asked.

"Not at all, sir."

"What, then?"

"Her youth. Changing my name."

"I know you're not for sale. But half of L'Acadie becomes yours. Whether you change your name or not."

"That's generous, sir."

"As for Euphemie, she's mature beyond her years. The Leblancs are passionate. She's had her loved ones torn from her. She needs a place to put her love."

"And if I should fail to love her?"

"I saw your eyes."

"You're perceptive, sir. No girl has ever had such appeal for me."

"Then there's nothing to stop you."

"The girl herself."

"She wants what I want, what I think best. I saw her eyes, too."

André considered keenly. This was the opportunity of a lifetime. The scandal they could live down. Both he and Euphemie were ready for love; each was attracted to the other. She needed protection; he needed a life. Here was one for the taking, filled with work and challenge.

Quietly he said, "I accept the proposition, sir. I'll marry Euphemie if she'll have me. In time, I may even change my name."

Chapter VIII

At supper, nearly speechless from her racing heart, which seemed to be tangled in her throat, Euphemie stole shy glances at André Guerra, knew that he was also glancing at her. He wasn't so very tall really, but he was slender and strong and would be enduring. His eyes were as black as her own, and once, when their eyes meshed, her whole body went hot, but his pleasant, firm lips gave no sign that he knew she was blushing. She'd never seen features so smooth, fine and handsome.

He spoke to her across the table in his quiet baritone, and her soft voice responded. He might see how rosy her face was, but he couldn't know how madly her heart was beating, or have any idea at all that she kept wondering how it would feel to be in his arms.

André, for his part, could hardly keep from staring at this delicate, beautiful young girl. She did indeed seem mature for fourteen; he noticed her eyes, her poise, the total lack of young-girl foolishness. This gentle beauty was standing at the very brink of womanhood, and if she consented, André Guerra would be privileged to lead her across its threshold.

Thus, even as he discussed life on the Delta, and the raising of sugar cane with Old René, feeling Euphemie's interest in what he said, André determined to make the courtship brief. Hopefully, she would agree to Old René's plan, and succumb to the attraction she seemed to feel toward himself. This was an unusual circumstance. It called for speed, not for dallying.

After dinner they had coffee in the drawing room, and at Old René's request Euphemie played the piano, her gentle touch on the keys drawing forth the beauty of the notes. When the music ended and the two men had chatted, André excused himself to go to his room.

Euphemie glowed. This handsome, perfect man was going to sleep at L'Acadie. It had been revealed at dinner that he was to visit for perhaps a week. As she murmured goodnight to him, he bowed over her hand, lips almost touching her fingers, and then he was gone.

Old René motioned her into the library and closed the door. Hippolyte greeted her kindly, and she put her hand on his arm in a loving gesture.

"What did you think of him, little dear?" asked Old René when they'd sat down.

"I—he's very handsome. Much more handsome than the

boys on the bayou, but then he's a grown man. And he has brains like you and Hippolyte. He can think."

"Precisely. I told you, darling, that Hippolyte and I have been making plans for you. André is the core of those plans."

Euphemie waited. Her heart was going fast, so fast. She wanted to hear more, but she was overwhelmed. She held her breath, afraid to guess what Old René would say next.

He didn't make her wait. "André Guerra has my permission to court you, to ask you to be his wife."

She stared, breath gone. She was trembling.

"But only if you agree, my darling. Only if you love him and feel that love for him can grow in you. Only so. André is vital to the future of L'Acadie. He can run the plantation; he is the best of men and would be, I am convinced, a fine husband to you. And he is attracted to you, has admitted his attraction. But you're not to feel pressed—you are to follow your heart. The time is short, true, but believe me, little sweetheart, a man and a woman—the right ones—can fall in love in a heartbeat."

She was dazed, wondering if she had already fallen in love, wondered if fourteen was old enough for love. Her wild heart told her that it was, that André was an exceptional man, but still she questioned their ages. And so realizing that she herself was a child-woman, she asked, "Is fourteen old enough to love, Grandfather?"

He regarded her, read her very heart. "In your case, yes, Euphemie. You've been old for your years always. And the tragedies you've withstood have matured you even more. I believe it is right for you to listen to your heart now."

"I feel drawn to André," she said. "He . . . excites me. I love to hear him talk, admire him, want him to be attracted to me. Maybe that is the beginning of love."

"I think it can be so interpreted, little darling. Now, to bed with you. In the morning, you and André may want to ride, or he might enjoy going on the bayou in the pirogue. And he is your guest."

She lay awake remembering stories André had told about the Delta, about New Orleans, places she'd never been. If life had followed its natural pattern, she would now be getting her clothes ready to attend Miss Pettigrew's for four years. Old René had been willing to send her, but she had not wanted to leave L'Acadie and the bayou country or Old René. They'd been, at that time, all there was to life.

But now there was André.

They rode after breakfast; they raced, each trying hard to win. It ended in a tie, both laughing. While they walked and cantered the foaming horses back to the stable, Euphemie, her shy tongue freed by the race, urged André to tell of his school days in New Orleans.

He spoke of his studies, of history which he had liked especially, and she was delighted. She discussed history with him brightly.

André asked why she knew so much history.

"Grandfather and Hippolyte," she told him. "They're wonderful teachers, both of them. Hippolyte is a wizard at figures, and he says I could be, too, if I'd leave the history books long enough!"

After lunch and siesta, they went out in Euphemie's pirogue, André at the oar. They went as far as St. Martinville but didn't tie up, saving a tour of the little place for another day. They talked now of sugar cane, and she astonished him with her grasp of how it was cultivated; he could hardly believe she hadn't actually worked in the fields.

"Grandfather wouldn't permit it. Papa wouldn't either," she said quietly, and didn't smile again. André cursed himself silently for bringing sad memories to one who had had so much sorrow, to the girl he admired and wanted more every moment.

After dinner on that nearly perfect day Old René suggested that Euphemie show André the Grape House. "I'll wager he's never seen anything like it," he said, smiling.

André smiled back. "I've never seen anything like L'Acadie," he said. "I'm looking forward to visiting the fields with Mr. Ramsey in the morning, too."

They wandered about the grounds in falling dusk. Going through a rose garden, André plucked a perfect white rose-bud, half-open, and gave it to her. She lifted it to her cheek and let its softness touch her skin and its fragrance come into her. It was the only time a man had given her a flower, and she knew she would press it between the pages of her white-bound Bible and keep it forever.

André exclaimed when they reached Grape House.

"Astounding! A grape arbor built like a house! I've never seen anything so unusual, a house of green leaves and purple grapes! Whoever thought of it?"

"My first ancestor, Gabriel Leblanc," Euphemie said proudly. "In winter when the leaves fall, you can see the posts and the rafters with dead vines over them, and it makes you sad. But in spring the vines turn green. Then there are leaves and after that, grapes. This is my favorite spot on all L'Acadie."

They went inside, sat in side-by-side chairs and looked through a window opening into the sudden dark that dusk had pulled after it, across the quarter mile of early starlight to Bayou Teche. Fireflies moved around Grape House and beyond, there was the heady smell of sun-ripened grapes, and from a distance, the sound of frogs tuning up for their nightly serenade.

André reached out and took Euphemie's hand, and she let him, her heart afire. He held her hand gently, and she let it rest, trembling at first, then at last holding onto his hand, too.

"Your grandfather told you," he said gently.

"Yes."

"Everything?"

"He told me you can run L'Acadie, which is a very important thing. He said you will be kind to a wife."

"Love. Did he mention love?"

She swallowed, pulse quickening. "He said I should . . . should . . ."

"Be able to love the man you marry?"

"Yes."

"And what did you tell him, Euphemie?"

"He meant you. I told him . . . that I feel attracted," she whispered.

"That's what I told him about you," he said. André stood and taking both her hands, drew her up into his arms, holding her as if she were fragile. He lowered his head and gently kissed her. She found herself kissing back with suddenly burning, trembling lips. He closed his arms about her and they kissed again. The trembling, pulsing delight was heaven to Euphemie, and André knew that she was beyond compare. They drew apart, though she was still in the circle of his arms.

"I'm more than attracted to you," he murmured. "I believe we have the beginning of love, if we nurture it."

Trembling, she loved the sound of his words. "My grandfather—I think he'd want—very soon—" She faltered, then stopped, overwhelmed by the realization that she was virtually proposing to him.

He cradled her head, stroked her hair, drew his fingers along the outline of her face. He kissed her again, warmly and slowly, and she responded and clung.

"I'm ready now," he said. "Ready to join my life to yours. I need only your consent."

"It's so very fast."

"We're truly attracted," he said, "and falling in love after marriage often happens. And that is the best love. But don't let me persuade you against your wishes, because if we marry now, you'll be a woman overnight, and God willing, there will be babies."

His babies. And hers. Such a strange, unexpected thought. But she found herself liking it, suddenly impatient for it to come to pass. Shyly, she confided this to him; shyly, but confidently, she agreed to marry him at once.

They were married in the drawing room at L'Acadie. The room was banked with white roses, Euphemie wore white, carrying roses in her arms. The only guests were the Heberts, Old René, Hippolyte and the Ramseys. The old priest blessed them, and smiled when they thanked him for marrying them by special dispensation.

Their wedding night in Honeymoon House was idyllic. When André offered to refrain from making love in order to lead her into wifehood gradually, Euphemie's natural spirit overcame her shyness.

"We'll do what is usual!" she cried. "I'm not a doll; I'm your wife!"

Afterward, they lay in each other's arms. He smiled, and she wanted to know why.

"People would call this a marriage of convenience," he said. "And it is. But I'm going to love you, sweetheart, by God, I am!"

"Me too!" she whispered, and he loved her again.

Overnight, she was radiant. They moved into L'Acadie and their happiness grew. Euphemie made changes in the house, putting her own mark on it. She was spirited with

André now, but she was also gentle and tender, and he returned these qualities in kind. They had love in their hearts, and they cherished it.

André spent hours in the fields with Ramsey and the hands. He used additional hours talking with Old René and Hippolyte on how to run L'Acadie, on how to run the Leblanc family. Soon all three men—old René, Hippolyte and Ramsey—learned to respect André's opinion and began to change a number of things to his way of doing.

Consuela was in and out of Carita's rooms often. Under Euphemie's guidance, the wench was better able to control her mistress, to calm the shrieking tirades, to lessen the constant efforts to escape.

Euphemie searched trunks for bits of silk, satin, and velvet. From these she made scarves and gave Consuela a new one every day.

"For Missy," she would say, "to arrange her emeralds on. This one, being gold, will set off their green fire."

Consuela was delighted. "Missy will be happy. She ain't had but one table covah, and she's tired of it!"

"There'll be a new one tomorrow," Euphemie promised, "a new one every day, something for her to look forward to. She'll take pleasure in these scarves as well as in the stones. We need to keep her occupied with pleasant things, to give her a chance to be a little happy."

Consuela stared. "You grown up so fast, Miss Euphemie!"

Euphemie smiled. "I'm a woman now with a husband twelve years older and a big house to run. And Old House and Honeymoon House, too. Also," she said, indicating the scarf, "I have Missy. When she tires of scarves, I'll make bags for the emeralds, and after that, new dresses. We'll keep her as busy and as satisfied as possible."

A few days later, Carita got loose again and began searching the library for her dagger. She threw books off the shelves, flinging them everywhere. Old René and Hippolyte couldn't stop her, nor could Consuela. But when the housemen, summoned by Mrs. Ramsey, started to restrain her physically, Euphemie motioned them aside.

Carita was shrieking, yanking books, hurling them. "That old devil! He's cut the pages out of a book and hidden my daggah! But I'll find it, and when I do—"

Quietly Euphemie laid a folded turquoise scarf on the

shelf Carita next turned to, and when the madwoman saw it, she snatched it up and began to unfold it. Euphemie stood close beside her.

"Isn't it pretty, Missy?" she asked calmly.

Carita stroked the heavy silk. She shot a keen, sane look at Euphemie. "I've nevah told you the story of the Journals," she said. "They wouldn't let me. I'll tell you now."

"First," soothed Euphemie, "why don't you see how lovely your emeralds will be on turquoise?"

Carita hesitated, then forgetting both dagger and story, permitted Euphemie to put an arm around her and guide her to the stairway and up to her rooms. Here, an apologetic Consuela whispered, "She tore the key from my belt, Miss Euphemie!"

Euphemie put her hand gently on the wench's shoulder. "You're not to blame," she said. "Just lock up now, and keep her interested in her new scarf."

Euphemie, soon pregnant, confided in André her wish to carry on the Leblanc name. "I've thought of a way," she said. "If we hyphenate the names and use Guerra-Leblanc, both will be kept forever."

André took her hand, kissed the wide gold wedding band. "What put that into your lovely head?"

"It's in my blood, I suppose, and just seeped into my head. L'Acadie has been Leblanc always, and would be now except—" She broke off. "Grandfather said he discussed it with you."

"Briefly."

"I—did he ask you to change your name?"

"That he did. It's a sensible request. My brother is carrying on the Guerra name, and the way things are, there can be no more male Leblancs."

"But there's Leblanc blood," she mused. "At least there's Leblanc blood."

André became deeply thoughtful. "But it hurts you," he said. "It really hurts for the name Leblanc to be lost. Isn't that true, my darling?"

"I—oh, André dear—yes. But it isn't your worry, your responsibility."

He closed her lips with a kiss. "I've given the problem

much consideration," he told her when he lifted his lips. "I'm going to change my name legally to Leblanc because I want to. No, don't protest. It's my gift to you, my gift of love."

Their first child, Marie-Louise, was born in 1857. André was fascinated by every aspect of the pregnancy, yet worried. Old René and Hippolyte were just like him. More than once, Euphemie laughed at their helpless concern until tears ran down her face. They hovered; they wanted to know if the baby was moving right; they wanted it to be born so they could see him—or her.

When Marie-Louise was finally born, all three of them insisted on seeing her naked, and were plainly relieved when they'd inspected her and found ten fingers and ten toes. Euphemie laughed at their anxiety, and André kissed her and let the baby be dressed.

Their son, Gab, was born in 1858. Again, the three men worried all through Euphemie's pregnancy. Again, they had to see the child naked before they were satisfied. This time Euphemie, greatly matured by motherhood, merely smiled at them.

Alone with André, she asked fondly, "You want our babies perfect, don't you? Well, they are. If we have a dozen, they'll be like Marie-Louise and Gab!"

Also in 1858, both Old René and Hippolyte became ill with failing hearts. Old René sickened first with a severe pain in his chest. The doctor came, gave him drops, ordered complete bed rest. Hippolyte volunteered to nurse him.

"You take those drops yourself," the doctor said, giving the ancient servant a sharp look. He listened to Hippolyte's chest. "And you go to bed, too. You fellows have been sitting up too late, talking too much. You've both got to rest."

Euphemie, now carrying her third child, insisted on nursing both of them. She had a fine bed installed beside Old René's bed, and gently ordered Hippolyte to get into it. "You can see the master, watch over him," she said. "All you need do is open your eyes. I'll give the drops. Mrs. Ramsey will sit with you some, and André will take his turn at night. We'll get you both out of this, fast."

The doctor came again. He listened to the ancient hearts, ordered the same drops, the same soup, the same care, and left. It was then when they were alone, Euphemie and the two invalids, that she knew Old René would die.

He lay motionless as he spoke. "I want you to know where the daggah is hidden," he said. "It's a place nobody knows of except Hippolyte and me."

"Yes, Grandfather. But later, when you're stronger."

"No, now. While I can."

That was when she knew, when her heart began to bleed, so she let him speak on. "There's a secret well built into the library floor," he said. "It's under the rug, and a leather armchair sits over it, my armchair. I don't think she can find it there. But you should know, you and André."

"Thank you, Grandfather," she murmured. "We'll keep the well a secret."

Suddenly he was asleep.

It was that night Old René died in his sleep. As he died, Hippolyte awoke, rose to his elbow, saw by lamplight that his beloved master had passed on, and began to weep. André, sitting with them, was alerted by the weeping, and discovered that Old René was dead. Hippolyte wept while André took the body away, wept alone with the empty bed, wept into the night, into death.

They buried the master and his slave, buried the two friends side by side in cypress tombs in the Leblanc cemetery. Family, slaves, neighbors, people from up and down all the bayous came, and all wept, not only for the two old men, but also for the passing of an era.

Celeste was born in 1859, inspected by André. There was little anxiety this time. "She's the most beautiful of all," he told Euphemie. "We'll never have another as beautiful."

In the next three years, Euphemie had three miscarriages and André began to take care that no seed enter her. When she protested, he said their family was complete, that his mind was made up, and she accepted his decision.

"We have a son," he told her. "Gab will carry on the name. L'Acadie is prospering. We haven't a worry in the world."

Chapter IX

Eldo was thirty years old when the war between the states, the Civil War, broke out in 1861. He was Master André's trusty and proud of it. He believed his master to be the best in the bayou country, and impressed this on his pretty, lively little wench, who was only twenty and afraid to have babies.

Eldo, six feet tall and strong as an oak, was a bit worried about the baby part. He'd even spoken to the master about his worry, rubbing his big hand across the cropped wool on his round head.

"Dicey an' me, us bin married two yeahs," he said. "An' no suckah."

Master André smiled. "Don't be impatient. You've plenty of time. You're both young."

"She 'fraid to have a suckah, suh," Eldo blurted out. "An' I 'fraid fo' her."

"How so?"

"I so big an' she so lil' an' del'cate. She could die tryin' to push out my big suckah."

"Small women manage, Eldo. It seems to do them no harm. But if you're worried, there's a way . . . if you're willing to do without a family."

"That anothah worry I got, suh. Dicey, she don' push out suckahs, mebbe you think she ain' doin' her duty."

The master laughed. "Dicey's one of the best housemaids we have, the mistress says. She'll be happy enough not to have to let her go. The two of you please us very well as you are. If the baby question worries you, don't be afraid we'll be displeased if you have none. The choice is yours."

That was just one example of how the master was. He let Eldo be his companion, too, not quite the same as Old René had taken Hippolyte for his bosom friend, but enough that there was closeness between them.

Together they explored the network of bays and bayous and lakes, and the master told of things Eldo already knew, and of others he didn't know. Eldo knew the temperature hardly ever got below fifty-three degrees; he knew he'd sweat in January. And he saw with his own eyes that the swamps varied from swales covered with hardwoods to cypress-tupelo. He saw Spanish moss draping cypresses and even pecans, elms and water oaks. There was wild cane, growing thick; Eldo believed the dirt would grow anything a man stuck into it, that it would grow rice and tobacco and indigo. Anything.

Trapping was still good, and sometimes they trapped. "Old René told me," André said, "that in the early days out in the marshes, muskrats were as thick as ants in a hill. The muskrat's a heavy breeder, three to five litters a year. The best market was in New Orleans, still is. Back then, the 'gator was numerous too, and there was lively trade in the hide."

When Eldo hunted with the master, they found most of the deer in wooded swamps. They saw wildcat, raccoon, and mink. The country was still alive with swamp rabbit and gray squirrel, with beaver and otter on some of the swifter bayous. There was wild hog, mostly tough.

Eldo made a great, happy sigh at all the riches of the bayous. "It like the Garden of Eden," he said. "I wouldn' evah want to leave."

And then he remembered this Civil War the master had mentioned, saying the northern states wanted to fight the southern states and free the slaves. Eldo couldn't understand why the north wanted to do that, not even when the master explained about something called politics. Any mention of the war bothered Eldo, and he turned his mind to the bayous he loved. He fished with his master for redfish, croaker, sheepshead, mackerel, and in season, they hunted ducks—mallard, pintail, teal, and blue geese. And when Eldo was doing this, the war didn't matter.

But the war began to seem more like the snakes, mostly harmless. It was a far-off thing and didn't touch him no way. Unless the North come marching up to L'Acadie, they were safe. And if that happened, they'd deal with it like the way they done the moccasin, or the cane rattler. Cut it down and stomp it dead. If it come. But it was such a far piece.

It never occurred to Eldo that bayou folks would go north. Not until the master solemnly took him one morning to the meeting at St. Martinville.

"Whut this meetin' 'bout, suh?" Eldo asked as he oared the pirogue along.

"It's one of many we've had," said the master. "At this one, we'll all speak up and say what we'll do for the war. Go and fight or stay at home and help."

"Go to war an' shoot guns?" quavered Eldo.

"That, yes. Other things, too. You'll hear. And you can make up your mind, too."

"'Bout whut, suh?"

"About going or staying. Some slaves are going with their masters."

This was the first Eldo had known any white master meant to go off to the Civil War. Much less any slave.

"Why the slaves go, suh?"

"Mostly to be with their masters. A few go to fight for their freedom."

"Whut they do with freedom, suh?"

"That's what we all wonder, Eldo. It's a thing we may never know if the south wins."

Eldo oared silently, head thick with new knowledge, trying to understand what the master had said, and what he had not said.

Now the master asked, "If I were to go to war, Eldo, would you go with me? Go against the northern army, be my orderly, risk your life with mine?"

The shock of this drove into Eldo's great, strong body. His powerful hands gripped the oar. He didn't know what to say. His impulse was to say yes, but he knew that when Master André asked a straight question, he wanted a thought-out answer, and Eldo's head was churning so badly that he couldn't think.

"You don't have to decide now, maybe not at all," Master André said. "I'm still weighing what I'll do myself."

Confused though he was, Eldo suddenly knew one fact, and he spoke it out. "I don' undahstan' Civil War, suh," he said. "But if you go 'way, I go with you."

It was then the master gripped Eldo's shoulder and gave it a squeeze. He didn't say a word.

There were many bayou men at the meeting place, and each man, it seemed, had brought his most trusted buck along. Eldo stood with the other slaves; open-mouthed, they watched their masters march in formation, back and forth, in step, each with a rifle over his shoulder. Some, Master André among them, didn't march, but stood in a group and watched; pride was on some faces, indecision on others.

Master André, now thirty-one, looked stone-faced. Eldo reckoned he was making up his mind. He felt fear sweep him that the master might grab a rifle and begin to march, too, and that would mean he'd decided to go off and fight.

Eldo knew instinctively that the marchers were going to fight. Other slaves, bunched with him, whispered together.

"My mastah," whispered one, "he bravest one. Nobody keep him home, not even de mistress an' chillun. He want me to go wif him, say it my duty, that the mistress look aftah Lulu an' the suckahs. He sweah we won' git shot, that we come marchin' home, an' the North be on the run wif they tails between they legs."

When the marching ended and the talking began, Eldo was aquiver. He didn't want to go away, but if the master did, he had to. What kind of trusty would he be, stay home, let his master be shot, even killed? He jutted his chin. He'd done his deciding, no matter how Dicey might cry.

Master André was in charge of the meeting. He stood there, so handsome. You couldn't tell there was a thing wrong to look at him. But Eldo knew different. The master was tore up inside.

"Before we take a vote on what we'll do," André said clearly, "I'll state my own position. Others can do the same; perhaps a vote won't be needed. I've pondered the situation from every angle, taken into consideration the size of L'Acadie, and see the way I can best serve in this war. And it is not to bear arms and kill. It is to stay on the land, double the labor of my slaves, double the land under cultivation, and raise corn and other grain and foodstuffs for the Confederate Army."

"That's fine," said one of the Heberts. "But can you

double your work, can your slaves manage? A man's body can take just so much labor, then it collapses. What if that happens?"

"It's my responsibility to see that it doesn't happen. I'll talk with my people, explain the need, grant them the right to come to me if I'm overzealous and work them too hard. If such time comes, I'll ease off, but we'll still produce for the Confederacy."

Other men spoke, some pledging themselves to raise food crops, among them both Heberts, some saying their consciences told them their duty lay to drill and go north to fight. Eldo, relieved that his master would not be shot and killed, that Dicey would not have to weep, resolved to do the work of three bucks raising crops. He knew what his master and the others were up to—stuff the bellies of southern soldiers with good southern grub and they could wipe out the North in a week.

The master told Eldo to assemble all L'Acadie slaves outside the cabins that night after supper. They gathered early and did some talking of their own before the master appeared.

"Whut if de mastah change he min' an' go?" Old Granny asked, one of the torches showing the veil of wrinkles which covered her small black face.

"Mistah Ramsey, he still be ovahseeah," replied Eldo. "Mis Euphemie, she a great lady, but she know how to run L'Acadie. We be all right if he goes, but he won't go."

It was then the master appeared. He stood before his people in torchlight and explained the war as best he could. He told them how they were going to have to work. When given their turn to speak, each slave pledged to work twice as hard on the land and win the war with grub.

It seemed to Eldo that the war went on forever. The first thing he knew, after working until he was one solid callus, a year had gone by and it was 1862 and the war was still being fought. After that, it was 1863 and 1864 and 1865 and the war went on, Eldo laboring, as did the others, black and white, with no idea that 1865 would see the end of fighting.

During those years, word came of St. Martinville men killed in battle, of men from all the bayous killed, wounded.

Some came home, mustered out with wounds that would never let them work again. A foot cut off, an arm, even two arms. It was pitiful.

There was some social coming and going during these years, the white folks visiting, the blacks doing the same. But their gatherings lacked zest. Every person, white or black, had a sadness from the war, a loved one killed or wounded or simply vanished, buried on some unknown battlefield.

The Negro preachers gave fiery sermons. The slaves shouted and wept and sang, according to the mood of the preacher. The white people went to Mass on Sunday, listened to the priest, prayed.

Eldo noted the attitude of the slaves during these years. Some remained bewildered and frightened; some were excited, wanted the North to win so they could be free to do what they pleased. Even the Negro preachers were divided on this aspect of the war.

And when the war ended, dozens of freed slaves left the bayou country. A few from L'Acadie left, though many remained, not knowing where to go or what to do with their freedom. The bayou men who had survived the war came home and tried to resume a normal life; this was impossible because of the unrest among the newly freed blacks.

In 1867 Congress enacted the Reconstruction Act, which divided the South. Eldo explained to his people, who were restless, worried, torn. "All the south, 'cept Tennessee, is split into whut they call five military districts. The Army Commander is the big boss. We do whut he say."

In 1868 he explained, "It's been a year now and six states—Arkansas, No'th Car'lina, South Car'lina, Louisiana where we are, Alabama an' Florida—have been let back into the Union."

"Whut dat mean?" demanded Old Granny.

"People that was for the south can't vote, an' us new nigra votahs ain't been learnt how, so the state gov'ment's been grabbed by northern carpetbaggers an' southern scalawags. These white men got no honesty an' they're greedy as hawgs. Claim they goin' to reconstruct the South. I don't know how long it'll last—the mastah says it could be long as eight more years, an' I b'lieve him. He one good, smart white gentleman."

Dejected, those remaining at L'Acadie went to their cabins. Word had drifted back through disillusioned slaves who had gone to New Orleans that they were faring worse than when they were chattels.

André, telling Eldo he was concerned about both L'Acadie and the ex-slaves still living there, called a meeting which included every black man, woman and child. They stood in rows, waiting, pitifully few in number. The master stood before them. Eldo waited proudly beside him, convinced that whatever his master said, it would be to the benefit of the people.

"I'll start by asking," the master said, "if any of you have plans to leave L'Acadie. Or if you have plans of any sort, now that you are free."

Some of the people shifted uneasily. Not one spoke, not one held up a hand to ask permission to speak.

"So," said the master, and his voice sounded tired, as well it might. He'd worked the fields these years, as hard as any buck. "I have an offer. It is the best I can do. You can take it or leave it."

Silence. Waiting.

"I'm willing for you to continue to live in the cabins you now occupy," the master told them. "Each of you will have a garden patch in which to grow food, and you're free to hunt and fish and get a ration of milk and eggs when they are available."

"Whut we do fo' dis?" sang out Old Granny.

"Work in the sugar cane as you did before the war. Work in the fields growing feed for the cattle. Only now you will work as free people, conduct yourselves decently, take pride. There will be no master-to-slave orders, no punishments, no serving white people except to earn your pay. No need to ask permission to go see friends on other plantations after work. You will be expected to work regular hours—the white man has always done that to earn his wages. You will do the same; you'll be paid by having use of the cabins and with the food you get, and a share in any cash money from the sugar cane at the end of the season."

"An' clothes?" asked Old Granny. "Who buy dem?"

"You will, as free people. You can sell vegetables from your gardens if you find a market; that will bring some money. And if you find a job that pays money, take it, do all you can at L'Acadie, and you'll still get cabin and food until you can support yourself elsewhere. The Heberts and one or two other plantation owners are offering the same to their people, and I heard that Rivard Plantation is doing the same."

"'Bout workin' away fum here," put in Old Granny, "whut chanct us got to git payin' work?"

"Very little," the master said sadly. "Very little."

Chapter X

The Leblanc children attended private school in St. Martinville. The Heberts sent their children to the school, and the widow Rivard sent her son, Riel, whose warm, outgoing nature made him liked by all.

It seemed to Riel, now seventeen, that he had always loved Marie-Louise Leblanc. He adored her long black hair, her great black eyes, her spirited nature. He wished his own light brown hair and eyes, both touched with gold, were like hers, dark and enticing and perfect.

But when he blurted this out to her one day, she stared. "Why, Riel Rivard! Who ever heard of such a thing! You're perfect the way you are—you're handsome as a picture in a book! And you're so strong, your hands are big and powerful. And there's a golden aura all about you! Don't evah let me heah you wish for black hair again!"

He was transported. His secret love thought he was handsome! She admired everything about him! The world was perfect.

"And you're tall!" she added. "And built just right!"

"I—I like the way you look, too," he stammered. "You're beautiful."

They gazed into each other's eyes, smiled, blushed.

Then the bell rang and they had to return to class, but Riel forgot not one word of what she'd said. He believed, stealing glances at her, that she, too, had forgotten nothing.

Gab, aggravated at his sister that night, cried out before their parents and Celeste, "if you treated me half as well as you do Riel Rivard, we wouldn't fight! Always hanging around him!"

André took this outcry very seriously. "You'll not associate with the Rivard boy, Marie-Louise," he said sternly.

"Why not? He's nice; he's smart; he's—"

"Sounds like you want to marry him," taunted Gab.

"And if I do?" she responded defiantly.

"Enough!" André commanded.

"But why, Papa?"

Euphemie tried to explain that which she did not herself understand. "His family, dear. No father, and his mother has kept to herself all these years. I thought you liked Charles Hebert. Isn't he a nice young man?"

"He's all right, I guess. But Riel's . . . different."

"We'll ask Charles to dinner," Euphemie smiled.

Marie-Louise made a little face.

"They're old, they don't understand!" she whispered to Riel next day when they took their lunch baskets to the secret place in the trees. They want to divert me with Charles when it's you I—well—love. There! I've said it, and now you know!"

Dumbstruck that his beloved had shown her heart, Riel put his lunch aside and took her into his arms. She nestled to him, her arms stole around him, she tipped up her face, and they kissed. It was a trembling, warm kiss on both their parts, and they could hear each other's heart knocking.

Riel felt passion, burned with it. Clumsily, because he had never before done such a thing, he cupped one sweet breast in his big hand. She sighed, nestled, and they kissed again. Kissing on and on, their clumsy young hands wandered, explored, touched, and now Marie-Louise was afire; she gave only a faint moan when he penetrated.

At the end he whispered, "You're mine, body and soul! Say it, so I can hear and know!"

"I'm yours, body and soul," she murmured.

Tremulous, they tried to eat, failed. It was almost a relief when the school bell rang. Each had a need to be alone, to dream over the wondrous state in which they found themselves.

Next day, their love was better, experienced. For Marie-Louise, it was still a bit frightening, yet exciting, putting shivers through her, but this time she touched glory at the end. For Riel, it was blissful heaven.

They talked of marriage. "In June," he said, "at the end of school. We'll live at Rivard."

"When will we ask them?"

"Ask who, ask what?"

"My parents, your mother. Ask to be married. It should be in May, so Mama'll have time to sew for me."

He agreed on May, enveloped her body with his own. He'd promise her anything she wanted, see that she got it, see that she would get everything that would arise in all their wonderful life to come. They would be happy forever.

Gab saw them go into the trees every day, and warned his sister. "You'll get into trouble, bad trouble. Stay away from Riel Rivard."

She tossed her head. "I can take care of myself!"

"If you don't quit, I'll tell Papa."

She spun to him, instantly pleading. "Oh, please! Not that, Gab, please, pretty please! We're going to speak to Mama and Papa in May! They'll know all about it! That's a really truly promise! Just wait till May!"

"That's two months."

"Gab, please! We're going to get married!"

"They'll never let you!"

"They will, I know they will! Don't tell, Gab. Promise?"

Sullen, he promised. "But when May comes," he threatened, "if you don't tell them, I will. And you be careful in the trees. Riel's a man more than he is a boy, and you're only a young girl. He can get you into trouble."

"But he won't, Gab; he loves me!"

When they knew that she was pregnant, Riel took Marie-Louise to L'Acadie. Her parents were surprised to see him, but treated him kindly, nonetheless. They sat in the library—André and Euphemie, Riel and Marie-Louise, the parents on the divan, the young people in the chairs once used by Old René and Hippolyte.

"I know you wonder why I'm here," Riel said, "ma'am . . . sir."

"Yes," André responded soberly, "we do."

"I'll come right out with it, sir . . . ma'am. Marie-Louise and I love each other. We want to get married. There is going to be a baby. We'd planned to wait until May to ask permission, but now with the baby, we can't wait."

André, stricken to the bone, went ashen. Euphemie paled, sat so still she seemed not to breathe. She looked, bewildered, from Marie-Louise to Riel to André. She tried to speak, but her lips wouldn't move.

Riel watched their elders anxiously. Marie-Louise stared at her fists in her lap. The only thought she had was relief that Gab wasn't here.

At last André spoke. "You're telling us you want to get married? Asking, because of the condition you . . . ?"

"Yes, sir . . . ma'am. We'd planned to ask in May, but this other . . . we're asking now."

"The answer is no," André said harshly.

Riel leaned forward. "But, our baby! I don't understand why. Would you explain, sir? Briefly, if you want, but explain?"

"Incest!" André cried, the word torn from him.

"How can that be, sir?"

"You want an explanation."

"Yes, sir. I do."

André cast a despairing look at Euphemie, who was staring at him, aghast. Her heart had gone still; her mind, for no reason, flew to Carita, locked in her rooms. Her eyes clung to André; she waited.

André looked at Marie-Louise, his beautiful daughter, his perfect firstborn in whom there had been no blemish. And now she was filled with blemish. He looked at Riel, stark white and shaking.

He pulled in a breath and then he spoke, crushing his words mercilessly into them all, changing their lives in one splinter of time. "Incest," André repeated. "This is incest."

"How can it be, sir?"

"Bloodlines."

"What do you mean, sir? What bloodlines? Marie-Louis is Leblanc. I am Rivard. There is no mixture."

"Mixture there is," André said sadly, knowing he was about to stab Euphemie to the heart, about to devastate his daughter, about to wound this earnest, intense young man.

"Listen carefully, Riel," he said. "It bears telling only once. Your father was René Leblanc. He was lover and protector to Olive Rivard, his octoroon placée, whom he brought from New Orleans. Riel, you are their son. René sired you, and he sired you, Euphemie, by another woman." He took her nerveless hand, held it.

"No!" cried Riel.

André gave him a steady look. "There's more," he said, and gazed now at Euphemie. "This makes you, darling, half-sister to Riel Rivard." He moved his eyes to the stricken Marie-Louise, and there were tears in them. "And it makes you, my sweet, Riel's half-niece. Hence the incest. Also, through his mother, Riel is part black. The child you carry, my little darling, will put black blood into the Leblanc family."

The room seemed to throb. André was devastated at what he had told and what he must yet tell. The others were motionless, speechless. The tall clock between the windows marked off what seemed lifetimes—tick-tock, tick-tock. They could only exist, these people, helpless as he despoiled their lives.

"Now comes more," André said at last. "It was written in the Leblanc Journals which Carita read. The first Leblanc, Gabriel, found a runaway wench on his property, loved her and sired Old René. The child showed nothing of his mother's blood and was raised white, and it was Old René who made certain that no more black entered the Leblanc stream. Until now."

Euphemie whispered, "You're saying that I . . . that my children . . . !"

Her hand had gone icy in his. He held it firmly, to warm it. "There is only one sixteenth black in you, my darling, one thirty-second in our children."

"And in me?" croaked Riel.

"About two-sixteenths."

"You married me . . . knowing?" whispered Euphemie.

"Old René told me, asked that I keep it secret unless need arose. As for your having the blood, it makes no difference to me."

"Now I understand why you inspected our babies when they were born," she said.

"That mere drop of blood," he told her, "doesn't matter. In spite of it, Leblancs are white. As you are, Riel," he added. "You've been reared white, you are white except for that invisible trace. As to your child, it isn't the addition to the blood which troubles me most. It's the incest which makes marriage out of the question."

"The baby," Riel asked hoarsely. "What can we do about the baby?"

André shook his head. "I don't know yet."

Again, as each absorbed the horror of this situation, the silence held only the ticking of the old clock which had marked so many L'Acadie hours. Hours of joy, of tragedy, and now, hours of utter, helpless shock.

Euphemie was numb. Even the hand André rubbed so lovingly was numb. Her tongue lay in her mouth, useless. Somewhere under the numbness was grief, over Marie-Louise, over the fact that she, Euphemie Leblanc, had lived a lie, that she must continue to live a lie. She wanted to think what to do with the baby, but her brain was numb, too. She could only sit, her one salvation André's hand.

André, feeling her icy coldness, felt he was a killer. He had murdered the hearts of three people. He was the head of the family. It was up to him to guide them through this crisis, and he would. After his mind cleared. After he could weigh and measure and decide.

Riel grew more rigid by the moment. He felt that if he went any stiffer, he'd fly into splinters. His head, his whole body, was of no more use than a piece of ungiving iron. Grief and rage lay at the core of the iron, he knew. He began to shake again, but he couldn't control himself. He tried to swallow, and it was no use. He'd have to sit quietly until he came out of it by himself, gradually. Vaguely, he heard the clock mark off time.

Marie-Louise couldn't even think. Her ears were ringing, she felt sick at her stomach; she almost swooned, but somehow avoided it. She couldn't look at Riel, staring at her as if he didn't see her. She wondered if she ever did love him, a black, and then she remembered that she, too, had the blood, and wished to die.

Riel, mind stirring at last, knew that he was losing Marie-Louise, his love, but he could not accept what André

Leblanc had related. Not that André was a liar, but what André believed to be true was false. All rigidity left him. He, Riel Rivard, would prove that this blood thing was false, would prove that he and Marie-Louise were not related, would prove that he had no black blood so they could marry and have their child. He felt his jaw harden, his eyes go steady, gazing alertly at André.

André gazed back, the pain over what he'd told boring deeper. It would remain always, a soreness and a regret. He had, in a sense, betrayed them all, first by keeping the secret, then by changing their lives without mercy. Even now, he prayed that he could find a way to guide them back into contentment. The boy Riel was beyond his reach. But the others, Euphemie and Marie-Louise, he could comfort and help.

He stood, bringing Euphemie to her feet. Marie-Louise stood, as in a dream. Riel got to his feet.

"Gab and Celeste are to know nothing of the blood or the baby," André told them. "Only the four of us in this room."

"And my mother," Riel said firmly. "She's the one who can clear up the mistake."

André gazed at Riel, inexpressably sad.

Chapter XI

Riel raced home, running the three miles, wishing he'd brought the pirogue. But he'd needed time enroute to L'Acadie to think, to decide on the right way to state their case, his and Marie-Louise's. And he had failed completely. Not because he hadn't been able to think and speak clearly, but because of the impossible, unthinkable mistake which André Leblanc accepted as truth.

His mother would know. If only his feet would go faster,

he'd be with her sooner, and she'd know the truth and give it to him. And with her truth, he would prove it was fitting and right for himself and Marie-Louise to marry.

Despite the state he was in, Riel was again impressed with Olive's beauty as he burst into the drawing room where she was polishing a glass lampshade. He saw the dark blond curls high on her head, the heart-shaped face, the delicate features firm and unlined; saw the question in her light green eyes; heard the soft richness of her voice.

"Riel, what is it? What's wrong?"

"Plenty!" he gasped. He stood slightly straddle-legged, staring into her face, wild with suspense, unable to continue.

"Where have you been? What happened?"

"I've been at L'Acadie talking to André Leblanc!"

He saw the color drain from her. His heart, still racing from his trip, went into a new, faster beat. Why would she pale if she knew nothing of what André Leblanc might tell?

Slowly, she folded the cloth she'd been using, put it on the table. "Sit down," she urged, gently. "Catch your breath, then tell me."

He sat on the divan, sprang up, paced, all the while struggling with his breath. She was sitting on the divan herself, beautiful as a Madonna, pure and chaste, accused by André Leblanc of the lowest filth. The need to tell her, to ask, all but choked him. At last he stopped in front of her.

"It's about Marie-Louise Leblanc and me," he said. "I've got her pregnant, we want to get married, and her father said we can't because it would be incest!"

Olive went completely white. Even her lips faded. "What did Mr. Leblanc say, my son?"

"That Euphemie's father and you—that you were his octoroon placée—that Euphemie Leblanc is my half-sister."

Olive sat, unmoving. After all the years, after her meticulous behavior, her infinite care to do nothing to harm Riel's future, there was this. He'd been told, and by the Leblancs themselves. She'd been so careful to give her son the best, only the best, of his heritage.

"He said you were René Leblanc's mistress, Mama, that he brought you to Rivard from New Orleans. It's a lie, a mistake, isn't it?" He stared into her eyes, seeking the answer he wanted, must have.

"It's not a lie, Riel," she murmured. "Or a mistake."

He stared wildly, boring into her eyes, boring past what she'd said, seeking the truth he meant to pull forth. But she gazed steadily back, tears in her eyes. "I never wanted you to know," she whispered. "I never wanted it to touch you."

"It's true what he said?" The words were unbelieving, the tone a rasp.

"Completely true," she replied. "I can't lie."

"Yet you lived a lie. And I did."

"Not you, son, never you. It was my doing."

"Why, if you were octoroon, would you be placée?"

"My mother was quadroon," Olive said simply. "My father took her for placée and freed my brother and me. We were given a choice. We could pass for white; my father stood ready to put us in foreign schools so we could live in Europe as white. My brother chose England; I suppose he's there now. I went to one of the quadroon balls, my mind not yet made up, met René Leblanc . . . and chose him."

"They say he had black blood himself!" Riel spat angrily.

She inclined her head. "He never knew of it. I learned it reading the Leblanc Journals that Old René Leblanc entrusted to me shortly after you were born. He told me to use them as I saw fit for your future; they told the story of the black blood in the Leblanc line."

"Where are the Journals? I want to read them!"

"I burned them."

He stabbed her with a look.

"Perhaps I shouldn't have," she said softly, shaken by his harsh look.

He kept at her. "They were my birthright, and you burned them! Why?" he demanded, hating her, repelled by the very sight of her. He had to hold himself back to keep from grabbing her shoulders, from striking her. She was at the heart of his difficulty with Marie-Louise, she and she alone.

"I burned them because René wanted you never to know."

"René! What does he matter?"

"He was your father. I loved him."

"And he used you!"

"He loved me, asked me to marry him when he was left a widower."

"And why didn't you?"

"It wouldn't have been suitable for me to pass myself off in such a marriage. I am an octoroon, even though no one can tell."

"And all the time he had the blood!"

Trembling, she lowered her head.

"Why didn't you tell me what was in the Leblanc Journals? Why didn't you see how wrong you'd been? Why did you wait until I had to find out this way?"

"Because René wanted you never to know. Because he wanted you to be raised white, to live white, so your children could live the same."

"Pah! What he wanted! The white man who wasn't white!"

She sat silently. She thought of Marie-Louise, of the child she carried. Olive was torn by remorse, helpless to aid the girl, to aid Riel, her devastated, desperate son. And what about the baby which could not possibly be born but yet had to be, because it now nestled innocently and trustful in its mother's womb?

Riel paced, stopped. "Tell me," he damanded, "tell me what was in the Journals. Tell me everything."

"Sit beside me, and I'll try," Olive said.

He sat on a chair, leaned forward, fists between his knees. His eyes, flecked with gold, were hard as any rock. "Talk, Mama," he said. "Don't leave out a thing."

Meticulously, she started at the beginning of the Journals written by Gabriel Leblanc, continued with the volumes written by Old René. She left out no facet, no sin, but gave it all to him. When she finished, she said, "That is almost verbatim, my son. I read the Journals many times."

"You sinned when you burned them," he told her fiercely. "You robbed me of my birthright, which was little enough, thanks to you. And to him."

"I burned them," she insisted, "so you'd never know. Everything, no matter how you may regard it now, has been for you. Because you are nearly white, René wanted honor and respect for you."

"You've made a real crisis, Mama. There's Marie-Louise, the baby. What happens to them? I'm responsible; I did it; I've got to make it right! It's up to me to force things to be right!"

"How, Riel, how? She's your half-niece!"

"I'll take her to another country, to Cuba where nobody knows us! We are forced to carry on your damnable lie for the baby. The baby can't suffer for what you and René did!"

"It can suffer for what you and Marie-Louise did, son. Unknowingly, innocently. But you did it, just the same."

"I don't know what you're talking about!"

"If you'll only listen, Riel. When a baby's parents are closely related as you and Marie-Louise are, their baby may be born deformed or with no intelligence whatsoever. It could be just a helpless lump of flesh as long as it lives! Or others, born later, could be like that! It's an impossible risk!"

"I don't believe it!"

"Have I ever lied to you, aside from the one thing?"

"Regardless. The baby is started, and it's up to me to take care of it. And Marie-Louise! Cuba's the only answer!"

"And where will you get the money to go? How will you make a living when you get there?"

"You can mortgage Rivard. I can work in the cane fields."

"I'll try to borrow money," Olive said. "It won't be easy now, after the war. Money is hard to get."

Riel stalked out of the room.

He returned to L'Acadie the next day, determined to marry Marie-Louise whether her parents consented or not. He would take her to Cuba. Who needed Rivard, L'Acadie, the bayou country or anybody in it? He and Marie-Louise would create their own family, alone and unaided except for money from Rivard, which he would one day inherit anyway.

At L'Acadie he was again admitted to the library. He faced André Leblanc full on. "I've got a plan that will solve everything," he told the other man. "But I need Marie-Louise to be here when I explain it. What I'd prefer would be to see her alone first."

"To that I say no," André replied. "I'll have her mother bring her in, however. Whatever you have to say must, under the circumstances, be heard by us, her parents."

Riel nodded. It was the best he could do. At least he'd see his love.

When Euphemie and Marie-Louise came into the room, the girl wouldn't so much as look at Riel. She was pale, her lips trembled, and she hung back so that Euphemie had to urge her into a chair. Then Euphemie drew up a stool and sat at her daughter's feet, holding her hands.

"You can speak now, Riel," André said. "Let us know what's on your mind."

Riel, filled with apprehension over Marie-Louise's attitude, held himself stiffly. His words came out, not reasonably and confidently as he meant for them to do, but in a blurt, a blast. In one miserable sentence he said that he was going to marry Marie-Louise, take her to Cuba, and work in the sugar cane and make a home for their baby. And then he fell silent, miserable.

Marie-Louise sprang to her feet. "I won't marry my own uncle, Riel Rivard!" she cried. "I won't go away from the bayou country with you or anybody else!"

"Can't you see?" Riel pleaded, going to her. "It's the only way! What else can we do? You can't have a baby with no—"

"Oh, hush! You and your silly plans! I don't understand what I ever saw in you! You put me in this mess, but I won't let you get me out. I can do that for myself! And I hate you for what you've done, and never want to see you again!"

When he moved closer to plead, she shrank from him. "Don't you dare touch me, you dirty . . ."

She meant 'nigger.' The realization pierced him, mortally wounded the love he had for her, and it lay bleeding unto death. He turned away from her, stunned, wondering how he could live with such pain.

"Darling," Euphemie said, putting an arm around her daughter, who turned away when her mother would have kissed her cheek. "Riel means well, darling. Some boys wouldn't assume responsibility at all. We must respect his desire to do what seems right to him."

"I don't c-care!" wailed Marie-Louise, pulling away from Euphemie. "Last night, you told me to think, and I have! I've got it all worked out, and it's easy! Put me in Honeymoon House, tell everybody on the bayous—even the slaves, too—that I'm in a decline like my great-grandmother Catherine died of! And that nobody but my wench and the doctor and you and papa can see me!"

"Impossible," said André. "It's too risky. It would travel the grapevine like wildfire. Gossip would start. And people know that gossip often has some basis in fact."

"But what could they prove? If you say I'm in a decline, and nobody can see me because I'm so sick, they can't call you liars! And I can fix my wench Gracie so she'll never, never tell a soul, not even that stud Cal she's so crazy about!"

"Sweetheart," pleaded Euphemie. "Don't you see what a wild plan that is? We'd never succeed! Besides, last night your father and I decided on the most sensible thing to do."

"Just what?" demanded the girl, black eyes afire. "Exactly what?"

"We decided I must take you on a tour of Europe. Your father can manage the money, just barely. The baby will be born there, in London perhaps, and boarded out and grow up with no scandal attached to it. When you recover, we'll come home, and there won't be the least chance of anybody knowing, ever."

"I won't go to Europe!" screamed Marie-Louise. "I won't go to Cuba! I won't travel with my stomach all big! If you try to make me go, I'll kill myself! I'm the one having the baby, and it's to be my way or not at all!"

"Your way," Euphemie reasoned, "people are going to want to call on you, dear. They'll think it odd if no one is allowed to see you, and then you suddenly appear after the baby is born, pretty and healthy as ever. There simply will be gossip."

"I don't care! They know my great-grandmother died in a decline!"

"She died of consumption, darling."

"But she had declines. And that's what I'm going to have. I've got it all planned, and you won't listen!"

"We'll listen," André said grimly. "Talk."

"I've already told my wench I'm enciente," Marie-Louise announced.

"No!" Euphemie whispered. "Gracie will let it slip!"

"Not her! You know how wild she is over Cal. They want to get married, and I promised her a white-folks wedding if she keeps the secret from everybody, even Cal. And I promised her a wedding ring. But she doesn't get any of it until I'm rid of this baby, and then only if nobody at all finds out. And Gracie wants all that—she's a greedy wench!"

"That's bribery," André said. "Now she can blackmail you all your life."

"She won't! And if she tries, nobody'll believe her!"

"There's still gossip," Euphemie reminded.

"Gracie won't let it out, I tell you! I promised her that three-room cabin. All the darkies want that cabin, Papa, because it's the biggest, and you won't assign it because there would be jealousy. I promised it to Gracie and now I can't break the promise or she will talk. We have to do it my way!"

André stared at his daughter, unbelieving. Euphemie, pale, looked from Marie-Louise to André to Riel. Riel, scarcely able to believe Marie-Louise capable of such a scheme, tried to catch her eye.

She shot one glance at him. "Well," she demanded, "are you going to tell that I'm having your baby, or are you going to let me handle this the only way it'll work?"

"The Europe plan is sounder by far," André cut in. "If only you'd kept your lips closed to Gracie!"

"Only I didn't! And if I go traipsing off to Europe, she'll tell because she won't have her wedding things, and then there will be gossip."

"I hope to God," André said, "you didn't tell her about the blood."

"Do you think I'm crazy? Of course I didn't!"

"I think," Riel said, heart aching on every word, "that Marie-Louise should do what she wants. You know for certain that I'll not tell any of it."

"He's right!" Marie-Louise cried. "Gracie and I talked about this all night long. She's smart, for a wench. She wants to marry Cal so bad and live in that cabin and be my maid forever, she'll never talk. She can tend my needs, tell the other blacks how sick I am, and they'll tell the blacks on other plantations. And Papa, you and Mama will tell all the white people the same thing. They'll believe it. There's no reason they won't. Please, please do it my way!"

"It's based on lies," André warned.

"The European trip would be a lie, too," Euphemie put in quietly. "Let's try her way. We're almost forced to."

"There's still the problem of the baby," André said.

"Give the baby to Riel, he's so anxious to raise it!" cried Marie-Louise. "I never want to see it!"

Jaw hard, Riel spoke. "I'll take the baby," he said. "I'll keep its ancestry secret from all but my mother who already knows."

Reluctantly, because this seemed the only solution, André agreed. "You'll give it your name?"

Riel nodded. "I'll get my mother to adopt it. It will be Rivard by name and by blood."

Chapter XII

Riel quit school the next day. He told the schoolmistress that he was needed on the plantation and she accepted his statement. All the plantations needed every available worker.

The schoolmistress also accepted, with surprise, Euphemie Leblanc's note that Marie-Louise had begun to go into a decline and the doctor felt she had best stay at home and build her strength. The schoolmistress had noted that Marie-Louise seemed subdued, but not that she looked ill. Well, Euphemie Leblanc was a perceptive mother, and there was the family history of a great-grandmother who had gone into declines, finally dying. Heaven forbid that such a fate should come to sweet, spirited Marie-Louise.

And so, quite innocently, the schoolmistress did her share in spreading news of Marie-Louise's decline, thus giving it authenticity. Everybody had heard of Catherine Leblanc and her tragic declines; it was wise of the Leblancs to give their daughter the best of care. Most even approved of the family's decision to permit no visitors.

All the girls at school sent cheerful notes; some of the boys, too shy to write, sent messages. A few people, among them the Heberts, did ask to call on Marie-Louise, but when Euphemie explained that she was to have no excitement at all, they sent soup instead.

Consequently, the bayou country accepted Marie-Louise's story as true. Old Dr. Gilbert would never give a hint of the situation. He came to see Marie-Louise every few weeks, said that she was having a normal pregnancy, advised strongly that he be called at the time of birth.

Marie-Louise tossed her head. "That's too dangerous! You tell Mama and my wench what to do! And Old Granny'll help—she'll keep her mouth shut! We don't dare risk having the blacks see you rushing in, staying a long time! They'd begin to talk, and it'd get on the grapevine and everybody on the bayou would be suspicious!"

The old doctor tried to prevail on André, but he shook his head grimly. "Marie-Louise is determined. The problem is whether she can undergo a midwife delivery safely."

The white-haired doctor nodded. "She's in beautiful condition. She should deliver easily. However, I'd much prefer—"

"We have to keep it secret, doctor."

The old man sighed. "It's months yet," he said. "My prediction is that she'll thrive right to the end. I'll give Euphemie instructions, but if trouble starts when she goes into labor, call me."

André agreed, but he was troubled.

Marie-Louise soon tired of hiding. "I don't see why I can't go for a walk in the rose gardens!" she exclaimed. "Nothing shows yet!"

"Yo' good health, it show," said tiny, dimpled Gracie. She smiled placatingly, and the dimples showed more. "Nobody gonna b'lieve yo' in a de-cline, they see yo' all rosy an' purty! Yo' got to stay hid!"

"The Grape House, then! We can sit there after dark. Nobody can see what I look like then!"

"I reckon that be all right," Gracie said doubtfully.

"Of course, it's all right! When did you set yourself up as mistress, saying I can't do this, can't do that?"

"It yo' own notion, Miss Marie-Louise, fo' me an' yo' to stay in Honeymoon House, with you seein' nobody 'cause yo' in a de-cline."

"Oh, hush! It's hard enough to— What about Gab and Celeste? Do they ask about me?"

"Mistah Gab, he want to know if you in a bad de-cline, an' I said whut the doctah told—that it a real bad de-cline, but it not dang'rous."

"He's suspicious! Gab's suspicious! What else did he say? Anything about boys?"

"He nevah did. Or Miss Celeste."

"That's one good thing."

"Yo' ain' never mention no boy, even to me."

"That's something you have no business knowing!"

"No, I reckon not."

As time dragged on, Marie-Louise became increasingly restive. She got big in the stomach, the baby kicked and sometimes that hurt, and she developed a tendency to waddle. She cried frequently.

"I can't stand it!" she wailed to Euphemie. "I can't! Look at that!" She gestured to where Gracie was putting away hated, voluminous nightgowns which she had washed and dried in the kitchen so their size wouldn't be noted.

"You must be patient, darling."

"I want to ride, to dance, to have fun! I never ever meant to get into this mess! I wish we'd gone to Europe! I wish I hadn't got so scared I practically forced you and papa to let me do it this way!"

"It's too late to change now, darling."

"Not even in black night with me in a cape? We couldn't go to Europe now?"

"No, darling. There's Gracie, too. You made promises to her."

"You wouldn't tell, would you, Gracie?" wept Marie-Louise.

Gracie began to weep, too. "Yo' thought it up yo'se'f, Miss Marie-Louise! Whut you'd give me if I stay with you, an' all! An' I ain' tol' nobody, not even Cal! Why, jus' las' night some of the people ax me how you doin', an' I say it be weeks yet be'fo you well. An' aftah that, Cal got real fierce. He say he tired waitin' fo' me, that you takin' an awful long de-cline, an' he got othah girls wantin' him, an' I didn' tell him a word of whut's really goin' on! I let him kiss me sweet, an' he calm down an' say he wait, 'cause I the purtiest wench he know, but it was scary an' it was hard to keep my promise when I might lose Cal!"

Still weeping, Marie-Louise recognized the import of what Gracie said. She realized it was impossible to go to Europe with her stomach so big, because it would seem strange indeed to bayou folk were she suddenly to abandon her rest cure for the rigors of travel.

Gracie blubbered, "Now I don' know do Cal want me or jes' the big weddin' and the big cabin! I don' know is he waitin' fo' them or fo' me!"

"Hush, both of you," Euphemie soothed. "Time will pass; this will end."

"If I kin jus' tell Cal!" wept Gracie.

"No!" sobbed Marie-Louise. "You promised. And if you tell him, you get nothing!"

"Then she'd be free of her promise," Euphemie pointed out. "You have to keep faith with each other. It would do you equal harm if you didn't."

The two young girls, mistress and maid, gradually stopped weeping, wiped their eyes, blew their noses, stared at each other with new eyes. "Trapped," Marie-Louise said. "We're trapped with each other. All our lives."

"You're friends," Euphemie told them, "going through a stormy period. Believe me, your friendship can deepen the way Old René's and Hippolyte's did. You'll be as close as they, when you're old, after you get through the next few weeks."

They gazed at her solemnly, then at each other, managed a smile. It was at this instant that Marie-Louise knew she loved Gracie, and that Gracie knew she loved her mistress and could never betray her, even to Cal, husband or not.

The bayou folk never forgot, not for a week, that Marie-Louise was in a decline. They sent her jellies and broths; they sent her gossipy notes. Every day Celeste gave Gracie a hand-picked bouquet for Marie-Louise; Gab filled a basket with the wild greens she liked to eat and gave them to Gracie to cook.

Riel, in these months, fought the ache in his heart. He took charge of Rivard, and helped by those of the plantation's ex-slaves who had elected to stay, he gradually pulled the operation under control. He couldn't grow as much sugar cane as in the past—there weren't enough field hands to cultivate and reap it, but at the end of the growing season he knew there was going to be a small profit.

Riel himself worked harder than any buck, any wench. Driven, devastated by Marie-Louise's rejection, by knowledge of the black blood in his veins, by the fact of incest, by his mother's perfidy, he worked as much to forget as he did to bring in crops.

As he worked, he brooded over what he had done, his bringing to light incest and black blood. He'd committed incest. He'd ruined Marie-Louise. Somehow he would set the whole horrible situation right. He knew he could never marry Marie-Louise, but some day before he died, he would resolve everything. How, he couldn't think. There was a foggy pattern, an undefined map, at the bottom of his mind, but he could not yet bring it into focus.

He had another brief talk with Olive.

"It's getting near time for Marie-Louise's baby to be born," he said.

"Yes," she answered sadly.

"I told them I'd take it, that you'd take it."

"It's the least we can do, son."

"I told them you'd adopt it."

For a heartbeat, she was silent. "Of course," she agreed. "But have you thought how we can explain a baby?"

"Use that sea captain you're supposed to have been wife to," he said bitterly. "Say the baby's a nephew of his. Or niece."

"That's a good solution," Olive agreed. "I'll be happy to adopt your baby, my son."

For an instant, only an instant, the edge of his anger and hatred toward her dulled. And then his feelings sharpened against her once more.

When enough time had passed, he made secret trips to L'Acadie to find out if Marie-Louise had given birth. Heartsick, ravaged by her hatred of him, resentful of what René Leblanc and Olive had made of him, filled with pity for his unborn child, he made the useless trips, then went home. He waited, brooding, discarding one idea after another, seeking the right one.

His motive was to spare Marie-Louise any more hurt, then see to it, somehow, that the Rivard family built into something fine and honest and admirable. How, he didn't yet know. But this building of his family was to become his life's work.

In early dark one night, he was outside Honeymoon House. He was about to leave when the activity began. He hid behind a tree and watched. Gracie burst out the door and raced for the big house. From the cottage came only silence.

Riel's heart swelled. Was his darling, his ruined darling, in there alone, holding back her moans, stifling them, keeping her secret even in her labor? He started to rush to her, but forced himself to draw back.

She wouldn't want him.

After a silent eternity, he saw a figure run into the lamplit kitchen, followed by a man. It was Euphemie, and with her, André. They disappeared, then Gracie came trotting back, Old Granny with her, and they crossed the kitchen and disappeared.

Riel choked on his own breath. He coughed, hand over mouth, to avoid strangling.

As in a dream, he left his tree, crossed the grass, moved into the kitchen. At the bedroom door he stopped, trembling.

Marie-Louise was arched up from the bed, Euphemie holding her hands, Old Granny pushing her hips flat to the mattress. Gracie was wringing her hands, not a dimple showing.

"Hot watah!" demanded Old Granny. "Scissahs!"

Gracie bumped full into Riel as she rushed to the kitchen. He steadied her, stepped inside. She ran to the stove, and soon he was aware of the rocking sound of the iron teakettle.

"Moan, sweetheart," he heard Euphemie plead when Marie-Louise arched again, dropped so her hips struck the mattress. "Don't try to hold it back!"

The girl rolled her head from side to side. "No," she gasped, and bit her lip. Her breath was another labor. Her body arched again.

"Yell, Missy!" urged Old Granny. "It easiah!"

"Nobody . . . must know . . . you not . . . tell. Mama . . ."

"You heard her, Granny," André said sternly. "Only those of us in this house are to know. The missy has had a decline, that's all you need say. Do you understand?"

Old Granny slanted him a glance. "Ain' bin scandal 'nuff, Mastah? Ole Granny, she die wif dis night lock in her heart."

It was when Riel moved aside to admit Gracie with the teakettle and scissors, that André saw him. He felt anger, then sympathy. "This young master," he told Old Granny, "is here to take the baby. That's a secret, too."

Old Granny slanted another look, nodded, bent over the bed. "She have hard time," she muttered. "She don' stretch right. She goin' labah long time."

"If I could help, sir?" Riel asked André.

"Keep watah hot," ordered the old midwife, and Riel took the teakettle and made for the water barrel. He set the filled kettle on the stove, went back to the room, watched.

He saw the agony his love had brought to Marie-Louise. He saw her lips bleed, saw her palms bloody from digging her nails into the flesh. He quivered when he realized that not only was her face streaming sweat, but her tortured body was as well. This he had brought her, this she endured without a moan.

Before dawn, Old Granny pulled forth the scrawny, limp body. She held it by its ankles and smacked its buttocks and shoulders, but it didn't cry. In the lamplight, there was a blue tinge to it.

She put it into Riel's arms because he was the nearest. "Stillborn boy," she said, and turned back to Marie-Louise. "She need us now. She goin' to have a time wif de aftahbirth."

"We'll send for the doctor," André said, only to be hushed by Euphemie, Old Granny, Marie-Louise herself. "I'll not have her suffer any more," he told them grimly.

"Stay heah; she got to suffah, Mastah! Granny bring huh through. Granny had lots of aftahbirths. She be all right—it jus' take time. Trus' Granny."

When André moved toward the door, Euphemie stopped him. "Trust her, darling. The worst is over. Don't ruin what Marie-Louise has gone through; don't make it all for nothing."

He hesitated, stayed.

"Sir," Riel asked, "may I take the baby home?"

André, dazed at the sight of his dead grandson in its father's arms, thought swiftly. This way, Marie-Louise would have no little, hidden grave to remind her, nor would it ever be discovered and talked about.

"Go," André said. "Now."

As Riel stumbled the three miles homeward in dawn light, it seemed the dead baby quivered. He stopped, looked into the little face, saw the wizened lips part, stir. He broke into a run, heart in his throat. The baby was alive! His son lived!

He hurried into the kitchen as Olive and Nette, her personal maid for years, were cooking breakfast. They rushed to him, took one look at the blue infant. Olive lifted the naked little body into her arms, Nette brought a heavy towel, and they wrapped him.

"That won't do it," Olive said. "We've got to rub him."

She hurried into the drawing room with the child, laid him on the divan, knelt. Olive began rubbing around his heart, while Nette rubbed his legs, his toes and fingers and arms. Riel watched in wonder. Working together without letup, rubbing and dribbling drops of warm milk between the tiny lips, Olive and Nette brought life into the frail new body, and soon the infant began to breathe in a shallow, but regular manner.

"He has a bad heart," Nette said, rubbing the tiny toes, her hand under the towel which covered him.

"We'll send for Dr. Gilbert," Olive said. "This baby needs more than we can give him. He needs medicine, some kind of drops. Special foods."

"And he needs love," whispered Nette.

"He'll get it all," Olive said, her eyes meeting Riel's. He had stood ready to help, not knowing what to do. "Send someone for the doctor," she told him. "Don't go yourself. I'll tell Nette who he is, for she must know, but the others at Rivard need only know what we tell them."

After the doctor, the drops, the milk with melted butter added, the rubbing, the rocking, the love, the baby strengthened, tiny bit by tiny bit. One day he smiled and Olive and Nette wept, smiling back at him through their tears.

Riel told the Rivard people, knowing word would travel the bayou grapevine, that the baby Felix was an orphan, the nephew of Olive Rivard's deceased sea captain husband.

"Mastah Riel's father?" one black asked.

Riel frowned, decided, spoke. "That's right," he said, anger slicing through him as he added to the lie.

Felix would always have a weak heart, the old doctor told Olive, would always need the drops. "He'll be in pain at times," he said. "He is in pain even now as a newborn baby. But with careful nursing, he'll improve."

Olive watched Dr. Gilbert with the child, noted the

gentleness of his fingers. Does he know? she wondered. Surely they must have had him to see Marie-Louise when she was pregnant, perhaps he even delivered the child. But no. He would have detected life; he wouldn't have put the child aside as stillborn. She had no idea of the birth scene; Riel had told her nothing, and she wouldn't anger him by asking.

Of one thing Olive was certain. If the doctor knew Marie-Louise had borne this child, if he suspected Riel was the father, the secret would die with him.

Days passed, weeks, and Felix's looks changed. Brown-haired and brown-eyed, his features now promised to be handsome. His skin was white as Riel's without the tan the sun laid on. She rocked him, held him to her, loved him, the grandson of herself and René Leblanc.

At this time, the Rivard blacks were suddenly agog about the big wedding the Leblancs were giving Gracie and Cal. There was to be a white wedding cake and a gold wedding ring. The happy couple was going to move into the three-room cabin. But the Rivard people had to do their admiring and exclaiming from afar, because none of them had been invited to the wedding.

Chapter XIII

During the months of working the fields with his people Riel agonized over Marie-Louise, over his mixed blood, over the fact that he and Olive had lived white all these years—dishonestly, because they carried the taint of Negro.

He spent sleepless nights haunted by the problem of the blood. By day, he studied Olive, so beautiful and gentle, and thought not Mama, but octoroon. She should have been some white lady's faithful serving wench, not a white man's toy, a man who wasn't really white at that.

Riel felt guilt over his changed attitude toward Olive. He

did love her, angrily, but he could no longer respect her. What she had done seemed not gallant nor courageous, but deceitful. And the thought of Olive and deceit being impossible to reconcile, he felt a continuing resentment, a growing hatred toward her.

It always came back to the same thing. Because of the lie she had already lived and still was living, his entire life was a lie. And he could not forgive.

Rarely was Riel merry now; usually he was deeply sober. He brooded over Felix. The baby was as white as any child, whiter than most because of his pallor, his delicacy. Riel felt both aversion and pity for Felix, whom Olive had adopted legally and who was rightfully Felix Rivard. He didn't feel like a father toward the infant, nor even like a brother. Pity and regret and kindness, those emotions he felt, and for these things the frail baby loved him and held out his arms and Riel would hold him for a moment.

His determination to make the Rivards a family of worth drove him night and day, but the solution eluded him. So he worked the earth, pondered, was friendly toward the blacks. But when real warmth toward anyone rose, especially Olive, he crushed it down and remembered only lost joy, incest, the ailing Felix. Then his anger toward Olive would revive as he brooded.

The time came when he could delay the future no longer. He had to come to a decision. All the facts were burned into his soul; he must deal with them.

Meticulously, he brought that dim plan he'd carried so long at the bottom of his mind into focus. And from it, there came to him a careful, thoughtful decision. A spelling out of its consequences indicated shame and pain for Olive; his whole family would be looked down upon, despised, and even persecuted at first.

Riel announced his goal to Olive.

She was in the drawing room, darning table linen. He sat down, facing her. Seeing her placid face, her pleasure that he had come to sit with her, he almost faltered. But he clung to the fact that his was a considered decision, not just a blind lashing-out at fate.

"They're marrying Marie-Louise," he began. "She grew up, I guess, when she had the 'decline.'"

"I heard. The grapevine."

"Do you think she loves him?"

"Probably. She's very young. She needs to recover from what happened."

"I don't grieve over her any more," he said. "But I'll never get over it. The blood, I mean. It changed my life. And will change yours."

"How do you mean, it will change our lives?"

"It's been a long time. I've spent it thinking. There is only one answer."

Olive's darning dropped to her lap, her hands rested quietly on it. "And that is . . . ?"

"I should think you'd know. Do you expect that I'll continue to live a lie? Hide my black blood in my white, never admit to it, never be proud of it? Do you expect that I'll hide what I am from my children? That I'll marry a white girl, deceive her, see that Felix does the same, make sure the Rivards are 'white'? Throw away the heritage you gave me, Mama, you and René Leblanc?"

His words kept slamming into her racing heart, terrifying her. Her hands trembled in her lap. She sucked in her breath. It was dry, and hurt her lungs. Her head began to spin. She had to answer him; he was waiting. She had to reply to her son, to his fierce words. Had to ward off the panic his words had driven into her.

"There's such a good start, Riel," she pleaded. "You're so nearly pure white that your children—"

"You're forgetting the throwback, Mama, the coal black baby born to a white mother and father."

"I can't believe in the throwback."

"And you can't change me, Mama."

"What is it you mean to do?"

"You have it backward about my children. I said I'll not hide black blood in white, and I say now that I'll pour my white blood into black. The Rivards from this day on are going to be Negro. Because I am going to marry the blackest, prettiest, smartest girl I can find. Felix will, too, when he is strong enough to deal with the truth."

Olive's heart pounded so that the thin gauze of her dress moved. "You can't marry a black girl!" she whispered in horror. "You're white . . . white!"

"But I'm not white."

"The law won't let you marry a black girl!"

"The law won't keep me from it, I promise you!"

Feeling as if he'd beaten her with his fists, Olive stared at her son, suddenly a strong, willful man. Despair knifed through her for the years with René Leblanc and the ambitious plans he'd had for Riel. Her whole inner body, her very soul, ached from all the years of pretending, of 'passing', of keeping herself remote from the bayou community but respected by it.

She thought dully of the horror her acquaintances would feel over her blood and Riel's, thought of the shame and embarrassment of appearing in public as an acknowledged black. Nausea swept her. She understood Riel's belief that their life had been a lie, started to cry out her understanding but he gestured her to silence.

She remained quiet. Overwhelmed by his implacableness, by his intentions, she went sick to the marrow. She dare not argue lest she lose all his love as she had lost his respect. She felt impelled, driven, to do whatever he wanted. He seemed to be the stern father, she the frightened child. And she loved him so deeply, now was so in awe of him, that there was only one way—his way—to retain even a drop of his affection.

She asked, aching throat so dry she could hardly speak, "When do you mean to do this thing?"

"The minute I find the right girl, Mama," he told her quietly. "The sooner the better."

PART II

1875—1894

Chapter XIV

Charles Hebert had been in the drawing room with his father Robert when the subject of travel came up. At twenty, he enjoyed these evenings; while his father smoked a cigar; they spoke of many things.

This night, as soon as they got comfortable and the cigar was going, Robert said, "You're a handsome young man. Do you know that?"

Charles reddened, gestured. He'd given himself an occasional glance in the mirror, knew he wasn't homely with his light brown hair and eyes, his olive complexion, his strong Hebert build, his strong Hebert features.

He grinned at Robert. "I look just like you," he bantered.

"Except for some wrinkles and white streaks in my hair. Your mother told me from the day you were born you'd be another Robert Hebert, wanted to name you that, but I talked her out of it."

They smiled together sadly for the woman they had lost.

"I've had a thing on my conscience," Robert said. "That you missed your college years in New Orleans."

"That wasn't your fault, pa."

"I know—the war between the states. My consolation was that you were too young for the Army; you were only eleven when the war began, fifteen when it ended. Your mother was grateful. Even at the last she said, 'He's safe, Rob! Oh, keep him safe!'"

Charles nodded, remembering. He knew how important he was to Hebert Plantation, the only child, the son to carry on the name.

"Why worry about college now?" he asked. "I'm satisfied, learning more about sugar cane from you every day."

"You have a need, son, before you settle down, that you don't realize. I've arranged for you to have a year away from the bayous. To give you a change, to enrich your life."

"Whatever for?"

"Every man needs, once in his life, a time of change, a respite, a period of freedom in which to do as he pleases. You missed college which would have supplied you with much of what you need. I have the money. I've sold your mother's diamonds; they brought enough to go wherever you want in comfort."

"Go where?" Charles was bewildered.

"To college for a couple of years in New Orleans."

Charles shook his head. "I'm beyond that, pa. You and Mama taught me here at home."

"Travel, then. Spend a year on the continent."

Charles felt a stir of interest. "Not the whole continent," he said. "Paris, maybe. Remember how I read all those Paris books in your library? Mama used to tease me so; she said I was wearing them out!"

"If Paris is what you want, there's money for passage and a full year in the city."

Charles' excitement flared, quieted. "It's also money that can well be kept against hard times," he said.

Robert insisted. "We're doing as well as any other grower. I'll be sorely disappointed if you don't have at least one year of being young and carefree. It means a great deal to me, Charles. Why, André Leblanc plans to send Gab to college in New Orleans for a year, for the same reason. We discussed it."

"How will he get the money?"

"He has a bit put aside from before the War. He inferred as much, because he said he's already prepared to send Gab after he's matured a bit more."

Charles didn't give in to his father's wishes that night. They talked about it for a month. Charles finally admitted that yes, he'd like to go to Paris, and from that admission on, Robert was not to be denied.

Immediately, he told André Leblanc and others the news, and within two days everybody on the bayous knew that Charles Hebert was going to spend a year in Paris. Some were shocked because Robert had sold his wife's jewels; most approved. More than one set of parents regretted they couldn't do the same for their sons; a few who could have managed travel for one son found themselves unable to consider it because they had two sons, and couldn't favor one above the other.

Charles allowed Robert to supply him with a modest travel wardrobe, carrying everything in one bag. He secured the money in his pocket, keeping easily available a small sum for immediate expenses after he paid for his passage in New Orleans. As his ship set sail, his eyes stung.

Did any son ever have, he thought, a father as thoughtful as Robert Hebert. Then Charles set his face forward, ready for his year, resolved to memorize every detail for Robert, to fill their evenings with tales of Paris.

It was July 15, 1870 when Charles set foot in Paris. He walked from the train station, carrying his bag. Excitement surged through him; he was in Paris at last! He walked the wide boulevards lined with chestnut trees, passed hotels, some of which looked inviting, some imposing, all too grand for his pocket.

Robert had said before Charles boarded the small boat in St. Martinville, "Don't be afraid to spend. I expect you to be penniless when you get back."

But today, walking the boulevards, Charles was on the watch for some hotel which was small and plain and cheap. What did he need of a fine place? All he'd use was the bed for a few hours of sleep each night, and the wash basin, and then he'd be out roaming the city.

He would dine at some fine restaurants. Robert had made him promise that. "It's like going to Antoine's in New Orleans," he said. "Expensive, but an experience not to be missed. You're to do these things, for such things become a part of you. You never lose them. Memories, come home filled with memories."

Pa was right, Charles thought, seeing fine carriages

drawn by shining, matched horses, moving fast in two directions. He gazed at couples strolling along, the women young and attractive, wearing fine silk dresses with bustles and tiny hats, their hair caught artfully in the back, allowed to fall in puffs, braids or twists. Charles had never seen anything so fine. The ladies' escorts wore sack coats and fairly full, long trousers. They wore tall silk hats on their parted hair, and paid courtly attention to their ladies.

All seemed to be speaking excitedly, and Charles wondered if something had happened or whether this was a Parisian trait. He took note of people in carriages and they, too, were animated and talkative. He marked it down to the excitement of Paris itself, thinking excitement was in the blood of these people, wondering how they ever got any sleep at night.

It never occurred to him that he looked slightly out of place in his new plain trousers, his American version of the sack coat, his plain bayou hat. If he had thought of his plain and sturdy garb, he would have decided he was well outfitted.

He walked and stared, wondering where all the people came from. He was from Bayou Teche where there were few people, and Paris had a population of two million. He started paying closer attention to strollers he passed.

They were excited, really excited, talking so fast and, though their French differed from the Acadian French of the bayou, he did keep hearing the words "war" and "Prussia."

Charles frowned. War? He stopped, set his bag down, stood in the shade of a chestnut tree, his hand on the protective railing built around it, and openly studied people. They were more than excited; many were upset. There was no laughter in any of the talk. And not a smile on any face.

Across the boulevard was a small hotel, very plain. He decided to go there, and engage a room if the price wasn't too high. He'd ask the concierge, using his Bayou French, if anything out of the ordinary was taking place and, if so, what it was. He picked up his bag, stepped out and began to thread his way carefully through the fast traffic of the carriages.

He was almost across the boulevard when a black carriage, drawn by runaway horses, careened around a corner. A girl in white who was running across the boulevard got in its path and instantly was knocked to the pavement.

Charles dodged between two speeding carriages, flung his bag onto the sidewalk, gripped the girl under the arms and pulled her to the walk. She'd fallen face down, and in his haste he dragged her that way, the toes of her slippers scraping the pavement.

Once at the walk, he helped her to a sitting position. Her skirts had ridden up over her knees, both of which were skinned and bleeding, her delicate stockings torn.

People gathered round as Charles whipped out his handkerchief and began to pat away the blood, first from one knee, then from the other. As fast as he patted, it flowed anew, running down her slim, shapely legs.

Charles assumed from the anger and exclamations of those gathered around that the carriage which had knocked the girl down had gone on its way. He heard some cry, "Police!" then go into a tirade when no police appeared.

Two of the ladies urged Charles aside and took charge of the girl's bleeding knees. Each bandaged a knee with a handkerchief from her escort, then both helped the girl pull her skirts properly down. From the constant chatter, Charles realized that the ladies were blaming the war for what had happened to the girl.

What war? Charles wondered, but didn't ask, because the ladies had gotten the girl to her feet, then had moved on with their escorts, leaving Charles alone with her.

This was the first real look he'd had at her, except for those lovely legs. Now he saw that she was young, a mere girl indeed, and beautiful as she stood holding her crushed bonnet against her soiled white dress. Charles suddenly wanted to find out about her.

She was slim and shapely; her short, black hair was fine and soft-looking, cut so that it was feathered all over her head and around her face. Her features were fine and perfect, her dancing eyes deep blue and almost dancing.

"Monsieur!" she exclaimed, then continued in English, "thank you for saving my life!"

"I'm glad I could help," he said, amazed to hear English from a girl in Paris. "I doubt if I saved your life."

"Oh, but you did!" she cried, utterly serious. And then she smiled, and this seemed to set all of her features dancing, though she hadn't stirred. "You saved my life which makes me your responsibility, or so some say! And I can't thank you properly unless we sit at a sidewalk cafe and drink coffee! Or does my boldness offend you?"

"Indeed not! Where shall we go?"

"To the square. Bring your valise. Did you just arrive?"

"Not an hour ago."

"It's a long trip from America," she said, as they started to walk.

"How did you know I'm from America?"

"It shows in your clothes. And your speech. My mother was American. It's easy for me to tell."

"I speak French," he told her, "but it comes from what the Acadians spoke in Nova Scotia long ago. It seems different from Parisian French. I can hardly understand the people here. And they talk so fast."

She laughed, gave a little skip. He glanced down at her slim feet. Dancing feet. One would never know she had two bloody knees, he thought.

At the sidewalk table he ordered, but the waiter barely understood Charles' French. Charles grinned at her and she smiled back. He forgot the traffic on the boulevard, forgot the people who kept passing by. This was the most exciting girl he'd ever seen. He had to know all about her.

She laughed brightly. "You haven't told me your name. I'm Suzette Duval; I'm eighteen and on my own in the world!" Sadness tinged her eyes; laughter ceased. Then suddenly, as if aware of this, she laughed away her unexplained sadness.

"I'm Charles Hebert, twenty," he told her. "From the Bayou Teche in Louisiana."

"Louisiana, in America?"

"New Orleans is the nearest city."

"Then you know about war; you had a war!"

"And my side lost."

"Paris won't lose."

"What do you mean?"

"All this excitement! Today, just today, France has declared war on Prussia! And we'll win!"

"Why did France declare war?"

"Spain has no king, and the crown was offered to Leopold of Hohenzollern and he's a relative of William I of Prussia!

That would bring Spain under the influence of Prussia, which France will not tolerate!"

Charles was entranced by her. He didn't want to talk about war, he wanted to tell her how lovely she was, and to see her, again and again. He wanted to tell her how everything about her danced—her loose hair, her eyes, her slim feet.

But she kept talking about the war. "My papa would have been very serious about it," she explained, "but Mama would have wanted to go back to Charleston. Papa had a stroke, he didn't live. We'd have talked about this war, oh, how we would have talked!"

"I'm sorry about your parents."

"Thank you, Charles. They were wonderful, and I miss them. And I miss my Aunt Harriet who moved to London. She quite disapproves of me, a girl alone in Paris, pursuing my art studies! But we mustn't talk about me—it's the war! You must understand! Adolphe Thiers, one of the French leaders, is opposed to this war!"

"Why is he opposed?"

"Because we have no allies!"

"Why doesn't Leopold withdraw?"

"Oh, he has! Then Paris demanded an immediate declaration of war because otherwise France could lose her power and her place in the world!"

"I see," said Charles, not understanding at all.

She let him walk her to her apartment on the Left Bank. It had three rooms; she had shared it with her father. Her canvases were stacked all around the biggest room, and as she showed them to him, he saw that they were mostly landscapes.

He described Bayou Teche, telling her that a lifetime of painting could never capture its beauty. And in the telling, he conceived the idea of marrying this enchanting girl and taking her home with him, but it was too soon to speak. He had to satisfy himself by saying, "It would keep a hundred artists busy all their lives, and they'd never get it all on canvas."

He did ask to see her again. "I enjoy your company," he said. "And if you'd show me through the Louvre—I've seen paintings in books, but now I want to see the real thing."

She accepted with delight.

They went the next day. He knew nothing about artists' techniques, so she explained, and because she loved to paint and he was falling in love with her, he paid close attention. Also, as he viewed the paintings through her eyes, he developed a taste, and appreciated them more. But it was her own paintings he liked the best. He told her so, and she smiled and thanked him but said in time he'd see the vast difference between her work and that of the masters.

The days flew past, filled with talk of the war, with Suzette showing him more of Paris, the old, exquisite buildings. He realized he was falling more deeply in love which he feared to mention, for she was so intent on the war, on Paris, on her determination that France should win.

On September 6, General Louis-Jules Trochu became commander of what was left of the French army. Adolphe Thiers, a white-haired, square-faced politician, did not accept a position in government, but instead went to visit London, St. Petersburg, Vienna, and Florence, trying to enlist foreign support for beleaguered France.

"He'll get help!" declared Suzette, starry-eyed.

As Paris prepared for attack, Charles and Suzette saw the Tuileries stable and garden turned into a vast military park, saw graves dug at Montmartre to prevent the possible spread of disease.

They watched trainloads of treasures be shipped from the Louvre to Brest for safekeeping, and the empty galleries turned into another arsenal. The partly finished Opera House was converted into a military depot; most of the theaters became hospitals.

Trains seemed to bring people in as fast as they took them out. Men, women, children scurried up and down the streets, carrying or wheeling or dragging some kind of vehicle. Charles helped Suzette store her paintings in a sturdy stone warehouse, hearing distant rumbles as the bridges of the Seine were blown up.

Suzette existed in a state of excitement, as did all of Paris. "The Prussians will lay siege to Paris!" she declared. "Everybody agrees on that! And all are getting ready!"

This was in January, and the weather was cold. Puzzled by this war, aware that fuel was running low and people were cutting down the trees along the boulevards for firewood,

Charles tried to get a clear picture of the conflict from the excited Suzette, could not.

"Won't Paris be hard to surround?" he asked as they chopped up a small tree to use for firewood in her apartment. "With a thirty foot wall around the city, and outside it thirteen forts—"

"Fifteen," she corrected. "And we have over a hundred thousand men in the Army and Navy, and another two hundred thousand National Guard and a hundred thousand Gardes Mobiles."

About this time she warned him to get out of Paris while he could yet her big eyes pleaded for him to refuse. He took her hands, kissed her gently on the lips. "I don't pretend to understand this war, Suzette," Charles said. "Later—"

"Let's not talk about later until we win!" she cried. And because she was so intense, he kissed her again and said no more.

The next day she told him, "Authorities think there's enough grain in Paris for eighty days, and coal, too, so they don't want people cutting any more trees. They've driven forty thousand oxen and two hundred fifty thousand sheep into Napoleon III's Bois de Boulogne to slaughter for meat. Nobody is to go hungry!"

The Prussians advanced steadily, throwing two wings around Paris, north and south. There were skirmishes but no big engagements. Balloons were now sent out with people aboard. Pigeons also carried messages to the outside world.

Paris, now under full siege, unable to fight, suffered acute boredom. There was nothing to do but settle into the dull, tedious discomfort of waiting out a siege.

Suzette had much to say; there were no dull moments for Charles, who was with her constantly. "Shortages have appeared way too soon," she declared. "There's not enough fresh milk for the babies, think of it!"

"Meat and bread seem to be lasting," Charles said.

"But we have to stand much longer in line to get it," she reminded him. "Sometimes I think we spend our lives standing in line!"

"That's because we do it for some of the tired mothers," Charles reminded in his turn. "Well, tomorrow's Sunday, so there'll be no lines."

Sunday, they joined the favorite occupation of hundreds, taking to the walks near the defense zone and listening to the occasional firing, and talking to each other and to those nearby, the favorite topic being Napoleon and Eugénie and the whole imperial regime.

Thiers, having failed in his mission to win allies, returned to Paris. He wanted the Parisians to accept the German peace terms and, in February, went to Versailles to discuss preliminaries of peace.

As a result, thirty thousand German troops were permitted to occupy Paris, limited to the area between the Avenue des Ternes and the Rue de Faubourg St. Honoré on the north and the Seine on the south. This kept them in the wealthy district, away from the working class where trouble might foment. Much to the troops' disappointment, ratification of terms made their stay in Paris very short, lasting only three days.

Paris was in turmoil. Suzette, ever on the edge of excitement, tried to explain, but the situation was so complicated that even she didn't understand it thoroughly. As for Charles, he was bewildered. He took the only course open to him because he loved this girl—he stayed on her side of every controversy, knowing her to be honest, though fiery.

Out of Thiers' talks at Versailles rose the new Parisian government. Suzette and the other Parisians considered this government traitors who had sold their country to the Germans, traitors who acted as if they were ready to accept a king.

This swung Suzette to the army of poorer citizens. "We're joining them, Charles!" she cried. "We must! We can't tolerate a king; and we can no longer permit thousands of children only eight years old to work! We're forced to join the Commune!"

"But Marx—"

"Communards have nothing to do with Marxism! They want only fair and equal treatment for all! Say you'll join with me, Charles, oh, please!"

This time, because he wanted to put a stop to child labor, not because Suzette pleaded so hotly, Charles agreed.

The German bombardment began January fifth. Twelve hundred projectiles fell on Paris. Fourteen hundred buildings and homes were damaged. Four hundred people were killed or wounded.

Charles, trying to get Suzette to safety, felt a numbing blow on his right ankle. He ran on, hobbling, until Suzette, alarmed, persuaded him to stop behind a stone warehouse.

He sank to the ground, looked at his ankle. The stocking was ripped, blood oozed. Suzette, pulling his shoe and stocking off, spied the shell fragment embedded in the flesh.

"A doctor!" she cried. "You've got to see a doctor!"

She turned her back, tore off an undergarment, bound the ankle. "Can you walk if I help you?" she asked.

Charles managed a smile, stood.

They found a makeshift hospital and got in line. There were all sorts of wounds. Charles turned his eyes away, unwilling to witness the suffering of others. Suzette gazed at each one, saw the shattered arms, the gaping, bleeding belly wounds, the head injuries, the wives and husbands, the crying children. Charles stared at his treacherous ankle, cursing himself for being unable to help the others.

He insisted on being the last one treated. The doctor was fat, dark-haired, weary. "Keep off the foot all you can," he instructed when he had removed the shell and bandaged the ankle. "You'll feel the effect of this all your life, but be able to function."

Suzette wept when Charles refused to stay in her apartment. "For just a week, until you can walk!" she begged. "Charles, I'll not be able to sleep or eat if you don't! You got this wound taking care of me, now you can at least let me take care of you!"

Because he was so in love with her, because she was so distraught, he gave in. She established him in her father's old room, stood in line for meat, made him a substantial soup, watched him eat it all. She tried to find milk for him, could not. They settled into a routine, Suzette nursing, Charles insisting on hobbling about more each day. Slowly, he improved.

On March eighteenth, Thiers sent a badly trained detachment to seize the two hundred cannons the Parisians held. A crowd of Parisians gathered, armed, and drove the troops away. Paris was now in open insurrection, Parisians fighting Parisians, turning against Thiers, who wanted to bring peace to the city by compromise.

Charles and Suzette left the armed crowd, went back to

her apartment. His ankle left a trail of blood, and she insisted on trying to support him as he walked.

Home again, she bathed and rebandaged the ankle.

"I can move back to my hotel now," he said. "Your reputation—"

She laughed. Again, everything about her seemed to dance. "We won!" she exulted. "We chased the troops out of Paris, and you talk about my reputation! Who pays attention to what we do? There's a war, a siege! Please stay here, Charles. I need you!"

Unable to wait longer, desire for her strong, even with the pain, he captured her vital hands. "I'm in love with you," he said. "Surely you know that!"

"But of course, Charles! And I with you!"

"When all this ends, will you marry me?"

"Certainly!"

"And leave Paris and go with me to Bayou Teche and be wife to a grower of sugar cane?"

"I'll be delighted to be your wife!" she replied, and they kissed with clean passion. She was so beautifully clean-minded, so truly honest. And this was evident in her paintings, clean of line, vibrant with suggested movement of tree, of flower.

He moved into his hotel despite her protests. They were together every waking hour, their precious love growing, as they did what they could to help in the siege.

Thiers, still wanting compromise, remained with the Germans at Versailles. Before March ended, Versailles began another siege, the second in three months, and Charles and Suzette, like the other thousands, settled in to endure.

By the middle of May 1871, the Versailles troops numbered well over a hundred thousand. Thiers, leading them, took the offensive against Paris, street by street. The besieged ones barricaded streets only to see them captured as Parisians fought Parisians.

Charles and Suzette helped barricade still another street. Communards set fire to public buildings—Tuileries, the Louvre, others. At the end of the attack, Versailles was the winner.

Charles, still limping, found that the end of the fighting was only the beginning of the bloodletting. As he and Suzette tried to bring a wounded Communard with a bloody hole in his chest to safety, they were jerked away from him by soldiers and held, despite their struggles.

"Dirty Communards!" spat the one holding Suzette. He gave her a vicious shake.

"Don't do that to her!" shouted Charles in English, forgetting they couldn't understand his words. They understood his tone, however, and the one holding him drove a fist into his eye.

Charles staggered, heard Suzette cry out in French that he was American. The soldier gripped Charles again. Charles yanked free, drew his fist back, crashed it at his captor. The fellow dodged, lunged to grab Charles again, was faced by a flaming Suzette, who had twisted away from her grinning captor who was now watching.

"Non!" Occasionally, recognizable words came to Charles. "American . . . big country . . . soldiers come. . . ."

Abruptly, Charles' captor let him go. Charles ran to Suzette, held her in his arms. He had to get her out of this mob of soldiers and prisoners, but it was a wall of bleeding, shouting humanity, and they were jammed into the midst of it.

Soldiers were lining up prisoners, line after line. Charles managed to stay with Suzette, clutching her. He noted that the street ran with blood.

Suzette, shrieking, got the ear of a soldier. She pointed to Charles and screamed that he was an American, a visitor. She shrieked that if he were harmed, the United States would come in a body and kill every Frenchman.

Another soldier had stopped to listen. He looked at the first soldier, shrugged, yanked Charles away from Suzette. The soldier shouted in French and Charles understood his gesture to leave if not the word. He grabbed for Suzette, ready to run.

A uniformed arm shot out, yanked Suzette back. Charles lunged for her, but failed even to touch her, for three soldiers tackled him, dragging him away through the crowd. Suzette continued to fight wildly to escape, but failed.

The three held Charles, and he still fought. A fourth one laid hands on him, and they held him immobile. He got a flash of Suzette's captors shoving her into a line so violently that she fell back against a fence with a jolt. He saw soldiers' rifles lift, heard the crack of their fire, then Suzette was out of sight, lying on the ground next to all the other prisoners in line with her.

The soldiers fought more prisoners into a line. Charles' captors flung him to the ground. Face battered, ankle a rage of pain, he crawled to his knees, pushed to his feet, staggering, fighting a way through the packed soldiers to where Suzette had been.

He was knocked back by snarling soldiers. Though he struggled to reach Suzette the whole time the rifles cracked, cutting down Communards, Charles never penetrated far enough to see the bodies on the ground.

Because he had to, he waited until the killing ended, waited until the soldiers left. And then he went limping and searching for Suzette, moving along the fence where she had been standing when last he saw her. There he found her, at last.

She was lying on her back, arms flung out, feathery hair stirring in the breeze, a look of peace on her face. Her dancing feet were quiet. He laid his ear over her heart, and it was silent.

He spent the night beside her, surrounded by the thousands of dead, wanting to bury her himself under their favorite chestnut tree, but a burial crew of soldiers appeared at dawn and ordered him away. He tried to explain, but they couldn't understand. He pointed to Suzette's body, but they shook their heads and drove him away, threatening him with rifles.

He glowered, letting all hatred show, but there were too many soldiers, and they were relentless. There was nothing he could do but let Suzette be buried with the others.

Later, when they had finished and her body had been buried in a mass grave, there was no way to find her. She was lost to him forever. If he could have done so, he would have killed every soldier in Paris in order to avenge Suzette.

Finally Charles went to the army headquarters. He told one who understood English that he was American, that he never wanted to see Paris again. The official was displeased and frowned, but gave him an official exit paper. He went to the stone warehouse to get one of Suzette's paintings, his favorite, a bridge across the Seine, but the inside of the warehouse had been burned and there were no paintings. After that Charles departed, leaving part of himself behind with Suzette.

At Bayou Teche, he was greeted with the information that his father had died of a heart attack only a month ago. He found that he was sorely needed to take over running the plantation.

With a bleeding sadness which he believed would never heal, Charles put on his old, familiar bayou clothes and set to work.

Chapter XV

Charles, grieving for both his gallant Suzette and his father Robert, worked every waking hour. He made careful farming plans and saw that they were carried out; he himself labored as hard as any helper. And still grief gnawed and ate at him, so he worked, toiled until he was too exhausted when darkness fell, to do anything but sleep. And often he couldn't sleep, could only dwell on the tasks he would do tomorrow, could only dwell on Suzette, on Robert.

During the days, he forced his mind to stay on the job at hand—planting, chopping weeds, clearing irrigation ditches. Intent on such work, he kept his mind off his lost ones. He never went out, but stayed at home to work and to sleep.

Months flowed into a year, two years, more, and still he lived so. One night on the verge of sleep, the memory of Suzette came stealing—her sweet spirit, honesty, talent for painting—and with it, a sort of comfort. And the knowledge that Robert had made it possible for him to know Suzette came stealing, too, and the sharp edge of his grief began to dull.

With this scrap of comfort, he felt a wisp of solid thought. What he'd been doing, enshrining Suzette and Robert, was morbid and unhealthy. He owed them and himself the peacefulness of loving memory.

The time had come. He must return to being Charles

Hebert, the Charles of Bayou Teche. That night he slept profoundly, woke refreshed, eager to go into the fields.

He worked as hard now at getting back to his natural self as he did on the land. He even went to a party at the plantation of George and Mae Lefleur.

It was a modest party, showing the effects of the war, the food and drink simple. The women and girls wore calico, but the dresses, Charles thought, were as smart as any he'd seen in Paris. Talented field hands played their violins and there was dancing and merriment.

Marcel and Laura Gaboury were there with their youngest daughter, Honoré. She was red-haired, lively, extremely pretty, and she let Charles see she was attracted to him.

Charles felt awkward, because he'd had no contact with a girl since Suzette, but he asked Honoré to dance, and she accepted happily. They danced to the violins, and the rhythm got into Charles so that he danced with scarcely a sign of his limp.

"You've stayed away from parties a long time, Charles Hebert!" Honoré accused teasingly.

"Yes. Well, there's been a lot of work."

She smiled, her brown eyes shining, held his eyes, and they danced on. When it was time to whirl her around in the figure of the set, his arm stiffened and he deliberately relaxed it, forcing himself to meet her laughter with a smile, as they danced on.

He should feel no antagonism toward this girl who couldn't be more than seventeen. It wasn't her fault that she was the only girl he'd touched since Suzette. He threw off his gloom, smiled at Honoré as they went into the waltz.

"You should be dancing this with one of the younger fellows," Charles smiled. "They'd give you a whirl; just look at them!"

Honoré tossed her bright head. "You don't get rid of me!" she declared. "You waltz better than any of them!"

"Not with my limp," he laughed. "Don't try to flatter me!"

"Everybody knows you got that limp in Paris in the fighting! Not a girl here would stay with her partner if she had a chance at you! You're the best catch of the Teche!"

As their banter continued, he realized that his grief had

indeed quieted and that one day he was going to need a wife. But not this flame-haired young girl.

In bed, he felt the need of woman. He knew that it was past time for Hebert Plantation to have a mistress, a warm, ready partner in his arms, a mother of children to carry on his name.

He fell asleep more quickly than usual, glad that he hadn't asked to see Honoré again, yet sorry, remembering her downcast look at the end of the party. But she was too nice a girl, too attractive, and it would be unfair to waste her time, knowing that he had already decided against her.

All week he reviewed the available Teche girls; he recalled those on other bayous, a few on the Delta—Antoinette, Chloë, Noel, Lavon and others. All were bright and pretty; he went to parties they attended but not one appealed to him.

He kept remembering Marie-Louise Leblanc; he hadn't seen her in several years. He recalled her beauty, her appeal. At one time he'd been tempted to court her, but she was too young, a schoolgirl, and he was doing a man's work on the plantation. But he also recalled that she'd been mature for her age, too.

He knew that she'd suffered a decline, but was now recovered, and found himself thinking of her nearly every day. He hadn't forgotten how black her hair was, how white her skin—in appearance she was rather like Suzette—and this appealed to him. They were two different girls, of course, but he liked the hint of resemblance and saw no reason to let it hold him back.

Accordingly, one day, he dressed in his best and went to L'Acadie. At the front door he asked to see André Leblanc on a matter of importance. Charles was promptly admitted and shown into the library, where the elder man was sitting at his desk, papers spread out across its top.

André got up and extended his hand to Charles. "You've been a stranger for a long time, Charles," he said. "I'm happy to see you."

"And I to see you, sir."

"We haven't really talked in years."

"No, sir. I haven't been in a talkative mood."

"And now you are?"

"You might put it that way, sir. There's no good in delay. I've come to ask your permission to court Marie-Louise. If she will permit me to call on her and renew our acquaintance, I'd like to take her to the next party."

André grew deeply sober, searched Charles' face. "Marie-Louise has been ill," he said, as if reluctant. "She has only now fully recovered."

"Yes, sir. I've heard she hasn't been well. Will it be long before I can see her? With your permission and her consent, of course."

Still puzzlingly sober, André agreed. Charles noted his subdued manner, wondered, then concluded it was left over from the father's concern for the daughter's health.

The next morning Charles received a hand-written note from Euphemie. It was an invitation for him to have supper with the Leblancs that night.

Again he wore his best. After he greeted André and Euphemie, Marie-Louise moved into view from behind her parents, and his head swam at her beauty, her long, fine black hair, her black eyes, her slim, curved figure. She was a replica of Euphemie, her mother, considered to be the most beautiful woman in the bayou country.

Charles saw that in Marie-Louise, though she smiled, there was a sadness, a Madonna quality that Euphemie didn't have. She was the most beautiful girl, in short, he'd ever seen, and intelligence shone through the sadness in her eyes, enhancing her.

It struck him that her decline had added depth to her nature. That here was the girl he was going to marry, if she would have him.

After supper, they sat alone in Grape House. He asked about her illness, and if she was entirely recovered.

Marie-Louise, unexpectedly and strongly attracted to him, wanted to throw herself into his arms. He was a man, a real man, older than herself, and he was handsome and strong. She hoped desperately that he would court her, as he'd told Papa. She wondered if he could hear her heart racing.

"I'm entirely well!" she declared. "It's as if I'd never been ill!"

"I heard it was rather serious."

"We caught it in time."

There. She hadn't told a lie. She wanted not to lie to Charles Hebert.

He could feel her vibrancy; there was an aura of health about her. Yet there was an underlying seriousness which disturbed him. He dismissed the thought. It was natural for her to be serious about a long decline.

"You stayed in Honeymoon House the whole time?"

"Yes. It was lonely, but quiet. I rested; believe me, I rested! Now you," she urged. "Tell me about Paris."

"Tell what?"

"The siege of Paris! Oh, I know it's old stuff to you, but it's new to me. Was it awful, going on a pleasure trip, ending up in a war? I know that's why you limp! Or would you rather not talk about it?"

He told her about the war, told of cutting down trees for firewood, told of the thousands shot to death that terrible May. There was a hint of tears in his voice.

"Was there ... a girl?"

He didn't want to talk about Suzette, but he didn't want to lie to Marie-Louise, even by omission, so he let it come pouring out, even the part where he had failed to save one of her paintings.

Marie-Louise put her hand on his and pressed. "I'm so sorry," she said. "But you're over the worst part, aren't you, Charles?"

"I suppose I am, or I wouldn't be here with you. I wouldn't be so overwhelmed at your beauty, so glad you got well."

He appreciated her understanding, but wondered. The Marie-Louise he remembered had been sweet but strong-willed and not particularly understanding. Had her illness changed her this much, or was it just that she was older now?

Something had changed her, and whatever it was, he felt grateful for it. They talked on into the night, into other nights, with him waiting for the moment when he might dare to kiss her. No, more than likely, to propose.

Chapter XVI

From the time Riel Rivard learned of his black blood, only one thing would satisfy him and that was to change the situation, to make the Rivards respected. And, once he'd conceived his plan, only one desire consumed him—to create a black family. It was an obsession with him, he recognized it as an obsession, but would not swerve from his objective. He ignored the fact that he was hurting Olive, that he might hurt his descendants. Only one thing mattered. The Rivards must be black.

And after the setback with Marie-Louise and Riel, only one thing would meet André Leblanc's purpose—to keep his family white.

Each man had taken a stunning blow; each vowed that nothing similar was to happen again. Both were tense, protective of their objectives, and each understood that this burden was to taint their lives.

André, in town for trading one day, met Riel on the street. As if at a signal, they stopped in their tracks, spoke. They were dimly aware of shops, pedestrians, a passing carriage, but their full attention was on each other. A big, tan, well-fed dog came over to them and, embarrassed by the unexpected meeting, they both patted the dog. When he trotted on, André said, "We need to talk."

"That's right, sir. I have a need to talk to you."

André suggested that they go into the small cafe nearby. Riel nodded. "I can still go in. Nobody knows about my blood yet. I wanted to tell you I'm going to let it be known."

André frowned, but understood Riel's wish for honesty. They entered the cafe. The proprietress brought them coffee, excused herself and went into the kitchen.

"The child," André said unhappily. "You disposed of it?"

"Yes," Riel said shortly.

André looked sad. "Perhaps it was for the best."

Riel didn't reply. He asked how Marie-Louise was.

"She's well. Fully recovered. Taking an interest in life." André cut off, didn't tell that she was seeing Charles Hebert; there was no need to hurt Riel further.

"What did you want to talk to me about, sir?"

"The blood."

"What about it?"

"My family is white. I need your assurance that word won't circulate to the contrary."

"I have no reason to tell, sir. No wish to discuss your family with others. I have my own problems."

There was an awkward silence.

"Just as important," André said, "is that the two families be kept apart, have no contact whatsoever."

"That's what I wanted to say to you, sir. I have plans for my family. As I said, I'm going to let it be known the Rivards have black blood. No one will make a connection between the white Leblancs and the black Rivards or expect them to associate with one another."

Thus, no promises were made, but the two men, André mature, and Riel maturing, reached an understanding. Their connection was severed and would so remain.

Chapter XVII

The nearer Marie-Louise's wedding day came, the more elated she felt. What an escape! She might have married her own uncle! And missed out on Charles, who had been to Paris, who went through that awful siege and was a grown man from it, who was handsome and kind and whom she loved more every day.

She chattered to Euphemie, with whom she had a close love, as tiers of lace were stitched and patted into place on the wedding dress, making a wealth of frosted white. "Nobody knows, Mama! And we kept our word and gave Gracie her wedding and her cabin!" She hugged Euphemie, who smiled tenderly. "I vow, Mama, you're so young you could be my sister! I adore you!"

Feeling sad, Euphemie gazed lovingly at her daughter. "The baby, dear," she ventured. "Do you ever think about him?"

Marie-Louise's black eyes went somber. "Of course I do. But I daren't let myself brood over him. An incest baby would never be right in the head. It would be horrid, like Carita playing with her emeralds and running away and always having to be hushed so she won't drive people daft, wanting to tell her story of the Journals!"

Euphemie, stitching at the lace, recalled Marie-Louise's behavior when Charles, seven years her senior, came to ask for her hand. Before he arrived, André questioned his daughter. "What have you told Charles about your decline?"

"Nothing, really. I just let him go by what he'd heard, that I was run down and Mama made me rest and now I'm well. And he said I'm more beautiful then he remembered, that it might improve the looks of a lot of girls to take a rest cure!"

Frowning, André said, "He must be told the truth."

"Papa! Then he might not want me!"

"Even so."

"You mean you'll tell him?"

"Certainly. Surely you realize you can't base your marriage on a lie."

"How about the blood? If he doesn't know about it, then that's a lie, too! I'll make him such a good wife, Papa! And as years pass, I'll let him know!"

"He must know now. And, since you haven't told him, I must."

"Then I'm going to be there!"

Consequently, willfully, she had been present.

Charles, holding her hand, said to a white-lipped André, "We want to get married, sir. With your permission and that of your wife."

Silence covered the room. This caused Charles to feel that André was unfavorable toward him, and he worried over the impression he was making. Euphemie, knowing André's intentions and Marie-Louise's fear, sensed Charles' discomfort and her heart went out to all of them.

Marie-Louise, trembling, was terrified that she'd soon lose Charles.

André spoke. "There are things you must know, Charles," he said. "Vital, serious matters."

"Not you, Papa!" Marie-Louise cried in desperation. "I'll tell him! It's our lives!"

"Tell, then."

She searched into Charles' bewildered face and a great hand seemed to fold her heart and draw it painfully tight. Her fear was so great that if she did speak, Charles would leave—like a gentleman, but with finality, forever. If she made wifely love to him once, she could show him with her woman's knowledge, all of love. And after that, tell, explain.

"Well, Marie-Louise?" André prodded.

"After we're married, Papa! I swear it!"

"That won't suffice. You can't expect Charles to marry you, aware that there are secrets. You can't expect him to go blindly into marriage, one that you may well destroy."

"I know, I do know, Papa." She gazed pleadingly into Charles' steady Hebert eyes. "Papa thinks you wouldn't marry me! But you will, won't you, Charles? There are things you must know, bad things, and I want you to know them! But I'm not bad, darling! Foolish, yes, but I've grown out of that! One thing was my own fault, but not the other! You will want me, no matter what! I *feel* it!"

Stunned, Charles took both her offered hands. He looked into her tearful, truth-filled eyes and wished she'd speak now, that she would trust him. He thought of Suzette and her honesty. He searched Marie-Louise's face; there was a purity and honesty which matched that of Suzette. But doubt overwhelmed him. Why couldn't she speak now, why ask trust of him, yet fail to give it herself?

Here she stood, a lovely, pleading girl whom he had come to love. He crushed back his qualms. "I have to trust you," he said. "If you believe these things won't destroy us, I'll chance it. We'll be married first."

Yet, even as he spoke, seeing the tearful relief on her, his fears returned. He felt he'd done the wrong thing. But his word had been given; he would keep it.

Marie-Louise kissed his hands, weeping. Could she hold him, even after marriage? Was there forgiveness in him, along with kindness and warmth and integrity? Was there, oh, was there?

On their wedding night, Charles' heart was a lump in his throat when he saw her nude beauty. Her slender, gently curved body was so lovely it transcended even the beauty of her face and hair. He did note the long marks on her abdomen but was so caught up by her, so intent on love-making, that he didn't wonder about them.

Naked, they kissed, naked they sank to the bed. There he experienced all of glory, and so did she. They lay welded and Marie-Louise, awash with love and fear, whispered, "I wasn't a virgin, darling." She held her breath, heartbeats shaking her body. She felt him stiffen; her heart slowed to almost nothing, and she could scarcely breathe.

"I ... found out," he said tonelessly. "Is that what you had to tell?"

"That and more, my darling."

"It couldn't have been your fault." Charles waited, wanting the blame not to be hers. At least that much. And she sensed this, drove herself to continue.

"It was as much my fault as his," she murmured. "We were children, in school. I was sixteen; he was seventeen."

"Girls marry at sixteen."

A great throb jolted through her. This wasn't going well, not at all. It was almost as if they'd not made love and reached delight. Even so, she plunged on. "There was a stillborn baby. That's why I have the marks on my stomach."

His arms loosened from her, and she shrank into herself. What was he thinking; what would he do? She ached to plead, but could not. Whatever happened, she must bear it. She waited, longing for him to speak, to give some sign that he would listen so she could finish what she had to tell.

Charles' ears roared, then began to quiet. He wondered why this possibility hadn't entered his mind before marriage. But the worst he'd anticipated was that she'd been involved in some prank at school. Not this, not a baby!

His mind flew to Suzette and how he'd yearned to make love to her and had not. He felt a tinge of sympathy for Marie-Louise. But he didn't want to feel sorry; he wanted to love purely. His jaw stiffened.

She sensed his further withdrawal. She whispered, trembling against him, knowing that now he might recoil from her. "I wasn't in a decline. I was having the baby."

She knew that André had been right. Charles should have been told. He'd done nothing to deserve being trapped in a marriage which he did not, could not want.

At last he spoke. "And you came out of it wanting a husband, any eligible male. And I was the handiest."

"No!" she moaned. "I wanted you! For yourself, your handsomeness, your kindness, your goodness, and because I loved you! Do love you! Charles, darling Charles, can you forgive me, ever, for having that poor little dead baby?"

She touched his hand, and his fingers closed around hers. His hand was so warm, so safe! She wished she could touch his heart, bring it to remember how things were between them just a few minutes ago. What was he thinking? Not, pray God, of a kind way to tell her he didn't want her!

His mind was beginning to function. She'd been only a schoolgirl. At the time, frightened, she'd gone into hiding to carry the baby. And now, she was brave to tell him. Still, it had happened. It was not a thing to forget in a moment. He wondered if he could ever forget.

He became aware that she was speaking of the Leblanc Journals, revealing their terrible secret.

She told him all she knew, felt him move a bit away from her. She'd been a senseless fool, a selfish child, to insist on marriage first.

Understanding flashed through Charles. She'd had a child. She had Negro blood. She needed protection, not rejection. How many marriages could survive these shameful secrets? Would years of love—and there was love in him for her—overcome these things? If he could rid himself of confusion, then he'd know what was best for the two of them.

She moved, lay against his arms which held her loosely. "I was foolish," she sobbed. "I thought I was in love when it happened, but I wasn't! Not until now! You've got to believe that, Charles! My love for you is real."

The knowledge of incest pierced Charles like a sword. The black blood he discounted. It was the fact that Marie-Louise's own half-uncle had despoiled her that sent rage shooting into every cranny. He reared up in bed, swung his feet to the floor.

"I'll kill Riel Rivard!" he shouted. "To think that he'd—his own blood—killing's too good for him—I'll make him suffer first!"

Marie-Louise gripped his arms and pulled him back onto the bed. She hung onto him. His muscles were like iron. She knew he was only waiting for her hold to slacken and he'd go off looking for Riel.

"He didn't know, Charles. He didn't know about being kin! He didn't know he's part black until Papa told him! And if you do confront him, even though I hate and despise him, it'll ruin everything for us, destroy every chance for you and me!"

The truth of her words struck him like a blow. His muscles went limp. He turned to her, studied her, now weeping and lovely in the lamplight. His love stirred.

"I'll not confront Rivard," Charles said, through his teeth.

"And us? What about us? You know everything now!"

His love stirred more strongly. She'd be a true and abiding wife. Her lesson had been hard-learned, but he knew as he saw her tears that she was ready to be his wife.

"We stay together," he said. "But you are never to see a Rivard, any Rivard. And our children," he continued, "are to have no contact with their children."

"And my black blood?"

"It is all but bred out. You are to forget it."

She shook violently, weeping now from relief that he accepted her. Weeping, too, from the knowledge that her love for him would grow to worship.

After this night of love, of confession, of shock, of panic, they drew closer together each day. Nights were times of glory. Tenderness arose between them and was to deepen every year of their lives.

Charles called on André three days after the wedding. The older man received him in the library, closed the door, face him anxiously.

"You needn't worry, sir," Charles said promptly. "Marie-Louise told me about the baby, about Riel Rivard, about the strain of black blood in the Leblancs. I was shocked; I had serious doubts about the marriage."

"And now?"

"It's resolved, sir. We love each other. And we'll keep the black blood a secret. Set your mind at rest."

Chapter XVIII

Celeste, youngest child of André and Euphemie Leblanc, was their loveliest. She had the same long black hair and pure white skin as her mother and sister, the same fine features, though they were more daintily chiseled, and her black eyes were more luminous and showed tiny flecks of gold. Her lips curved and were always smiling, her voice was musical and merry, her nature was happy and generous. Her delight was to make people happy, for in so doing her own heart remained light. She wanted only to spend her life cheering others, except, of course, she hoped to marry, to revel in the love of a good and true man.

She spent much time with Marie-Louise after she married Charles, and the elder sister teased the younger about men. "You're too shy, darling," Marie-Louise said, "too retiring around men. If you'd only smile at the young men, you'd be knee-deep in suitors! Why don't you, honey, and see what happens?"

"I'm in no hurry," Celeste laughed. "Besides—"

"I know. Papa and Mama want to protect you. It's enough to drive the men away!" She looked rueful, for she knew why Papa and Mama were so careful with Celeste. Marie-Louise put her arm around her sister, kissed the lovely cheek.

This same evening, Ramon and Felicity Hanin, of Creole blood, gave a party at Magnolia Plantation. They were in their forties, childless, and delighted in having young people come to their home.

Dark-haired, dark-eyed Ramon greeted the Leblancs, held both Celeste's hands, his features glowing. "Celeste, you beauty!" he exclaimed. "You should always wear white! It makes you so ethereal!"

"I nearly always do wear it," Celeste smiled. "Mama insists, says it suits me."

What Euphemie actually said was, "White makes you virginal, bridelike. I think you'll be able to wear it always." Of course, Celeste couldn't repeat such a thing, so she smiled again, unaware that the smile enhanced her beauty as if lighted by a thousand candles.

Felicity, looking younger than forty, embraced Celeste so vigorously she set her own blond, natural curls aquiver. "As usual," she declared, "you'll be the beauty of the party! But I don't think you'll have an opportunity to sit out many dances this time. There's a gentleman here who deals in precious gems, and believe me, he knows a priceless jewel when he sees it!"

Celeste felt her cheeks go hot at the implication.

"And who is this gentlemen?" She laughed to hide her confusion. She wanted desperately to sit in a corner and observe, at least for a time.

Instead, she let Felicity put an arm around her and guide her through the merry guests. At the end of the room was a cluster of girls. At their center was a tall young man. Her heart quickened nervously; she had no wish to vie for the attention of this man, regardless of who he was, but Felicity moved her inexorably forward, wound a path through the group of smitten girls, and stood with Celeste before the object of their adoration.

He was over six feet tall, about twenty, and had a smooth, muscular build. Celeste caught her breath at the aura of his strength. He had clear, eager features and ash blond, curly hair. His merry, blue-gray eyes turned sober and seeking when they met Celeste's luminous eyes. His lips were strong, friendly, firm.

In spite of herself, Celeste's heart quickened.

"This," Felicity said, "is my one and only nephew, Anton Veco! He's his father's right hand in the biggest jewelry store in New Orleans, the best appraiser of gems in all Louisiana! Anton, darling, this is my favorite young friend, Celeste Leblanc!" She stood back and waited. They gazed at each other, speechless. "Well," Felicity cried, "at least shake hands!"

Anton Veco's head suddenly felt light. He'd never seen such a girl! He wanted not only to shake hands, but also to draw her into his arms, yes, right here with all the guests watching, and ask her to love him! He wanted to put the best diamond in his store on her finger, and with it a wedding band. He wanted to do it now before someone beat him to it. He reached out and took her hand, her firm, lovely hand, and pressed it gently.

"Celeste," he breathed. "What a perfect name." Celeste, his heart clamored, what a perfect girl!

The warmth of his hand shot up her arm, across her bosom, and lodged in her wild, racing heart. She'd never dreamed that one night she'd be introduced to a stranger, and that from the first instant, her heart would no longer be her own. She'd never dreamed that any man would look at her with eyes so filled with excitement and reverence.

"Come with me," Anton said, and took her arm.

Celeste moved with him through the sea of guests. She was aware that the cluster of girls stood staring. It seemed this was but the beginning, that she would always go where he led, go with love, for this clamor in her must be love. Yet there was a tremor lest she was imagining things, lest he was a flirt, lest he singled out a girl at every party, then when the festivities ended, would drop her and wait for the next girl.

She glanced shyly up at him, met those blue-gray eyes, and her fear stilled. For in his eyes she glimpsed the same fear, the fear that she would leave him for another partner.

He guided her to an alcove furnished with a love seat. The alcove was deserted, the love seat empty.

"Shall we?" he asked, indicating the nook. "We must talk."

She breathed, "Yes, oh yes!" She wondered if that were the right thing to do, to let him see how carried away she was. The other girls had been open, even brazen. Did her reply make her the same?

Anton seated her, settled beside her, took her left hand into both of his. Again, a thrill shot up her arm straight into her heart. She felt his gaze on her, lifted her eyes, and their look clung.

"Do you want to dance," he asked, "or talk?"

"Talk," she whispered. She was frightened at what he

might say but had to find out. She couldn't bear to feel this way about him unless she knew. Her heart skipped a beat. Surely, oh surely, he wouldn't toy with her!

He stroked her hand. "You're the only girl I've ever seen," he told her softly.

"How can that be?" she whispered. "The rooms are filled with girls!"

"That they are, and beauties, some of them. But none like you."

"I don't know if I understand," she whispered.

"Your heart understands. You're the only girl I've ever . . . loved."

Her heart filled her bosom, beat at the soft interior walls, moved the thin white material of her dress. "L-love takes time!" she stammered. "Two people can't just meet, and look at each other and be in love!"

"We can," he said firmly. "Others have. It happens. We have plans to make."

"Even if—doesn't the man—propose?" Her lips were numb, but she must know what he meant.

"I am proposing," he said. "I'm asking you to be my wife. Oh, I know you'll want time, want us to get acquainted, and I'm willing to do that while the banns are being published. I'm speaking up the instant I meet you so none of the young blades here will beat me to it. Will you marry me, Celeste?"

She was in such turmoil. Love had hit her like a blow. She was stunned by it, stunned by his urgency and haste. Besides, now her heart seemed to be in her throat and she couldn't speak. But she did nod assent, her eyes locked to his.

He moved his gaze to her lips, let it remain. Then he lifted her hand and kissed it. "Thank you, darling," he murmured. "You've made me the happiest man alive."

She felt hot all over, wished he could enfold her in his arms, kiss her lips, but of course he couldn't, not here, not with all these people. She lifted her eyes to his again.

As if he'd read her mind, he murmured, "The time will come! I'll drown you with kisses, my darling!" And she burned hotter still because he'd known her unmaidenly thoughts.

People began to notice them on the loveseat, and began

to tease, urging them to dance. They danced every waltz, neither of them accepted another partner, and sat out the rest.

They exchanged facts about themselves. He eagerly told of school and his love for jewelry. She told him about Carita for he had a right to know, but he'd heard the scandal already and said it didn't matter to him.

She brought up Carita again. It was important, very important; that he didn't really mind. "Carita gives some trouble," she said, "but mostly she's happy with her emeralds. She has dozens."

"She should keep them," Anton said. "They're worth a fortune."

"Yes," Celeste agreed. "Papa smiles about it. There's been so little money since the war, and Carita plays with thousands of dollars in gems; she has lots of diamonds, too."

"You're beautifully honest to tell of her. Some girls—well, they'd be ashamed."

Celeste's eyes widened. "We're not ashamed of Carita. She couldn't help it that she lost her mind and did those things. It's mostly when she wants to find the dagger that she makes a fuss. But Mama can quiet her, and sometimes I feel I could. But Mama doesn't want me to try, not yet."

Suddenly she felt she had talked too much, and said so. But he declared she hadn't, captured both her hands, asked to go to Mass with her next morning.

Blushing furiously, not knowing what André and Euphemie would say to Mass, let alone marriage, she consented. Suddenly, the party was breaking up. Anton asked to see her home, and she longed to say yes, but told him reluctantly that first she must explain to her parents how she and Anton had become acquainted and that they were going to Mass together.

"Papa is particular," she said.

"Good for him! Anyway, I'll be asking him for your hand. So go on, my darling, go home with them. Tomorrow will come, far away as it is, and we'll be together!"

She told her parents about Anton as they returned home. Euphemie said, a smile in her voice, "I'm not surprised, darling. Nobody will be surprised. That young man, I'd say, is besotted with you!"

"He's in a mighty big hurry," growled André.

"Now, André," Euphemie said, "it's all right! The Hanins

are the best blood, and so is Anton. Wouldn't you be in a hurry," Euphemie teased, "if you were a young man and saw a girl like Celeste?" She put her arm around her daughter, squeezed her briefly. "You see this young man if you like, darling. He's the finest!"

After Mass Celeste and Anton ate Sunday dinner with the Hanins. Then he oared her to St. Martinville where they strolled, sat on a white bench under a magnolia tree, strolled again. For the first time, she realized how beautiful the little town was, and thought that love had given it an extra allure.

She trembled inwardly and constantly. His clear, low voice made her tremble, the touch of his fingers on her elbow. So this was love, this tremulous glory, his insistance that he ask for her hand at once, that their banns be published immediately. He spoke of their love constantly.

"How can I know I love you?" she asked wonderingly. "When I don't know, really."

"The softness of your eyes when they look into mine; the golden flecks that rise in them like tiny suns. a quiver to your lips, darling girl, lips I'll kiss without stopping when we're married. The way the pulse in your throat races, the way your hand quivers when I touch it."

"Anton, oh, Anton!"

"Can you deny any of it?"

"No," she replied shyly.

That very night Anton asked André for Celeste's hand. André frowned, not because he didn't approve of Anton, but because he was going to take her away to New Orleans, but he gave his consent.

Monday, Celeste oared across the bayou to spend the day with her older sister. She found Marie-Louise smocking a baby dress. "You are a goose!" Celeste teased, herself as happy as she was aquiver. "Making a baby dress when you're not even enciente!"

Marie-Louise blushed. "Married women get enciente," she said, not letting her thoughts dwell more than an instant on the stillborn baby.

"It wouldn't put you into another decline?" asked Celeste seriously.

"Of course not! I'll have a dozen babies if I choose! But where have you been? I haven't seen you."

"If you'd come to the Hanin party and to Mass yesterday, you'd know!" Celeste blurted, face pink.

"You're blushing! What is it—a man? Ah, a deeper blush! Who is he?"

Celeste had meant to tell it casually, but she began to tremble, and Marie-Louise had to pry the information from her, bit by bit.

"Anton Veco!" she exclaimed. "Of Veco Jewelers?"

"Yes."

"Celeste! You met him! At the party?"

"Yes. He was supposed to be guest of honor."

"What does that mean?"

"He spent the evening with me. Oh dear, I do hope Felicity isn't angry with him!"

Marie-Louise's eyes sparkled. "I almost wish I hadn't let Charles talk me out of going to the party so we could—" She colored, touched the baby dress. "Before you get excited about the first rich, handsome jeweler you meet," she warned, "be sure what you want."

"I know now. I want a husband who loves me as Charles loves you; I want a home like yours.

"Marrying Anton Veco means you'd have to leave the bayou."

"I don't mean a plantation, darling, but a home!" Celeste breathed. "It can be in New Orleans. I shan't mind at all."

"You talk as if it is all settled. Is it? Even Papa's consent?"

Celeste nodded, happy tears in her eyes.

"But love, darling! That takes time!"

"I love him so much already that—"

"That what?"

"—if papa had said no, I could never, never, never have married any other man! I don't know how to explain it, but we—fit. It has to be Anton or nobody."

They talked and sewed all day. They planned future visits to one another. They would bring their children every time, all of them. In this excited talk, a pang took Marie-Louise as she glanced at the baby dress she'd laid aside. Suppose she never did have a baby? Suppose God punished her for being glad her one baby was stillborn? She couldn't throw off that feeling, not even when she began to plan a party for Celeste and Anton.

As soon as the engagement was known, a round of parties began. In the midst of these, André called Anton to him and sketched the story of the Leblancs, warning him that Celeste had one thirty-second black blood.

Anton was shocked, not so much by the fact that Celeste had a "touch of black," as André called it, but that her beauty was so pure and showed no trace of what Old René had passed down. He promised never to let Celeste know the truth.

Anton had written his father Stephen and asked him to bring two of their finest rings for the wedding. When it was time for Stephen to arrive, Anton began to feel slightly ill with pains in the abdomen, but did not see a doctor, attributing his discomfort to excitement over his upcoming marriage. He said nothing to Celeste, but she noted a difference in him.

"What's wrong, darling?" she asked one day.

"Nothing at all," replied Anton. He had just suffered a long, hard twinge. "Why do you ask?"

"You looked pale."

He laughed. "Do I look pale now?"

She gazed at him. He'd never looked taller, broader, stronger. She didn't have to decide between his great strength and his handsome good looks. He had both; she was the luckiest girl in the world.

The next day he was definitely pale, and she sensed that he was in pain. She pleaded with him to go to a doctor, but he laughed and refused.

"I find it hard to sleep," he confessed, "and that is because I'm eager to be your husband."

They were alone in the L'Acadie drawing room, and he drew her into his arms. Tenderly and for the first time he kissed her, tracing butterfly kisses along her eyebrows, down her perfect nose, coming to rest, sweetly, gently, on her lips. Quivering, she returned the kiss, ever so gently. Their tenderness grew warmly passionate, and she burned for more, and he held her firmly at arm's length. "I ask you," he demanded, "could a sick man kiss like that?"

Stephen Veco arrived next morning, and they met his boat. The father looked much like the son, only twenty years older and with gray at the temples.

"You're to call me 'dad'," he ordered. He turned to Anton, and as he embraced his son, demanded. "You sick?"

Celeste winced. Anton must indeed be ill; his own father surely knew how he should look!

"It's being in love with this beauty, Dad," Anton said. "As soon as the wedding's over tomorrow and we board the boat, me a married man, nobody'll mention sickness again!"

Anton put one arm around Stephen, the other around Celeste, and she felt both relieved and disturbed. One thing she decided firmly. Once she married Anton, she'd watch him very closely indeed. She'd be with him twenty-four hours a day, and she'd be able to detect any illness.

For the wedding in the little church, Celeste wore fine white voile, carried a huge magnolia blossom, and Anton wore white, too. Then they went, followed by the guests, directly to the *Magnolia Blossom*, which was ready to sail. Celeste could hardly breathe, she was so excited at being Mrs. Anton Veco. The wide gold wedding band and two-carat diamond felt heavy and strange on her finger, but she loved the feel because Anton had placed them there.

They stood on deck, waving to those ashore, as the vessel pulled away from the dock. Anton's arm was around his bride's waist, and he could feel her supple body move against him as she waved. A spear of pain sliced his middle and he stiffened, waving, smile set and jaw hard.

He hadn't slept last night. If the pain kept up, if it threatened to disturb his wedding night, he'd see the doctor on board and get a powder. Maybe he'd been a fool not to see a doctor in St. Martinville, but he hadn't wanted Celeste to worry.

The pain, thank God, passed. He relaxed, then stiffened. He wouldn't give in, for he could not bear to see that look of rapture on Celeste become one of concern and fear.

By the time they'd gone to their bedroom, the pain returned. Harder. Again he overcame it.

Celeste, talking happily about the wedding, admiring her rings, moved about the room, looking at everything. "It's perfect!" she exclaimed. "And the rings, most of all. Do you know, darling, my favorite is the wedding band. Because it says I'm your wife! The diamond is my next favorite, because you gave it to me with love!"

"You'll have other jewels," he told her, sweat popping out on his brow. Then as the pain vanished, weakness followed. "Pearls, I think, lots of pearls. They fit the purity of your beauty."

"You mustn't spoil me, darling," she said. "Carita was the one who wanted jewels. I don't care to have so very many."

He turned his back to her, mopped his brow with his handkerchief. When he turned back, she was struggling with a trunk, trying to open it.

He did it for her, his normally strong fingers feeling weak. He set his jaw, threw his weight onto his hands, opened the hasps, and she began to unpack her trousseau, hanging it up in the wardrobe.

"If you'll open your trunk," she said, "I'll hang your clothes up. We're the only bride and groom on board; we've got to look neat!"

He managed to laugh with her, managed to unlock his trunk and get it open without her noticing that he had trouble. Then he started to lift out a coat, and she pushed him gently aside, saying this was a wife's chore. He was glad enough to let her do it, for his whole inside felt as if a chunk had been cut out of it.

"I don't think we need to change for dinner," she said, hanging his things away. "Actually, that's one reason I wanted to dress simply for the wedding so we wouldn't have to change to travel clothes, then change again for dinner."

"Splendid idea," he said, realizing he couldn't have changed his clothes just now, even if his life depended on it. Later he'd— He felt himself sway, fall, heard Celeste cry out his name, and then there was the great, bursting pain and the agony, and from very far away Celeste calling, "Darling! Oh, darling, the blood—there's so much blood!" And next, her voice, fading as everything went black. "Help . . . my husband . . . blood . . . !"

There was a doctor. Thank God, there was a doctor. He was young, dark-haired, with quick, gentle hands.

The steward cleaned up the blood from the floor. The

doctor, aided by Celeste, undressed the unconscious, moaning Anton, and she saw his dear, strong body devastated by this terrible illness, and saw there was more blood.

"What is it, Doctor?" she cried. "What's wrong with him?"

"He's got a bloody flux, a looseness of the bowels with much pain and blood. Has he complained of pain?"

"He has complained of nothing! He looked pale, I tried to get him to see a doctor—"

"Quickly, Mrs. Veco, the pan!"

But it was too late. Blood poured out of Anton's mouth, soaked the pillow. At the same time it flowed out of his body lower down, and the berth was awash with blood.

"Save him!" Celeste cried. "Doctor, save him!"

"I'll do my best," the doctor said, and turned to his black bag. But before he could get anything into Anton's mouth, more blood came.

There was only darkness and cramps and outpourings from his body. If there were people about, he didn't hear them. There were no thoughts in him; the great, recurring cramps crushed away everything, crushed away time, crushed away life.

Celeste cradled his head to her blood-soaked wedding dress. He wasn't moaning now. The first rays of light crept into the room, illuminating Anton's face which was still, so still.

"Mrs. Veco," the doctor said softly. "It's over."

The Magnolia Blossom, once a honeymoon boat bound downstream, nosed in to shore and *The Delta Rover,* bound upstream, likewise nosed in. When they sailed again, Celeste Veco was aboard *The Delta Rover,* taking the body of her bridegroom back to St. Martinville.

Celeste buried Anton in the L'Acadie cemetery, her family and Stephen Veco at her side. But no tears formed in her. Everybody else wept; André wiped his eyes and tried to put his arm around Celeste, but she stood away from him, erect and stiff. Only Marie-Louise did she allow to touch her, and then only briefly.

Afterward, she moved into Honeymoon House. Gracie offered to look after her, and she accepted. Daily, she rowed across the bayou to Marie-Louise. She found comfort with her sister, more even than she found with Euphemie.

"My one true love is gone," Celeste told Marie-Louise. "There'll never be another."

A week later, Carita got loose. Seeing Celeste, she cornered her, and told her the story of the Leblanc Journals. Celeste managed to lead Carita back to her suite, soothing her. Sadly she watched Carita, now forty-five and still beautiful.

When the madwoman was safely locked away, Celeste rushed to Marie-Louise. "Are the Journals true?" she asked. "Oh, please just let it be her poor, tormented mind!"

Celeste was kneeling beside Marie-Louise's chair. The elder sister stroked the other's cheek. "The Journals are true, darling. You were never to know, you and Gab. Carita's mad, that's certain, but she did read those Journals and their truths are imprinted on her mind. She wants the dagger, Papa thinks, to kill the widow Rivard. It's hidden where she'll never find it."

"Anton . . . did Papa tell him of the blood?"

"He did. And it didn't matter to Anton, not a whit."

It was then, unexpectedly, that Celeste's tears came flooding out. She wept because Anton had loved her enough to overlook black blood, wept because he was dead, wept that they had never been true husband and wife, not even once. She wept until Marie-Louise became alarmed and put her to bed and kept her the night.

When Celeste stopped at L'Acadie next day, Carita was calling for her, and Celeste listened to the Leblanc story again. On other days, she heard it repeated until every nuance was etched in her mind, and she pitied the people who had lived the story.

Because of Celeste, Consuela was able to get a bit of freedom from her mad mistress, the mistress whom she loved and who, she never tired of relating, was once the most beautiful woman in the entire bayou country, in New Orleans itself.

André warned Celeste not to let Carita drain her strength and she replied that she pitied her step-grandmother. "She may have been spoiled, Papa," she said, "but I understand her. She loved only one man, and hasn't looked for another."

"But," André said, "you're young and beautiful and sane. Anton would never have wanted you to live out your life alone."

"No, Papa," she answered. But she knew that she would never marry again.

Chapter XIX

Riel, his mind intent on finding a wife and making Rivard self-supporting, was alone in the fields. He was vigorously weeding, sun blazing down, his face running with sweat, his shirt sticking to his back. He dropped his hoe, took off the shirt, laid it aside, and turned to pick up the hoe again.

Two horsemen had appeared out of the blue; he hadn't heard a sound. They reined up their scruffy horses, glowered down at him.

"Good morning," he said. "I didn't hear you come up."

They didn't reply, but dismounted, walked the rows of cane, staring at the healthy growth, came back.

Riel's pulse raced. He'd seen enough, knew from their aggressive walk and the arrogant, threatening expressions on their faces that they were carpetbaggers.

The taller man, dressed in dirty work clothes, was about forty and a little under six feet. He had coarse features and thick, dirty, tan hair with an unruly wave to it. He glowered at Riel with fierce brown eyes.

The second man, a bit older and somewhat shorter, was dressed the same. He had lank black hair and bruised, gray eyes. His mouth had as ugly a twist as the first man's.

Riel waited. He'd spoken. They had come onto his property. It was up to them to reply, to state their purpose.

"You Rivard?" growled the coarse-featured one.

"I'm Riel Rivard, yes," Riel admitted, picking up his hoe. He stood it on the ground, held it erect. He didn't like these men, didn't like their swagger. He didn't like the rough challenge in the first man's coarse, heavy voice.

The second man grinned maliciously. "Riel Rivard! Purty fancy name fer the likes of you!"

The first man smiled maliciously. "I'm Silas Mercer," he grated. "My friend's Henry Dodds. Them's names fer ye to remember." He raked a fierce look over Riel. "I thought Riel Rivard was a nigger."

Riel held his voice even. "I've got black blood, if that's what you mean."

"A white nigger!" chortled Dodds, and both carpetbaggers smote their legs and brayed with laughter.

When it had subsided, Riel said evenly, "And you are carpetbaggers."

"That's what they tell us," said Mercer, "smartest men in the south today. Silas Mercer an' Henry Dodds. That's our names, remember 'em good. We aim ter be the biggest men on the bayous! We don't complain now, an' we're jest commencin'! We got things rollin' our way, an' afore long the money'll be rollin' in!"

"It doesn't roll very fast, these days," Riel said.

"Fer us it will!" Mercer bragged. "Me, I bought the plantation south of ye—it's Mercer Hall now—seven hunderd sweet acres. Dodds bought the next two places south of me; he's got a total of two thousand acres. Got a bargain. The folks was sick of bein' pore an' moved to New Orleens."

Riel had heard of these sales. He'd not known, however, that his new neighbors were carpetbaggers. Watching the two surly men, he braced himself. More was sure to come. They weren't through with him.

"Me'n my fam'ly's moved into Mercer Hall," said Mercer. He turned, gazed toward Rivard's plantation house, which stood on a little knoll. "That'd be a likely place fer us," he mused. "Yes, indeed, t'would."

"It's not for sale," Riel told him coolly.

"What right's a nigger got to own a plantation?" Mercer demanded, turning back, face ugly, filled with hatred.

"My mother owns it. My father was a white man."

"But he ain't around no more."

Riel stared into Mercer's narrowed eyes, didn't reply. He ached to fight this man, almost flung his hoe aside to attack, but held back. He couldn't fight the bully, and it was his own fault. He'd let word out in town about the blood. Consequently, if he fought Mercer, it would be black man assaulting white.

Anger and frustration raged in him. He wanted to beat Mercer's arrogant face into a pulp. He wanted to kick him off Rivard. Yet, despite his inability to do so, he was proud that he had boldly acknowledged his blood.

"Ye got five hunderd acres, right?" asked Mercer.

"Correct."

"I'll pay ye five hunderd dollars cash money. Right out of my personal carpetbag. Today. Ye git yer fam'ly the hell off t'morrow."

"Thank you," Riel said grimly, "but no."

"Ye got no appreciation!" exploded Mercer. "Ye ought ter be proud that a white man'd talk bizness with ye at all! Six hunderd, an' that's as high as I'll go, so drop th' dicker an' make yer sale."

"No, thank you," Riel forced himself to say evenly. He met the look of Mercer, of Dodds. They glowered, obviously enraged that he showed none of the subserviance they expected.

Both were flushed. Mercer started for Riel, but Dodds held him back.

"He ain' worth it, Silas! Leave him rot!"

"No nigger kin own a plantation!" roared Mercer. "Never could, an' sure as hell can't now!"

"Several black men do own plantations, Mr. Mercer. Three own plantations near New Orleans, and owned slaves before the war. They have legal papers to prove it, as my mother has."

"Then I'll talk to yer mammy! Take me to her. I want ter git this done an' over with!"

Motioning for them to follow, Riel started for the house. As Mercer and Dodds rode their horses at a walk their heads turned, eyes greedy on the rich soil, the flourishing sugar cane, the productive kitchen garden.

At the front of the house they tied their horses to the hitching posts and followed Riel across the veranda, swaggering. Mouth grim, Riel led them into the drawing room where Olive was sewing.

Olive rose to meet them, bewildered, yet she looked at them graciously. Riel, instantly aware of her quiet confidence, felt proud, but ashamed, knowing how cruelly he had been treating her. For a moment, that pride he felt for her and his anger battled in him, and anger got the edge. But for her liaison with a white man, they would not now be involved with these carpetbaggers.

"Mama," he said. "Silas Mercer, Henry Dodds."

The men stared. Olive looked as beautiful as she always did. Obviously, Mercer and Dodds weren't accustomed to anyone like her. Riel could almost read their minds, feel their shock at her whiteness, her grace, the gentle smile she gave to put them at their ease.

"This is my mother, Olive Rivard," Riel said. He went on coolly, "These men are carpetbaggers, Mama."

Her smile faded, but the graciousness remained.

Mercer swaggered to Olive, stopped. He raked a suggestive look over her figure. Riel's hands sprang into fists; deliberately, he relaxed them. Black and white, he thought, black and white. He stiffened his jaw. He'd tolerate only just so much. If Mercer lifted a hand to Olive, he'd kill him.

"Yer sucker here," Mercer drawled, "tells us that he don't own this land. He says ye own it."

Olive paled. She held her head proudly, chin up. "That's right, Mr. Mercer," she said.

"I'm payin' ye seven hunderd fifty dollars fer it," Mercer said roughly. "Git out the paper, an' we'll sign. If a nigger kin write! That's a good one!"

Dodds guffawed.

Riel tensed to spring at Mercer, but Olive caught his eye, and he restrained himself. This was part of his black heritage; he'd have to teach his future family to deal with it.

Olive said quietly, "The price you mention, Mr. Mercer, is only a fraction of Rivard's value. Furthermore, it isn't for sale at any price. It's my son's heritage."

Mercer argued, and so did Dodds, but Olive was firm. Finally, deeply enraged, the carpetbaggers turned to go. "We'll make it too hot fer ye to stay," Mercer threatened. "Make ye glad ter git half of what I'm offerin' now!"

"Rivard is for my son," Olive repeated.

"Ye'll pay fer yer stubborness!" Mercer promised. "Silas Mercer don't give up till he gits what he wants!"

When they were gone, Olive let her fright show. "What can they do to us?" she asked.

"Insult us, bluster, threaten, make any kind of trouble they can dream up. Legally, we're sound. Rivard is yours, Mama."

"No, it's yours," she murmured, grateful for the moment of the old familiar warmth, aware that it would fade again into resentment.

"It's not mine really, not yet."

"I'll have papers drawn up tomorrow," she said.

He made no objection. He'd now be on a firmer footing with men like Mercer and Dodds. His word would carry full authority.

As he once more turned cold and withdrawn, Olive ached with disappointment. Suddenly she was frightened by this new Riel, master of Rivard.

Chapter XX

Riel, relieved to have Rivard as his own, sternly crushing back his hurt over Marie-Louise, continued to actively seek a wife. He wouldn't do it in a hurry, but carefully.

He proceeded as he would have gone about buying a wench. Not wench—girl, he corrected himself. He wanted a fine girl of sweet nature and lively mind, with a proper build to give him a son, and very, very pretty. He wanted someone capable of becoming mistress of Rivard. Consequently, his eyes were always open now, looking girls over, weighing, considering.

He had one last task to accomplish before he could ask any girl to marry him, even if he found her soon. There was something Olive must do for him. One morning after breakfast he approached her.

She was dressed in soft green, ready to go to the Rivard schoolroom. The children would be there in half an hour, and she meant to place their lessons on their desks before they arrived.

"Mama," Riel said politely enough. "In the drawing room. There's a thing we must talk about, and the sooner the better."

She tried to read his face. Her pulse started to race. He had something serious to discuss, and he expected her not to like it.

He saw her probing eyes, her concern. He steeled himself. He must get one further concession. It was the hardest one and the most important: she would resist.

They sat together on the divan. Riel, noting her pallor, knew that she was afraid, and regret flashed in him. He made his tone almost gentle.

"Mama, this has to be faced. My . . . plan."

"Yes, Riel, yes, son?" A wild hope sprang up at his gentleness, a prayerful hope that he had reconsidered, that he would live white, after all. The word he'd dropped in town that he was black would fade into gossip, oh, it would! She watched him closely, lips ready to tremble into a smile.

Recognizing her false hope, Riel again felt that flashing regret, but continued with what he had to say, prepared to deliver the blow. "You've made me sole owner of Rivard," he began.

"It was planned so. You're a man now, young, but a man. It's time you be master of Rivard. You've been doing a master's job, and doing it well."

"You've had no regrets? About Rivard?"

"None," she said, abruptly fearful. But she remained silent. She'd not give up hope, not toss aside the lifelong struggle to raise him white, wouldn't permit words spoken in the recent weeks to affect the belief that he would, after all, adhere to her way, René's way.

He stared at her without expression.

Surely, oh, surely, this child of the love she and René had known could not cast away his upbringing and carry out an anguished threat! Not René's son!

Riel shattered that thought. "You haven't forgotten what I said about marrying a black girl?" he asked, his tone cold.

A great hand seemed to thrust into her chest and grasp her heart, her struggling heart. She could scarcely breathe. Desperately, she clung to the belief that he had reconsidered, that he had given up his impossible plan to marry black.

"Mama?" His voice was hard now, cold.

"How could I forget?" she asked, "that you would threaten, even in hurt and anger, to destroy what your father and I built for you! You don't mean it, Riel! You couldn't mean it, not now, not after time has passed and you've considered!"

"You built nothing for me. I'm destroying nothing but deceit. I'm going to marry as I said."

She stared in disbelief. Why, dear God, why? Tears rose in her, but she held them back, her body one aching throb. Her life, the happy years with René, the love and care she'd lavished on their son, her every thought for his good, his happiness, his future, came crashing down. As in a dream, his next words fell on her ears.

"It isn't easy for me to marry a black girl," he said angrily. "Because for a white man to marry a black woman is against the law, as you know. Further, thanks to you, I'm not considered to be a black man, even though, also thanks to you, I am black."

In her roaring despair, she found one lifeline. The law! The law would keep Riel from doing this mad thing, and in years to come, he would be glad it happened so. She clasped her hands in her lap to still their trembling.

"You don't comment," he said. "You think that the law will stop me?"

She met his eyes, the throbbing lump in her dry throat about to choke her. Eyes pleading, she nodded.

"Not so, Mama. You don't get your way so easily. You have only to go before the law with me and sign papers that you are an octoroon. You have to tell the truth. You never thought it would come to this, Mama, but it has. It has."

The shame of what he demanded encompassed her. The shame to herself and to him. The shame to René, dead now and in his grave, René who would never know his loving plans had been destroyed, who had never even known of the blood he carried. She dug her nails into her palms.

"No, Riel," she said. "I can't do it, son, I can't. René arranged things so perfectly, and I've followed his wishes. No, I can't do what you want."

"My father's name doesn't belong in this," Riel said flatly. "Just yours. If it brings shame on you, it is, after all, your own fault. I mean to have children, and they are not to live a lie. You will sign the paper today. I've had an attorney draw it up. He's expecting us this morning."

"And if I refuse to sign?"

"I'll no longer consider you my mother. I'll cohabit with a black girl. My descendants will be illegitimate at first, but they'll be black and can marry black. I'll achieve my purpose, one way or another."

"If I'd no longer be your mother, what would I be? Where would I be?"

"At Rivard. You'd live in the house." But without respect, his tone implied. Without love.

She sat trembling, defeated by this beloved son, the son now so utterly a stranger. For him not to be a son to her who had borne him, who had memorized his every baby smile and boyish mischief, she could not endure. Better the other. Better anything but not to be his mother. Numb, gazing at Riel she whispered, "I'll sign the paper."

He took her to St. Martinville that day. She was aware of people on the street, of the attorney's office, the desk, the middle-aged man with the kind face who put the pen in her fingers.

"You're certain you want to sign this?" he asked.

She nodded, signed, and they left.

They walked down the streets to where the pirogue was docked. As in a trance, Olive moved with pride, as she'd always moved. Riel helped her into the boat. This was her last appearance in public as a white woman.

Riel sat across from her, working the oar. She looked at him, seeking a softening of his attitude, but there was none. She knew that if she wanted his love, she'd have to win it. The task before her was enormous—to truly make friends with his black wife—to love his black children. To be a black part of a black family. That would stir to life, pray God, his old love for her.

Riel, watching her, had a glimmer of understanding of what it had meant for her to sign the paper. "There will be other things," he told her. "I know I'm turning your life upside down, but it must be done. And you have to endure it and deal with it. Like the lady you are."

Her breath hurt. So there was still an instinctive understanding between them. He had spoken her thoughts, though in different words. He'd even complimented her, said she was a lady. She clung to his words, unable to look into the future and predict what else he might require of her.

She thought of René again. With a stroke of the pen, she had made herself, her descendants. René's descendants, black.

Riel had the notice of Olive Rivard's octoroon blood published in the weekly paper. The paper went into the homes of the bayou folk, and was read from the first page to the last. Few missed the Rivard legal notice, and those few were promptly told of it by friends. It was received with shock and consternation; it was read and reread and discussed without end.

Pablo and Clio Sanchez took turns reading it to each other over their dinner table. Never before had Clio allowed the newspaper at table.

Pablo, forty-two, finally laid it, folded, beside his plate. His heavy build, now run to rolls of fat, lips fat and red, oozed shock. "Unbelievable!" he exclaimed. "A woman like that, such a beauty, raising her son properly, deceiving the whole countryside!"

Clio, thirty-eight, black-haired and black-eyed, stared at her husband. "You see, now?" she cried. "Arla Brewer knew what she was talking about! She always said there was a mystery about that woman!"

"For once she was right," Pablo agreed. "But that the Widow Rivard, so proper and reserved, that she would be—"

"Well, she is! The proof's right there in the paper! And she sent that boy of hers to school with white children, raised him white!"

"What I don't understand," Pablo reflected, "is why she published this notice. Peculiar, that after all these years, she'd—"

"We ladies always thought she had something to hide! She'd never go to a party, kept to herself even at Mass. Now we know why! She meant for that boy to marry white and fool everybody! But she didn't get away with it!"

"But she did have it published, Clio. Why?"

"Does it matter? Nigras never have logical reasons for what they do! They just act!"

So the talk went through St. Martinville and all the bayou country. The general opinion was that Olive Rivard had been some white man's placée, probably that sea captain nobody ever saw, and maybe he'd meant to retire and live with her at Rivard, passing her off as white, and maybe he hadn't. But none of them could figure out why she'd had the notice published.

Even the ex-slaves, dumbstruck at the news, couldn't figure it out. They talked and talked. They'd never do such a thing, ever. If they could pass as white, they would.

Chapter XXI

Riel found the girl he wanted at Gaboury's Plantation. Boldly he oared his pirogue to the landing to take a look, just stroll around. He avoided the big house and made for the old slave quarters.

He saw her on the dirt road and followed her. She was tall, shapely, and had gleaming ebony skin. Her kinky hair was in tiny braids, the ends tied with narrow red ribbons. When he stopped in front of her, smiling, blocking her path, he saw that the short braids formed an attractive cap on her head.

She stopped just short of bumping into him, a look of surprise on her. Her face had broad bones, a good nose, lips narrow with an underlay of red. He liked everything about her.

"Hello," Riel said abruptly.

"H-hello, sir." She faltered. Her voice was music. Her hips were made for child-bearing.

"I'm Riel Rivard," he told her. "From Rivard."

She glanced at him quickly, excited. She'd heard the story about his black blood; it was hard to believe by looking at him. He was waiting. Politeness demanded that she speak.

"Y-yes, sir," she managed, cheeks warm from the way he kept staring at her. "I'm Deedee Johnson. Will and Bess are my pappy and mammy. They took the name Johnson aftah the war."

"What did they do on the plantation before the war?"

"Pappy was second butlah. Mammy was first cook. Now they work in the fields."

He read her nature, gulped it through his eyes. Intelligent, sweet, a hint of spice and sassiness, capable of love. Although she was conversing with a man who looked to be white, she conducted herself with dignity.

"You speak well," he told her.

"I've been to the plantation school, sir."

"Are you promised in marriage?"

Her lips trembled; her heart jumped. What did he mean, what could he mean?

"Are you?" he pressed.

"No, sir. I need to love a man."

As she spoke, her eyes, wide and black, lingered on his face. Not only was he handsome, but there was kindness in him. He'd be gentle with his wife. If he came here often— Well, it wouldn't be easy to keep from loving him, even if he didn't look black, and even if she'd always liked brown men. Until now.

He watched her keenly every second. She was attracted to him, couldn't move her eyes away. Her pulse was hammering in her throat, a dead giveaway. She moved, and he glanced at those hips again. His groin started that miserable aching.

He decided on the spot that she was what he wanted. "I'm nineteen," he told her, "and master of Rivard. It is my plantation."

"Yes sir, that's nice, sir. I'm eighteen." Now she could scarcely breathe.

"We farm the land at Rivard with ex-slaves. Many of our people stayed after the war. Or came back."

"We have that here too, sir. Labor in exchange for cabin and food and a share of the harvest."

"I want you to marry me, Deedee."

She gasped, a mixture of surprise, pleasure, fright. "Are you joking, sir? A white man—"

"No joke, Deedee. Haven't you heard yet? My mother is octoroon."

"Y-yes, I heard." She stared at him. She could feel her pulse, beating hard and fast in her neck, in her chest. "What would people think?" she asked, her mind a whirlwind of shock and deep attraction to this Riel Rivard, a feeling even now akin to love.

"Who cares what people think? I'm part black." He asked that they go to her parents, now working in the field. "I want to ask them for your hand immediately," he insisted.

She held back, studying him as he had studied her. He was so very white. She was so very black. Even feeling love being born in her this moment, she wondered if she could ever get used to the difference in their skins. She looked him over, up and down.

"You'll be mistress of Rivard," he urged. "You'll be mother to my heirs. You'll be honored, always. Surely your parents can't object to that."

She heard the throb of sincerity in his tone, warmed to him. He was offering her himself and all he owned. He was offering her his future. He had already leapt the color line; if she married him, she would have to adjust to it bit by bit, even learning to love him.

"Please don't think I spoke too soon," he pleaded. "I know it's sudden. But I also know what I want when I see it. I want your blackness, and I want your love."

Tears welled into her eyes, crept down her cheeks, but she didn't wipe them away. He didn't offer her a handkerchief, but probed deeper into her teary eyes. Helpless, feeling herself slipping into love with him, she struggled against agreeing so soon to marry him. Marriage on sight, she thought. Yet she dashed away her tears and took him to her parents.

They found Will and Bess sitting under a tree, sharing cold corn pone and lean fatback, drinking water to wash it down. They stood and watched in surprise when they saw Deedee and Riel approaching.

Riel studied them as they neared, eager to see what blood, through Deedee, would go into his heirs.

Will Johnson was almost six feet tall, with wide, strong bones, ebony skin like Deedee's, and classic negroid features. He was muscular and exceedingly strong; his round head was covered with short-cropped wool.

Bess was the same age as Will, fifty, and her skin, too, was shining, ebony black. She was slim and shapely still, head covered with a red bandanna, features less negroid that Will's.

"What you doin' heah, Baby?" she asked Deedee. "Thought you was goin' clean the mistress' stove!"

"I'm all finished, Mammy," Deedee replied, a quaver to her voice. "I was going to clean our cabin when Mistah Rivard came by. He wants to talk to you, both of you."

Will and Bess were nodding, nearly bowing, but Riel put a stop to that by extending his hand. "I'm Riel Rivard," he said. "Of Rivard, and I'm part black."

Staring, they shook hands with him, and he asked if they all four couldn't sit down for their talk. The parents, making no effort to hide their bewilderment, assented.

When they were all sitting on the ground, Riel asked Bess, "How many more beautiful daughters besides Deedee do you have, Mrs. Johnson?"

Sadness replaced bewilderment on Bess's face. "I borned ten suckahs, all boys but Deedee, 'n she's my last," she said. "They was all sold off. By the time Deedee was borned, Miz Gaboury and her husband had bought us and they say we to keep Deedee till she marry."

"Which is what I want your permission to do," Riel told Bess, then he looked at Will. "And she won't be lost to you, if you consent. She'll live at Rivard. As my wife, she'll be mistress of Rivard; you can visit back and forth all you like. You can know your grandchildren and watch them grow up."

There was immediate silence. Bess and Will gazed from Deedee to Riel, back again. If they noticed that their fellow workers had returned to the fields, they gave no sign.

"Has ouah Deedee say she marry you, suh?" asked Will, troubled.

"Not yet, not quite. But she brought me to you, and that makes me hope. I told her I want to ask you for her hand, and that is what I'm doing now."

"She be mistress of Rivard," mused Will.

"Yes."

"You be good to huh?" Will's dark eyes pierced, and his thick lips firmed.

"I'll be good to her," Riel promised, wondering how any man, white or black, could be otherwise to the exquisite Deedee.

"We bin good to huh," said Bess, beginning to weep. "We love huh most as good as we love God! She ouah baby!"

"You love him, Baby?" asked Will.

"I just met him, Pappy! I feel different, but how do I know if it's love?"

"You love ouah baby, suh?" Will asked, frowning.

"It's a new love," Riel said. "I admit that. But every moment I'm with her, it deepens. I know myself pretty well, sir, have good reason to, and I can promise that every day and every year, I'll love her more. And will do all I can to win the same love from her."

"That how it's been with me'n you, Will," Bess said, wiping away her tears. "Remembah? One day we met, and next Sunday we jump the broomstick! And it bin good evah since 'cept foah havin' ouah suckahs sold away."

"That true," Will agreed. "But this is diffrunt. Theah's white blood, lots of it, and Deedee bein' mistress of Rivard. That a big job, but it hard."

"I'll help her," Riel promised. "I'll get my mother to teach her. She's a lady and knows everything there is to know about being mistress of a plantation."

"You mothah white as you," Bess said doubtfully. "I seen huh. How she goin' feel, you bring huh ouah black Deedee and say 'Learn huh to be a lady like you,' Deedee so black and youah mothah so white?"

Riel looked at Bess steadily. "It will be all right," he assured her. "My mother will do what I ask."

"But how she treat ouah Deedee?"

"With kindness, Mrs. Johnson. Because she is a kind lady; she wouldn't know how to be anything else."

He said the words, but did not allow himself to think on them. He spoke further, getting acquainted with Will and Bess, mentally approving the stamina they would add, through Deedee, to his heirs.

Before he left, certain things had been settled. Riel could come courting as often as Deedee said. He was to give her time, give himself time, to learn whether the instant attraction they felt would grow into love, to ponder whether that love was the kind Will and Bess had, strong enough to weather trouble.

And so, the courtship began. Deedee found she was

anxious to see Riel every night. He found himself thinking about her day and night, knew he'd never find another like her, told her so. He even went to St. Martinville and bought a plain gold wedding band with money he couldn't afford to spend.

Steadily, Deedee's worry about his white blood faded. Every time she saw him, her tender feeling toward him grew. The moment came when she let Riel kiss her, and right after the kiss she said yes, she'd marry him the next Sunday night.

Chapter XXII

On the night of the wedding, Mae and George Lefleur spent the night with Marcel and Laura Gaboury at Gaboury Plantation. All they could talk about was this unprecedented wedding.

"To think the Widow Rivard has been a nigra all the time, a placée." Mae whispered to Laura so the men couldn't hear them indulge in such scandalous words.

"Shocking! Earth-shattering!"

"It's bound to be that sea captain who died. She was trying to make folks believe he was her husband."

"And to think that Riel Rivard is marrying our Deedee, black as ink, this very minute!" fluttered Laura. "All our people are at Rivard, invited by the widow herself."

"Most of our people made the trip, too," Mae said. "You should have seen them—dressed up so you'd hardly know them! Some of the wenches even turned their dresses, sewed them back up by candlelight!"

The men, when appealed to, declared the marriage was a disgrace and the law shouldn't permit it. "But the slaves are free now," Gaboury said heavily. "They can do what they please."

"I don't know what the south's coming to!" wailed Mae.

"Carpetbaggers for neighbors, nigras for neighbors—it's enough to make a person want to move to New Orleans!"

"It's as bad there, maybe worse," said her husband. "I heard only today about some scalawags who tarred and feathered a nigra who talked back when his smithy job was given to a white man. They dipped the nigra in hot tar, plastered him with feathers, and left him to die. The Ku Klux Klan has done some of that, too."

The ladies, nearly swooning at such horrors, immediately agreed that the Rivard wedding should be the least of their worries. But they simply did not know what was going to become of the South.

"What we've got to do," Gaboury pronounced, "is hang on. This can't last. One day the carpetbaggers will leave, bound to. And nigras like the Rivards will lose their land, because it takes a white man to head up a plantation."

"But it takes nigras in the fields, too!" wailed Mae. "Oh dear, what are we going to do?"

"Wait," Lefleur said. "Work. Be good to the nigras who do stay. Prices will go up. The bayou country will come back into its own."

"Right," agreed Gaboury. "Let Reconstruction do its worst. We'll live decently again one day. Not in luxury, perhaps, but in pride."

"And now," Mae wailed on, "the nigras don't even call us Acadians! They've shortened it to Cajun! They call us Cajuns!"

"Nigras always change words," her husband comforted. "They mean no harm, dear. They soften words, so Acadian becomes Cajun. It's a natural thing."

So went the talk on other plantations, too—at the Heberts, the Corbets, the Leseurs—in homes up and down the bayous, where Reconstruction and poverty went hand in hand.

On this night, Riel and Deedee stood in the Quarters, lit by flares, before the black-suited preacher. Riel wore his dark suit, Deedee was lovely in gold calico, her hair braided with gold ribbon, and she looked to Riel like a rich, pulsing sunbeam.

The grounds of Rivard were thick with guests, black guests. They filled the big space in the Quarters, reached into the candle-lit plantation house, flowed into it and moved about, smiling, subdued, happy, impressed.

Olive, wearing soft green, stood at the front entrance

with Bess and Will Johnson, both in new, dark garb. She extended her hand to each guest, smiling, inwardly driving herself to be truly gracious to these people her son had adopted for his own.

Deedee and Riel joined the line and they, too, shook every hand. Olive stood grasping hand after hand, silently soul-searching. Deedee was beautiful, but the difference between her and Riel repelled Olive, and it hurt to see them standing together, husband and wife.

Again, in her mind, she heard what Riel had said this morning. "I see you're moving out of the master suite," he'd begun.

"Yes."

"It's the right thing to do, Mama."

The right thing, Olive thought miserably, to leave the bedroom in which she and René had made love, to leave the very bed in which Riel had been born, to leave the sitting room in which she and René had read together and talked.

"You're to have the biggest guest room," Riel had said.

"That's the one I chose," she had replied.

After the dancing began, Deedee, shy but glowing, came with Riel to Olive. "Riel told me about the rooms, your rooms. You needn't have moved out. Any other room would have been wonderful for us."

"The master suite was designed for the master and mistress," Olive told her quietly. "The rooms are rightfully yours. I want you to have them."

And she did want it. She smiled at the girl, who smiled back tremulously. Deedee couldn't help what she was, could never have resisted Riel. Olive saw Deedee's adoration for her son emanating from her like an inner light.

After the wedding night, there were problems for the newlyweds. Going to bed was a delight, but the next morning, Deedee was very quiet. She wandered, as if frightened, from bedroom to sitting room to bath and back again.

Riel, enchanted, loving the glow of the yellow gold wedding band against her black skin, noticed her mood. "What's wrong?" he asked. "Is there something you want changed?"

"I shouldn't have done it!" she blurted. "I shouldn't have married you!"

"Why not? Last night—"

"Was perfect. I loved you—in bed."

"What do you mean?" he asked, deadly quiet. "Don't you love me now?"

"Of course I do," she said simply. "It's just that now with the sun up so I can really see what a fine house you've always lived in—I don't know."

"Go on, Deedee."

"It's that the sun shows up our differences, don't you see? You, raised white in a mansion, me raised black in a two-room cabin. The two things don't fit. How can a white master truly be husband to a slave?"

"You're not a slave. And you seem to forget my blood, my mother's blood. I chose you for wife, and you gave consent. So did your parents. You love me, and I love you. What more can you ask?"

"That we live in a cabin in the Quarters until I get used to the idea of this house, us."

"Used to Rivard, the idea of being mistress? You're already mistress. There'll be no cabin. I've asked my mother to show you the way to run the house. Please don't bring up the subject again."

Her eyes met his timidly. "Yes, sir," she whispered.

Anger crossed him, but disappeared. "Riel—call me Riel. I thought that was settled. You are my wife, my equal."

He held out his arms, and she went into them. Enfolded there, she felt safe. And a trickle of courage returned to her.

At breakfast, Riel and Olive discussed one of the cane fields. Riel said he'd put the whole force on it today, clear out the weeds. As she talked, Olive tried to feed Felix in his high chair. When Felix turned from the spoon and smiled his angel smile at Deedee, it was as if a dam had broken in the girl and she spoke impulsively.

"Maybe, ma'am," she said, "he'd open his mouth for me."

Olive, surprised, gave the spoon to Deedee. Felix ate for her, smiling and gurgling, and Riel watched, a grin on his face. Olive felt a tinge of warmth for Deedee, yet regretted that her son's wife was black.

Deedee asked if she could help take care of Felix.

"Some of the time," agreed Olive. "Polly Landers is his nursemaid. She's only fourteen, but he loves her and she's careful with him."

"I don't know Polly yet," Deedee said, depresssed because she, the new mistress, didn't even know all her people. The enormity of what had been thrust upon her was frightening and she glanced, pleadingly, at Riel.

He smiled, then his mouth went hard. He recognized her fright and was displeased. Deedee braced herself to do what he wanted, to become in truth mistress of Rivard.

Polly, a skinny, black girl, came in to get Felix. "Aftah he baf, us go in de sunshine, Miss Olive," she prattled. "Us jes' poke 'round, have fun."

Olive introduced her to Deedee, then said, "He must have a nap, Polly, and be ready for dinner." Remembering Riel's displeasure, Olive turned to Deedee. "Deedee, is that what you want Polly to do?"

"W-what he's used to is best," Deedee stammered. Turning to Olive, she added, with a flash of courage, "You're Felix's adopted mama. Doesn't that mean you should be the one to say what he must do?"

Olive saw Riel's mouth loosen; she smiled at Deedee. At least Deedee had intelligence and judgment and intuition.

They went about their work, Riel to the fields, Deedee to tidy their house, then, following Riel's suggestion, to make the rounds of the cabins and get acquainted with the few not in the fields.

To Riel, as he strode to work, it appeared that his plan to establish a black family, a black dynasty, was working well. He was a bit troubled at Deedee's feeling of not belonging, but confident that his growing love for her and her increasing familiarity with Rivard would change that.

Deedee, finding no one at home in the Quarters, made her way to the field being weeded. She paused to speak with each worker, man and woman alike, and smiled and asked the names of those she didn't know.

The ex-slaves, on their part, felt strange toward Deedee the first moment or two. Then, because she was so black, so friendly, so outgoing with them, they were soon grinning, entranced. Riel, watching this, felt a pleasure which was almost joy.

As the first days passed, Deedee became more acquainted, felt more comfortable. She delighted in caring for Felix, coaxing at times to get him away from Polly.

She went to a party with Riel and the Rivard blacks, given at Gaboury Plantation by their blacks and had a happy evening. She scarcely noticed that the Gabourys themselves did not appear to look in on the party, but let the blacks run their own affair, which they did a bit noisily, but decently. Deedee was proud that all the girls, seeming to be unaware that Riel was white, wanted to dance with Riel, so he danced happily with them, telling Deedee later when they danced together that he was being made to feel at ease.

Gradually, too, as the first days passed, Olive came to accept Deedee as a good, intelligent girl, even to like her because of her love for Felix who was now crawling, on the verge of walking.

One bright morning, Polly announced that she was taking Felix to see the pigs. "He jes' love 'um big, bad, gruntin' hawgs," she grinned.

"Keep him well back from the pen," Olive warned.

"I does, ma'am! Dem hawgs fierce as de wild ones in de bayou! Polly allus take keer!"

After they were gone, Deedee went to the cabin of Meg and Joe Wilson. Both were laid up with aches, and Deedee spent quite some time with them, rubbing on a salve, making cheerful talk.

Suddenly, from the direction of the pigpen, came a piercing shriek. As Deedee ran outside, there came another and another, building into a continuing scream. Deedee, running at top speed, made for the pigpen.

As she neared, she saw Polly sitting on the ground, clutching her foot and shrieking. Beyond crawled Felix, headed straight for the pen where the three great, murderous beasts had reared up, grunting and squealing.

Deedee ran on, faster. If Felix got close enough to poke his hand through the slats . . . ! Without pausing, she simply threw her body forward and went flying toward the baby.

Felix was reaching out, a murderous boar coming at him, when she snatched him up and away. She tried to stop, but her momentum slid her foot and leg under the bottom slat, and she took the boar's slashing teeth along her leg before she jerked it free. She limped back to Polly, Felix in her arms crying at the top of his voice, Polly still screaming, and she saw Olive and Nette running from the back of the house.

"Stop it!" Deedee shouted at the hysterical Polly. "It's all right; he didn't get hurt!"

Polly's screams subsided into a loud crying. "I done turn my ankle, broke my foot!" she sobbed. "De baby, he git loose an' crawl!"

"It's all right, thanks to Deedee," panted Olive, just arrived. She took the baby, now howling loudly. "Nette and I were snapping beans on the back gallery; we saw the whole thing. You shouldn't have run while carrying the baby, Polly."

"We play horsie, Miss Olive! He like it! But Polly won' do it ag'in! Polly broke huh foot, Miss Olive, an' it hurt ba-ad!"

Olive gave Felix to Nette, knelt, Deedee beside her. "The foot's broken, all right," Olive said, after examining it, Polly crying out in pain. "We'll have the doctor come and tend it. You'll have to stay in the cabin while it heals."

"Who take care de baby?" Polly sobbed.

"The three of us," Olive said. Then turning to Deedee, she saw the gashed, bleeding leg. "One of the hogs?" she asked, and Deedee nodded. Olive took off her apron, began to sop away blood gently. "It's not too deep," she said, "but the doctor must tend it, prevent blood poisoning or worse. You did a brave thing, Deedee. You saved Felix from being killed by those hogs."

"I only pulled him out, ma'am. I wasn't in danger."

Olive met Deedee's tear-filled eyes, put her arm around her instinctively. "Thank God you were here, Deedee."

Now, drawn by the screams, workers were running in from the field. Riel was with them. Polly was sobbing again, this time wrapped in her mother's arms. Olive took Felix back into her lap, and Riel, alarmed, knelt beside Deedee, horrified by the sight of her leg.

Nette related to all of them what had happened. Riel sent a man to go for the doctor. He stayed beside Deedee and used his mother's handkerchief to bind the wound.

The workers muttered and shook their heads at the miraculous escape. "The new mistress save Mastah Felix's life," said one black man. "That boar almos' got Miss Deedee, but she save the baby. She one brave lady."

Yes, a brave lady, thought Olive with a jolt. Suddenly she was flooded with memories of Deedee's unfailing respect, her kindness, the way her eyes softened when they rested on Riel.

What a fool she had been! Riel could have searched the world and never found such a wife. Fondness for Deedee sprang in her again as it had earlier, and even with Felix in her arms, she enfolded the girl.

"Thank you . . . daughter," she murmured. "Thank you, and welcome to Rivard!"

"Today," Olive said, "if your leg isn't too sore, we'll practice setting the table."

"My leg is fine, ma'am."

"Call me Mama. Unless that is what you call your own mother."

"No, Mama. I call them Mammy and Pappy."

"Splendid! Now, first the linen cloth—we drape it evenly on the table. That's the way! And see that the folds hang just missing the carpet."

With trembling hands, Deedee stroked the starched white linen. Following Olive's example, she placed the flatware, the plates, the serving platters and bowls.

"With every worker needed on the land," Olive explained, "we don't have a butler to serve meals. You and Nette and I cook the food, then bring it to the table. Nette has a bad knee, so we don't let her serve. The food is put in front of Riel, as you have seen, and he serves the plates and passes them along. That's why we put the plates in one stack at the head of the table. You'll continue to sit opposite Riel at the foot—that's the mistress's place. I'll sit on one side and Felix on the other, when he's old enough to feed himself."

"And Nette, what about her?"

"She's old-fashioned; she started as my maid and housekeeper, won't sit at the table. At supper, she feeds Felix in the kitchen, eats all her own meals there."

Deedee gazed at the table. "It's beautiful. Knowing how to do it is—is—"

"Satisfying, dear."

"You know so much, Mama. Will you learn me?"

"Of course. In six months, you'll be a perfect mistress for Rivard!"

While they continued to prepare for the meal, Olive said, partly on impulse, but mostly because of her new affection for Deedee, "On Sundays we have a special dinner. You must invite your parents to dinner every Sunday so that they may see how you live and enjoy it with you."

Deedee began to weep. Olive held her, ashamed of her old, antagonistic feelings. She wondered, had she and René been blessed with a daughter, if she could have been any sweeter.

"To think that you'd invite Mammy and Pappy!" sobbed Deedee. "That you'd be so kind!"

"It's your house, too, dear. Much as I bemoaned your marriage at first, your parents are a part of this family now, a worthy part to have raised you so perfectly. Parents visit their married children freely, look on the children's home as a kind of second home for themselves. Forget that I was once mistress here. As for me, I'm grateful to be a part of the household. Unless—"

"Don't say it, Mama! You're to live with us always!" Deedee sobbed. She clung to Olive, who was bewildered at her own change of heart toward this girl, yet comforted by it.

Chapter XXIII

The following Sunday as Deedee shyly served her parents, Riel watched with satisfaction. He approved the way Olive conversed with Will and Bess, was proud of their reserved, yet friendly conduct.

He watched Will and Bess. Finally, sensing an inequality in the situation, he spoke. "Mother Johnson, Father Johnson, how would you feel about moving to Rivard at the end of harvest? To live."

They were dumbstruck at first, then Bess spoke. "You mean live in this house with all of you?"

"Yes, unless you prefer private quarters. You could have the overseer's house."

Bess and Will glanced at each other; communication flowed in the glance. Will shook his head. "No," he refused, "though we thank you kindly. We have an obligation to the Gaboury's. Visiting back and forth makes us happy, and hope it will be the same with you."

Deedee looked disappointed. Her eyes, however, glowed, and Riel knew that she was still pleased with the situation.

Soon Deedee found it necessary to give orders to women of her own color. Because it was her duty, she gave the orders, trying to be both firm and kind. At first the women seemed to hesitate, but except for one young girl who put up an argument, no one objected.

Deedee and the girl Loree stood in the back yard as Deedee outlined what was to be done. Loree having an eye for men, was unhappy.

"I don' like field work," she said.

"No one likes it too well," Deedee agreed. "But all the work must be done so we can all live. You know that, Loree."

"I'd ruther work in the house, be a maid. Or 'tend Mastah Felix. That Polly, she cain't walk good with her broke foot."

"She'll take care of the baby again when her foot heals. Besides, that was an accident," Deedee said uneasily. She knew she shouldn't explain, but she was new at this and facing resistance bothered her.

"She have 'nuther accident, you see."

"Regardless. We can't spare you from work on the land," Deedee told her, her heart beating wildly. "Miss Olive and Nette and I do all the cleaning and cooking, everything but the laundry, and Miss Olive also teaches the school. Among us, we tend the baby, and Polly's been promised that job back. There simply isn't anything in the house for you to do."

"I don' want to do no laundry, eithah!"

At her wit's end, Deedee wondered what Olive would do, faced by Loree. But then, Loree would never dare argue with Olive. Deedee had to deal with this herself.

"You don't have to do laundry," she said, "because we have a laundress. What you will do is work in the kitchen garden. That keeps you from the fields. If you argue about that, I'll have to go to the master about you."

"No'm," Loree mumbled, twisting her bare toe in the

dust. "De mastah, he git cross afore when I want to be house wench. He put me in de garden, too."

"Then I needn't speak to him?"

"No'm." A sullen look. "I work in de garden."

Silas Mercer came riding back to Rivard, spied Riel on the front gallery refreshing himself with black coffee. Mercer still looked filthy, his very bones seemed coarser, his hair more rumpled.

He slid off his horse, tied it up, stood straddlelegged, speaking no word of greeting. His manner indicated authority, as though he owned the place. His expression was ugly.

Riel, glad that Deedee was making the rounds of the cabins and Olive was in the schoolroom, stared at his caller. He burned with slow anger.

"What can I do for you today, Mr. Mercer?" he asked, deliberately not inviting the fellow onto the gallery.

Mercer glowered. "Ye kin listen to sense, that's what ye kin do. An' save yerself an' yer bride an' yer nigger mammy a pile of trouble."

Riel waited, anger building.

"Ye don't say nothin'," Mercer growled.

"What is there to say? I know you didn't drop in for a neighborly visit, and I've already said no to your proposition. I don't see that we have anything to discuss."

Mercer snorted. His face turned menacing, but his tone was arrogantly reasonable when he spoke. "I'm in a gen'rous mood today," he said. "I'll pay ye a thousand fer this plantation. That's on'y 'cause I've took a likin' to the house, want it fer my woman."

"My original answer holds," said Riel. "No sale."

"My woman is breedin', means ter keep on breedin'. I got to have more land. She's already got six childrun."

"Why do you want Rivard? Because it's rich and fertile?"

"Hell, all the land around here ye kin say that about! I want this perticular place because I like the house, an' the land joins what I a'ready got."

Riel held his silence.

"What ye up to?" Mercer demanded. "Holdin' out fer more'n a thousand?"

"I won't sell at any price, Mr. Mercer. Rivard is my heritage, will be my son's heritage."

"Yer nigger son!"

"That's right. My black son. A new Rivard with need for land, land which is mine and will remain so to hand on to him."

"What 'bout my six?" snarled Mercer. "I aim ter split what I git amongst 'em! I ain't no hawg, hangin' onto five hunderd acres fer jest one nigger brat!"

Riel stood still, looked straight down into Mercer's angry eyes. "Mr. Mercer," he said quietly, "be decent enough to take no for an answer, then get off my land. No amount of your money or that of any other man can buy Rivard."

"I'll go," snarled Mercer. "But no nigger gits away with orderin' Silas Mercer, a white man, off of property you ain't got no right to in the first place! Don't be a fool. Don't think ye've saw or heard the last of me! Ye'll rue this day. What Silas Mercer wants, Silas Mercer gits, an' right now he wants Rivard, house an' all." He gave one last snort, swung onto his horse, jerked the reins, and galloped away. Even the crude manner in which he sat his mount gave evidence of his rage.

That night two Rivard youths saw shadowy figures near the stable and the chicken house, heard the chickens cackle, ran for the big house. Riel, alerted by the boys, grabbed his rifle and ran to the chicken coop, but the intruders were gone and a search by lantern light showed that six laying hens were missing.

Furious, Riel sent everybody back to their cabins. At the house, he told Deedee and Olive of Mercer's repeated offer to buy Rivard, his own refusal to sell, and the white man's threats and rage.

"He sent men to steal our chickens, to get even?" Deedee asked.

"I'm sure of it. He'll try any trick to get me to sell."

The next night Riel posted men to guard the livestock and chickens, but the garden patch was the objective, and the watchmen heard no sound. Daylight revealed vegetables uprooted and flung aside, bean bushes torn from the ground, and sweet-corn stalks broken.

"If I'd had more guns for the guards," Riel said, "and had them patrol, we could have caught them, and proved they were Mercer's men. But it's just as well I didn't."

"Why not?" Deedee asked.

"I don't want to kill one of them," he told her. "They're only carrying out orders, Mercer's orders. Even if he came with them, which he's smart enough not to do, I don't want shooting. We're blacks; even though we're free, we can't do harm to a white man."

The next night, a shout from the front yard brought Riel and his womenfolk to the front gallery. Six white-robed men, heads hooded in pillowcases, sat their horses in a semicircle.

A few of Riel's men came running but stopped, frozen, when they saw the night riders. "Ku Kluxers!" someone shouted, and they all took off at a run, headed back to their cabins. Riel knew some would get their families and hide in the swamps, while others, after cautioning their wives, would return to help if they could.

Riel came down off the porch, one step at a time. Some of the horses shifted uneasily. Far off, a bull frog was drumming. An insect whined shrilly past Riel's ear. A mosquito landed on his brow and drank of his blood, but he advanced on the riders without so much as lifting a hand to brush it away. Pale moonlight lighted the clump of horsemen, glinted off their robes, revealed a sizable cross one rider was carrying balanced across his saddle.

"Who are you?" Riel asked. He stopped, waited for a reply. He was uneasy, frightened, but steeled himself for whatever might come.

Raucous laughter erupted. Riel recognized Mercer's coarse tone.

"If you think I'm afraid of you," Riel challenged, "you've come to the wrong place." He was sweating profusely; he was afraid. If Mercer would dress in white, come riding in darkness, he could also kill. Deedee, Olive himself—all would be targets. And the men would ride away and nobody would ever know who had done the killing. Riel's black workers might speculate, but nobody would listen to them. And Mercer would get Rivard.

Riel wouldn't back down, dare not. "Burn your cross, if that's what you're here for!" he shouted. "Frighten my people! They'll get over it; they'll not leave me!"

He knew they wouldn't. Those who did hide in the swamps would come trickling back once the danger was past.

There was no more laughter. Two riders dismounted,

rooted the cross into the soil and doused it with kerosene. Suddenly it was aflame; it reared there, red and flashing, its flaming wooden arms outstretched. The horsemen remounted, and all of them cheered and whistled and guffawed as they rode their horses in a circle around the burning cross.

When the fiery cross had become an object of beauty, a cross of pure fire, Mercer's unmistakable, brutal voice rasped out. "This ain't but a warnin', nigger! Worse is to come if ye don't sell an' git out of bayou country! We'll tar an' feather ye next time! Hot tar! Be expectin' us!"

Yipping and cheering, the six circled around the fiery cross one more time, and then galloped away. Soon the sound of hoofbeats faded. The cross blazed on, collapsing into red embers on the ground.

"Who was it, Riel?" Olive asked.

"Silas Mercer and Henry Dodds. Plus, I'm convinced, the renegade blacks they've hired to work on their plantations."

"I thought they were Ku Klux Klan."

"They used that for disguise. Only southerners are admitted to the Klan—not scalawags or carpetbaggers. What we need to do now is calm our people, set a regular guard, and try to get some sleep."

Early in the morning, Mercer and Dodds appeared again. Their faces were grim and threatening.

Riel met them on the front porch.

Mercer spoke right out. "My price has dropped to five hunderd."

"Why the drop?"

"Seems ye had trouble here last night. I seen a cross burnin'. Clean frum my place." He jerked a thumb at the ashes on the lawn. "Seein' that, somebody might think niggers was still here an' pester me 'cause I live here, I can't pay more. I ad-vise ye to take it or ye'll rue the day. Ye an' yer nigger wife an' mammy, all of ye."

Again Riel refused to sell.

"Don't fergit 'bout tar an' feathers. If the hot tar don't kill ye, an' somebody peels it off, yer skin comes off with the feathers, an' ye'll be in mis'ry fer weeks if ye don't just up an' die."

Riel repeated his refusal. At last, mouthing threats,

Dodds cursing and threatening right along with his companion, the two men rode off.

From the first night, Deedee had been all that Riel could hope for in bed, and this, added to her quickness in learning how to run the house, had entrenched her in his heart. And he knew from her response Deedee had come to love him with abandon.

Deedee became pregnant on their wedding night, and told Riel the joyful news as soon as she suspected. Riel's happiness soon disappeared. She worried about him. He walked the floor of their suite by the hour, face stern, and she sensed that he was frantic for the baby to be dark. She suspected that it would always be the same with each successive generation: the expected child must be darker than his father, must be blacker.

When Deedee was big with child, they awoke one night to find the plantation house on fire. Nette, up for a drink of water, found the kitchen ablaze, and roused the household. They fled, saving nothing but their lives. Olive carried Felix, wrapped in a blanket: Nette followed, steadying Deedee lest she fall.

Riel roused the cabins and all poured forth, men and women, striplings and girls, to fight the fire. They formed a bucket brigade, using buckets, small tubs, basins, night jars, bowls, passing the filled utensils along the line from cistern to house, flinging the water onto the flames. Olive, entrusting Felix to Polly, grabbed a bucket and labored with the rest. Deedee, ignoring Riel's warning shout, also took a bucket, as did Nette, and they all fought the roaring fire.

The only sounds were the muted voices of the fire fighters, the hiss of water on flame, the crash of a blazing rafter. There was the crackle of fire as the blaze grew and crept over the roof, down the rafters, into the windows, enveloping the furnishings inside, glaring and dancing with brightness.

Except for the light of the burning house, the night was dark. The fire showed figures, dark, moving, struggling without end to drown it. Sparks from the house shot up into a sky, where there were only stars. Children cried and were hushed.

Quickly, Rivard was a flaming skeleton with bones of fire. Now Riel sent the fighters to douse the nearest cabin, for a breeze had sprung up and sparks flew onto its roof and ignited. Another cabin also stood under a shower of sparks, so Riel divided the others between the two cabins, stood on their roofs, and soaked them with water from the bucket brigade. They used blankets to smother flames and, just as the men on the cabins stamped out the last spark and these cabins were safe, Rivard itself burned to the ground, the fiery boards drifting, burning, to lie melting to embers.

Nobody had come from any other plantation to help, nor had Riel expected them.

"We're too far from most plantations for the fire to be seen," he explained to Dedee. "The Mercers wouldn't come, because I'm positive Mercer had the fire set."

"Didn't we have a guard?"

"We did. They saw nothing, heard nothing. Mercer's clever."

"And you can't accuse him," Olive, who had joined them, said. "You have no evidence."

"What judge could bring himself to rule against a white man, for a black?" Riel asked.

He wondered if the Leblancs had seen the flames. But André wouldn't send help because of his and Riel's agreement to stay apart.

Riel established his family in the overseer's house which was vacant and sparsely furnished. Now that the fire was ended, he was beside himself with fear that Deedee would bear too soon, but she was free of pain, and laughed at this worry.

Next day, Mercer and Dodds showed up again, bolder than ever. They dismounted, tied up their horses, strutted about, viewing the smouldering ruins. Only the sturdy fireplaces and their chimneys remained standing.

"What happened?" Mercer grinned.

"You can see for yourself," Riel said coldly.

"How'd it happen?" asked Dodds, grinning.

"It was set. And no, I can't prove who did it."

Mercer guffawed. "Tell ye what, ye bein' a neighbor an' havin' such a bad run of luck, I'll pay ye four hunderd dollars fer yer Rivard."

Riel shook his head no, lips tight. "And where would we all go, my family, my people?" Riel asked, through his teeth. He ached to throttle both men, to kill them. Instead he said to Mercer the villain, the carpetbagger, the arsonist, "I repeat: Where do you expect us to go?"

Mercer shrugged his shoulders. "That's yer problem, white nigger. Ye'll have cash money. Country's full of niggers, they git along somehow. No killin' 'em."

"You had the fire set," Riel gritted.

Dodds roared with laughter. Mercer grinned; his teeth were big and yellow. "Better'n tar an' feathers, ain't it? Oh, they's more'n one way fer a man ter git what he wants. Ye takin' me up on the four hunderd?"

"No," Riel said, his rage growing. "I'm going to rebuild."

"Any house, old or new, kin burn! Two houses, three, any number! I got no objection to yer buildin' a new house."

"Will he ever give up?" Olive asked, when Riel told her and Deedee what had taken place.

He looked at Olive almost as coldly as he had at Mercer. "I think not, unless he buys some other place and uses up his gold. I don't think he'll burn us out again. He knows there's a chance, if he does, that I'll make an accusation, and the law just might pay attention. He doesn't want to get near the law. But he will try something, sometime, to wear me down."

He turned away, then called his people together and arranged a work schedule so that certain hours would be devoted to clearing away ruins, cutting trees, making boards and, as time passed, to rebuilding the house.

Within days, Mercer, bolder than Riel had given him credit for being, took Riel to court on the charge that Riel Rivard, Negro, could not be legal owner of a bayou plantation. Riel managed to get Gordon Lester, a young attorney he'd been friends with in school, to take him on as a test case. Marcel Cleary, a Negro-hater, was eager to represent Mercer.

Judge James Gerard, disapproving of the case, held the brief hearing in his chambers. "The issue is simple here," he addressed the four sharply. "Whether or not Riel Rivard has a legal right to Rivard Plantation. Cleary, you talk first."

"Riel Rivard is a self-confessed Negro," Cleary said. "His own mother signed a paper to that effect. When she or her protector bought Rivard, she was passing as white. She deceived the whole countryside, pretended to be white, pretended to own the plantation as a white woman. All land, your Honor, should be owned by whites. Now comes Silas Mercer, offering to buy Rivard from Riel Rivard, who has no more right to own it than his mother did, and he refuses to sell. Mercer isn't trying to cheat Riel Rivard. He sues only for the privilege of paying, in gold, for land Riel Rivard has no right to own because he is Negro."

"That will do," interrupted the judge. "Lester, what have you got to say for your client?"

"This, Your Honor," Lester replied quietly, and passed to the judge a legal document. "It is a paper showing that Rivard belongs to Riel Rivard, that he has every right to sell or to keep it, as he sees fit."

Scowling, the judge read every word on the paper, then glared at Mercer, at Riel, at the two attorneys. "This is the most foolish case of my entire career," he snapped. "The land belongs to Riel Rivard. Case dismissed."

Mercer, his face twisted and mean, stomped out of the chambers. Judge Gerard had him brought back, then fined him for contempt of court.

On his way out the second time, Mercer shot a furious look at Riel. So. There would, some time, be more trouble, Riel supposed, and wondered what the man would dream up next. It wouldn't be another fire. Even Silas Mercer wouldn't risk that after today's defeat.

Two days later, Riel heard that Mercer had bought the plantation across the bayou from Mercer Hall. This made him fairly confident that the fellow would no longer be a serious threat, because, by now, he had surely spent all his money and must get down to the business of planting.

It was when the first cypress boards were being hand-planed for the new house that Deedee's baby, a boy with skin color considerably darker than mulatto, was born. It was nine months to the day after the wedding.

Riel's joy over the dark infant was so deep he could hardly speak. Torn between joy over his son and terror because Deedee was ill with childbed fever, he lived in a daze. At last the doctor said Deedee would live, but never bear again, and Riel was content. He still had Deedee, his baby son would grow to sire others who would be even blacker.

Riel relaxed. He had his beloved Deedee safe for all time. He had his first dark descendant. All he need do was instill the proper thoughts into the boy, then sit back and wait for the next generation. He was happier then he'd ever been in his life. He even found himself speaking gently to Olive when she said the child was strong and handsome. He failed to note the deadening in her eyes, the fading of hope as he turned away from her, cutting short their conversation.

When Deedee was stronger, she wanted to name the baby Beau.

"I don't like that name!" Riel objected.

"It was the name of Mama Rivard's own father!"

"But he was a white man."

"Beau is a nice name! I like it for itself! Beau Rivard, that sounds nice!"

"No."

"Then let's name him Riel, the way I've wanted to!"

"No."

She began to weep, Deedee who was always so happy, so saucy when they were alone; she cried until she choked on her tears. It frightened Riel, and he was afraid she would hurt herself, tear herself inside. Finally he asked, "Why are you so set on that name?"

"It's pretty, and he's my son, too! I even let him have white blood put into him! You never thought of that, I bet! You've been so fierce, turning Rivards black, you never asked me if I wanted your white blood! And I'd rather have black, but I can't because you're white, and I love you!"

Thus Riel hit his first block in breeding his dynasty. Stunned, he realized the truth of what Deedee had said. He took her into his arms and begged forgiveness. "I can't undo putting white blood into your line," he said, "but we'll get it black as ink in time. We'll call the baby Beau."

At her smile, her excited plans to tell Mammy and Pappy when they came today what the baby's name was, Riel's love for her deepened. And his liking for her, everything about her, grew and strengthened.

It was settled. He had his dark son, and Deedee had the name she wanted for him. He had his new plantation house started, knew it would take months to build, but that one day it would be finished and somehow they would furnish it.

While Deedee was still recovering, he went to the bank and applied for a loan. The banker, Jules Gomez, frowned at the amount Riel wanted to borrow, using Rivard as collateral. Gomez asked to what use the loan would be put.

"I'll use some of it to plant more sugar cane, sir, a new strain. The increased yield from this new strain should pay the interest plus some of the principal."

"You have enough workers?"

"Enough to manage, sir."

"I hear you're building a new house."

"Yes, sir. We have most of the material on the place—cypress and oak. And my men have to work on the house, too."

"Surely you don't plan to invest most of such a loan in cane. That would mean extra workers."

"No, not a great deal in cane, sir. Some of the money would buy clothes for my people. The rest would go for glass windows, hardware for the house, things we can't make ourselves."

"H'm'm. Five hundred dollars for five years. And you think you can handle it."

"Just barely, sir."

When Riel left the bank, the loan papers had been signed and the five hundred dollars was on deposit in his name. Now he must work harder than ever before, but he had explained the loan to his people and how it would be used, and they had agreed to work with him on it, for in the end they too, would benefit.

"And," said Old Sam Boling, who worked his share and more, "we be buildin' Rivard to where it was before the war. And we'll git cash money."

Others agreed with Old Sam.

Riel's eyes misted at their loyalty. His own resolve strengthened, and wound into it was a solemn fact which he dare not forget. He had to repay this loan in five years because, if he didn't, he would lose Rivard.

Olive sat holding her new grandson. He had black, deeply waved hair that curled at the ends. She wondered, looking into his dark eyes, putting a finger into his fist, if she could love him as much as she loved Felix.

Deedee came into the room, holding Felix by the hand. She knelt, showed him the baby. "This is your little brother. He belongs here with you."

Of course Beau belongs, Olive thought, tears in her eyes. They're both Rivards, real half-brothers, though Deedee doesn't know. Olive kissed Felix on the head and Deedee, watching, felt an impulse to cry.

Chapter XXIV

André Leblanc, dedicated to his family, had been deeply troubled that he hadn't been able to afford to send Gab away for several years of college. Consequently, when his only son was in his late teens, André determined to send Gab for at least one year, using a portion of his modest savings to pay the cost.

"I'm too old now," Gab protested. "Most boys start when they're twelve."

"If there's money enough. I've arranged for you to take an examination and enter the form you'd be in if you'd started earlier. I expect you to cover two years' work in one. Do you find that overwhelming?"

"Not at all, sir."

"It won't leave you much free time or money for girls. However, you must relieve your, er, desires, for you are a Leblanc and have strong urges. Just avoid wenches. Is that a promise?"

Gab frowned, but he promised.

In New Orleans, he did exceptionally well on his examinations and was put in a high form. Here, with his quick reading and sure grasp of content, he made top marks though he carried a double load of courses.

In his free time, Gab explored the city, gazing at the mansions. Their side walls stood against the banquettes on which he walked; the courtyards and patios were hidden behind ornate iron fences which looked like lace. He studied the iron railings on second-floor balconies and windows; he smelled the magnolia and lilac, breathed them in.

He found the very names of the streets romantic. Often he walked on St. Charles Avenue, then turned onto Eighth Street, crossed Rampart, Burgundy, Dauphine, Bourbon, wound up on Chartres. He watched fine carriages, pulled by matched teams, pass smartly, sometimes with a gentleman and his beautiful, exquisitely dressed lady beside him: Gab supposed they had somehow saved their money from the war and, thus, could live so well.

He passed pedestrians, easily picking out which ones were scalawags and carpetbaggers. Along the cluttered waterfront he saw many Negroes, some neatly dressed by a master who paid wages, but most wore torn, ragged garb. Some of these blacks were begging: often he gave them a coin, all he could afford. He viewed the fine shops, noted that only a few ladies entered, though many looked and lingered at the small display windows. Money, he thought. If they had money, they'd buy.

Despite his admiration for all he saw, Gab knew he wouldn't be reluctant to go home at the end of the year. Beautiful as New Orleans was, he preferred the bayou country.

He kept on the alert for a girl. He didn't like the idea of going to a brothel, hadn't enough money. He sought, preferably, a clean, intelligent girl who could be persuaded to bed him. He approached one or two in cafes and was thoroughly turned down. But he didn't give up, and could think of no better hunting ground than a coffeehouse.

This particular day, he chose a crowded place, stood in the doorway, his gaze roaming the tables; not one was vacant. He wondered how so many people could afford to patronize the cafes and decided most people were like himself, having only a few spare coins but a desire for a bit of relaxation.

His gaze spied a table with only one occupant, a neatly dressed girl, her glistening black hair in curls, her dark eyes roaming until they met his.

They gazed at each other. Even from here, he saw her pleasant, rounded features, her rosy lips which turned up at the corners, the graceful way she held her head and used her hands. Wondering if she, like other girls, would admire the wave in his hair, he ventured a smile.

Amazingly, she smiled back. A slight smile, true, but one with warmth, and the smile gave a touch of real beauty to her face, also pretty in repose. He made his way to her, stopped at the table, gave a half-bow.

"I'm Gab Leblanc," he said, "from the bayou country, going to college for a year."

Her lips trembled slightly. "I'm Nanette Bellfontaine," she responded. "I've always lived in New Orleans, my parents are dead, and I teach piano for a living." She hesitated. "The tables are filled. Would you like to share mine?"

It was exactly what he wanted, and he said so. She gestured, smiling, and he pulled out the chair next to her and sat down. She ordered only a cup of coffee, Gab noted gratefully. He was low on funds today, but could afford that coffee and another for her, and two for himself. If they sipped slowly and talked fast, they might get acquainted, and before they parted, arrange to see each other again. He warmed at the thought, and a far ache came into his groin. She was perfect, if only she were willing. Yet he didn't want a roundheel either.

Nanette, speaking politely, was in turmoil. The instant she saw him, the moment he said he was from the bayou country, she wanted him. And when he said he was from L'Acadie, which she knew to be a fabulous plantation, she set out to win him.

She smiled a lot, letting her dimple show, and he smiled back. "You'll run L'Acadie one day?" she asked.

He nodded. "My father's been training me for it all my life. I'm the only son, so I get all the work." He laughed. "I don't mind it, really. I like the life. I guess it's bred into me."

"I'll bet the bayou girls are after you," she teased. She wanted to find out if he had a girl, had to know. "With that brown hair, all wavy. And those red lips!"

He grinned, embarrassed. "Girls?" He shrugged. "There's plenty of time."

"Your build is perfect! I don't care for tall, slender men, but shorter ones like you, with a strong build like yours." She flushed. "How I carry on. Please forgive me. It's my French blood, all French. It makes me impulsive. My piano teacher used to say it also put music into me. For this I'm grateful, because as scarce as money is, the better families still pay me to teach their young daughters to play piano, and I'm able to live."

"That's splendid," Gab said, liking her more every moment. "I may be from L'Acadie, but we're as poor as most. When I finish my one year in college, I'll return home and be just a hardworking cane-grower waiting for the Reconstruction foolishness to end so wealth can flow into the bayou country again."

The idea of marrying Gab already in her mind, Nanette invited him to walk her home. She had two bare, exceptionally clean rooms which smelled of scented soap and sunlight. Sunshine fell across the whitescrubbed floor.

"It's all I can afford," she told him simply. "But I like it. I can just barely manage rent and food and a new dress length now and then. But times are bound to get better here, too; then I'll get more piano pupils."

As he looked around, admiring what she'd done with the rooms, she gestured toward the bed. Her color was high, but so was her head. She was eighteen and mature for her age. She could not afford to waste time. If Gab said good-bye and walked out now, she might never see him again. And she wanted his wedding ring on her finger, wanted it fiercely with all her heart. Not that she loved him yet. That could come later, when she was safely his wife—if her gamble worked.

Gab stared at the bed, at Nanette. She moved her rounded hips slightly, provocatively, and his loins caught fire. She came to him, hips moving slowly; he opened his arms and she came into them, face lifted. He kissed her, more roughly than he meant to, this being the first time, but she pressed closer, her lips parted, and his tongue slipped between them. In that manner, embracing and kissing, she urged him toward the bed.

Oh let it work! she willed. Please let it work! Let him marry me!

Somehow they got out of their clothes and fell naked onto the bed. He entered her and she tried to help him; both were clumsy because neither had done this before. And then they moved, wildly, and nature took matters in hand and they reveled.

She wept afterward. "You'll think I'm a bad girl!" she sobbed. "And I want you to respect me, even love me."

"I know you're a good girl," he croaked. "I could tell."

"Mama used to say I was too impulsive," she said,

weeping less. "She was right, I know it now, but it's too late. Gab, do you think I'm nice enough to marry? You wouldn't be ashamed to make me your wife?"

"Not if I loved you. Because I feel you'd be true to me."

"Oh, I would! Are you going to see me again?"

"Of course. I like you. You can be my girl. I won't have another."

And he didn't. He and Nanette roamed the city, admired its beauties, dined at Absinthe House on Bourbon Street after Gab saved up enough money, played a game of choosing what fine house they'd like to own. She showed him the outside of the old Orleans Ballroom and explained how it had been used, and he listened, entranced, for such things had never been spoken of at L'Acadie.

"It's where they held the quadroon balls," Nanette told him.

"What were they?"

"Balls given by mulatto women who had quadroon daughters by white lovers, their protectors. These men set the mulattoes up in cottages down on the Ramparts, a section of New Orleans, and supported them for life. They freed the children born to the women, and the mothers presented their quadroon daughters at the balls, which were attended by young white men, and this way, in turn, the daughters chose protectors. Many of these alliances still exist, though since the war there have been no quadroon balls."

Gab remembered now some mention of these balls, but he'd never paid much attention. It seemed very strange to him and not an event he'd want to attend. Especially, he thought wryly, with Papa so rabid on the subject of wenches!

After each outing, they made love. Once he asked Nanette how she could afford so much time from her music pupils, and she said she didn't have all that many pupils yet, and that she'd even give up some of those she did have to be with him.

Despite her honesty and beauty and her open wish to marry him, Gab couldn't bring himself to give her the answer she wanted. He was not in love with her, and knew he never would be.

A letter came from home telling of Celeste's tragic marriage. He felt sad for his sister, but did not tell Nanette of it, feeling that to do so might make her too hopeful, that she would feel he was drawing closer to her.

As his year ended, she pinned him down about marriage. Being now seventeen, matured by heavy study, companionship, and love-making, Gab fell silent when she came right out and asked if he intended to marry her.

She gazed at him, troubled. "You don't answer, Gab. You probably don't know how to answer."

"No, I don't know what to say," he told her. "I believe there should be two-way love in marriage, the kind my parents have."

"And you don't love me."

"I'm fond of you."

"Say it all, Gab. We've always had honesty between us."

"Well, then, I'm just not ready to marry. And that's the truth."

"Not even if I waited."

"No."

There was a catch in her voice, but she pressed on. "I've met another man, a musician older than I am. He's attracted to me, hints that he's looking for a wife. If I stop seeing you and encourage him, will you be jealous, Gab?"

"Perhaps, a little," he confessed. "But you need a husband. I advise you to concentrate on this musician."

"Then," she said sadly, "I shall."

When Gab came home with no fiancée in the offing, André, anxious to see him marry early, arranged for him to correspond with a girl of good family in Vicksburg. He'd warned the boy so often never to consort with a wench that Gab quibbled at writing to some girl he'd never met.

However, he did write, their letters soon passed in a stream, daguerreotypes were exchanged, the young couple considered themselves in love, and the girl made plans to come to St. Martinville to visit her cousins and meet Gab.

He first saw Angelique when she appeared in the archway of her cousins' drawing room. Tall, slender, fineboned, she had platinum blond hair, eyes of delicate blue. Her features were finely drawn, her expression sweet. Her lips were pink and they smiled shyly. Gab had the thought that the Vicksburg cousin who raised her had done a good job. Orphan though she might be, she was a lady.

"You don't look the way I expected," Angelique said.

He gazed at her pure, white skin. She seemed as delicate as the finest china.

"You're more beautiful than your daguerreotype," he said. "I'm sorry if I disappoint you."

"I didn't mean that!" she protested softly. "I feel the same as you. You're handsomer than I realized!"

He took her hands, kissed her brow. When she drew shyly back, he said, "It's proper. I brought a ring, one my mother wore. If you let me put it on your finger, we'll be engaged."

She let him slip the big, lovely pearl onto her finger, and it fit. He drew her gently into his arms and kissed her soft lips, which quivered, then kissed shyly back.

They sat together, not quite touching, and spoke of the future. He had lost all reluctance to marry. She confessed that she was nervous about becoming his wife.

"You'll get used to it all," he assured her. "We'll live in Old House, the first one built at L'Acadie. It was small then, but it has been added onto and now it's large. The trouble is, you can't have a personal maid, but you will have Chloe, one of the wenches, twice a week to do cleaning. My mother arranged it."

Her eyes moistened. "You're so thoughtful, Gab! I didn't dare hope there'd be help with conditions the way they are now."

"You're to have Chloe. And Marie-Louise is giving us a party tomorrow night. She's already the most popular hostess on the Teche, says she has to keep busy because she has no children yet. My other sister, Celeste, helps get ready for the parties, but won't attend."

They married as soon as the banns were posted. The wedding was at L'Acadie with only the family and a priest present. The cousin who had reared Angelique was suffering rheumatism again and couldn't make the trip.

Consuela gave Carita her laudanum early, so Consuela could stand near the drawing room door and watch the ceremony.

After the ceremony, after the cake and wine, bride and groom ran to Old House. The wedding night was a success. Gab, aware of Angelique's fragility, was tender with her and at the end she wept with happiness. "W-we'll have many sons," she promised, "and they'll all look like you!"

After the wedding was over, André and Euphemie discussed the bride. "She's much too frail to take care of Old House," Euphemie said. "Even with Chloe twice a week."

"Can you let her have Chloe full time?"

"I think it's necessary."

"How can you manage it?"

"I can help Manda in our rooms more, and she can take over some of Chloe's work here."

"But I don't want you to be a drudge, darling," objected André.

"Hush, my fussing husband! In fact, I'll take over all the cleaning of our rooms and help Manda with the guest rooms. It'll keep me slender. You don't want me to get fat, do you?"

"Heaven forbid!" groaned André comically, giving in. And then he drew her into his arms and they made love even more passionately than did the newlyweds.

When Angelique became pregnant, she was sick all the time. She spent many days, uncomplaining, in bed. She longed for the baby to arrive; Gab was so excited, André and Euphemie talked about it constantly, and Marie-Louise was outspokenly jealous.

One day Carita managed to escape from her rooms and sped directly to Old House. She brushed past Chloe who tried to stop her, and flew up the stairs into the bedchamber where Angelique lay, white and ill. Angelique opened her eyes to see Chloe and Consuela lay hands on the haggard beauty in the doorway.

"No, please! I know who she is! Gab told me." She sat up, smiled at the tormented face. "You're Carita, aren't you?"

"I'm Carita Leblanc, mistress of L'Acadie, only they took my daggah to keep me from it!" The very blue eyes pierced Angelique. "Have you got it? Have you got my daggah?"

Angelique shook her head. "No, I haven't. And it isn't in my rooms. But you can look for it if you like; see for yourself."

Consuela laid her hand on Carita's arm; Carita shook it off. She moved toward the bed, probing Angelique with those eyes, and the girl in the bed saw sanity behind the wildness.

Carita stopped two steps away. "Are you really enciente?" she asked.

Angelique smiled. "Yes," she said proudly, "I am."

"Are you sick, evah so sick, mornin's?"

Angelique nodded.

"Does coffee taste awful, make you throw up?"

"Yes, it does."

"Do you get too weak to stand, can't walk?"

"Yes," Angelique admitted. "And the doctor says I must stay in bed those times or I'll lose my baby."

"No doctah evah told me that. I wondah why! And I was sick, oh, so sick, and nobody undahstood! But at noontime it would pass and I'd be bettah. Is it that way with you?"

"When the sun goes down I feel better," Angelique confided. "Not any sooner, and not necessarily every day."

"Then you undahstand how it was with me, how I suffahed!"

"I think I do."

"I feel sorry for you," Carita said, and there was a flash of complete sanity. "Youah sickah than I was. Are they good to you?"

"They're wonderful."

"That's because they want an heir," Carita snapped, the sanity fading. "All they want is to carry on the Leblanc name! I can tell you all about it, so you'll undahstand what's ahead. I know the whole story—I read the Leblanc Journals and remembah ev'ry word!"

Frightened by Carita's change of mood, Angelique remembered that Gab had said Carita was a raving maniac and not to be believed, no matter what she said. Now, the prospect of telling her story burned in Carita's eyes and, though frightened, Angelique felt compassion for her.

"Tell your story," she said faintly. She wouldn't let it bother her, and telling might give this poor, tormented woman relief.

Consuela sprang to Carita, put an arm around her. "Miss, no! Miss Angelique is too sick! See how pale she is, how weak!"

Carita jerked away, came right to the bed, sat on the edge. Angelique, gazing up into those penetrating eyes, again saw the tinge of sanity.

"Youah truly sick today?" Carita asked.

"I'm afraid so."

"You don't feel strong enough to heah the story of the Leblancs, just lie theah and listen?"

Consuela tugged at Carita's arm. "You can see it for youahself, Missy. She's evah so weak. Even her lips are white. She don't want to have to say no to you 'cause she's a gentle lady like you, Missy, jes' like you!"

Angelique began to tremble. She saw Carita note her trembling, saw the strengthening of lost sanity in her, saw a woman-to-woman understanding.

"Then I won't tell you the story this time," Carita said. "Youah too sick. But next time I will, because you have a right to know. And I'll not look for my daggah in youah rooms."

"Thank you," Angelique managed, her trembling worse. She was swept now, by fear of this woman, engulfed by pity for her. Tears covered her cheeks, and she longed to help Carita, who, Gab said, was beyond help.

Gab burst in at that moment. His look flew from the weeping Angelique to Carita who had risen and stood looking down upon the bed. He grabbed her by the arms. Instantly she began to shriek and struggle.

Angelique, rising up on her elbow, cried, "Don't, Gab! Please, for me. Don't!"

He paused, Carita still struggling in his grip. Suddenly she stopped, looked to Angelique for help.

"Gab, darling," Angelique said, "she did no harm. Just asked about my health."

"That's all? You're sure?"

"That's all, darling. She's ready to go back to her rooms, aren't you, Carita?"

Carita looked rebellious. "If I can look foah my daggah first."

"It's not in this house," Gab told her sternly.

"Honeymoon House, then! I haven't looked in Honeymoon House!"

Angelique wished they would let her look, let her see for herself that the dagger was not to be found. Yet she sensed that the more Carita looked, the wilder she would get, and said no more when Gab and the others led her, resisting, out of the room and away.

Later, Gab chided Angelique for talking to Carita at all.

"There was no way out of it," she told him gently. "Besides, she needs a friend, darling. There's sanity in her, deep down. After I'm strong—"

"You're not to have a thing to do with her!"

"She's gentle with me. After the baby comes, let me see if I can be her friend. Please, darling," she pleaded.

And he, loving her, reluctantly gave consent that she could try.

From that day on, she made plans to be Carita's friend, spoke of them freely. Gab fretted over this, unable to go back on his promise, wished it was time now for the baby to be born.

André waited in suspense for the birth of his grandchild. The baby would be pure white, he told himself a thousand times; it couldn't possibly show blood from generations long past. Look at Marie-Louise, at Gab, at Celeste, all white. He didn't even feel compelled as he had with Charles, to tell Angelique of the blood. Still, the months dragged for him and he waited, strained and anxious.

He knew when Rivard burned, regretted that it happened. He'd heard that Silas Mercer wanted to buy Rivard, wondered if the carpetbaggers had anything to do with the fire.

The waiting drew to an end, and the night came when Angelique at last bore a son. Exhausted, weak, too spent to moan, she let the gathered family name him René III.

Soon after giving birth, Angelique began to bleed, and within hours was dead. Gab kissed her cold lips, so deeply grieved he couldn't weep. He tried to be interested in the baby, but could not.

He stood while they buried Angelique in the family plot. He made no objection when Euphemie took the baby to L'Acadie, saying she would raise him if granted the honor. Gab looked at her stonily. "Go ahead, Mama," he said, voice breaking, but still no tears. "She would have wanted it."

Chapter XXV

Gab was devastated by grief, riven by anger—grief because he had adored Angelique, anger at God. Vaguely he had understood Celeste's quiet grief over Anton, but now was too ravaged by his own loss to feel sympathy for her any longer.

"No," he told Celeste a week after the funeral, "I won't go to Mass with you. Not tomorrow, not any other Sunday!"

"Why not, Gab?" she asked gently. "We need Mass now, need—"

"I sure as hell don't need God! Don't need His brutal, senseless power!"

"You'd find comfort, Gab. Angelique was taken for a reason, brother. Don't blame God."

"I do blame Him! Angelique was only eighteen years old, had all of life before her! I don't believe there *is* a God! If there's anything at all, any power, it's one of evil! It shows its colors every time it takes someone like Angelique! What did she do to merit death? She only bore a son, my son! Evil forced me to kill my wife with my own seed! I despise Him—I spit on Evil!"

"Gab! Gab! You'll feel differently, in time!"

"Never! I'll never believe in God again, never go to Mass! No matter how Mama begs and argues, no matter what Papa says! My mind is made up and nothing ever will change it!"

And so it was to be, though Euphemie still believed that one day he would change. André was of a different opinion.

"Don't tear yourself up over Gab, darling," he urged. "He has a strong mind: he's finished with the church. Now—" seeing alarm on her—"don't be frightened. He's a good man, a moral man. He'll do no evil; he'll cheat no one in business, break no girl's heart. Don't let him break yours now. Accept the man as he is. Teach his son, teach René to go to Mass. Gab won't object, won't interfere. He wants only to be allowed to follow his own course."

André's words were prophetic, for Gab, though he otherwise conducted himself normally, was never to enter a church again. Euphemie did see him make the sign of the cross on occasion, and from this took what small comfort she could.

Gab, meanwhile, was often angrier at himself than he was at the nonexistent God. He tortured himself for months, convinced he had helped kill Angelique with his seed. God was still the real culprit, for He could have spared Angelique. Gab wept at night, remembering how she'd planned to have many sons.

He worked harder than he'd ever worked, stripped to the waist, chopping weeds, clearing drainage ditches. He ate heartily, for his body demanded food. At night he went to bed at eight o'clock, his exhausted body dragging him into sleep. He was the first one up in the mornings, slopping the hogs. Following this pattern, he came not to weep at night, to mourn his lost bride, but to sleep like one drugged.

His family, disturbed by his early bedtime, tried to persuade him to stay up later. André challenged him to games of chess and backgammon. Soberly, Gab declined, then went to bed to sleep.

"I'm tired," he said truthfully. "I want to sleep."

"You sleep too much, son," Euphemie said anxiously. "It isn't right, isn't healthy. And you don't come to the nursery to see René put to bed."

Gab gestured. "I'll look in on him," he said.

"I should hope so!" exclaimed Euphemie indignantly. "He needs to know his father!"

Thus Gab forced himself to take René III into his arms nightly, to rumple his dark hair, look into his light brown eyes. His features were sharp for a baby, his voice piercing when he cried. Otherwise he was all Leblanc.

Why can't I love him? Gab wondered. Why couldn't he have looked like Angelique? If he had her hair, her eyes, I'd have something of her left. Without those, he's a nice baby, but not like a son.

Handing him back to Euphemie who was smiling, he wondered if he'd ever grow to love this baby. No, he realized sadly. How can I? He was the instrument used to kill Angelique. But he would be kind to the boy as he grew, try to be friends with him.

For the baby and for Euphemie, Gab moved from Old House back into L'Acadie. And continued his routine of relentless work followed by exhausted sleep.

Finally, after Charles's visits to L'Acadie, after Marie-Louise's frequent visits, Gab heeded their insistence that he cross the bayou to Hebert Plantation. "What did we ever do to you?" Marie-Louise demanded. "Have you struck us from your list? We want you for dinner, supper, any meal! We miss you!"

And he missed Angelique. Missed her with every throb of his heart, with all the sap of his young and healthy body. But at last one day, he did row across the bayou to visit his sister and her husband.

He tied up at the landing and, seeing no one at the front of the house, made his way to the back gallery. He found Marie-Louise there cleaning squash, Celeste helping, and Charles, in from the fields to refill water jugs for the workers, passing a word with them.

Charles was first to see Gab. "Well, look who's here!" he exclaimed. He left the jugs, gripped both Gab's hands, and they exchanged a double handshake. Charles was grinning happily; Gab felt uneasy, though his expression was friendly.

Marie-Louise set aside her work, ran down the steps, pushed Charles aside, and threw her arms around her brother. "Am I glad to see you!" she cried. "Now that you're here, just try to escape! You can go to the fields with Charles—I know wild horses wouldn't keep you away—but you're staying for dinner! Celeste and I will make your favorite chocolate cake, icing and all!"

"Better save your sugar," Gab warned, smiling a bit. "You'll need it for one of your parties."

"Piffle on the sugar! This is an occasion. You will stay, won't you?"

He nodded. Charles pounded him approvingly on the shoulder. "We'll make a day of it—work and chocolate cake. We've missed you, Gab."

Gab's face went stiff. "Not like I miss Angelique," he heard himself retort.

"Ah, no," said Charles. "We all miss her, Gab. She was exquisite, fragile as a china cup. She should never have borne."

Gab went ramrod stiff. All the old shock and grief slammed over him, covered and suffocated him. His world ended all over again.

He jerked away when Charles tried to lay an arm across his shoulders. Everything had a red haze, especially Charles's face. "You've defiled Angelique!" Gab shouted. "I'm going to kill you for that! What you said about her bearing!" He spread his legs, bunched his fists, slammed one at his brother-in-law, who jumped aside.

Charles, his own fists hard, limped away from Gab. They circled, eyes fierce on each other. Charles, not wanting to fight, remembered in a flash how he'd felt when Suzette was killed in Paris, spoke quietly, "Drop your fists, Gab! I meant no harm. But a fight is your due if you insist. How do you want it?"

"No!" cried the women. "Stop it!"

As if they hadn't spoken, Gab shouted, "With fists! I'm going to kill you with my bare hands!"

Marie-Louise and Celeste ran to them. Marie-Louise grasped Charles's arm: Celeste seized Gab's arm with both hands. Gab gave her a shove that sent her staggering; Charles did the same to Marie-Louise, only more gently.

Gab lunged forward, brought his right fist up from the hip, crashed it alongside Charles's ear; an instant later, Charles hammered a mighty blow to Gab's nose. They grappled, pushed apart, danced warily, Charles with his limp, eyes keen, fists up. They came at each other simultaneously, Gab splitting Charles's lip, Charles pounding twice at Gab's midriff.

They could hear the sisters screaming to stop, but paid no heed. They fought on viciously, Charles now as stirred up as Gab, each going for the kill. They heard their own women scream for help, and black men and women ran in from the fields. They turned on the black men who would have parted them and cursed and ordered them to stand back.

Gab's face was bleeding; Charles's fist slammed it again and again. Charles's head went thick; his ears stopped up. He drove his fists into Gab furiously, but the other's onslaught never slackened. Their eyes were swelling; Gab's face was a bloody pulp. They grappled, hugging and slugging, knees bent, all but giving way. They parted, rushed each other blindly, got in blow after crushing blow.

The workers moaned, making a kind of musical lament as they watched. Some leaned on the hoes with which they'd been working; one man leaned on a heavy shovel.

Marie-Louise, desperate, screamed at the man with the shovel, because he was burly and powerful. "Stop them! Stop them before they kill each other!"

His great black face knotted. "Cain't, Miss Marie-Louise," he mumbled. "Mastah Charles, he say no. I got to do whut he say."

"Well, I don't have to!" shrieked Marie-Louise. She yanked the shovel from the big Negro, causing him to almost fall, and advanced on the fighting men. They crashed to the ground, rolling and punching, with no sign of a letup.

She waited. Soon each man had a stranglehold on the other's neck. She lifted the shovel and brought it down mightily on Gab's head, then as he fell away and Charles bestrode him, she lifted the shovel again and slammed it onto the back of Charles's head. Now both men lay sprawled, unconscious.

She dropped the shovel, knelt between them, called out Charles's name, Gab's. Celeste knelt with her, examining each man for a pulse.

"They're alive!" she cried. "You men," she continued, motioning to the growing crowd of gaping blacks, some moaning and others silent, "you women, help us get them inside!"

They carried the two battered, bleeding men into the house, up the stairs, and into a chamber with two wide beds. "Put one on each bed," Marie-Louise ordered, and they did. "Gracie!" she cried. "Thank God you're here! Organize the women, bring water, bandages, salve!"

An hour later, the fighters' wounds had been dressed. Only Marie-Louise, Celeste and Gracie remained with the sorely beaten men, now conscious and glowering at each other.

"Two more minutes," rasped Charles, "and I'd have had you!"

Gab swore. "No, you wouldn't. You'd have been dead!"

"Hush!" ordered Marie-Louise. "If you don't, I'll send for the doctor!"

They glared at each other, said nothing.

"We've got to get to the bottom of this," Celeste said steadily. "Neither of you is a killer. Why did you try to kill each other? Gab, I know you have a temper—but Charles—I'm surprised!"

Charles, every inch of his body a sore, painful ache, was himself surprised. "I lost my head," he admitted. "When Gab came at me so viciously I felt as though I were being attacked by a mad dog, and the only solution was to fight back."

"Gab?" Celeste said, touching her brother's shoulder. "You're no killer."

"He defiled Angelique. No man does that and lives."

"He didn't mean it the way you took it!" exclaimed Marie-Louise. "Charles wouldn't be so cruel! And besides, he doesn't feel the way you say he does. You misunderstood."

Gab scowled, the creases in his face deepening, his swollen eyes mere slits. Charles scowled back.

"Charles, you owe Gab an apology," Marie-Louise said firmly. "We're going to clear this thing up! There'll be no family feud between the Leblancs and the Heberts!"

Charles tried to consider, his head a throbbing mass. It hadn't started out to be a fight, not on his part. Mumbling, he said so, adding, "It was only when you beat me up so, Gab, and kept yelling about killing, that I went out of control."

Gab heard the words. He mumbled a reply almost incoherently, but they all understood. He had wanted to kill Charles, had tried his best to do it. But not now, there would be no killing now. Angelique wouldn't want it, ever. Gab knew Charles wouldn't be his enemy, but realized, groggily, that the old warmth between them was dead.

Euphemie and André, troubled by the fight, came to visit the invalids. They spoke no word of reproach to either man, but went away saddened, for they sensed that the brothers-in-law had lost all closeness.

Gab, who had vowed never to marry again, healed from the fight. A few weeks later he found himself beset by sex hunger and thought of Nanette in New Orleans, wishing he could see her now. He began to observe various women in St.

Martinville, and one Paula Montgomery came to his attention, making his loins ache every time he saw her.

He finally met her in a shop where he went to buy a hank of sewing thread for Euphemie, who was making new baby clothes for René. Paula was buying a length of rose-colored silk. The shopkeeper introduced them, they smiled and chatted, and Gab eyed Paula as she watched the clerk wrap up her purchase.

Paula. That name suited her. She wasn't very tall, her fair head would come to his shoulder. She looked a bit plump, reminded Gab of a full-breasted dove. Her eyes were pale and blended with her fair, wavy hair. Her features were sharp, but not too sharp, she had a lovely, rose-colored mouth and light, winging eyebrows. Her chin was a bit pointed, her hands tiny; her voice was soft.

Forgetting to purchase Euphemie's thread, Gab opened the shop door for Paula when she was ready to leave. "I'm going your way," he told her boldly. "May I walk with you?"

"But of course. I know you're decent, because you're a Leblanc."

They strolled along past shops, pedestrians, Gab carrying her parcel. A carriage passed, then a cart piled high with wooden boxes clattered by.

"You're new in town?" he asked.

"I've been here a month. I came from New Orleans. George, my husband, was killed by a stroke very suddenly."

"I'm sorry," Gab murmured.

She inclined her head. All he could see was the blue hat which matched her smart dress. "I heard about your loss," she murmured.

A pang went through him. Angelique. He would never see her again. But this woman understood. She herself had lost a mate.

"How long have you been widowed?" he asked quietly.

"Almost two years. George had a leather business. I stayed in New Orleans long enough to sell it at a fair price. I'd been to St. Martinville on a trip and liked the beauty and peacefulness, and here I am with nothing to do but keep house, sew and read."

So. She was financially independent.

"Are you lonely?" he heard himself ask.

"Oh, so lonely, Mr. Leblanc! I can understand why women remarry, but in my case—There was only one George. I'm quite reconciled to being a widow."

"And I to being a widower," he responded, amazed and excited by the interests they had in common.

"You're very young to say that."

"I'm almost twenty."

"I'm thirty-two," she said.

Feeling guilty, untrue to Angelique, he smiled at Paula. "I see no reason why we shouldn't be friends. Perhaps even . . . more. What does age matter, actually? It's the meeting of minds as well as other things that matters."

"I quite agree, Mr. Leblanc."

"Gab."

"Gab. My own mother was eight years older than my father. They had a perfect marriage. He died young and she, too, remained a widow as long as she lived. And here is my house, Gab. Will you come in for a cup of coffee?"

He went in for the coffee, and thus, their association which was to last the rest of their lives, began. Paula was a delight in bed; they found dozens of topics to discuss together as they sat in her little drawing room. He took her to summer concerts. Townspeople treated her courteously, but remained at a distance because they sensed there was something more than friendship between Paula Montgomery, widow, and Gab Leblanc, widower.

Together Gab and Paula found pleasure and contentment and that was all either asked of the other. Gab played chess with André on the evenings he was at home, but was out quite late when he saw Paula. The eight o'clock bedtime ended.

André, ever on the alert, wary of the danger that Gab might use a wench, learned of his relationship with Paula. Both André and Euphemie were relieved.

"She is too old for him," André said.

"I disagree, darling," Euphemie said, after a moment. "The fact that she is older could be a blessing. She'll understand his youthful attitudes and in time, if it lasts, help him to mellow."

"Perhaps," André agreed. "For Gab's sake, I hope she fills his needs. And that he will fill hers as well."

Euphemie delighted in little René, who was a loving, but willful child. As he grew, he became more demanding, though in a charming manner. She made every effort not to spoil him. Always, she tried to spark Gab's interest in his son.

"Hold him, Gab," she urged. "Let him learn your touch. Kiss him, let him feel your love."

Gab tried, really tried, but his heart wasn't in it. Though he was fond of the child, René reminded him of his loss of Angelique. He held the boy awkwardly sometimes to please Euphemie, kissed his brow, but felt nothing.

"See how handsome he is!" Euphemie would urge. "Look at him, see for yourself! And don't tell me that all babies, all little boys, look alike!"

"He doesn't resemble Angelique," he said.

"That isn't his fault, Gab. He's his own little person. He does resemble the Leblancs."

At this point Gab didn't know whether to be disappointed or relieved that René had no look of Angelique. He didn't know whether he could endure seeing a little replica of his lost love trotting about L'Acadie, because it would be a constant reminder. Or would it be a comfort? He couldn't decide, and there was no need to mull it over. René was plainly a Leblanc.

And he had only to go to Paula to leave memory behind.

Chapter XXVI

Felix Rivard, natural son of Riel Rivard and Marie-Louise Leblanc, was both content and discontent. He'd always known about his frail heart which kept him from working the fields with Riel, the man he believed to be the son of his adoptive mother, but at times, in spite of the doctor and the family he attempted to work just the same. Unfailingly, the pain in his chest drove him out of the fields, and back into the house to the piano, which Olive had taught him to play expertly.

Music quieted his unrest. On good days, he wandered the plantation from one end to the other, taking pleasure in the wealth of cypress and magnolia and pecan. He loved the flowering shrubs, the unnamed wild flowers which bloomed year round, sometimes red, sometimes white or blue or pink.

When he was seventeen, he had discovered a spot of sheer beauty in the wilderness, and set about making it better still. Three saplings grew in a crude circle, making an outdoor room in their center; up their trunks clambered a rose vine covered with small red roses, the color of blood.

At once Felix conceived the idea of an arbor-room, and set to work. He guided the vines from one tree to the next, sent them weaving through the tops of the trees, forming a roof of roses. He planted cuttings at the bottoms of the trees, rigged sections of branches broken off other saplings, and formed a framework.

Now, two years later, his arbor was like a room in the small clearing. It had walls and roof and back, solid with green leaves and blood-red roses. The front he left open, vines hanging like a drapery, and when he sat or lay in his rose room, he was filled with the fragrance of roses and filled with contentment. This thing of beauty he had created was his cherished secret. He told no one, not even Olive.

Unknown to Felix, Riel talked about Felix with Olive one day.

"Exactly what does the doctor say about Felix, now that he's older?" Riel asked.

"It's still his heart, a faulty valve. It's a very serious condition. He couldn't survive any extreme strain."

"Will it kill him regardless of strain?"

"Perhaps not. If he doesn't work in the fields, doesn't exert himself. He doesn't know the true seriousness of his condition."

"Why isn't he told?"

"He must be shielded from trouble, from being depressed. If we keep him happy, his lifespan may last as long as any."

"He's been after me again to work in the cane."

"He can't, Riel."

"I told him no, that heavy work is out of the question. But he wants to do something; he's determined."

Olive pondered, a small frown between her eyes. "He's

been top student in our plantation school. He's finished that and more, all I've been able to give him on the side. He could help me teach the children. And he already plays piano for church services. Maybe he can give the people a concert occasionally. That would keep him busy."

Riel scowled. "It's plain he can never marry. The first night would kill him. Let him go on believing he's your nephew from the supposed white branch of the Rivards. There's no point in letting him deal with the problem of blood."

Olive nodded. Riel was still cool to Olive because he knew she would never feel as he did about turning the Rivards black.

"Maybe next year I can get a piano for the church," he said. He hadn't the money to buy another piano. He'd bartered work to get the old piano they now had in the drawing room. It had taken five years to complete rebuilding the plantation house. Riel had virtually stopped work on the house for one entire year, planting and harvesting one-third more cane, so that he could pay off his bank loan when it was due.

"As for the piano," Olive said now, filled with knowledge of her son's ceaseless labor, "we can move ours to the church. Riel can play it there all he likes, and the people will have music every Sunday instead of once a month."

Riel, accepting the offer, immediately got some of the field hands to help himself and Beau, now seventeen and so darkened by the sun he was nearly black, to move the instrument. Felix insisted on carrying the piano stool and the music, and it was he who decided where the piano should stand. When the others left to return to their duties, his fingers were already rippling across the yellowed keys, playing a piece which he had himself composed.

As he played, sadness came into the music, sadness that any field work put that awful pain in his chest. Not even Olive knew how he longed to work in the cane, to wield a hoe, a scythe. Perhaps this was why he'd never taken her to see his rose bower; the work it entailed, slight as it was, had caused him pain. He left the keyboard, went out of the church and made his way past the house toward his wilderness spot, his roses, feeling somehow bereft.

Why couldn't he be like the others? Why couldn't his heart be strong? Why did he have to be Olive's adopted son, not flesh of her flesh, blood of her blood? He wouldn't mind the Negro part. It was admirable. Look how Riel felt about it. He would feel the same if he could be of their blood.

As he approached his rose bower, his spirits lifted. Sometimes he brought a book along to read, but today he hadn't. He noted the white, star-shaped wildflowers underfoot, avoided stepping on them. They looked like stars, fallen from the sky, fallen past the trees and bushes to adorn the greenery below.

He was almost at the entrance to his rose house when he saw the girl. He stopped. She'd been standing in the middle of the room, her beauty framed like a picture, and now she stared at him in breathless silence.

He'd never seen a girl like her. She was small, weighing not more than ninety pounds, had auburn hair, black eyes and chiseled features. Her dress was deep green and clung entrancingly to her dainty, lovely figure.

She caught her breath when she saw the ethereal beauty of this strange boy. He wasn't tall, but was slim and tense. His skin was very white with a golden sheen from the sun; his features were pure, with a slight flare to the nose. His hair and eyes were soft brown.

"Hello," Felix said, and waited.

She smiled. Her free spirit was in the smile. Her chin suddenly hinted at a driving, determined nature. She was altogether sweet and, he thought, passionate. And she was spoiled, had to be, with all that beauty and spirit, that sureness with which she held herself.

"Hello yourself," she said at last. "I've never seen such a beautiful arbor, all roses, a little house! The white flowers on the grass even make a carpet in it! Did you make this house?"

He nodded, his excitement hot and fast. She liked it! This exquisite girl liked what he had dreamed up and brought into being with his own hands! He felt as able, as strong at this moment as Riel himself.

"It's perfect!" she cried. "I just found it today, and I've wandered all through here lots of times!"

He smiled on, at a loss for words. He was afraid she would leave, would go away, and he'd have only his bower.

Without her it had been a thing of beauty; with her, there were no words to describe its utter perfection.

"You, whoever you are," she said impulsively, "are so handsome you're spiritual!"

And she thought; he's gentle, too. He cares, cares about things! She gazed at him with seeking black eyes, waiting for him to speak.

"You," he said so low she could scarcely hear, "are lovely enough to be in the Garden of Eden!"

They continued to gaze at each other, two young, beautiful spirits, seeking, finding. As easily as they had met, Felix fell in love with her on the spot, and she with him.

"Do you want to ride in my pirogue?" she asked. "Or should we ride in yours?"

"I don't have one."

"How do you get about?"

"I walk."

"That's what my Pa said to do, too, but I made a big fuss and got my own pirogue. I explore wherever I please. I'm out in it every day."

"That's nice," he said. "But it's pretty all around this spot. We can pick flowers and search along the bank, wherever your pirogue is tied up. Sometimes I find a shell. I've found a few that are rare, according to the books."

"I'd rather stay here," she decided suddenly, and sank to the starred grass. "Come on in. Don't stand out there all day!"

Shyly he entered his rose bower, which he now thought of as theirs, and settled beside her. "That's too far away!" she complained. "Sit closer, I like to look at your lips. I've never seen a boy with such nice lips. Did you get them from someone in your family?"

He didn't know. He thought of Olive's lips. His were like hers, but he couldn't have inherited them from her because he was adopted. So he shook his head, forcing a smile, "I don't think so." He wasn't ready to tell her he was adopted.

"I went to school in St. Martinville," she said. "I never saw you there."

"My mother taught me at home."

"I liked school," she confided. "Some of the girls hated it, but it's fun to learn. My pa wants to send me to New

Orleans to school, but he never does, says I'm too wild. I think he wants me to get married, and I don't want to!"

A skip took Felix's heartbeat. He drew a long breath, fought off trembling. She couldn't marry somebody else, not this girl! She was created for the rose bower which he had made. They needed time to be together in it, to meet every day. He'd even tell her about his heart, if he must, and about being adopted. If only she didn't marry somebody!

She stretched full length, tugged at him, and he lay down beside her. Their bodies touched from shoulder to foot. Her breath kept catching the way his did, and when she turned her head to him, her cheek, soft as a rose petal, touched his.

It was inevitable that she would snuggle closer, inevitable that he would put his arms around her, his lips on hers. Their kiss held, clung, lasted.

It was inevitable that they fall in love. Even before they first spoke, they were on their way to love, and, after the kiss, neither knowing the other's name, they made young, clean, passionate love.

A great tide surged through him, out of him, carrying his love into her body, there to lie in warmth, waiting for more. His heartbeat became very fast as he loved again, and this time, with the surge came the pain, squeezing and stabbing, and he didn't know whether it was a part of the joy or the sickness of his heart. The third time, after he'd caught his breath, struggled for it, she held him to her, moving against him, and the surging was greater, the exquisite beauty shattered to glittering bits by unbearable pain.

The girl gloried in this, thinking his gasping for air was a part of love which she'd never known before. Again she drew him into her, rode to the crest, lay in his lax arms as he fought to breathe. She whispered, "Darling, oh, my darling! Please love me forever!"

They lay whispering. "We don't even know each other's names," she breathed. "I'm Frances."

"I'm Felix."

"I live at Mercer Hall. My pa owns it and Mercer Hall Two across the bayou."

"We'll get married," Felix whispered, ready now to tell all. "I'm Felix Rivard, but I'm adopted. I'm white as you are."

"Pa won't let us get married. He told me never to speak to anybody from Rivard."

"Why not?"

"The feud. Because Riel Rivard wouldn't sell Rivard to Pa, and Pa had to buy across-bayou to get enough land. And your brother blames Pa for your house burning down, blames him for other things."

"Riel won't talk about it. It must be bad."

"Oh, it is! Pa's fierce, hates anything Rivard. He says I'm to marry the richest man in all the bayou country. Someone who has a big plantation and can run it."

"I can't do that," Felix said bitterly. "I've got a bad heart. All I can do is teach school and play piano."

"We could run away to New Orleans! You could play and sing at a restaurant. You do sing, don't you?"

"Yes. Pretty well, my mother says."

"Well, that's what we'll do! The feud won't matter then!"

They turned to each other. They could no more keep from making love than they could command the sun not to shine. She knew nothing of his joy, of the killing pain. She must never know the agony of his love.

For Felix, this was Heaven. For Frances, it was a pure and shining glory of which she wanted more and more. Daily they met, and daily they made the pain and the glory, the glory for which he would willingly die.

Felix began to think seriously of eloping to New Orleans. He didn't want to hurt Olive or anger Riel, but there was no other way he could have his chosen wife.

When they knew she was pregnant, they sought a way to cope. "We shouldn't have to do this!" she cried. "We should be able to go home and tell and have a proper wedding! And go to New Orleans on a boat!"

"It would never work. Your father will look on me as black because of my mother's blood. Because of Riel, and Deedee and Beau."

"It's not fair! How much money do you have, darling?"

"About four dollars."

"And I have ten. Maybe we could sell the pirogue and get enough to live on until you find a job!"

"That's too risky," he said. "We'd easily end up living on the streets."

"I'll go to work on Pa, that's what! No matter how mean he gets, I always coax what I want out of him. I'm his favorite. He could give us money to last until you get a job, I know he could."

"Except I'm a Rivard. And he's set on your marrying a plantation owner."

She wept, and he comforted her. The comforting ended in lovemaking which all but brought about his own end. Finally the pain ebbed, and he could barely breathe.

Weeping again, she sobbed. "We've got to do something! We daren't ask to marry, I know that. Pa hates your brother so much that he'd get a potion for me to take, and he'd pour it down me, if he had to. We'll wait, try to think of a way. I'll wear a corset, and lace it tight. Then, when it's too late for potions, Pa'll have to let us go to New Orleans and get married! That way, there'd be no scandal; people here'd never know, and Pa wouldn't be shamed. He could say I'd married a rich man in New Orleans. He'd like that, Pa would, fooling folks around here."

With this frail plan their only hope, they parted under the roses, to meet next day and plan further. "If I can't get here," she warned on a sudden impulse, "don't come looking for me. Just keep coming to our rose house every day. I'll show up sooner or later."

"Why do you talk this way?" he asked, alarmed.

"Pa's been acting funny, like he's up to something. And he's been cranky about me being gone every day. He might just take my pirogue away and order me to stay home and do housework. The only way to handle him when he gets like that is do what he says. In time, I can sweet-talk him and do as I want. You just need to know, in case I don't show up. So don't be upset if I don't get here. Just remember, we can hold out as long as he can!"

Frances didn't come to the rose house the following day. Or the day after that. Felix waited for hours, listened for the faint sound of her airy walk, but there was only silence. He returned to their bower day after day, yearning to go to Mercer Hall openly, a man come courting, but held back because she'd been so insistent. But time was passing; their child was growing in her. He fretted and worried, willed and prayed each day for this one to be the day she'd return to him.

Olive noticed that he was troubled. She cornered him in the drawing room after supper. When he would have slipped away, she put her hand on his arm and he stopped.

"Felix," she asked firmly. "Are you taking your drops?"

"Yes, Mama," he said truthfully. "I never miss a dose." Actually, because of the intense pain of lovemaking, he'd been using a double dose. Because he was almost out of drops, he told her he needed more but did not tell her why.

She insisted that they go to the doctor next morning. The doctor listened to Felix's heart, thumped his chest, asked questions.

"Been suffering more pain, haven't you?"

"Considerably more, sir," Felix admitted.

"What seems to bring it on? Been working in the fields, rowing a pirogue, anything like that?"

"No," Felix replied honestly enough. But he couldn't tell the doctor, couldn't tell Olive.

"H'm'm," the doctor said thoughtfully. "What do you do, young man?"

"Teach, play piano, rove the plantation."

"Try not playing the piano for a while. That involves physical exercise. Go back to your normal dosage on the drops—double is too strong, can do more harm than good. Rove around the plantation slowly; sit down and rest. If there's a spot where you can nap in the sun, do it. If not, go to bed, once midmorning, again midafternoon. Rest is the best medicine. Come back in two weeks and let me see how you're doing."

Though Olive tried to draw him out as Riel oared them home, Felix said little. As the pirogue came to the landing, he spoke more freely.

"I won't go to bed," he said definitely. "I will lie down twice a day out on the plantation. I've a place just made for that."

"Where is it?" Riel demanded.

"It's private."

"Private, hell!" exploded Riel. "You go to this private place and have a bad attack, nobody knows it, nobody knows where you are even, how do you think you'll get help?"

"Just the same," Felix said adamantly, "it's a private place of my own, and I'm keeping it so."

Riel turned on him, then seeing the pallor of his son's face, he loosened his fingers. "Use the brain God gave you," he said. "You know what I told you is right. You could have an attack, and nobody would know in time."

"I'm not that sick," Felix maintained. "I admit I have been overexerting—"

"How?" Riel demanded. "What've you been doing?"

"Breaking off some branches," Felix improvised, giving Riel a truth two years old, "fastening them to other trees, making myself a rose bower. I've trained roses to climb the walls and roof."

Olive stared. Felix's rose bower sounded just like Gabriel Leblanc's Grape House, which she'd read about in the Journals! The hair on her neck lifted, knowing that this descendant of that Grape House builder had inherited the same talent, emerging in the form of a rose house!

"I'd like to see it, Felix," she said.

"One day," he evaded.

He couldn't take her there. Not ever. Frances might turn up. He felt guilt that his mother couldn't see his work of love, but the rose bower belonged to Frances now. He had given it to her, along with his love, along with the pain and the ecstasy of his body.

To satisfy Olive, who insisted he must rest from the trip to St. Martinville, Felix lay on his bed for an hour. He didn't relax, but lay taut, wondering, hoping, praying that Frances would come to him this afternoon.

But she didn't. The rose house stood empty in the sundappled wilderness. He took the drops and stretched out there and tried to rest, but there was no rest to be had.

Had they found out she was pregnant? Had they taken her to some black granny for a potion? Had her pa locked her up?

The next day he rested twice in the rose house, breathing the aromatic fragrance, but Frances didn't come that day, nor the next, nor the next, nor the next.

Chapter XXVII

The time came when Felix could wait no longer. He slipped down-bayou in Riel's pirogue one afternoon, every stroke of the oar a stab in his chest.

Frances, confined to her room by her pa, spent most of her time staring out the window at the bayou. Consequently, she saw Felix oaring toward the pier which was almost hidden by the double line of oaks between it and the house.

She hurried to the door of her room, cracked it open, listened. There was no sound of Pa's voice; this meant he was in the fields, for wherever Pa was, his voice could be heard finding fault, giving orders.

Silently, Frances went down the stairs, along the hall, across the gallery. The moment her foot touched ground, she began to run. She got to the landing just as Felix, breathing hard, was tying up the pirogue. "Why did you come here?" she whispered. "And rowing alone—your heart—"

"I had to come!" he whispered back. "It's been so long!"

She took his hand, drew him swiftly through the trees into a shrub-encircled space. She sat on the stone bench there, pulled him down beside her.

She could tell he wanted to kiss her; she saw that hunger on his lips. But there wasn't time. Pa might show up. She had much to tell Felix, and quickly, before they were caught together. Felix was still breathing hard, and she knew that it was bad for his heart, that even their lovemaking must hurt him, though he'd never said.

"I don't care if your pa does come," Felix said. "It's time we faced him. This can't go on any longer."

Suddenly, recklessly, she threw herself into his arms and they kissed as though starved. When he would have spoken, her love welled up and she closed his lips with her own, and they kissed until she was dizzy. Her ears were singing, and in this wonderful kissing time, she wished her pa could understand how fierce and necessary was their love.

Felix, also dizzy, his own ears singing, trembled as he held her and kissed on and on. He felt fed after unbearable hunger but his heart lunged and raced, and the pain in his chest became a double-edged knife.

He tasted her tears, accepted them into his mouth, let the pain cut. Frances was the only thing in the world he wanted—Frances and their baby. He'd make her understand that he must speak to her pa at once.

"It has been so long!" she whispered into his lips, still salty from her tears. "Oh, my darling, it's been so very, terribly long!"

"I waited for you at the rose house. Every day I waited, because you said to."

Voice shaking, she spilled out what had happened. "Pa and Ma took me to New Orleans for all those weeks to let me meet men!"

"What men?"

"Eligible men, rich men, even old men! Pa has got his head set that it's time for me to marry! And there aren't any eligible men on the bayous who'd marry a carpetbagger's daughter. That makes him yell and curse."

Shock and pain hit Felix simultaneously. His hold on her tightened. "But you didn't—"

"No, indeed I didn't! There was one, Armand Brewer, who Pa said if I'd marry him, Pa'd be a very important man. Armand wanted me real bad, and Pa tried to make me marry him. We had a big fight."

"And you won the fight?"

"In a way. To hush Pa, I had to tell Armand I needed time, that promising to marry a man is a very serious thing for a girl."

"What happened then?"

"Armand said he'd give me time, and Pa brought me home, ordered me to make up my mind fast, his way, and forbid me to use my pirogue or to leave the house until I said yes."

"What will you tell this Armand?" Felix whispered. He

could hardly breathe because of the pain in his heart and another, even worse, in his soul.

"That I can't marry him, of course. How can I marry him, Felix, with your baby in me? I belong to you!"

He held her, trembling with wracking pain. "Tell me every word you said," he pleaded. "Don't let me wonder and worry."

"I've already told you, darling. I said that I needed time. And they all had to agree, because I was stubborn. They were mad, especially Pa, and Armand was long-faced. They never let up on me to say yes, but I couldn't, Felix—our baby!"

"You seem thicker in the middle."

"I am, a little. Pa thinks I'm getting fat, eating too many grits, and that makes him mad. I eat the grits because it's the only thing that doesn't make me sick at my stomach. Ma, sometimes I think she knows!"

"They have to let us marry now. Maybe it'll even end the feud."

"Never! Only last night Pa ranted about Rivard again! How it should be his. If he finds out I'm enciente, he'll take me away again until the baby's born. Then he'll farm the baby out, give it away, anything! Just so nobody finds out what happened to his daughter! He's set on being an important man, and he won't let anybody, not even me, stand in his way!"

"Those things aren't going to happen," Felix said firmly. "Not to you, and not to our baby. We'll run to New Orleans on whatever money we have. If need be, I'll sing on the streets for coins until I get a job playing piano. At least we'll be together, the three of us."

"Yes, oh, yes!" she breathed. "You've got to leave now, before Pa comes in from the fields. Tomorrow morning meet me at the rose house; we'll bring clothes and we'll run! I'll sneak my pirogue out, and we'll make the trip to New Orleans, then sell it!"

They clung, kissing. They parted, Felix making his way back to the landing by going from tree to tree, Frances running back to the house the way she had come. He untied the pirogue, thinking about tomorrow. He still had his four dollars. And Frances had ten. He had no idea what price they could get for her pirogue.

It's not enough, he thought, pushing away from the landing, swinging the craft upstream. He took a strong pull on the oar; instant agony put another invisible oar through his chest. He pulled again. And again. His lips skinned back from his teeth; his hands clamped the oar.

Chest afire, he oared home.

Chapter XXVIII

Frances was late.

He waited, chest hurting. He took a dose of drops from the new bottle, put the bottle into his packet. He tested the strap he'd put around the bundle of extra clothing. His good shoes were in the middle, shined, ready to wear to work in the finest restaurant. His best suit was there, too, along with a change of plain clothing. He'd wrapped the Bible that Olive had given him in clean underwear. That Bible might be all he'd have, ever, of Rivard.

On he waited, listened to bayou sounds, felt the morning sun. Restless, he moved toward the bayou, then turned back into the rose-scented house. He dared not risk being seen, knew that he'd have to hide in the bottom of the pirogue until Frances oared them away from the Teche along a smaller stream.

She appeared at last, crashing through undergrowth, staggering across the clearing and into his arms. She was bleeding, her blood puddling on the ground. He lowered her to the grass, cradled her, trembling in his trembling arms. Her hand clutched his shirt, driving pain into him as she sobbed out her story.

"Pa did know! But I wouldn't tell him who the father is! Pa hit me, and I didn't tell! They decided to take me to a voodoo woman tonight, and I threw a tantrum. I said I was only fat, and finally Pa acted like he believed me.

"After Pa finally left me in my room, he and Ma stayed

up nearly all night, fighting. I waited till they got in bed, and then I went to Old Granny in the quarters and gave her my whole ten dollars and—

"Now there's no baby. If you'll bury it, nobody'll ever know, not even Pa and Ma!"

"But we were going to New Orleans! We were—"

"Bury it!" she screamed. "I can't stand any more!"

"Where is it?"

"Back toward my pirogue! Hurry!"

Hysterical, frightened, she seemed not to care that she had killed their baby. Felix tore off his shirt, gave it to her to staunch the blood, and left her in a sobbing heap, then rushed toward the bayou, all the beauty around him a mockery, even the croaking of frogs seeming to mock and taunt, getting into his chest with the pain.

Before he reached the bayou, he began to search, looking for any disturbed spot. Very soon he found his baby—a tiny little body, a boy. He covered it with leaves, went back to Frances.

"Take me home!" she pleaded. "I can get to my room without being seen. I'll claim the bleeding is my monthly. Then later, when I'm well, we'll run away to New Orleans!"

She tried to walk; her knees crumpled and she sank to the ground. So he carried her, letting his heart bulge. When they got to the pirogue, he sat her down in it and took the oar.

They didn't talk. She was weeping, and it took every ounce of him to oar the pirogue downstream. Even with the help of the tide, he could scarcely manage. But he'd do it. He'd deliver his beloved to her home where she wanted to go. She was the one who was suffering. He thought of the little form under the leaves, shuddered, pulled relentlessly on the oar, over and over.

At the landing, she sobbed, "Next week! This same day! At the rose house!" And then she crawled out of the pirogue and went staggering behind trees up the driveway to the house.

He tied up the pirogue and, seeing no one, staggered homeward on foot. No, toward the leaves. His awful pain full spread, unable to think, he returned to his aborted son, took off his trousers, wrapped the fragile form in them, stumbled on past tree, bush, garden, to the house, to Olive.

Olive took one look at him, wearing underwear only, his face drawn and white. She ran to him, saw what he carried, and blanched. "Felix," she whispered. "Oh . . . Felix . . . !"

He almost dropped his little burden; Olive caught it, held it close. Her eyes flew from it to Felix, and she quaked.

"Your drops," she said, "where are your drops?"

"They're in the pocket of those pants."

She laid the bundle on the divan, opened out the trousers, ran her hand into a pocket, but the small bottle wasn't there. She felt for the other pocket.

Riel, coming in at that moment, caught sight of the small form atop the trousers. He crossed the room, stared down at it in shock.

"Whose dead baby is this?" he demanded.

Felix, driven by physical and emotional agony, gasped out the facts. "Frances Mercer . . . love . . . each other. She . . . "

Heavily, he lifted his hand, indicated the aborted baby. "Ours . . . "

"God in Heaven!" whispered Riel, furious. He didn't notice that Deedee and Nette had entered the dining room with dishes of food, that they stood, staring into the drawing room, that they saw the infant corpse on the divan, that they listened.

"Not once, but twice," Riel's whisper raged on, "we've had this. Now I'll have to deal with Mercer, and this time—"

"Frances . . . won't . . . tell," Felix gasped, face blue. "Never . . . tell . . . "

"I'm your father, your blood father! Do you understand that, Felix!" Riel shouted, wild-eyed and merciless, man bereft of reason. "You're part black, and you've given me a dead white grandson, and I must have black! Do you understand? I must have black!"

"Riel!" Olive cried, finding the drops. "So cruel!"

"He needs to know his blood should not be put with white."

Felix swayed and Olive, already on the run for him, steadied him and poured some drops past his blue lips. "Swallow, darling . . . swallow them!" she urged.

Felix, tears wetting his pain-wracked face, moved to clutch his unfinished son, closed his arms about the raw little body, wilted, fell to the rug. Olive dropped to her knees, lifted and cradled his head, and holding his baby, Felix breathed once more and died.

And that was the way they buried Felix and his son, the baby in his father's arms, wrapped in a tiny white blanket once used for Riel, later for Felix, thrown around him by Olive the night the house burned.

Riel went about his life fiercely. He lived for the day when Beau would marry and produce a black son. The motive for my life is hard and clear, he thought. I must live down the incest with Marie-Louise, must remedy this matter of my blood. I must build a black dynasty, a Rivard dynasty. Nothing can change me. Nothing.

Riel's goal had become an obsession, one which would grow worse. He did not recognize this change in himself, this obsession, nor did he care.

Riel was never warm toward Olive now. Sometimes, as the months passed, Olive had the feeling that he wished she would die so he wouldn't have to face her whiteness.

André Leblanc heard that the orphaned white boy at Rivard had died, and was convinced he knew that boy's identity. Saddened at Marie-Louise's unhappiness because she had borne no children in her marriage, André grieved for her Rivard son, his grandson.

He heard that Frances Mercer, the carpetbagger's daughter, had married and gone to New Orleans to live. He didn't notice that she seemed not to return to the bayou country to visit.

Part III

1894—1896

Chapter XXIX

René Leblanc III, eighteen, six feet tall, yanked on his clothes. He glared into the mirror, but didn't notice his strong build, not today. He whipped the comb through his light brown hair, his brown eyes flashing, and regarded his handsome, angry features with no satisfaction. He was in trouble, and it was a silly, easy girl who had put him there and he wasn't going to stand still for it.

She was downstairs now with her parents. His father Gab was there too, and his grandparents, André and Euphemie. It was André who had ordered René to join them. So, instead of going to the fields as he normally did, he had to dress up and face these people.

Constance. He set his jaw. He would not let them force him to marry Constance Jerome. He was a full-grown man, under André and Gab in plantation work, true, but his personal life was his own and he was going to keep it that way. He threw the comb down on the dresser, turned on his heel and strode for the door.

He found them standing uneasily in the library. He wondered why they weren't seated, then realized they were all too upset to compose themselves on chairs and divans. Well, they weren't the only ones upset; it was his whole life they were bent on meddling with, and he was going to stop them in their tracks.

He swept a glance over Constance and her parents, who

were standing together. Dick Jerome was in his forties, pale-faced with a receding hairline, but no beard, and was exceedingly fat. His wife Mary was a graying wisp, her hair only a shade darker than her silvery eyes. They're not of our class, René thought resentfully.

René moved his glance, avoiding André's steady gaze, Gab's anger and Euphemie's troubled sadness. He hated to hurt Euphemie, but it couldn't be helped.

Constance looked as she usually did—blue eyed, pretty, blonde, quiet. She was too thin, and René wondered why, at one time, he'd felt he must have her or burst. Now he could see that she was vapid and that her blonde looks fell far short of beauty.

His glance had taken only seconds, but already the silence of the others worried him. Why didn't Jerome come out with what he had to say, get René's answer, take his family back to where they belonged? He stood, his expression cold.

It was André who finally spoke, addressing Jerome, cutting to the heart of the problem. "You have said, sir, that you have reason to demand this interview." He raked Jerome with a look, raked it quickly at all present. For a moment there was silence. The leather-bound books glinted richly on their shelves; the tall mahogany clock went on with its assured ticking.

René, too, defiantly glanced at every face. The three Jeromes looked strained, the father angry, the mother on the verge of tears, Constance chewing at her lower lip. Euphemie was pale and sad, Gab angry, André intent, awaiting a response to what he had said.

At last Jerome nodded assent, one set of double chins sinking into the next set. Mary Jerome paled; her chin trembled. Constance drew herself very erect, tears sliding down her cheeks. She clasped her hands across her stomach, a telltale gesture.

René winced inwardly and angrily at her. Well, her tears would have no effect on him. He'd never been able to feel patience for a weeping girl; he wanted them smiling, laughing, gay, reckless. Constance could weep until she stood in a pool of tears, and it would never change him. This was his future at stake and she was not going to run it, no matter what. Imagine a lifetime tied to such as her!

"She's pregnant, then?" Gab demanded of Jerome.

"Tell him, Constance," Jerome growled.

She choked on tears. "Two months, sir."

"And you're accusing my son René?"

"Accuse ain't the word," growled Jerome. "Statement of fact is more like it."

Euphemie suddenly cried out, "René, why do you just stand there? Do you know this girl, or don't you?"

"I know her," he replied grimly.

"Then if you—if she— Speak up!"

"There are two sides to every question, Grandmother."

"Then state your sides, both of you!"

"Oh, René," Constance sobbed, "they m-made me come here! I don't want to force you, I know you get stubborn! I know you say there've been others, but it was only you! Just you! And you told me you loved me, you know you did! Don't you remember what you said, how you felt?" Tears streaming, she gazed into his adamant face, then whirled to her father. "I won't have him forced, Pa, I simply won't!"

René squirmed inwardly. He had considered himself in love with Constance. In bed. But it had been that way with every girl. He even thought he was in love with the wench that time. Trouble was, once he'd bedded a girl a few times, the love soon faded and he'd be ready for a new girl. Not ready for marriage, just ready for bed and fun. And certainly he was not ready to marry Constance who had bored him long before the end.

Gab stepped to René, gripped his shoulder, swung him roughly so they faced each other. "Could you be the father?" he demanded sternly. Gab waited, glaring into his son's stubborn eyes, aware that André had been more a father to René than himself, yet it was for him to ask; it was his duty.

"Yes, sir," René admitted, "I could be. But I never promised her marriage. It was her own free will. And I'm convinced she had other men."

"How can you say such a thing?" cried Euphemie. "If there's the least chance, it's your duty."

"There's no future for me in a forced marriage," René said, speaking slowly and distinctly. And stubbornly. "Even out of duty, and even if I were, beyond a doubt, the father. And there's no future for Constance and her baby. It would just be three people tied by accident or circumstance or a complete wrong, none of them satisfied. It would be an unhappy household."

"No, it wouldn't be like that!" sobbed Constance. "You'd never regret it! I'd do everything exactly your way. I'd love you till the day I die! I'd be so eager, so laughing, making jokes the way you like, that you'd love me again! I know I've been crying and pleading with you lately, and it's turned you against me! But I'd stop all that, and it'd be like it was in the beginning! You'd see!"

René made a chopping motion of refusal, firm in his conviction. He watched her fall back a step, watched her mother hold her, dry her tears, saw Constance stand trembling in the clasp of loving arms.

Jerome, fists clenched, started toward René, who stood ready to let the father vent his ire. He owed her family that much. But Mary Jerome protested softly and caught at her husband's sleeve, and he stopped. His face had gone red, and he was breathing heavily, mouth twisted angrily.

"And what's my little girl supposed to do?" he asked, his eyes burning across all their faces, stopping on René, boring and vicious. "Bear a fatherless child and live her life in disgrace?"

René didn't know what to answer. He was the only one who could save Constance from her dilemma, but he would not sacrifice his entire future happiness to do so.

"I assume," André said carefully, "that you've questioned your daughter thoroughly, Mr. Jerome? That there is no possibility of there being another man?"

"Oh, sir!" wailed Mary Jerome. "How can you say such a thing? We've never even allowed Constance to see another man alone, just your grandson! And we trusted him because he is a Leblanc, and the Leblancs are honorable people!"

"But you don't think we're so honorable now," André said quietly.

"No, sir, I do not! Not when your grandson seduced our daughter, made her love him, got her into trouble, and now refuses to marry her!"

"How do you feel, René?" asked Gab. "Are you refusing because she's not good enough?"

"No sir, not exactly. To be honest, it's boredom. She'd be as bored with me; we have nothing in common now."

"But she's got the Leblanc heir in her!" Jerome thundered.

"Stop and think of that! This here's not just a question of my daughter, but of your descendant!" He broke off, glaring from André to Gab, and back again.

"That's true," Euphemie said. "René, if the child is yours, what Mr. Jerome said is true. You're responsible. We're all responsible."

Silence clamped them for a moment. Each face held its own expression. Euphemie showed concern; Mary Jerome had a look of desperation. Jerome himself looked still more furious; Gab and André were solemn, reeling under the words that Jerome had hurled at them. René felt his own face, set and stubborn. He was more determined than ever not to be trapped.

Finally, Gab spoke. "René. You are to marry Constance. We'll get a special dispensation. You've got an innocent girl into this situation; you've got a new Leblanc life started, and that baby is going to be raised a Leblanc!"

"No!" Constance tore out of her mother's arms before René could speak, before he could refuse or give in. "I can't stand any more of this!" She spun to René. "Are you willing to marry me now, after hearing what they said about the baby, are you?"

René looked her in the eye. "No," he said.

"That's settles it!" she cried. "He doesn't want me, he doesn't want his own Leblanc baby! So you can all just stop it! Even if you could force him to marry me, I wouldn't marry him, not now! I'll have my baby and raise it myself! It doesn't need the Leblancs, especially him! Ma, Pa, I want to go home, back to New Orleans!"

When Jerome started toward René again, Constance flung herself at him and his arms went around her. "It's what I want, Pa! If you'll have me, you and Ma, after what I did!"

"Of course we want you, baby," the father said, melting. "You're a good girl; we know that. We'll take you home to New Orleans. We'll say that you're a new widow. There won't be any scandal; I'll see to that. Nobody's going to look down on my little girl."

"Constance," André put in. "Stop. Think. Is it your duty to have your baby raised Leblanc? Would you be willing if René—"

"Never! The way he's acted today has opened my eyes, and I don't want René any more than he wants me! That makes the baby mine, all mine! It'll never be a Leblanc, it'll be whatever name I pick out as a 'widow.'"

"Then," André persisted, "René must at least support you and the child." He turned. "René, are you willing, or do you have to be forced?"

René scowled. "Of course, I'm willing," he snapped. "Even though the child may not be mine." He looked at Constance, who met his eyes coolly. "It won't be much money," he explained, "because I don't get very much. It'll take every dollar, but you can depend on it. If a time comes when there isn't cash, I'll make it up to you the next time."

"That'll be fine," she said. "I don't like taking money from you, I want you to know that, but it isn't fair to expect Pa to support us. Whatever you send will do."

After some discussion, Jerome agreed to this, and he and his family prepared to leave. They didn't shake hands, merely nodded to one another, and then they were gone.

As soon as they were out of the house, André demanded of René, "Have you a mistress now, my fine fellow?"

"No. Of course not."

"Leblanc men don't do what you did," Euphemie said quietly, anger trembling in her voice. "We certainly never expected such behavior from you. You owe it to that girl—she's a good girl—to marry her and give your child its rightful name. Constance is educated, she's white—"

René exploded. "Enough, Grandmother! You heard how she feels! As for her being white, I never want to hear another inference that the Leblancs have black blood! It comes from that crazy woman upstairs, from her insane notions!"

"They're not insane," André snapped. He included Gab as he continued. "It's time you know, past time. What Carita says is true. I had the facts from Old René himself. That's why it's vital that no Leblanc man touch a wench, ever!"

René snorted. Gab paled. For a moment he felt tainted, then swiftly figured the generations and realized how little black blood he carried, and how much less his son had.

When André again warned René, he answered angrily. "So I'll marry white! But not Constance, not any girl as easy as she was! My wife is going to have substance! She'll carry on the name of Leblanc so that all will know!"

Faithfully, René sent all his bits of money to Constance. This left him nothing to spend on girls, which surprisingly, did not bother him. Despite his aching hunger, he was averse, for the time being, to bedding any girl at all, no matter how willing.

In two months a letter came from Constance.

"René," she wrote. "Just a word to let you know I received the money you sent and have bought material and am making baby clothes. Ma and Pa won't take a cent of Leblanc money, say I'm to use it all on the baby.

"But I'm not going to do that. I've met a man two years older than you are, and with better sense. He's a bookkeeper and very smart and makes a good living. His name is Carl Dysart, he knows about the baby, and wants to adopt it, so it'll be raised a Dysart. He wants me to stop taking money from you, says if he ever meets you, he'll kill you for what you did to me.

"So don't send any more money. Carl doesn't want it and I don't want it. Use it any way you see fit. I only hope it won't be to ruin another girl. And you don't need to think you really ruined me—I've got Carl. In a way, I should thank you. If you hadn't got me pregnant, I never would have met Carl and found out what love really is. We've been married a week now, and I'm happier than I ever could have been with you in that big house. Constance."

René galloped through this letter in delight and relief. The only thing in the whole affair which had troubled him was the certainty that he was the father of Constance's baby. Now, though it might carry Leblanc blood, it would have a good upbringing, a good life. It would never suffer because of him.

He showed the letter to his father and grandparents. Celeste had been across-bayou when the Jeromes were at L'Acadie, so neither sister knew of his escapade. Euphemie and Gab and André read the letter but made no comment. Euphemie did say, "I'm happy for Constance."

René, once his surprise wore off, accepted the providential events in Constance's letter as his just due. Now he had money to spend when he wished, now he could ask a girl out. But he didn't ask a girl out immediately. He began to think in terms of getting a wife, a regular bed-partner. Then, if he got her pregnant, there'd be no trouble, no lamentation, only rejoicing.

Heady over his release from Constance, he again took joy in his work with the sugar cane. It was his opinion that he, of all Leblanc men, liked growing cane the best. He particularly liked to use the hoe and the scythe, took pleasure in the play of his strong muscles, growing ever stronger with use, and soon forgot Constance.

But all this was no help to his Leblanc hunger for women. Soon he began to dally with girls again. Any girl he wanted, he could get. He noticed, too, that more than one nubile black wench eyed him, but, his family being so obsessed by color, he left the wenches alone. He took only white girls, and with each one was extremely careful to spill his seed at the peak of each encounter so no pregnancy would result.

Chapter XXX

René also enjoyed the social life on the bayous. Reconstruction was falling far short of making the planters rich again, but slowly, in the face of all odds, they had started to rebuild that which was gone. This meant not only financial progress, but a return to the parties and merry-making which had added joy to their lives before the war.

René and others his age didn't miss the elaborate, luxurious gowns the girls and women had worn to balls and dinners long ago. They enjoyed the prospect of a simple dinner at someone's home, crowded with guests, the women in dresses which had been turned and remade, the girls in calico. The girls were as fair, their lips as smiling, their manners as perfect as those of their mothers a generation ago, and René, hearing Euphemie and André agree on this, was surprised. Of course the girls smiled and were gay; weren't they admired and courted by men their own age who also smiled and exhibited perfect manners?

All in all, except for a few of the older generation bemoaning what was lost, the bayou folk enjoyed as active a social life as ever. The one thing they gave up, though only temporarily they assured one another, was the month-long house party.

There was talk on the Teche, some weeks after René had the letter from Constance, that a wondrous beauty had returned from school in New Orleans to live with her parents, Pablo and Clio Sanchez, at Cypress, the big plantation downstream. She was reputed to be a regular heart-breaker, and René, invited to a dance in her honor, looked forward to it eagerly. He was especially careful with his appearance when he dressed to go, having one of the black boys polish his shoes twice before he was satisfied with their sheen.

All the rooms at Cypress, a big, sprawling one-storied house with chunky columns, had lamps burning when the Leblanc family, except for Celeste, arrived. Light spilled out onto the lawns until it was swallowed by the cypress trees which had been so carefully nursed to maturity away from the bayou.

With the light, spilled forth music, voices, laughter. It settled over René like a wave as he entered the once fine, but now shabby hallway; he looked out over the many guests moving there, in the double drawing-rooms, and even in the dining room.

Pablo Sanchez, host, gripped René's hand. "Welcome, my boy," he said congenially. "Ramona's out somewhere in all that crowd, but you be sure to hunt her out, hear? She's so excited to be home, seeing everybody, we couldn't make her stand here at the door!"

"I'll find her, sir," René declared, and took the slim hand of Clio Sanchez, noting that she was curved and seductive yet. She inspected him, smiling. "You'll do!" she laughed. "You're handsomer every time I see you! Pablo's right; you'll have to seek out Ramona. She's mixed into the crowd somewhere."

René wandered away from his family, pausing to speak every time a girl caught at his arm, which was often. He was idly seeking Ramona Sanchez. He doubted she was as breathtaking as gossip reported; girls seldom were. However, if blood meant anything, she might be handsome at that—her father was pure Spanish and her mother pure French. Ramona was pure Creole, and some of them were beauties indeed.

He side-stepped, trying to avoid colliding with a girl in white whose attention was on the front door where still more guests were arriving. But he stepped the wrong way; she veered suddenly and came up against him, right into his arms which went around her inadvertently.

"Oh!" she gasped. She looked at him with dark brown eyes which held all of seduction. "To think that I'd run right into your arms, and you so handsome!" She swooped a look over him, her red, passionate lips smiling; she tilted her head, and the heavy, straight black hair moved like a silken curtain at her shoulders. "Yes," she murmured, voice seductive. "You're the handsomest thing I ever saw! I'm Ramona Sanchez, and if you don't tell me this minute who you are, I'll explode!"

He moved his hands to her shoulders, and she let them remain. "I'm René Leblanc," he said.

"Of L'Acadie?"

"Of L'Acadie."

The Negro fiddlers began to play then, the crowd miraculously spread over the rooms, and the dancing began. René still had his hands on her shoulders, holding her, and she moved languorously. He ached instantly.

For a heartbeat, they stood like that. And in that heartbeat, he knew he wanted her to keep forever. Because everything in him recoiled from the thought of bedding her as he had all the others, he believed that he had, at last, truly fallen in love. On sight he loved this Creole beauty, and he was not going to let anybody else get her.

He took his hands from her shoulders, but caught one of her hands and they stood, hand in hand, as others danced around them. "Have you promised this dance?" he asked.

She nodded, with that smile, her seductive eyes on his. "And there he comes," she added, nodding to the side.

René saw a young man trying to make his way through the dancers. "You want to dance with him," he demanded, "or hide with me and talk? We've got a lot of getting acquainted to do."

She laughed, low, throaty, and it, too, was seduction. "Hide!" she said. "Talk!"

Still hand-in-hand, she led him away from her oncoming partner, put a whole roomful of dancers between themselves and him, tugged René across the hallway and into a small library. Here she closed the door and turned the key in the lock.

"What if someone finds us locked in together?" René asked, excited, yet stunned at her boldness.

"Pooh on them! It's my father's house, and I do as I please! I think the room's perfect for getting acquainted in!"

He gave it a glance, saw books, elegant but worn carpeting, leather furniture. There was a grandfather clock here, too, as at L'Acadie. The clock made him feel at home.

They sat on a divan facing each other. A green-shaded lamp cast light on her lovely face. Her mobile features were as seductive as everything else about her.

"You first!" she demanded. "Tell me about you!"

"I live at L'Acadie, work there. Some day, it will be mine. That's my life story."

"No girls?" A flash of intensity.

"Girls? None that count, until now."

Ramona gave him a slow look. "Before you ask, all men are for me until I choose one. Mama and Papa sent me to New Orleans when I was a little girl to have city advantages, but I got sick of conditions there and came home."

"You like it better here?" René asked anxiously. She had to prefer the bayous, simply had to! He needed time. He wanted to see her often and his life was tied up here. He couldn't follow her to New Orleans. He wanted her here, where he was.

"I'm wild about the bayous," she said. "And the parties!"

He gave a great, deliberate sigh.

"What's that for?" she demanded, working her eyes.

"Relief that you like the bayous."

She smiled, seductively. "And I like bayou men, all of them," she murmured. He tried to kiss her, but she evaded. He knew, then, what her nature was, and it challenged him. She was a temptress of men, but she'd not feed their passions. She'd hold herself untouched for her husband.

Ramona decided it was time to rejoin the party. Reluctantly, he agreed. He danced with her, and it was like holding a piece of thistledown in his arms, she was so graceful.

He danced with other girls, then returned to dance again with Ramona. He noted that when he had other partners, she watched him from under lowered lids. It gladdened him that she noticed.

Before he left that night, he had her promise to go to a dance with him the next week. After that, they attended a concert in St. Martinville. There were more parties. Now they were a couple, his trousers stiff half the time, her asking about L'Acadie until he got sick of it. She seemed to be more impressed by the plantation than by himself, he thought angrily.

He couldn't get her to talk seriously until he locked themselves into the library during a party. "What do you want?" she asked pertly. Her hands were on her hips; she gave a roll with those eyes.

"You're mine," he said sternly and bluntly. "Your shape, your good looks, your voice, your eyes—all mine."

"You sound as if you think you're my husband, and we've only been seeing each other three months," she said, and smiled.

"I'm going to be your husband, and damned soon! You're drawn to me same as I am to you. I can tell. I've been with girls before."

"I'll just bet you have!"

"That's ended. I was looking for you, and now that I've found you, I'll duel any man who might try to get you away from me!"

This intrigued her, and now, when he tried to kiss her, she met his lips openly. Hers were hot, throbbing, as he was hot, throbbing, all of him. But he controlled his hands, even his lips, kissing her ardently but with respect. For she would be his; she was trembling in his arms even now.

Before they went out to dance, she had promised to marry him.

Next day, when he told the family of his engagement, Euphemie was delighted and André was pleased. Celeste left her place at the table and came to kiss him.

Only Gab had a word of warning. "Pablo's spoken to me about Ramona," he said. "She's a good girl, but you'll have your hands full with her. She's very spirited. It seems, too, you became engaged awfully fast."

René laughed. "Fast is the only way to catch Ramona," he declared.

When René, on their wedding night, was preparing to bed her, Ramona pulled away. Both were naked in the simple, lovely bedchamber of Honeymoon House. He tried again, but she would not so much as let him touch her.

She glared at his need. "So that's how a man is!"

His eyes were aglow over the perfection of her. "Darling, I can't wait!" He gulped in her total allure through his eyes—the provocative, uptilted breasts, the deep-rose nipples, the shapely legs, the dark glory between her thighs.

"I can't wait!" he repeated.

"You have to wait. I'm not some doxy! This ring gives you no right to jump on me like an animal. I want things understood between us first."

"What things?" he demanded.

Their words were interrupted by Carita, her shrieking voice going on and on, all the way from L'Acadie to Honeymoon House.

"What's wrong with her now?" Ramona demanded.

"Who knows? Usually, when she keeps yelling, she wants the key to her rooms so she can get out and search for the dagger, the one she—"

"I know what she did with it. I just wish somebody would give it to her, so she'd hush."

"That would be fatal. She might kill again."

The shrieking stopped, and René knew that Consuela and Celeste had got some more laudanum down her. Ramona knew this, too.

"What if Celeste marries and leaves?" she asked. "Don't expect me to help with that crazy woman!"

"Celeste won't marry. She's turned down two fine men. She's satisfied to live at L'Acadie, be part of the family affairs."

"I'm tired of hearing about family!" Ramona blazed. She turned on René, eyes afire. "You're mine, René Leblanc! Forever! I know your reputation, don't think people haven't told Mama about you! Besides, I can smell the way you've been. Well, now you're married to Ramona Sanchez, and I require absolute loyalty!"

"My reputation is in the past," René said hotly. "Leblancs are loyal to their wives. I want only you."

"Tonight, yes. But the future! You're handsome as a god, otherwise I wouldn't have married you. Also, I'll one day be mistress of L'Acadie. When I've given you a son, and one is all I'll give, your nature will be to look elsewhere. And that I'll not abide. You're never to look at another woman. Not even look, understand?"

René had never seen her so lovely; her anger made her more seductive. Her eyes flashed on every word she spoke, and those tempting lips firmed under the words they formed. Even her breasts jutted, commanding, as she sparkled with anger.

"You are jealous!" he exclaimed.

"Completely. If you dally, I'll know. And I'll kill the woman who dallies with you."

Stunned, he vowed to be true to her. For always.

Only then did she let him take her, which he did in a frenzy. She met him wildly, as frenzied as he. They didn't talk, didn't speak. Their sport was faster and harder with each encounter, until both were spent. Then they lay quietly, resting before resuming the passion which they accepted as love.

This passion grew, fostering a hot and angry link between them. At parties she let her jealousy show, not caring who saw it. One night, at a party Marie-Louise gave, René danced twice with Lottie Perez, one of the most attractive girls present. This was one dance too many for Ramona; she broke up the second dance by telling Lottie to go steal another partner. Ramona herself finished the number with René.

Once home, she accused him of being smitten with Lottie.

He laughed, honestly denied it. "Marie-Louise asked me to dance with Lottie again," he protested.

"Why? Just exactly why?"

"Lottie's afraid Clyde Hanson isn't as attentive as he used to be. She thought it might do him some good to see that other men, even married ones, like to dance with her and enjoy her company."

"Marie-Louise!" There was an impatient flash to Ramona's eyes. "Why does she have so many young girls and men at her parties?"

"Oh, she invites everybody, you know that. And, if she'd

had children, some of them would be that age now. She cries, at times, because she's childless. Celeste told me."

"Well, tonight—"

"Ramona, I told you—"

"No, I'm telling you! If you dance with her again, give that Leblanc blood a chance to come to a boil, make one wrong move..."

Her eyes slitted; her lovely mouth twisted.

Now there was an ugliness about her. René's skin prickled. He watched her closely, and this angered her more; her ugliness strengthened.

Anger and alarm warred in him. He'd never seen her this jealous, and over nothing. For no reason, he thought of Carita, wondering if she'd been jealous of that other René.

"Promise! Promise never to dance with Lottie again," Ramona hissed. "Or do you want to bed her, do you want her to be the one I kill?"

Chapter XXXI

Ramona came to childbed as she did everything else, with passion and anger. The first pain sent a tentative finger through her at the noon dinner table. She dropped her fork to the plate with a clatter.

Celeste, sitting on her right, glanced up. She saw how white Ramona had gone, saw the shock on her, the anger. "What is it?" she murmured, so as not to disturb the men who were discussing work for that afternoon. Euphemie had noticed, too, from her place at the foot of the table, and lowered her own fork.

"Pain!" gasped Ramona loudly.

All at the table looked at her.

"Well, do something!" she cried. "Don't just gape! I had a pain!"

"How hard a pain, dear?" asked Euphemie, rising. "There's plenty of time," she reminded. "From the first small pain to the last big one, Ramona," she said kindly, "sometimes hours pass." She eyed her closely. "There. You see? It's gone. Now, eat what you can."

René, alarmed, looked from his mother to Celeste. They both nodded calm assurance. But he saw Ramona's distress, and some of it got into him.

"We should be doing something!" he insisted. He went to Ramona, knelt beside her. "Where did it hurt, darling?"

She began to cry. "Inside, where do you think?"

"Is it hurting now?"

"No, but it'll come back, you know that perfectly well! I want my mother!" she wailed. "I want my father! They wouldn't just sit there when I have a pain, they'd make it stop!"

They all gathered round her. "We'll send for your parents, dear," Euphemie soothed. "We'll send for them and for the doctor right away. You shouldn't be frightened at one pain, dear. It may be hours before you have another—tomorrow, even. First babies take their time about being born."

"You mean I've got to stand this s-suspense until tomorrow? That I can't know when the next pain's coming, that I just have to let this damn baby make up its own mind when it's going to try to kill me?"

"There, there," murmured Euphemie. "You don't mean those things! The baby has nothing to do with it."

"It's got everything to do with it—o-h-h-h!" She doubled over, her fists going into the mashed potatoes on her plate.

René, shaking, looked wildly at Euphemie and Celeste who were taking all this quite calmly. The baby was about to be born, Ramona was having pains, and they acted as if there was all the time in the world!

"The doctor!" he yelled. "Send for the doctor!"

Euphemie and Celeste, after Ramona's short pain ended, began to clean the mashed potatoes off of her hand with table napkins. André, smiling, went to the bellpull. When the kitchen wench appeared, he instructed her to tell two men to leave by pirogue for the doctor and two others to fetch Ramona's parents.

Ramona's parents and the doctor arrived at the same time. Ramona, crying out at every small pain, rushed into her mother's arms, into her father's arms. After their arrival, she wouldn't let René touch her.

"You've done your part!" she screamed. "If you'd only kept your hands off me! Well, see to it that you keep them off now! I've got my Mama!"

They were in Old House, Ramona refusing to bear her child any place but in her own bed. "I like my bed!" she fumed. "Don't keep trying to take it away from me! I need every comfort I can get!"

Surprisingly soon, the pains were five minutes apart, four, then quickly were strung together in one continuous pain. Ramona shrieked until she was hoarse, until she could scarcely breathe, and still she shrieked, words coming out, always words.

"Don't fight it, my dear," Doctor Landro said. "Help me. Help me so I can help you."

But she only screamed the more, fought him, fought the pain and every drop of sweat that wet her body, and every pain, she blamed on René.

"Animal!" she screeched. "Beast! Get away from me. I don't want you in this room! You've done this to me!"

At L'Acadie, Carita heard the shrieking, and she, too, began to shriek, to search for her dagger. With it she was going to stop the screams, kill them. Consuela readied the drops. Carita didn't want to take them, but Consuela persuaded her, telling her the screams would then stop, and she swallowed them and was soon asleep.

At Old House, Euphemie, seeing how disturbed René was, how he, too, suffered every pang with his laboring wife, was flooded with sympathy. "She'll be all right, dear," she assured him. "This is just part of what happens to every woman. When it's over, she'll forget the pain, you'll see."

But Ramona did not forget. Sheet-white, her lips a colorless slash, she glared at him when he ventured to her bedside after the birth of their baby son.

"Don't try to kiss me!" she hissed. "No more babies, René Leblanc! Never, never, never!"

He stroked her hand. She jerked it away.

"Have you seen the baby?" he asked. "Mama says he's a true Leblanc and Papa says he's perfect. He's almost strutting. Imagine Papa, of all people, strutting! And your parents were so happy, they cried."

"Don't try to get my mind off what you did to me! I bore the pain, I faced death to give you a son, and you're strutting! Well, you'll never strut again!"

"Mama said you'll forget the pain, Ramona."

"Never! I'm too smart to forget! Smart enough to make you see to it I never have another baby!"

"All right," he promised. "You've done your share. We have a son. What did you think of him?"

"He's a Leblanc. Your mother promised me a wet nurse."

He nodded, realizing now that Ramona was not going to be a tender, loving mother, that he dare not be a doting father, for she was capable of being jealous of her own child.

"We're a family now," René said, feeling her out. "You and Pierre and me."

"He'll have his nurse," she replied carelessly. "We'll see him, but the nurse will raise him, then he goes to school. And I'm to come first. Especially now, after what you put me through."

When Pierre was six weeks old and thriving, René, who sneaked into the nursery as often as he dared, set about keeping his promise to Ramona. In order that she should have no more babies, René took her to Granny.

Old Granny produced a bottle of brown liquid. "Yo' take one swaller ev'ey night, dey be no baby," she squeaked, in her worn voice. "It work wif Ole Granny, an' it work wif some of de wenches, an' even white ladies. When dis gone, come back fo' mo'. No cause fo' Missy to suffah evah ag'in. Ole Granny's granddaughtah, she know how to brew dis up, too." Ramona believed in the potion, but René still planned to practice withdrawal.

As they started back to Old House, Ramona watched René closely, for there were wenches about the Quarters; she caught him sliding a glance at one who passed, skirt flipping, slim ankles on view, saw the wench's sidewise, inviting look. Instantly, her jealousy was in full cry.

"You want that wench, damn you!" she gritted. "I saw you look at her! What's been going on, with me sick and it your fault? How many times have you bedded her?"

Before he could speak, Ramona spun, ran after the wench, and struck her in the face. "Get to your cabin!" she screamed. "And stay there!"

The wench, cheek bruised, fled.

René, who had run after Ramona, gripped her arm. "Are you out of your senses?" he demanded. "That girl's a bride! She's crazy in love with her husband!"

"She's a wench, not a girl! And how do I know you haven't been with her? This very morning even! While I was having my bath, you could have—"

He yanked her along to Old House, up the stairs into their bedroom. "Take your clothes off!" he ordered as he began to undress.

She took two swallows of the potion, stoppered the bottle, set it on the dresser; she got out of her dress, her undergarments. He was nude now, waiting, readier even than on their wedding night, for Ramona had held him off the last five months of her pregnancy and now six weeks on top of that.

He remembered the black girl's ankles and his need grew, not for Ramona this time, but for the black girl. Or was it for Ramona alone? He didn't know, and he didn't give a damn.

Ramona threw herself on the bed, opened to him, and he came down onto her. And she cried, "You think you're the only one who needed this? And I had a baby to carry, besides! You'll never know what I did for you, no man could!"

Their bodies joined, and they moved together with all their original frenzy, and more. Time after time. Peak after peak. "See?" he mumbled once. "Could I have done this if there'd been a wench this morning?"

One afternoon, as Consuela opened the door of the master suite, Carita suddenly knocked her down, gave Celeste a shove which threw her off-balance, went flying downstairs, outside to Old House. There she came on René and Ramona just after one of their bouts of lovemaking, began screaming about her dagger, searching for it.

Celeste and Consuela were right behind her, Consuela with the drops; they tried in vain to lay hands on Carita, but she kept eluding them.

When Carita spied Ramona she stopped and stared, then screamed, "You're a new one! Who are you? Well, no mattah! Have you heard the true story of the Leblanc Journals, have you?"

Something, some mad truth about Carita, caught Ramona's

fancy. "Don't!" she cried at René, who had grabbed Carita and was holding her as Consuela advanced with the drops. "Let her loose, René Leblanc! Let her talk! I want to hear this!"

Unwilling, but wary of Ramona's temper, René let Carita go. Seeing that Ramona was willing to listen to her, Carita screamed the story of the Journals, the Leblanc passion, the mixed blood, all of it. When she finished, she quieted and let Consuela and Celeste lead her away, the dagger forgotten.

Ramona began to laugh. She turned a look of victory on René. "Now I've got you! If you ever stray—"

Angry, stunned, he asked, "The blood doesn't turn you against me?"

"Don't be silly! You're white, except for one thing. Everybody knows that Negroes are studs, and now all the Leblancs have got stud in them! Let's see who gets undressed first—hurry!"

They were nude at the same time. Laughing, she gave him a shove, caught him off-balance, pushed him onto the bed. In a flash, she bestrode him.

Chapter XXXII

Even as René III was getting married, Beau Rivard was troubled. Beau had always been told by his father that he was to marry young and pick the blackest, sweetest, smartest girl around. Riel had been talking about this constantly of late, and Beau didn't like to hear it.

Nearly six feet tall, hair black and deeply waved, his brown features smooth, he was chased by every girl on Rivard. And he didn't want a single one of them, nor did he want any of the girls on other plantations where he went to parties.

But Riel kept talking girl, girl, girl. He worried Beau. He scared him. Riel was his pa, sure, and Beau loved him, but Riel was so set on breeding the Rivards black, that seemed to be the only thing he thought about, except for Mama and crops.

Riel never smiled, only at Mama, treated the rest of the family, including Beau, as if the only thing that mattered was for Beau to marry right. And those black and white chickens he experimented with, that was scary.

Beau had noticed the girls from plantation to plantation, but nice as they were, he couldn't pick a wife. He didn't know how and he didn't want to, not yet. And he was beginning to be afraid that Riel would suddenly produce a girl and say, "Here she is. Marry her." Whether he took to her or not. And he was afraid to defy his father, who was so fierce.

Beau was in his room dressing for field work. He clenched his powerful hands, so like Riel's, loosened them. He couldn't strike his pa, never, no matter what.

It wasn't that he didn't like girls. Beau could just look at a pretty one and want to bed her. The trouble was Pa and breeding black. Pa was unreasonable about that, needed to get it off his mind. Suppose Beau found a really nice brown-skinned girl and wanted her and no other, what then? Could Pa keep him from marrying her, make him marry a girl with skin black enough to suit his plan? His wild, senseless plan?

One day when Beau was alone in the Quarters, waiting for Riel to come from the house, three strangers appeared.

They were ragged, dusty and barefoot. The man looked to be forty, was six four at least, had dull black skin, Negroid features, and cropped black wool on his head. His lips weren't so very thick, and showed some red. His hands were tremendously powerful, great muscles rose up his bare arms. Beau had never seen such a mammoth, strong man; he marveled at his size and at the look of kindness and intelligence on his broad face.

The woman was very black, had a slant to her black eyes, and was tiny and wiry, strong in her own way. Her shift, though dusty, hung neatly and her faded tignon was smartly tied. She had a thin face which held both anxiety and friendliness, and when her eyes met Beau's, she ventured a smile and he smiled back.

The girl with them made Beau stare openly. She had coal

black skin, couldn't weigh over a hundred pounds, and her hips drove him crazy. Her buttocks sort of jutted out and up at the back, sassy as anything, a temptation to any man. She wore her short, kinky hair in a halo which looked merrily wicked; her black, flirtatious eyes shone, lighting up her finely molded features. She was a real beauty, even barefoot, even in rags.

None of them spoke; they seemed to be waiting for Beau to speak first. They all looked so pleasant. Beau wondered if they were hungry. Since Riel wasn't here yet and they were waiting, he addressed the man.

"Who are you, sir?" he asked, with courtesy. "How can I help you?"

"Our name is Clark," replied the man in a deep, velvety tone. "My wife is Birdie; this is our daughtah. I need to talk to the ownah of the plantation, if you please."

"I'll bring him," Beau said. "Wait here."

The man nodded, and Beau ran for the house, wondering how many families had already passed through Rivard. He knew Riel had fed them, sent them on their way with a packet of food. One family had been put to work on the land, and was still here, content, and among the best workers on the place.

When he came back with Riel, the Clarks were waiting in the exact spot Beau had left them. The girl was making marks in the dust with her big toe, and this caused those hips to move and provoke; Beau felt a deep ache, and didn't look away.

"My son says you want to talk to me," Riel said. "I'm Riel Rivard."

"I'm Hercules Clark, sir. We need work."

"What kind of work have you done in the past?"

"I was a blacksmith down on the Delta, sir. I lost my job to a white man who was friendly with the scalawags. After I had to leave the plantation—they said they couldn't put me down from smith to field hand—I went to New Orleans. I couldn't find a job there, either. Did get a few days as a dock hand, but that's all. I heard about the bayou country, how men and women are needed to farm the land, and decided to come here and try for work."

"You speak exceptionally well."

"Thank you, sir. The mistress held classes for slaves who

wanted to learn. She was a kind lady, cried when we had to leave. Our girl here, she went to school on the plantation, but didn't take to study like her mammy and me."

Riel, liking this strong man, recognizing the wiry strength of his wife, studied them keenly. He was ever on the alert for help to farm more of his land, and he needed energetic workers. "It's still hard for black people to make a living," he said, and Hercules Clark nodded. "I don't know of any smith jobs. We have a smith at Rivard."

"We'd work the fields for cabin and grub, sir. All three of us."

"My people also share in the cash profit."

"That's kind of you, sir."

"They earn it, and it's the only way I can grow cane. I can't pay wages, but my workers do get a bit of hard money at the end of the season."

"Can you use us, sir?"

"I feel I can. I feel you're hard workers and will hold up your end of an honest bargain."

"That we will, sir. We're ready to start now, this morning."

"Have you eaten?"

"Enough, sir. We had cold corn pone made from some meal I did a day's smithing for."

"But you'll need rations today," Riel said. He noted their ragged clothes. "And decent garb. Come to the house with me now. The mistress will outfit you and supply rations."

"Sir, hadn't we bettah work first? Earn the right to rations and clothes?"

Liking this Hercules, Riel gave a tight smile. "No, but walk over here—I'll show you the field which will be your responsibility to clear, plant, weed, water, and harvest. It's of good size, for it will take that much extra cane to make it possible for me to pay you a share of the cash. You must earn your own share. I can't take even a cent from the others to make up a payment, however small, for you."

"That's a fair deal, sir," said Hercules. "And this way, the othah workers won't be sullen 'cause we're here."

During the conversation, Beau and the girl eyed each other, smiling now and then. Beau wondered if Riel had noticed her blackness and what he thought of it. As far as he could tell, his pa had merely glanced at the girl.

After the Clark family had been given food and clothes,

Riel took them to their field, which stretched weed-grown and wild for quite a distance. Beau thought it was too big a field for just three people. Then he reconsidered. He himself was responsible for a field half the size and helped in other fields, as well.

The Clarks were satisfied with their field and pleased with the two-room cabin Riel said would be theirs. In the cabin, Beau saw his pa look at the girl again, his eyes sort of lingering on her. Beau's pulse went faster. Good. Now Pa knew how black she was, how beautiful. The other qualities he insisted a girl should have—brains, the will to work, living clean—Pa'd need time on those. Beau found himself hoping Pa would like everything about the girl, because she was the very first one he'd felt like getting to know real well, ever, the only one he'd be willing to consider marrying.

When they started to the big house for clothes, the girl hung back, switching her hips.

This excited Beau; he burned where he shouldn't.

Teasing, she asked, "That white man you Pa?"

"Yes. But he isn't white. He's got black blood in him, and my ma's black as you."

"What youah name, dark boy?"

"Beau. Beau Rivard."

"That's a pretty name."

"What's your name, besides Clark?"

"Tansey. Just Tansey."

She looked him over, slowly switching her hips. She dearly loved to see a new, handsome man. She looked Beau over again, liked what she saw, flirted her eyes at him. She'd already slept with three different black men and found out that, though they all did the same thing, each was special in one way or another, and she wondered what Beau would be like. She saw the hump in his trousers, knew what he was feeling, and found it exciting.

While twisting her toe in the dust, twitching her hips, driving him crazy, Tansey and Beau talked about whatever came to their lips. She told of the long, weary walking she and her parents had done between here and New Orleans, of the occasional boat ride when her pappy could hire on in exchange for passage for three.

"Pappy heard 'bout Rivard," she said, " 'bout Riel Rivard

workin' his people fierce but fair. So he decided to come here. He's really a worker, my pappy. All of us are."

"My pa works hard, too," Beau said, "and so do I. Mama works in the house and in the vegetable garden. My grandmother works in the house and teaches the school. We hang on, Pa says, do a little better every year." He broke off, plunged, forgetting Riel and his requirements. "My wife, she'll have to work, too."

Tansey stared at him for a long moment. Then she said, "If you wanted, any girl'd marry you."

Chapter XXXIII

The Clark family worked their field from dawn to dusk six days a week, Sunday being a mandatory day off at Rivard. They worked at a steady pace, even Tansey keeping up with her parents. Every day, Beau, making rounds with Riel, saw that another wide swath of weeds was gone, or that land had been turned and cane planted, or that ditches had been cleaned.

Riel allowed at table one day that if the Clarks continued as they had started, they were going to be one of Rivard's most valuable families. "I wish more like them would come," he added.

"Me, too," Deedee agreed. "Think, darling, if we could have a good family like that in every cabin! It'd mean—"

"It'd mean we'd be farming at full capacity," said Riel. "I doubt that will happen overnight." Riel flashed one of his infrequent smiles. "Why don't you give them a welcome party, invite people from other plantations? The Clarks have been working extra hard, and so have all our people, trying to keep up with the Clarks. I think it's time they had some entertainment."

Consequently, the party was set for the following Saturday

night. The women took the afternoon off from the fields, each to cook her specialty for the party, and put the last festive touches to the dresses they'd been turning and repairing at night.

Riel provided milk for drinking, using all the milk produced in one entire day by his herd of eight cows. Deedee and Olive baked a three-layer cake, using the last of the sugar in the icing, making a row of white roses around the edge at the top. This was placed on one end of the linen-draped trestle table, set up near the dance area, the piano from the church next to it, along with stools for the fiddlers.

Right after dusk, the guests arrived by pirogue. Flares had been lighted and placed about the Quarters, candles burned in every room of the cabins as well as the main house, so there was light in the smallest cranny. Deedee, Olive, Riel, and Deedee's aging parents, greeted the guests from other plantations as well as the Rivard folk, welcoming all into the house. There was much hugging and squealing, shuffling of feet in good shoes, and a great deal of laughter. The Clarks were introduced to everybody, and soon mixed into the crowd as if they'd always belonged.

When it was time, Olive sat at the piano, the fiddlers tuned up, and the dancing began. For one magic moment it seemed to Beau that this was some never-never land—flares burning everywhere, the sky so filled with stars he felt like he could pick a couple, all the girls so pretty.

And Tansey. Tansey in a bright red, calico dress made from the things Mama had given them; Birdie had tucked here and pleated there, and under it, a skirt edged with lace that showed when she whirled. And whirl she did, trying to take her choice of partners from all the boys gathered round her, the new girl, while the other girls stood off to one side, pouting.

Beau, slicked up in his Sunday trousers which matched his skin and a white, starched shirt and spit-shined, brown shoes, pushed through the crowd around Tansey. He'd known every fellow would be after her; he'd also known he wasn't going to stand for it. She was for him.

"I get first dance," Beau sang out. Because he was the owner's son, he knew the fellows would give way. But they did it laughingly, turning to the waiting girls who had cast flirting looks at them, and soon every one of them was paired off.

Beau felt his pants go tight when he put his arms around Tansey, breathed as steadily as he could. Tansey, fully aware of his condition, danced her eyes at him, acted innocent, switched her hips until he was half-crazy. As they stepped to the rhythm, he felt that he was in a dream, a flare-filled, starry dream where there was only music in his veins and Tansey in his arms.

Olive, playing the piano, also felt removed from the real world. The music got into her and throbbed like a second heart, and her mind wandered where it would. This was what Riel wanted, and she wanted him to have it. Sadness crept in with the music. After all the years Riel had been married, even her fondness for Deedee, her love of his dark son were not enough to make up for what had happened between them, their estrangement. René, she thought, oh, René, that this could be! Her face now expressionless, she played on.

She saw Beau dance by with the new girl, saw the bemusement on him. She's black enough, Olive thought, Riel's obsession sweeping her. Then, deliberately, she shook off the feeling. Riel was her son, her love, her life. It's my imagination, she told herself. It's only because he's so intent on his goal. Buried deep, he loves me, he must.

Tansey danced with all the boys. She saw one young hulk, almost as tall as her pappy but broader and blacker, that she hated on sight. He had muscular arms big as young tree trunks and the way he stood straddle-legged was sickening instead of being exciting. He had a very big face; his features were like bumps—a big bump of nose, big bumps of lips, great, knobby ears on a very big, round head covered with close-sheared wool. Everything about him was big and ugly.

He danced with no one, but just stood, his great arms folded, staring at every move Tansey made, especially her hips. She switched them extra, just to let him see what he couldn't have and was never going to get.

Suddenly when she was dancing with a skinny fellow, the big ugly one scooped out a tremendous hand, swung her into his arms, and began to dance so strongly she had to follow or fall against him. When she had her balance, she pushed at him, trying to get free.

He held her with muscles of steel. He was sweating, and his body smell was getting on her dress; it made her sick at the stomach.

"Let me go!" she hissed.

"Oh, no. Yo' givin' me de res' yo' dances!"

"No!"

"W'y not, lil' black wench?"

"You—you stink, that's why!"

"Dat 'cause I de blacksmith. Take powahful, sweatin' man to be de blacksmith."

"My pappy used to be a blacksmith! He took a bath ev'ry night! He nevah stunk!"

The big one roared at the idea of a bath. "Yo' soun' like de mastah. 'Go jump in de creek, Boisy,' he say. 'Wash dat smell off.' Sometimes I does. But hell, nex' day I work at de forge an' de stink come right back!"

"You need a bath ev'ry day!"

"Boisy take bath afore he bed yo', lil black wench. Dat whut yo' want, he do it."

The very idea of bedding with this one revolted her, and she said so. He roared again. "I might even marry yo'," he rumbled. "I single man. Girl whut gits Boisy, gits all man!"

He set her to one side when it was time to eat and went to fill a plate for each of them. She'd danced only once with him. There'd be no second time, even if she had to ask Pappy to chase Boisy off.

He'd no sooner left than Beau appeared with two filled plates. He took her away from that spot, settling in the midst of a group of young couples. His heart was thumping. He'd gotten up courage to draw his pa aside and ask if Tansey was the kind of wife he should marry.

Riel had scowled thoughtfully. "She's black, she's a beauty, and she works hard. She's a smart girl, too. And she comes from good stock. Most important, she's too young to be anything but clean, with Hercules and Birdie for parents. Could be, Beau, could be. If you can get her."

Beau could hardly eat, he was so anxious to propose. He didn't notice Boisy glowering at them, unable to break in on Tansey while the owner's son was her partner. Nor did Boisy get to dance with her again, for Beau had whispered his proposal, Tansey had whispered her acceptance, and they danced every dance together after that. Boisy ended up by eating four plates of food, drinking a gallon of milk. He'd bide his time. By hell, he would.

Beau and Tansey were married a week later, the wedding celebration exceeding even the dance. Riel took a precious gold coin and bought a wedding ring of genuine gold.

The same people were at the wedding. The groom again wore his best clothes. The bride wore a new, bright yellow calico dress made with ruffles. Deedee had saved the length for some special occasion and, though she had doubts about the girl her son wanted to marry, gave it freely helping Birdie make it.

Riel, at peace with himself for the moment, watched the black preacher marry his son to the coal black girl. This was the second step of his plan. Beau was all man, filled with the juices of youth, and Tansey was at her most nubile. Riel expected a grandchild within a year.

Deedee stood beside Riel, knowing his thoughts. Uneasily she noted how the young men's eyes clung to Tansey and later, during the dancing, she didn't miss how Tansey threw them sidelong glances. Then Deedee looked at the Clarks' happy faces and chided herself; they were the salt of the earth. Of course their daughter would be true to Beau and make him a good wife, of course she would.

Olive, seeing Riel's expression, was happy for him. She glanced at Tansey's blackness, looked away. She'd get used to it in time, as she'd gotten used to Deedee, whom she no longer thought of in terms of her color. And Tansey's child would also be Beau's child, and she loved Beau devotedly. How could she not love his issue?

Later, nurturing her own stirring of friendliness, Olive embraced Tansey, kissing her on the cheek. Riel, standing with them, had a faint impulse to kiss Olive, did not. He dared not let her think that he might give up the relentless plan which, to her, seemed madness. So he confined his impulse to a smile, but even that put a song into Olive's heart.

From this night on, Riel's obsession deepened. Some called him crazy, he knew, but he felt completely sane. He had conceived a mission to make Rivards black, was carrying it out, and would stay on that course. Let the world scoff at his black dynasty; it made no difference to him. His family would soon be pure in blood.

The newlyweds were given the overseer's house for their own. It had six rooms, and Tansey was delighted with it. She flitted from room to room, Beau pleased with her happiness.

Their lovemaking was perfect from the start, but despite this, Tansey was restless. Now she knew what Beau was like, but what would the next one be like? Well, that could wait. For now, she was busy with her six rooms.

Beau found her scrubbing the floors every day. "They're already clean," he protested. "You did that yesterday in the whole house."

She sat back on her bare heels, slanted a smile up at him. "It's my honeymoon. Your pappy—"

"Call him Pa."

"Your pa says I'm to have a week off field work and do what I want. And what I want is to play with my house. Latah, I'll scrub once a week like Mammy."

Beau relented, couldn't help himself. She could wrap him around her finger, but he didn't mind. "Just so you're not too tired at night," he grinned. "You've got a hungry husband in bed."

They laughed together, and that night she made him extremely happy. Herself satisfied, she lay in his arms, yet knew she'd crave other men—the chase, the conquest, the peak—those things she wanted, and she would indulge herself.

Trouble was, her monthly didn't come, and she was pregnant. She decided, reluctantly, to wait about other men until after the baby was born.

Chapter XXXIV

The moment Riel learned Tansey was pregnant, instead of showing happiness, he became more taut than ever. Deedee saw this at once, knew it wasn't a good sign.

She spoke to him about it as they dressed to call on the young couple. "You act as if you expect the baby to be white," she said gently. "Actually, you know, there's not a chance of it."

"There's always the throwback," he said tightly.

"I don't believe in the throwback, Riel."

"That's what Mama said once, but it proves nothing."

When they arrived with Olive at Beau's home to make their congratulatory call, Riel was stiff and troubled. Deedee, whose hand rested on his arm, could feel the uneasiness in him, and longed for a way to comfort him.

After they were seated in Tansey's painfully clean living room, the young couple and Tansey's parents, Riel came right to the point. "Is it true, Tansey, what Birdie said?" His voice was so tight it seemed ready to snap in two.

Tansey, fearful of Riel to start with, went suddenly nervous, which was completely unlike her. She clasped her hands in her lap, stared at them, nodded.

"How far along are you?" Riel asked, ignoring the pressure of Deedee's fingers. He didn't care about manners. He was here for facts.

"About t-two weeks, sir," Tansey faltered, staring at her hands. She was in a tumult. She didn't want to explain how she knew about the baby so soon, didn't want to mention her monthly, not to a man, not even to her pappy. That was a private thing to a girl.

"How can you know?" Riel demanded. "So soon?"

Deedee murmured the facts, cheeks burning. All were embarrassed, especially Beau, who flushed, looking black for an instant.

"That's welcome news," Riel told them, fiercely tense, ignoring their embarrassment. "I'm expecting a very black grandchild. Perhaps you'd better not work in the fields until after he's born, Tansey. I don't want to run the risk of a miscarriage. This baby is the most important thing at Rivard, understand?"

"I like to work in the fields," Tansey said. "The othah breedahs do, and it don't do them no hurt."

"This case is different."

"Tansey's a strong girl," put in Deedee. "If she doesn't work, at least garden, it won't be good for her or the baby. She needs exercise, sun, and breeze, not just house-keeping and cooking. She might put on too much weight. The field work that the other women do keeps them slim and strong; when delivery time comes they can push, help the baby be born. And in three days they're up and about. You know all that, Riel. And you apply it to the other women. Tansey is no different."

Beau laughed. "Scrubbing floors," he told Riel. "That's what she does every day she's not in the field. She gets no sun, no breeze. That's not good for anybody."

"I feel for Mr. Rivard," Hercules put in now. "He wants a strong baby—a real black baby—and so do we. Meaning no offense, Birdie and I ain't anxious to have white blood show in our grandchild."

Birdie nodded her agreement, took sides with Deedee on whether Tansey should work in the fields. "Tansey's a sweet girl, and she's my only daughtah, but she needs to be busy and not with just a house. She needs the kind of life she was raised in—growing things. It won't hurt her, Mr. Rivard."

"Riel. I told you."

Birdie smiled. "Riel, then. I tell you with truth that Tansey be bettah off working outside."

"For how long?" asked Riel.

"To the very end. It will keep her muscles strong, muscles that she needs in birthing. Ask her. She'd rather be in the fields than laying 'round the house."

Riel turned his eyes on Tansey. "Mammy's right. I don't want to just stay around the house."

"It needn't be like that," Riel persisted. "It could be a learning time."

"I don't want to go to no school!"

"Not school learning, but the other. Deedee could show you how to be mistress Rivard, so that when the time comes, you'll know how. Olive can help; she helped Deedee. You could even learn to play the piano. We need a second piano player at Rivard."

Olive, who had long wondered who would take her place at the keyboard in years to come, spoke up. "Whether you go to the fields or not, Tansey, I'll be happy to teach you piano. You'll be good at it, with your sense of rhythm. I've watched you dance."

Tansey burst into sudden tears. "Ain't it enough I give

you-all a ba-by?" she sobbed. "Have I got to quit work I like, for work I don't want? I don't need to know how to be mistress, not yet! I just want to do what I been doin' and have my baby, and still work! I want to be like ev'rybody else!"

"You can't be like everybody else," Riel said sternly. "You're the future mistress, like it or not. Stop crying! You don't have to study anything now, and you don't have to stay at home. You will work in the garden with Deedee—that's hard enough work. It'll keep you busy and healthy."

They all approved, even Beau. Nobody asked Tansey if she liked gardening; they just told her what she had to do. She knew she'd simply pine in the gardens, because gardens were worked by women only, never a man to exchange exciting looks with.

Well, let them do it to her. She wasn't going to pick out a man until later, anyhow. When her time came, after the baby was born, she'd put up a real fuss to get back into the fields with men. She was going to have a little fun, not just keep house and tend her baby and garden. She'd work hard, do more in the fields than ever before, but she'd have her fun—secret fun. And she'd have the other, too—being married to the future master of Rivard.

"I wonder how dark the baby will be," Riel speculated, slightly less tense now. "Do you think, Hercules, it can be really black like Tansey?"

Both Clarks shook their heads, undecided.

"Deedee? Mama?"

Olive's heart warmed. He'd included her. She'd figured the odds mathematically and was ready. She started to speak, then shook her head. "It's not my place to predict, son, but Deedee's. We've discussed it at length."

"It may well be black as Tansey," Deedee said, smiling at Riel. "It could happen."

It was barely possible, Olive thought. Perhaps inheritance would carry through very strongly in this generation. Hoping it would, but not at all certain, she met Riel's look unhappily.

He returned it, aware that the flashes of warmth he felt for her had become rare. He thought of her with most of the old resentment intact.

He lay awake all that night. Having long ceased to pray,

he willed fiercely that Tansey's baby be coal black, that he need not suffer through still another generation striving for that goal.

After his sleepless night, he took Deedee and Tansey to the special chicken pens he'd built over a year ago. At that time he'd bartered his best laying hens for a fine, red-combed white rooster and two shiny-feathered black hens with equally red combs. As they neared the pens, Deedee saw that the chicks in all the pens had feathered out and were getting little red combs. She felt suddenly uneasy about all these chickens.

Tansey stared at them, then at Riel, wondering if he meant to assign the care of them to her.

"Note that white rooster and his black hens," Riel told the women, and they looked, waited for what he meant to say next.

"Both hens are black like you, Tansey. The rooster is white like me, almost..."

"Y-yes, Pa."

"See how the chicks have feathered out. What color are they?"

"Some are dull white, and some dull black, but most of them are speckled, black and white."

"Good! Very good!" Riel exclaimed, and Deedee shivered. She hadn't dreamed that he was this obsessed. Chickens!

The next pen held a speckled rooster, two shining black hens, and a variety of chicks—dirty white, dull black, speckled.

"The speckled rooster is like Beau," Riel explained. "The black hens are like you again, Tansey. See that shining black little rooster, Tansey—that's your baby. If chicks can hatch this black from black hen and speckled rooster, then you and Beau can have a coal black baby!"

The two women were horrified, silent, as they followed Riel to another pen. "Here's a black rooster, one that hatched out like the little fellow I just showed you," Riel said. "That's the way your baby will be, Tansey, when he's a man. See? His hens are black, and all the chicks are black, only one of them dull in color."

"Riel!" breathed Deedee. "How could you?"

"I had to, Deedee. I'll end up with all black chickens at Rivard. There won't be even one mixed color in the lot."

Tansey's throat was dry. What was he up to?

"What can chickens prove?" asked Deedee, wanting to cry.

"What I've told you about Beau and now Tansey. By breeding black into each Rivard generation, all the white will disappear. These chickens prove it. They're a guidepost, a way to show if I'm wrong, so I'll not repeat the mistake in the Rivard family."

Tansey looked at his burning eyes, and a shiver took her. She'd never seen such eyes. So hard and not to be argued with. So she didn't argue, and she noticed that Deedee didn't, either. They both just looked and listened.

"The chickens are an experiment," he said, "not an insult. Already the experiment points to some proven facts. By marrying you, Deedee, so black, Beau resulted, darker than mulatto. There's a chance that his baby and Tansey's will be very black, like that one little rooster."

"You say my baby has got to be like that little rooster?" quavered Tansey. He was a crazy man, had to be.

"Or so I'm hoping. With you as mother, Tansey, the next Rivard can be pure black. And when he has a son by a black girl, the line will revert to its origin."

Tansey stopped listening. She couldn't make heads or tails of it. She didn't understand half of what he said, and was now in such a state she could scream. You'd think he was the one carrying, not her. He really acted crazy.

She was sure glad to get to work in the garden. She dug into it with a spade, made a little, long ditch, dropped in beans, covered them with dirt. She felt sick at her stomach, him saying they were all like chickens, even her baby. And when the baby was big enough to chore, she'd see to it that Beau kept him away from tending chickens.

She told Beau about the chickens. He thought it was funny. He began to laugh. "So that's what he's up to!" he howled. "I never knew him to care about chickens before! I asked him once, and he told me to mind my own business. I got the idea he was trying to breed a flock that would lay more eggs. But babies!" He doubled up, laughing.

She began to cry. He put his arms around her, soothed her with sex. "Don't pay any attention to his chickens," he told her before they slept. "It means nothing. It fills his time. What happens with our baby has nothing to do with chickens!"

Deedee, living with Riel, feeling him so tense beside her

in bed, suffering from his sleeplessness, was frightened by the experiment. She tried to persuade him to forget it.

"You've already proved your point," she murmured in his arms. "What's the use of going on with it?"

"I want it perfected. Want to know that I'm going to succeed. I can't live long enough, can't live through enough generations to see that the black will hold, once established. When I've produced pure black flocks for three successive generations, then I'll be satisfied."

Thus, Deedee had to endure his growing tension. He never explained to Olive the purpose of his chickens, and Deedee cautioned Tansey and Beau to keep it to themselves.

"It would worry Mama Rivard, and it would worry your parents, Tansey. He's explained the experiment to me, and I know that by the time your baby is born, it will be finished and done with. Chickens breed fast, and he's pushing these."

They promised not to tell, Tansey crying out to Beau later that she didn't want her mammy and pappy to know his pa was crazy. "Now I got anothah job," she cried on, "to cure him of his craziness by havin' a real black baby!"

Deedee was convinced that Olive suspected the experiment, but said nothing about it. She became tense, hoping fervently that the expected baby would be very black, hoped it for herself as well as for Riel. She was used to his being white now, used to Olive's white skin, rarely noticed that they were different, but was happy that she'd had the black blood to pour into Beau, and, through him, into his child.

Meanwhile, Deedee caught signs which promised trouble. As she walked to the garden each day with Tansey, she saw the sly smiles the girl gave the unmarried men on their way to the fields. And she noted how their hungry eyes clung to Tansey's switching hips. And, always watching now, she saw Tansey's hungry eyes on an occasional worker from some other plantation and the response of the man, even though Tansey was plump with child.

Sensing that Tansey wasn't to be trusted, she continued to observe. Unfailingly she caught the sly glances, the secret smile on the girl's lips, so stayed close to her daughter-in-law in the garden lest she slip away, pregnant or not, to some hidden spot with one of the field men.

Beau, she thought. Riel. Well, she was alerted. She would see Tansey never got the chance to consort with any man but her husband. After the baby was born, Deedee would keep Tansey permanently in the garden with the women. She would see to it that Tansey spent hours in the plantation house, learning to be mistress, that she spent other hours learning to play the piano, practicing two hours a day, that she learn to sew, darn, and do fine needlework.

Nights, after the field work was done, she needn't worry about. Beau was young. He was passionate. He would keep his wife busy in her own bed.

Chapter XXXV

Celeste, thirty-seven, had reached the zenith of her beauty. Purity and kindness emanated from her. Her calm acceptance of life's events transcended even that of her mother, Euphemie. It was to Celeste that Marie-Louise let grief over her childlessness show. However, she never confided the fact that she'd borne a son out of wedlock.

Celeste had long since moved back into L'Acadie from Honeymoon House, because Euphemie pleaded with her. "We're a family when you're here, darling," she said. "Your papa and me and Gab. And you have such influence over Carita."

Tonight, Celeste was entertaining Berend Dixon, thirty-eight, a yard goods dealer from New Orleans. He'd come to St. Martinville to vacation and see the bayou country, had met Celeste at Mass, and lingered. After that first day, it seemed to her that everywhere she went he was present—tall and slim, ethereally handsome, his hair so blond it looked like spun gold, his eyes a bit slanted and melting gray. His features were finely cut; his lips were curved slightly at the top, seeming always to tremble on the edge of a smile. His voice was soft, with a caressing quality.

Celeste felt drawn to him, accepted him as a friend, saw him at parties which she now attended, saw him at Mass. Today she'd suggested he have dinner with them.

When they were alone for a moment, Euphemie looked at her youngest child in surprise. "Are you . . . is he . . . ?" Her voice trailed off, eyes both troubled and hopeful.

"I just like him, Mama, truly like him as a friend. And he's lonely. He boards with the Baxters and they're lively and interesting, but other people he knows only casually from parties."

"Yet he's invited to the parties."

"Oh, yes. He's charming, a good conversationalist, and a splendid dancer. Some of the girls are making eyes at him."

The men joined them and, though the weather had been threatening since morning, the air muggy, wind coming in gusts, they sat down to dinner. André and Gab were concerned that a hurricane was blowing up; Berend agreed.

"My staff will close the shutters both at my house and office," he said. "They know what to do. However, even if a storm hits here, it'll probably blow itself out before it reaches New Orleans."

"Let's hope so," said André. "If it builds up here, we'll be closing shutters and boarding up. The cabins have shutters too, so all our people need do is stay inside. The cabins are strongly built, fastened to sturdy posts driven into the ground. They can withstand wind almost as well as L'Acadie itself."

After dinner, André and Gab decided they should batten down, for the weather was worse. Berend offered to go along, but they genially waved him aside.

"You stay with Celeste, get her to play that new music she has," Gab said. "We'll not be more than an hour, maybe less."

They departed, Euphemie excused herself to check upstairs, meaning, Celeste knew, to see that Carita was stable; and after that she'd run to René and Ramona and the baby in Old House, insist that they come to L'Acadie.

Celeste and Berend found themselves alone in the drawing room. He smiled when she sat on a divan, took his place beside her.

"What about that music?" he asked.

"Somehow I feel you're not in the mood for it," she said, and smiled back. "Not with the unrest in the air, the possibility of a storm. We get some really bad ones here."

He laughed softly. "No music," he agreed. "Now that

I'm alone with you, not at a party with dozens of other people, may I speak freely?"

Comfortable with him, yet with a far uneasiness in her, she consented. "Please do."

"I made this trip to St. Martinville to view the scenery, to take a pleasant vacation," he began. "I stayed on to see you. To court you."

"Berend!" She was instantly, deeply upset. "I—I don't know what to say!"

"Nothing, for a moment. Let me speak, please. I've stayed just to see you, to court you at parties, at church, because I'm in love with you and want you for my wife. I want children from you, want you at my side always. I can take good care of you, give you luxury even. I've already given you my heart."

Celeste found it hard to breathe. Sadness filled every vein. Sadness for him and for herself. What he felt toward her seemed to be what she'd felt for Anton. She tried to speak, to explain, could not.

"I know your tragic past, Celeste. It's become a legend in St. Martinville—the handsome bridegroom who died on his wedding night, leaving his lovely bride a widow. I know you've rejected other suitors in the past. There've been none recently?"

He knew. This handsome, kind man knew of Anton. She yearned to put out her hand to him, to let him hold it, did not. Anton, her heart stroked, Anton.

"No one has proposed to me lately," she murmured.

"I don't ask you to love me, Celeste. I understand your reluctance. I, too, lost a mate ten years ago, and until now... But you'd see. Fondness would come. Companionship. Even love. Unless you find me not likable?"

"Oh, no! I like you very much."

"So. It's been how many years, Celeste?"

"Eighteen. But it seems like yesterday. When Anton died, the bottom fell out of my world."

When he would have spoken, she gestured. "Yes, I know. My life isn't natural, but I'm satisfied. I fill my time with my family and friends. I'll never be able to put another man in Anton's place."

"That's the way I felt about Rhoda. Until I saw you."

"Then I could be just an impulse, don't you see? I find it hard to believe you'll ever be able to replace her, with me or any other woman."

He looked infinitely sad. He reached for her hand, and she let him hold it. He traced Anton's rings on her marriage finger. "I should have known," he murmured, "when I saw these. A woman doesn't wear a dead man's rings unless he's still in her, heart and soul."

Tears stood in her eyes. Slowly she pulled her hand free, and he let it go.

He stood. She stood with him.

"I'll leave St. Martinville tomorrow," he said, "unless a hurricane does strike. Then I'll leave as soon as the boats run. I don't suppose you'd want my address?"

The tears rolled out of her eyes, two of them whispered down her cheeks. She shook her head. "No, but thank you. I won't change my mind."

He looked longingly into her eyes, murmured courteously about her parents and saying good-bye for him, and then he went swiftly for his rented pirogue.

Celeste, trembling, wandered upstairs in search of Euphemie, to do what she could to help.

"Has Berend left?" Euphemie asked.

Celeste nodded, wiped her cheeks.

Euphemie, fifty-four and still beautiful, looked at her daughter keenly. "He wants to marry you, darling."

"Yes. He proposed."

"And you sent him away."

"I had to, Mama. Anton . . ."

Gently, Euphemie embraced Celeste. Then she spoke with purpose. "The men say it's going to be a hurricane—they're on ladders now, closing the upstairs shutters. René's helping. They'll do Old House next, bring Ramona and the baby over here, then they'll shutter Honeymoon House and board up the old kitchen house. Some of the blacks are helping, others are battening down the cabins and the barn."

"Then we must get in a supply of water," Celeste exclaimed, starting down the stairway at a trot, her mother following. "And candles, we'll need candles if the kerosene supply runs out!"

Swiftly, they worked; swiftly, the men and blacks worked.

The storm had begun; a hurricane would soon strike. The wind now came in great, howling gusts.

Ramona, Pierre's nurse, and Pierre himself, came in on the first wind-driven slant of rain. They stood in the kitchen, taking off dripping wraps. Ramona was excited, laughing.

"René told me this is going to be a bad hurricane!" she exulted. "He promised! It should be fiercer than what we had in New Orleans. Do you think it will be, Mama Euphemie? Celeste?"

"I don't want to spoil your enjoyment," Euphemie said, "but if it turns out to be no hurricane at all, a storm only, that's what will make me happy! But I'm afraid, after what André said last trip in it's going to be bad."

Celeste hoped Berend would get back to St. Martinville before the rain drenched him. She thought about Charles and Marie-Louise, knew they were making the same preparations there as here. Knew all the people up and down the bayous were closing shutters, getting cattle into barns, fetching water, preparing for the moment when the full force of the hurricane would strike. Then they'd stay in their shuttered houses, venturing out in the calm center of the storm to check on things, scuttling back inside when the second half of the hurricane threw itself at them.

At Rivard, Riel was beside himself. Tansey was having birth pains. He'd sent for the doctor, and now had to order Beau to leave Tansey to help board up. He cursed himself for not starting the work sooner, for it had been exceedingly hot and humid all day. That was the first warning. Then had come the hot gusts of wind, and sometimes a spatter of rain, warning number two.

Now, instead of standing watch on his grandchild's struggle to be born, he had to deal with shutters. Hercules was at the barn door, and he fought it open to admit them with the ladders, fought it shut after them.

They checked the barn, left two men to stand watch over the cows and the chickens which they'd caught and turned loose inside. Beau was first out into the rain, Riel treading on his heels. Then, shoulder to shoulder, they went at a slogging run to the shuttered overseers house where Tansey and the women were.

As they burst into the kitchen, Riel heard Tansey's voice, shrill, moaning, screaming, and he ground his teeth so hard they hurt at the roots. He rushed for the bedroom. Damn little fool, why didn't she moan and push? She was screaming and that meant she was fighting the birth, meant she might kill the baby in the birthing.

Wet and streaming, Riel leapt into the bedroom, Beau behind him. "Make her stop!" Riel bellowed at Deedee. "Make her stop screaming!"

Deedee and Birdie and Olive stared at him blankly, turned back to the girl writhing on the bed. "Yo' yell, honey pie," croaked the old midwife, called in to help until the doctor arrived. "Yo' yell an' push. Us git dat suckah out, see if us don'!"

A broadside of wind hit the house. The house shivered and popped. Rain burst over it, began to seep under the kitchen door.

Carita knew what was going on. Oh, she did! She'd been through another unbearably hot and humid day once. That time she'd taken the Leblanc Journals down from the shelf where René had put them. And the awful storm which blew, that terrible hurricane, had tried its best to tear L'Acadie to shreds, to get at the Journals and rip them to pieces, but she hadn't let it. She'd read on and on to the very end.

Now there was another hurricane. She looked into her emerald-studded hand mirror and saw herself at twenty-four. Consuela said she was sixty-seven but Carita could see she still looked the same. Those lines cutting from nose to mouth to chin, that was the hurricane worrying her, nothing else.

She put the mirror down, listened to the storm. Yes, she knew all about hurricanes. That was when René, stud René, her husband, rode to his mistress and stayed with her while she had her baby.

But it wasn't going to work. They had hidden her dagger, but she knew where the kitchen knives were. Slit-eyed, she waited until Consuela unlocked the sitting-room door to bring in two pitchers of water. Then Carita grabbed one pitcher, smashed it over Consuela's head and, while the wench lay on the floor, stunned, ran for the stairs. Celeste, carrying a lamp, saw Carita dash. She set the lamp on a table and gave chase, but Carita got to the kitchen, snatched a knife, turned it on Celeste.

"I won't be stopped!" she shrieked. "I won't read the Journals, not this time! I'm going to kill her, kill that woman at Rivard, and I'm going to kill that bastard baby!"

She fled into the rain. Let Celeste get men to chase her; she'd outrun them all. This time, she'd finish what she'd started! On she ran, the wind at her back, pushing her and giving her wings, and she sped toward Rivard, remembering, knowing where it was.

Rain gusted, drove. Now she was riding the wind, going faster than any horse could have taken her. She was light and graceful, as always. She knew how to give herself to the wind.

Rain soaked her hair, ran through her dress and plastered her undergarments tight. Her feet sank into great puddles. Lightning flashed and thunder boomed, exciting her. The hurricane was deadly but playful. But not deadlier than Carita Leblanc. The hurricane gamboled and whirled and stabbed, stabbed the way her knife soon would stab. Both the hurricane and the knife would leave behind death and destruction.

Running, she had to turn, and somehow the wind changed. Now she had to fling her streaming, sodden body against the rain-drenched wind, straining and pushing toward Rivard. Her body was heavy and hard to manage, but she was only twenty-four, and it didn't matter.

Something struck her across the middle, knocking her flat on the watery ground. She was on her back in a pool of water, rain pouring without end. She struggled to a sitting position; lightning crashed. She pushed away the small tree limb which had hit her, and knife tightly clutched, slipping and sliding, got to her feet.

As she went, held back by the wind, she saw by the flashes of lightning trees whipping forward, tops hitting the sodden ground, leaves flattened under the downpour. She saw trees uprooted. A flying bush hit her in the face; she fell sidewise this time, fought harder to regain her footing.

They were chasing her. She couldn't hear them, not above the roar of thunder, the howl of wind, the crash of rain, but they were following her. They always did. But this time she would get away. She would finish the job.

She knew what this night was—that other, long-ago night, and she would kill them all. She flung her entire weight on the wind and it held her up, but still she made progress. This was all she had to do right now—take one step at a time. On and on.

It was René III who first grabbed her. She recognized his shout, so like that other René, the one she had to kill again, tonight. Someone else grabbed her wrist, gave it a wrenching turn, got the knife, but not before she cut him, whoever he was.

Another pair of hands laid hold on her. There were three of the enemy. Three to keep her from what she had to do. She twisted and yanked and tried to bite and kick, but they overpowered her. Now, ignoring her vicious struggling, they dragged her back the way she had come, face up to the rain, heels making tracks in the mud.

She began to scream, to shriek.

She knew they had gotten her back to the house, knew it was Celeste who gave her the laudanum, knew that André and René III and Gab, his arm bleeding, held her. She saw Euphemie and that new one, Ramona.

The men carried her upstairs and laid her on a couch. As her mind clouded over, as it went under, she was faintly aware of hands stripping, drying, patting, dressing.

When she slept, they sat beside her, listening to the hurricane as it roistered on and on, as it reached its still, windless part, as it blew afresh, and, at last, lessened, whirling away.

Carita slept on. Celeste returned to her room, exhausted. Consuela, a lump on her head from the pitcher Carita had thrown, sat with her mad, pitiful sister and wept.

Chapter XXXVI

At Rivard, the hurricane slashed and smashed, but those within the overseer's house paid no attention to the storm. Their ears were attuned only to the moans and piercing screams which came from Tansey's room.

Birdie stood gripping one of Tansey's hands; Beau gripped the other. The old midwife hovered over Tansey, her voice a constant murmur, a singsong litany of "push down, honey . . . push . . . push . . . like when yo' shit . . . harder . . . push . . ."

Deedee and Olive stood ready to help; Hercules stood in one corner out of the way, head back, eyes closed, lips moving. Prayer was written on his face, in his stance. Three black women moved in and out, bearing scissors, steaming water, white cloths. They were silent, quick.

When the old midwife told them to put a knife under the mattress to cut the pain, they did so, the sharpest knife to be found. They added their voices to that of the midwife, urging Tansey to "push . . . push . . ."

Riel stood in everyone's way at the foot of the bed, immovable. The doctor hadn't come, couldn't come, not in this killer hurricane. Riel had to depend on the midwife, on Deedee, on Olive.

Deedee came to stand with him. "If we go to the side of the room," she said, "it'll make it easier for them to help Tansey."

"She's got to help herself," he said grimly. He pulled away from Deedee's hand, moved up the bed, stooped over the writhing girl, her hips lifted from the mattress, her words a constant scream.

"Stop it!" he yelled. "Do what you're told! Push, damnit, push!"

Her hips smacked onto the mattress, stayed there. The

screams cut off. She pushed visibly, pushed so hard her lips skinned back and the cords of her neck stood out. She was sweating profusely.

"Harder!" yelled Riel. "That's not good enough—harder!"

He was aware that the midstorm lull had come and gone. The wind, now blowing from the opposite direction, was noisier, rougher. The wind slammed tree limbs against the shuttered house, got its windy hands on the corner of the roof and yanked until the house shivered, then slid away, seeking easier game.

And all the while, Tansey, crazed with fear and pain, heard faintly and far away Riel's inexorable shout, "Push! Harder! Shit the baby out; do it now!"

The storm blew its wrath, shouted its laughter at what was taking place in that room. Gradually, it passed; its sounds abated, faded, were gone. Only the downpour of rain was left.

It was then that Tansey's baby shot forth into the midwife's hands, and Riel saw that it was a boy, blacker by far than Beau, blacker, if possible, than Tansey herself.

Riel gripped the footboard of the bed. He trembled; he shook; he wept. Emotion, wilder than the hurricane just gone, tore through him. He bent forward, clinging to the bed, sobs gulping and wracking him as violently as the hurricane had raged over the bayous.

Deedee and Birdie cleaned the baby, dried him. The other women cleaned Tansey, cleared away the afterbirth. Beau hovered between Tansey and the baby and went to neither, not knowing where to turn or what to do.

"I want to see him bare," Riel said now.

"Hold out your arms," Deedee told him. "Take your grandson."

He held his arms stiffly, like sticks, the baby on them. His eyes swept the sturdy, squalling infant from head to toe. Yes. Black, by God. He'd done it. This one was all black. The son of this child would lock in the blackness.

He became aware of Beau, gazing at the baby. "What are you going to call him?" he asked.

"Tansey likes the name Ben," Beau replied. He touched the baby's heaving little chest with one finger. "Shouldn't someone make him quit crying?"

Deedee, smiling at the ineptness of men, took the baby.

Birdie helped dress him. Deedee held him over her shoulder, patted his back. The crying ceased, and he began to nuzzle.

When Tansey had viewed and accepted him and he was sucking at her breast, Riel drew a chair to the side of the bed. "You're a true Rivard now."

"What you mean?"

"You're as black as any Rivard ever will be, and you've given us a black heir. When he marries a black girl, there'll be no part of the white left."

He was right back at it, scaring her again. What if Ben had taken after Beau? Papa Rivard wouldn't be sitting here so friendly then.

"No part of the white that is left shows," Deedee said gently. She looked down on the plump, newly born infant, flooded with love for him.

Olive gazed at her first great-grandchild in awe. Her heart beat numbly. He is so very black, she thought.

"See, Mama?" challenged Riel, a flash of the young Riel on him. "It's worked, just like the chickens, only better! You guessed about the chickens, I know you did!"

"I . . . suspected," she agreed and smiled because of his joy, a sad smile.

Deedee studied the two of them. She understood Olive's feeling, for she herself felt as strongly, though in reverse. Deedee's descendants were regaining the black blood they had lost; Olive's descendants were losing—had already lost—all their white blood.

Unknown to Ramona, René was on his way to bed an enchanting little seamstress named Alberta Smith when he spied a lovely wench flipping along the street. She was carrying a baby on her arm, but that he ignored.

He'd rarely seen such enticing hips. Their shape and the switch they made aroused him. He walked behind her, watching those hips, noting how her hair was in tiny braids, each braid laced with narrow red ribbon.

The wench knew someone was behind her; he could tell by the extra flip she gave. Suddenly she turned and looked up at him; he saw the lovely face, the provocative smile, and burned.

Tansey, free to leave the plantation on the condition she

take Ben with her, smiled on at René. "Please, sir," she said breathlessly, great dark eyes roving him, lingering at the hump in his trousers, "could you help Tansey?" She gave him her special look. He was hot and handsome, all of him, hot and handsome for her.

"What can I do for you?" he asked.

She indicated the ribbons in her hair. "I don't know where to buy these. I pine for some yaller ones, and Beau, that my husband, he give me some money, but I don't know what store."

He watched her closely. Those slanting glances said more than her lips, told him she was ready to be intimate with him, that he had only to speak.

"Are you always this charming to white men?"

"Nevah before." She stared at her bare toes. "And I don't even know youah name. I'm Tansey Rivard."

"I'm René Leblanc," he said, and waited.

She recognized the name. She was impressed. Her eyes became more enticing.

"You like your fun, don't you?" he asked.

"Yes, sir. I got a mothah-in-law watches me close, but I'm goin' to have my fun. I can fool her."

"Then you'll meet me where we can have fun?" I'm a fool, he thought, remembering Ramona's jealousy, yet Ramona hadn't suspected about Alberta. How could she possibly know about Tansey? Once was all he needed with the wench. It was perfectly safe.

Eyes dancing, switching her hips as she rocked the baby, who had begun to fret, Tansey said, "I know a wondahful place! It's on Rivard land, right where it joins Leblanc land. It's got a rose arbor on it that'd look like a little house if it was cut back. And it's hid. Nobody knows how to find it but me." She went on, giving him landmarks, and when they parted, they agreed to meet there the next day.

She went into the shop he pointed out, and he decided to skip his visit to Alberta. He didn't want her now, didn't want to take the edge off his anticipation of Tansey.

When he got home, for no reason he knew, Ramona accused him of having a mistress. Her eyes were flashing; the heat of her rage licked out at him.

"What do you base that accusation on?" he demanded. "I bed you every night. You keep me drained."

"Oh, no! Don't tell me you haven't got some little doxy you see in St. Martinville! You go to town a lot more than you used to!"

He finally calmed her by taking her to bed. Their lovemaking was more frenzied than it had been in weeks. At last she had had enough.

"There," he chided, stroking her breast, "if I'd been with another woman this morning, could I have done this so many times?"

"That's what you always say! But you're an animal; there's no end to the times you can go at a woman! Don't ever try to deceive me, René Leblanc. You've been fully warned!"

He thought of tomorrow's assignation with Tansey. He stretched luxuriously. Tansey in the morning, Ramona at night. Not bad. He began to look forward to it.

He found the rose bower ten minutes before Tansey got there. He studied the shaggy beauty of the flowering house, compared it to Grape House, wondered if that Gabriel Leblanc had built this, too. Perhaps Gabriel, too, had met some wench on Rivard land.

Tansey was running when she arrived. She had the baby with her. He was nursing her full black breast as she ran, the motion seeming not to bother him at all. She sank to the ground within the rose house, rocked him to sleep in her arms, drew the nipple out of his lax mouth. René grew hard. He'd never seen a tall nipple, black as coal, before. He watched her lay the sleeping baby down.

"Why did you bring the baby?" he asked.

"To fool my mothah-in-law. She got me workin' next to her in the garden. I s'posed to take Ben to the house to feed him and stay for his nap. She acted like she wan't going to let me, scowled somethin' fierce, but fin'lly said I could have an houah. So I ain't got much time. We got to hurry!"

She took off her shift; she was naked underneath. Everything about her tilted up and out—hips, breasts, even the wool-covered mound. He tore off his trousers and entered her as she spread for him on the grass.

Boiling fire rode his veins, pounded in his ears, puddled and bubbled in his throat. She threw her hips up hard, giving a twist with each thrust, and he met it with a twist of his own. She felt him in her, big and almost hurting, but that added to her wildness and she tried to move faster than he did and could not. Within seconds they fused, his weight boring her into the ground, both of them mad with delight, the scent of roses masking their sweat.

She pulled away, grabbed her shift, put it on. Reluctantly, he reached for his trousers. Whereas he could satisfy Ramona three times, he felt he could deal with this torrid black beauty five times.

"Tomorrow?" he asked.

"If I can get my mothah-in-law to let me loose," Tansey promised. She snatched up her baby and was away, running lightly back toward her work.

René got home to find Carita at Old House, raving, shrieking at an angry, horrified Ramona. Consuela and Celeste were trying to draw Carita away.

"How did she get loose?" asked René.

"She ordah me to fix her bath," Consuela explained. "When I bent ovah the tub, she grabbed the key off my belt and ran!"

"She was hunting for the dagger!" cried Ramona. "Then she wanted to tell me about the Journals, and I wanted to hear! And every word made me more furious at you, René Leblanc! She just got to the part about her husband and that big hurricane, the part where she killed everyone, then turned the dagger on herself!"

"Where is he now?" Carita screamed. "Where is that stud, René? I know he's here."

"It's a different René now!" Ramona spat.

"No, there he is!" Carita whirled, glared at René III, then flew at him, fingers arched. He floored her with one blow, and they got her back to L'Acadie and under laudanum.

Ramona, who had followed, raged. "I told you I never wanted to see that hag! But she found me, filled me with all those lies. Or were they lies?"

"Nobody knows," René said warily. He looked at André, who had heard the commotion and come to investigate. "Are the Leblanc Journals true, Grandpa?"

"Unfortunately, yes."

"Then she did kill with an emerald dagger?" exclaimed Ramona.

"She did, Ramona. And she's searched for it, in her

madness, ever since. Old René hid it where she would never find it."

"And you know where?"

"Yes."

"And Mama Leblanc knows?"

"She knows."

"And René's pa?"

"No. Not Gab."

"Then I've a right to know, and so does René! We're the new generation! If something should happen to you—it's worth a fortune, I know it is!"

"True," André admitted, "and it's time another generation knows. When L'Acadie was built, a secret floor well was installed in the library. The boards fit perfectly with the rest of the floor. The dagger is in that well. Over it rests the carpet, and at that spot sits the leather chair Old René always used."

"What else is in the well?" Ramona demanded.

"Nothing. Just the dagger."

Triumphant, Ramona smiled when André left, then turned on René. "Where did you go this morning?" she demanded, suddenly back to her earlier suspicions.

"Down-bayou in the pirogue. Studied our shoreline to see if we need to build up our levee."

"And do we?"

"In a few places, yes. I'll get a couple of the men to start work on it Monday."

"How do I know you didn't go to some doxy?"

"Ramona," he said reasonably, "I wasn't gone long enough to row to St. Martinville, meet some imaginary woman, and then row back home. I was gone just long enough to oar down-bayou to where our land ends, look about a bit, and oar back. And find you with Carita on your hands."

"She opened my eyes, now that I know the Journals were true! You are just like her René, a stud, unfaithful to your wife."

"Don't let a crazy woman tear up our marriage, Ramona," René said earnestly. "I want you for always." And indeed he did want her, all her fire, all her passion. He'd broken off with Alberta.

And Tansey was just for now.

Chapter XXXVII

Tansey, her sport with René still undetected, now used the same ruse with Deedee every day. Deedee, though she didn't trust the girl, believed she only had enough time to feed Ben, let him nap shortly, then return. It never entered her mind that one black man, then another, slipped into the overseer's house and into bed with Tansey, or that many days Tansey went running to the secret rose house and back. When Tansey's milk dried up and she had to fix a bottle, it was only natural that she needed a bit more time and this, in good conscience, Deedee granted, though she still saw Tansey's sly glances at men.

Growing more uneasy, Deedee decided the best thing was to keep Tansey in sight at all times. "It's time to start your training," Deedee announced one day. "We'll both take off from garden work and devote ourselves to the big house."

"You mean you goin' learn me to be mistress now?" wailed Tansey.

"Precisely. Beginning tomorrow. The first thing we'll do, each day, is wash the breakfast dishes; next, we clean the house."

"I already do them things! And take care of Ben and work in the garden! I don't need to be trained!"

"There's furniture polishing—that's a real art—and making beds so they look beautiful. Also, there's setting the table different ways for different occasions, and arranging flowers. You'll have lessons on how to entertain gracefully, using the house instead of the Quarters, and between all this, you'll learn to play the piano and take care of Ben."

"That keep me busy ev'ry minute!" Tansey let her horror show.

"It's a heavy load I know," Deedee said. "Last of all, you'll have to learn to cook and sew."

"I already a good cook from my mammy!"

"Indeed you are. But there are special dishes, and cakes and jellies. And you'll have to learn to deal with the tenants' wives, and also learn how to speak properly."

"You mean I got to go to school?"

"Of course not. But you'll spend time at the big house with Mama Rivard and me. Pay attention to the way we speak, and the way Beau and Riel and your own parents speak, and you'll learn."

Suddenly, Tansey flared. "Maybe I ain't good 'nuff to be mistress! I already keep a clean house and cook and garden and take care Ben."

"You're the future mistress of Rivard," Deedee said patiently. "You have responsibilities. Please. For Beau and Ben."

Tansey scowled, thinking fast. "We-ll. Maybe. If you'll let it wait till Ben's walkin' and talkin', then I'll do it. But no school."

Tansey watched Deedee consider. What she'd said about Ben was a long time off. She could bed men for awhile longer. After that, well, she'd settle down to being a lady, she really would.

Deedee studied Tansey. Better to wait another year, she thought, keep a constant watch, than anger the girl so she'd never cooperate. So she agreed to Tansey's terms.

They continued the garden work, with Tansey going to the house to feed Ben. Sometimes Deedee walked part way with her, saying it rested her back, but in reality Deedee wanted to keep Tansey under observation a bit longer.

One day when they passed Boisy the blacksmith, Deedee saw the extra flip Tansey gave her hips, caught the intense, starved look on Boisy. When he spoke to Tansey, she ignored him, snubbed him openly, yet she flipped her hips again.

Deedee pulled in an unsteady breath. Did her son's wife truly dislike Boisy, or was she leading him on? If Tansey was going to become a reliable Rivard mistress, she had to become trustworthy. Perhaps she already was. But Deedee wondered. And she worried. And kept watch.

As for Boisy, he felt if he didn't get that little twist soon, his enormous, strong body would burst wide open. He, too, started to keep watch on Tansey, soon learning that the only time she was away from the mistress was when she fed her sucker. So he began to leave his forge to see where she went, and mostly it was to the overseer's house which was now hers and Beau's. But other days, she took her son and ran straight for the wilderness.

On one of these days, Boisy followed. Hidden in a clump of bushes, he watched Tansey strip, sucked in his breath at her tits and butt, watched her go wild in the arms of a white man. Then she grabbed up her sucker after putting her shift back on, grabbed his empty bottle, went running back to Rivard. Afire for her, Boisy followed cautiously.

He didn't know who the white man was, didn't care. Boisy the blacksmith was more of a man; he could make that hip-slinging wench go crazy and fall to her knees begging for more. And he could do it faster than the white man.

As he stole through the trees, he heard something moving off to his right, so hid behind a great oak and peered forth. The mistress was going back toward Rivard, too, coming from near where he'd been; her face was frowning and upset.

Deedee's pulse was drumming heavily. She'd become very suspicious today—Tansey was too anxious to take Ben to the house for his bottle—and she'd worked her way to the edge of the garden where she could hide but still see the overseer's house. In no time at all, Tansey appeared, carrying Ben and the bottle, and she was running. Across the quarters she ran, past the growing corn, into the trees and untamed growth.

Deedee dared not run in pursuit lest Tansey hear her, but she walked swiftly and lightly, following the sounds the girl made. From a screen of wild rose vine, she saw the shaggy rose house, Ben off to one side sucking his bottle, the naked Tansey in the arms of a white man, that René Leblanc III. Deedee held her breath until it stabbed, and then she crept away and returned to the garden and began to work.

She dared not tell Riel, so set up over Ben. She dared not tell Beau, so crazy in love with Tansey. She dared not confront the girl herself, for she would weep and deny, even go to Beau with her lies. That would reach Riel, and that must never be. She, Deedee, had the job of straightening out her son's wife, of protecting Beau and Riel, of keeping the name Rivard unsullied.

She was weeding furiously when Tansey came back with the sleeping Ben, put him in the shade, returned to her own weeding. Her expression was normal, even content. She hoed weeds methodically, gathered them into small heaps to be disposed of later.

Working, Deedee decided on the best plan she could think of. She'd let Tansey leave the garden just long enough to fetch Ben's bottle to the garden, where he could drink it. She'd see to it that Tansey had more garden work, keep her busy every second. And in the evening when she was supposed to cook Beau's supper, if she still strayed then Deedee would have to confront her. She would promise to tell Riel and Beau what Tansey had been doing unless she changed her ways. That, she was convinced, would bring Tansey up with a jerk. Because Tansey was afraid of Riel.

One evening, early, Ben fussed and cried and chewed his fist, and there was no quieting him. "He hungry," Tansey said.

Deedee instantly suspected that Tansey had given him less milk in the last bottle so he would cry early for the next. And this might give Tansey a chance to slip away. Still, Beau was due in from the field in less than an hour, so she relented.

"You'd better feed him," she said. She smiled at the kicking, squalling baby. "My, he's mad!"

"I won't come back," Tansey said. "It soon be time to cook Beau his suppah."

Deedee hesitated, nodded. She'd work at the end of the garden Tansey must pass to get to the rose house. In a way, it was a test. If Tansey stayed at home, it was an indication she may have broken off with the white man.

Boisy, leaving his forge to get a supply of iron from the stable, saw Tansey go into the house with her sucker. When she was inside, he made his move. It was the first chance he'd had; hell only knew when he'd have the next one. Now he'd show her what a man he was.

He sneaked into her kitchen door, found the room empty. From the front of the house, came the sucker's squall. He moved to the bedroom where the noise was, paused in the doorway.

Tansey was stooped over the sucker's bed, changing his clout. A bottle of milk stood on the table near at hand.

Boisy dropped his trousers, stepped out of them, reached her in two noiseless strides. He stooped, caught the bottom of her shift and had it up and over her head before she even knew anybody was there.

She whirled; her eyes flew wide. She opened her mouth to scream, but he had one treelike arm around her in a flash, and one big hand over her mouth. Not a sound came out of it, not a whisper.

"Yo' got a real man holdin' yo' now," he said. His penis surged up, hit her in the belly, and he moved, grinding it against her. Then, standing away slightly, he moved so it waved in the air. "Evah see one like dat?" he challenged. "Boisy goin' shove it in yo', make yo' happiest wench on de plantation!"

Eyes wild, she tried to bite him. He pushed his hand against her lips so cruelly they parted, bruised, and then he pushed against her teeth until they ached, doing it so she couldn't open her mouth.

She squirmed, tried to kick, but he held her. The sucker squalled on. Boisy thought if he dast move his hand from her mouth, he'd poke that bottle into the sucker's mouth, quiet him down, but if he did that, she'd screech. Well, once he got his cock into her, there'd be no screeching; she'd be too busy, too crazy for more.

Lips splitting from his hand, teeth ready to pop out of her gums and into her throat, Tansey struggled. He took his hand off her mouth, but before she could scream, he clouted her in the head.

"Yo' want more of dat, yo' jus' yell," he growled. As he spoke, he scooped her against his tremendous, sweaty torso, stepped to the bed, dumped her.

She flew to a sitting position. He struck her alongside the head, knocking her back down. "Don' spoil yo' own fun," he warned. "It don' spoil my fun, 'cause Boisy like it when a wench fight. It make it dat much bettah when she beg fo' dis!"

Tansey tried to get off the bed. Grinning, he held her down with one hand, with the other moved his great, hard penis back and forth.

"Know who de real mastah at Rivard is?" he chortled. "Dis cock! Not but a wench wan' it! An' yo' wan' it!"

"No!" she whispered with numb, bleeding lips. "No!"

"Dat's de way, hol' yo' voice down. Yo' wan' it onct it git into yo'." He straddled her. She bucked, trying to throw him off, but he held her flat across the mouth with one great hand, captured her wrists with the other, rammed his mammoth member into her inner recesses. Pain shot to every point in her body. He pounded, and every blow of his stinking body put pain through her, but she couldn't scream, couldn't even moan louder than his bestial growling. Finally, she managed to get her teeth onto the side of his hand and sank them in until they grated against bone. It didn't stop him. On he pounded, and on the baby screamed.

Somebody would come. The black she had an assignation with. Somebody would save her. Somebody would know; she never let Ben cry this way. She was sore, so sore; she felt she was bleeding, and still the beast who rode her tore and pounded and growled and cursed his delight.

She tried to twist away from him, but this he took as enjoyment on her part and rutted even harder. She found it was easier just to lie there and let him do what he was going to do anyway.

He was crushing her, ripping her, smothering her with his weight and his stink. She gasped, trying to breathe, letting go of the hand she had bitten. No other man had been like this. No other man had made her dirty and full of pain and shame. This animal was ruining her; Ben was hungry and crying. And nobody, nobody at all, came to see what was wrong.

Never had Boisy had a juicier wench. He liked the way her flesh sprang back when he took his weight off, ready to crash down onto her again, thrust after thrust after thrust. He'd never felt so powerful with a wench; he was taken by shudders of raw passion when she fought to get out from under him. He went crazy with joy when she lay still to let him do what he would.

Tansey, near fainting, existed in a world of torture. Blood from his hand wet her neck, her face. She was bleeding, too, down below. He went rigid at the last; she felt shudder after shudder jerk through him, and then he left the bed and put on his trousers. And she lay, spent, motionless.

"Dat wuz sumpin', baby," he growled. "Us do it reg'lar, now dat yo' know. Us de bes' pair on Rivard. Boisy be back anothah day, mebbe tomorrah. Yo' be ready."

He was gone.

Heavily, she pulled herself up and sat on the edge of the bed. Ben squalled on. Numbly, she swiped at her bleeding mouth, stared at the blood running down her legs.

Naked, bleeding, throbbing, pain raging between her legs, she moved to Ben's crib, took the bottle, pressed the nipple into his mouth. His dimpled hands clutched the bottle and he sucked noisily, the last tears drying on the sides of his face.

Trembling, she picked up her shift, put it on. Where had Mama Deedee been, with the baby crying so? Mama Deedee was always there, watching, keeping her busy. Sometimes Tansey felt Mama Deedee was keeping her from men. Only not today.

Nobody had come. Nobody at all.

Chapter XXXVIII

Sobbing, Tansey got to the kitchen, filled a pan with water. She stripped off her shift again, reached for homemade yellow soap, wet a rag and began to rub soap onto it. Blood kept running down her legs; the broken lip hurt and her head thumped.

She didn't even know when Beau got home until he shouted, "Tansey, what's wrong? What happened to you?"

Rag in hand, water running off it, she turned. He saw her ravaged face, the lump rising on her forehead, the broken lip, the blood on chin and neck and breasts. He saw the blood creeping down her legs.

She screamed when she saw him, screamed and screamed. Sobbed, gulping. She swayed and would have fallen, but he grabbed her by the arms. He searched into her face, saw the panic.

"What happened?" he yelled, again and again, but she could only scream and weep. Ben began to cry again, but Beau ignored his shrieks. Finally, Beau slapped her, a ringing slap on the cheek which rocked her head.

Her screaming stopped. She stared at him, blubbering.

"What happened?" he roared. "Tell me, and tell me now!"

Words tore out of her. "Boisy, he done it." She began to scream again. "Snuk up . . . from behind . . ."

That was all Beau needed. He'd seen Boisy look at Tansey; he knew Boisy was a stud. He let go of Tansey, rushed out the door and along the path. He was unaware that stragglers coming in turned and followed him, and others from the cabins followed, too, drawn by his maddened look, by his pelting run.

As Beau neared the blacksmith shop, Boisy, whistling, was clearing up for the night, standing newly sharpened hoes on end, leaning a new scythe against the wall, pausing to stroke the rawhide whip he used for sport, making sure it hung neatly from the loop at its handle.

Beau came to such an abrupt stop he had to catch his balance. "Step out here!" he yelled at Boisy. "I know what you did to Tansey, and I'm going to kill you!"

Boisy stayed where he was, socked big fists onto his hips. A huge grin split his face, showing wide yellow teeth. "Kill ovah dat lil' hot wench?" he rumbled. "W'y, Boisy ain' de on'y one, Beau. She got othahs, an' she got a white man she love out in de woods. I bin followerin' huh."

The field hands, both men and women, heard the exchange. Tansey came, screaming and bleeding, Ben on her hip, her shift on backwards. "Be careful, Beau!" she shrilled. "He'll kill you!"

Even as Tansey screamed, Beau swung, crashing a fist into Boisy's nose. Boisy rocked back, caught his balance, nose bloody. "Boisy warn yo'," he bellowed. "Yo' fight Boisy, yo' daid! He twict yo' size, an' he powahful!"

Beau's reply was another crushing blow, this time to the neck, and Boisy staggered and wove before he steadied, and then he lowered his head, came at a run for Beau who was plunging at him, and rammed that head into Beau's belly.

Beau doubled over, but somehow kept on his feet as he ran backward, digging his heels in to reverse his direction. Boisy was on him before he could move forward again, pummeling him in the ribs. They grappled, Beau smashing his fist under Boisy's heart, bringing up a knee, driving it into the blacksmith's groin.

Women screamed; children cried. More workers arrived on the run finding them now on the ground, rolling and punching, trying for each other's neck. Four strong men dove onto the fighters, heaved to pull them apart and could not, they were so viciously intertwined.

Deedee, rushing from the house, got there as Beau and Boisy fought to their feet, hugging each other, trying for the kill. She flew at them, hands out to stop them, but was swept aside and landed on the ground, her chin striking the earth so hard she bit her tongue severely, and blood flowed out and over her chin.

Tansey saw this, but her eyes were stuck to Beau and Boisy. She knew Boisy would kill Beau, and there was nothing anybody could do about it. Teeth chattering, she let Birdie take the whimpering Ben, and continued to watch. She knew that women were helping Deedee up, that Olive was staunching the blood from her tongue but, terror-stricken, Tansey didn't offer to help or try to separate Beau and Boisy.

They were still on their feet, eyes deadly on each other, weaving for position, arms held out from sides, hands ready for the neck.

Beau was large and very strong. Boisy was mammoth, even stronger. They closed again, but Beau was quicker. He got his fingers around Boisy's great neck, went for the windpipe; a split second, and Boisy had Beau's neck, crushing down on the windpipe. Like a macabre dance, they swayed and stepped, swayed again, crushing each other's windpipe. Sweat was rolling down their faces, across bared teeth, down their chins and onto their hands. Sweat covered their torsos. Their feet braced on the ground, moved only as one or the other forced movement.

Gradually the struggle became one-sided with Beau destined to lose. Again, workers pulled and shoved and yanked to part them and were kicked away, but the kicking loosed the holds on the necks and the two stood free for an instant. Then Boisy grabbed the razor-sharp scythe and came at Beau. Beau leapt aside, seized a hoe.

With desperate speed, lips skinned back, Beau chopped at Boisy's arms, cutting one of them deeply. Boisy, his face that of an enraged animal, lifted the scythe again, Beau chopped at his other arm, and the scythe landed on the ground, blade up. As Boisy dived for it, Beau hit him between the shoulders with the hoe. Boisy crashed down, landing on the terrible blade, landing on his throat, partially decapitating himself, and was suddenly dead.

Riel, last in from the fields, rushed to the crowd to see what was happening. He pushed through stricken men, sobbing women, silent children. He saw Boisy, dead, blood puddled about him. He saw Beau, gripping the hoe, staring open-mouthed at Boisy.

He saw Tansey, bloody. He saw Deedee, blood coming onto her chin, Olive swabbing it with a handkerchief. He turned questioningly to Beau, who couldn't speak, who only shook his head.

He stood before Olive, spoke to her.

"They fought over Tansey," she told him.

Tansey, sobbing, had followed Riel. "He raped me!" she screamed. "Boisy raped me! Pappy," she screamed to Hercules, who had come to be with her, "he raped me! He ought to have been killed!"

A voice from the workers called out. "Boisy said she had a white lovah!"

"That's a lie!" gasped Beau, throwing the hoe aside.

Riel, dumbstruck, clenched his fists to keep his hands off Tansey. Whatever had started this, he had a gut feeling that it was her fault. All of it.

He walked to Beau. "You did fight him, son?"

Beau nodded, breath pumping.

"We'll have to call the sheriff," Riel said.

"It wasn't his fault!" cried Deedee, running to him, words slurred from her bitten tongue. "It wasn't Beau's fault! Sanctity of the home! That's the law, isn't it? Boisy came at Beau with the scythe—Beau only tried to protect himself! What happened was an accident! Beau didn't kill him—Boisy fell on the scythe when he was trying to kill Beau! That's what happened!"

Beau, beaten mercilessly, was too groggy to think. He

stared dully from one person to another, gaped at Tansey standing between Birdie and Hercules, wished that Tansey would come to him, but she didn't.

Deedee had come, was standing close enough to touch him, and she grasped his arm and continued to scream in defense of him. She screamed at all the people, at Riel, at the swiftly gathering dusk of night, telling them Beau had done no wrong, and Boisy had died by accident.

"He'll have to stand trial," Riel told her. "We'll have to wait."

"I won't wait!" shrieked Deedee. She snatched that whip of Boisy's, that killer whip he'd used as a toy, and advanced on Tansey. "It was you!" she screamed. "All of this was over you! I should have done this long ago! Let go of her, Hercules. This is justice!"

She grabbed Tansey's arm, yanked her away from her parents, and flung her bodily into the clearing near the dead Boisy. A groan ran through the crowd. Birdie thrust Ben into another woman's arms and started for the clearing. Hercules overtook her, brought her back.

"Our daughtah did wrong," he rumbled. "She's been with men. I've seen her go. This is the only chance to save her—this, tonight."

Birdie began to weep and tried to get away from Hercules, but he held her, watching in horror.

Tansey cowered, bloodstained, terrified, weeping, wailing, trying to speak but unable to because of her sobs.

Deedee screamed, "This is because you fornicated on my son!" And she lifted the whip, swung the rawhide up and over her back, then brought it down, its lash cutting into Tansey, wrapping around her shoulders, breaking her flesh.

Tansey's scream rose to a shriek, held without letup as Deedee yanked the rawhide, unwound it from Tansey's shoulders, swung it back and up, then straight at the shrieking girl, this time wrapping the lash around her body, deep into her breasts. When she pulled it away, blood circled Tansey, and with the next lash, blood circled her hips, and the last time it cut her legs.

All the while, a moaning lament rose from those who watched the snap of the whip, the dull, cutting thud of it into flesh. Birdie and Hercules were weeping, and once Birdie cried out, "Run, Tansey . . . get away! It's enough, Deedee . . . enough!"

Beau, jolted into action, sprang to Deedee, tried to wrest the whip from her. She jerked it back, brought it crashing down on him, lacing around his legs. Riel tried next to get the rawhide, but she brought it around his shoulders, crying, "Are you going to let her ruin your plan? Are you?" And he fell back, as she resumed her whipping of Tansey, the rawhide wrapping and rewrapping around her body.

Again Beau tried to stop it. This time, Riel held him back. "Your ma's got a reason!" he shouted, and Deedee lashed on.

When the girl fell to the ground, Deedee cast the whip away. "That was for the rose house!" she panted. "Let's see if you'll be welcome there again!"

Chapter XXXIX

Law officers took Beau away to jail. Four strong workers dug a grave and buried Boisy. He had no one, not even a brother, to mourn him. The four stood a moment with bowed heads, and that was his service. Afterward, they returned soberly to their cabins.

Riel, who had watched, stood with Hercules. When they moved to part, Riel said dully, "I'd appreciate it if you serve as blacksmith from now on," and the black man said that he would.

That same night, his son in jail for murder, Riel oared to St. Martinville, went directly to the home of Gordon Lester, the attorney who had helped him years back.

Lester greeted him with surprise and took him into a square, luxurious, sitting room. "I'm alone tonight," he explained. "Hannah and the boys are spending a few days with her parents. What can I do for you, Riel?"

Riel sat on the chair indicated, looked squarely at his old schoolmate, and bluntly, in few words, told what had happened. "Will the law give my boy a trial?" he asked, when he had finished. "Does the fact that slaves are free entitle him to one?"

Lester considered. "Yes," he said, at length. "It'll be a test case, being the first in the bayou country since the war, but he can stand trial. The charge should be manslaughter rather than murder, if, as you say, the actual death was an accident."

"Beau meant to kill, in the heat of passion. But the way it happened was an accident. Boisy fell."

"The hard part will be getting a jury," Lester said.

"Does that mean you'll defend Beau? I'll pay. It'll take time, but I'll pay. I don't want to harm your career—you're the best attorney here—but I don't know where else to turn."

"I'll defend him, Riel," Lester said. "It'll be a challenge."

"How long will it take? How long will Beau have to stay in jail?"

"I'll get the trial date set soon. But don't forget—it's only a trial. If the jury finds Beau guilty of manslaughter, he can be in prison for years. If it finds him guilty of murder in the first degree, he'll be executed."

Riel nodded slowly. This trial endangered not only Beau's life, but the success of the Rivard dynasty. If Beau were to be executed, Riel would take over the rearing and training of Ben. The long, slow process would start again, with himself getting older. But first the trial. Lester would try, really try, to save Beau.

Back home, Riel found that Deedee had brought Ben to the big house.

"Where's the girl?" Riel asked.

"In the overseer's house. Your mama and Nette and Birdie are covering her with salves. They can't get her easy—she cries all the time, says she's on fire."

"Do you think she had men—even a white one?"

"I know she did. But no man'll have her after this."

He grunted.

"Well?" she asked. "Is Mr. Lester going to defend Beau?"

"He is. That's the one thing in our favor. He's the best defense attorney in St. Martinville."

"And the fact that he's defending one black man for killing another black, will that go in Beau's favor?"

"We haven't gone into that yet. I'm to go back to his office tomorrow."

"Tansey's no good, Riel! She'll sleep with any man! As soon as she's well, get rid of her! Keep Ben, keep Hercules and Birdie, but not Tansey!"

"It's for Beau to say whether Tansey stays or goes. He's head of that household."

"You think she'll settle down?" scoffed Deedee.

"After rape, after a killing, after a whipping that will scar her for life, what else can she do?"

Word of the killing traveled the bayous, and with it word that there was to be a trial. Everybody, even André Leblanc, was stunned.

The Lefleurs discussed the shocking news with the Hanins, just as it was being discussed on all the bayous. "What are we coming to?" cried Mae. "Why, when the darkies were slaves, the master tended to the punishment if one nigra killed another!"

"Not now," moaned Felicity. "Now they get a court trial, just like white folks, and who cares that nigra got killed, and who cares if the other nigra is executed? It'd be two less uppity nigras around!"

"They'll have a hard time getting a white jury," Lefleur predicted. "Surely the judge won't go so far as to allow nigra jurors."

"White men'll have to serve, want to or not," said Hanin. "But I predict they'll be angry white men sitting in those seats!"

"Talk has it that Prosecutor Ellis Crawford's fit to be tied!" squealed Mae. "I heard he came right out and said he'd as soon prosecute a wild hawg as a nigra! But he's got to do it!"

So went the talk, and so went the feeling. Beau Rivard didn't stand a chance, and he didn't deserve one.

Riel and Beau had two sessions with Gordon Lester, giving him the facts about the killing. It ended with Riel offering the attorney a fine, butchered hog and a butchered steer as fee, and Lester agreed. "I've eaten Rivard meat," he said. "I'll be only too glad to have my own supply."

Within two weeks court convened to hear the case of the State of Louisiana versus Beau Rivard, charged with the murder of Boisy, surname unknown, Negro blacksmith. Attorney Lester and Beau appeared from an inner room and sat at the defense table. Beau didn't so much as glance at the courtroom or try to seek out any face, not even Tansey's. He sat at the table with Lester, murmuring with him, sometimes nodding, other times shaking his head.

Prosecutor Crawford strode in and sat at his table, a rangy, sun-tanned man with a great wealth of white hair, piercing eyes, and a tremendous, permanent frown.

The bailiff moved about the front of the room. The court stenographer arranged his paper and pen on a small table near the witness stand.

The jury filed in, André Leblanc foreman, Charles Hebert behind him, their faces serious. The other jurors, all angry-looking whites, followed and took their seats.

When the judge appeared, all rose until he was seated, then resumed their places. There was a rustling sound, but no whispering.

André, gazing out over the room, saw that, with the exception of Rivard blacks, it was crowded with white men only. He studied Riel's expressionless face. The boy had chosen the hard way to live and breed; now the man must deal with the results of that boy's choice.

The judge addressed the witnesses—all of them black—directing them to remain closed in the inner room until called to testify. They filed out. Riel stayed where he was, because he'd not been present at the killing, thus couldn't testify. A few scattered Rivard blacks remained, also.

Crawford spoke first, for the State. He described the scene of the murder. Two black men, their kind not long free, had wanted the same woman. The husband, who admittedly had a right to her, had murdered in cold blood the alleged lover. The State would present its case and let the jury, comprised of honorable citizens, decide the accused's fate. With a flourish he laid his legal pad on the table and sat down. Beau listened to Crawford as though in a dream. None of this seemed real.

His father listened carefully; the prosecutor had said what Lester had predicted. Riel sat, impassive, containing his anger and anxiety. He studied the jurors. Would they vote his son guilty; would they impede the Rivard dynasty? Not André Leblanc, he thought hopefully; he was a just and thoughtful man. Not Hebert; he was known to be level-headed and fair in all his dealings. He studied the faces of the other jurors. Only God could predict how they would vote.

Lester rose and made his rebuttal. He portrayed Beau Rivard as the wronged husband who, in fighting his wife's rapist, had had the misfortune to see him fall on a scythe and be decapitated. The defense pleaded accidental death.

The Prosecution's first witness was called. He was a very black, wiry but strong man of forty. He sat on the witness seat uneasily.

Crawford now stated that all his witnesses were hostile, being black, and that judge and jury must hold this in mind as he proceeded with his case. The judge scowled and ordered him to proceed.

Crawford addressed the witness. "Your name?"

"Hiram, suh."

"Hiram what?"

"Hiram Ross."

"Were you present when Boisy the blacksmith was killed?"

"Yas, suh."

"You were present during the entire fight? You saw it all?"

"Yas, suh."

"Tell what happened that night of June tenth, 1895, when Boisy, the blacksmith was murdered, slaughtered by the son of his own employer."

"Objection!" Lester shot to his feet.

"Sustained."

"I'll rephrase the question, Your Honor. Now, Hiram, tell what you saw and heard between Boisy and Beau Rivard that night. Just use your own words."

"I work de cane dat day. Aftah work, evahbody was goin' to de quarters. I was in front, an' seen Mastah Beau when he first come up to Boisy."

"Did they talk?"

"Yas, suh."

"What did they say?"

"Mastah Beau was mad. He say, 'Step out here! I know what you done to Tansey, an' I'm goin' to kill you!'"

"Then what was said?"

"Boisy, he laugh. He say Tansey meet white man in de woods."

"What did they fight about?"

"Mastah Beau, he say Boisy rape Tansey."

"Did you see Boisy rape the wench?"

"No, suh."

"Do you know anybody who saw it?"

"No, suh."

"When did they begin to fight?"

"Right away, suh."

"How did they fight?"

"Wif' dey fists, at first. Den dey try to choke each othah."

"Yes. Go on."

"Some of de workahs try to part dem an' couldn't. Boisy, he grab de new scythe and go at Mastah Beau, den Mastah Beau he grab a hoe, and dey fight. Boisy, he drop de scythe, jus' as Mastah Beau cut him wif' de hoe, and he fall on his neck on the scythe and be daid."

"In other words, if Beau Rivard hadn't struck at Boisy with the hoe, he wouldn't have fallen?"

"Objection!"

"Sustained."

"You may cross-examine," snapped Crawford, and sat down.

Lester strolled over to Hiram, who was trembling. "Now, Hiram," he said. "Did you ever see Beau Rivard fight Boisy before?"

"No, suh, nevah."

"Did you ever see him fight anyone?"

"No, suh."

"Would you say he is a peace-loving man?"

"Objection! Asking for an opinion!"

"Sustained."

"Who else, besides you, watched the fight?"

"Evahbody, suh."

"Did you see Tansey Rivard watching?"

"Yas, suh."

"Did she look different than usual?"

"Yas, suh."

"In what way did she look different?"

"She was cryin' and she was bleedin'."

"Did she try to stop the fight?"

"I don't remembah, sir."

"When Beau Rivard hit Boisy with the hoe, did he push him toward the scythe?"

"Objection!"

"Sustained."

"What was it Beau Rivard did with the hoe?"

"He jus' hit Boisy."

"What did Boisy do?"

"He fall on de scythe."

"How did Beau Rivard look then? Pleased? Sorry?"

"Objection! What facial expression the Accused wore has no bearing—"

"Overruled. Answer the question."

"He look surprised, suh."

"Your witness," said Lester, and sat down.

A murmur had run over the courtroom. Crawford, his face thunderous, advanced on his witness. "You say Beau Rivard looked surprised."

"Yas, suh."

"Who taught you the difference between expressions?"

"I don' undahstan', suh."

"Who gave you lessons in telling the difference between a look of surprise and a look of satisfaction?"

"N-nobody, suh. It jus' seem dat way."

"Did Beau Rivard try to help Boisy after hc fell on the scythe?"

"No, suh."

"What did he do?"

"He jus' stood theah. Evahbody jus' stood."

"You didn't try to help Boisy?"

"No, suh."

"Why not?"

"His head was almost cut off, suh. He was daid."

Crawford faced the jury triumphantly, turned to the judge. "I've finished with the witness, Your Honor."

"You may step down," said the judge.

Looking frightened, Hiram got out of the chair and went to the back of the courtroom.

The trial ground on. André Leblanc listened carefully to each witness.

Crawford used Belinda Jones to bring out the whipping

Deedee Rivard had given Tansey. "After Boisy was dead, what did Deedee Rivard do?"

"Well, she was bleedin' . . ."

"Why was she bleeding?"

"She tried to part Beau and Boisy while they was fightin', and she bit her tongue."

"So she was bleeding. What did she do? Just stand there?"

"No. She blame Tansey fo' what happen, an' she grab dat rawhide whip Boisy had, an' she whip Tansey f'um head to toe."

"Did she say why she was doing it?"

"She say, 'Dis is 'cause you forn-cated on my son!'"

"Objection. This has no bearing on the case. The deceased was dead at the time it happened."

"Your Honor, my purpose is to prove that the Accused had cause to attack Boisy and try to kill him, and that the death was deliberate and planned!"

"Objection sustained."

The prosecution's last witness was Joe Blanchard, a square-built worker from Rivard. He was obviously a reluctant witness, but he answered Crawford's questions clearly. According to his testimony, Boisy's death had been premeditated, accident or no accident being the actual cause of death.

Riel's heart seemed to freeze. He sat like stone, endured.

Lester spoke quietly as he called his first witness, Deedee Rivard. "Mrs. Rivard, were you present on the evening of June tenth, 1895 when Boisy the blacksmith and your son Beau Rivard had an altercation?"

"I was."

"What was the cause of this altercation?"

"Objection!"

"Overruled."

"Tansey Rivard, my son's wife, said Boisy had raped her. She was bleeding."

"Did Boisy deny raping her?"

"He did not. He admitted it in a taunting way."

"What did Beau Rivard do then?"

"He attacked Boisy with his fists."

"Objection! Deedee Rivard wasn't present on the scene when the fight began! She cannot know, of her own knowledge, who hit first!"

"Sustained."

"Very well. When you arrived on the scene, they were fighting with their fists?"

"Yes."

"And in trying to part them, you were knocked down?"

"Yes. And bit my tongue and bled."

"Who grabbed the first weapon?"

"Boisy."

"What was it?"

"A new scythe."

"When did Beau Rivard get a weapon?"

"Right away."

"What was it?"

"A hoe."

"And they fought until Boisy dropped the scythe?"

"Objection. Leading the witness."

"I'll rephrase. What happened to the scythe?"

"Boisy dropped it."

"What did Beau Rivard do then?"

"He had the hoe up, in mid-strike, and it came between Boisy's shoulders, and Boisy fell on the scythe blade and died."

"Your witness," Lester said to Crawford.

The Prosecutor stood straddle-legged in front of the witness chair. He glared at Deedee.

"Beau Rivard had the hoe moving 'in mid-strike' when Boisy dropped the scythe?"

"Yes."

"Was it an accident that he had the hoe raised?"

"No."

"Was it an accident that he chopped the hoe down between Boisy's shoulders?"

"N-no."

"Your witness," Crawford said triumphantly to Lester.

Lester questioned Deedee gently. "Did your son put out his foot to trip Boisy and make him fall?"

"No."

"Did he use the hoe in any manner to guide Boisy's fall so that his neck would land on the blade?"

"No."

"Objection. Opinion of the witness."

"Sustained."

"How did your son act when Boisy died?"
"He was stunned."
"What did he say?"
"Nothing. He was speechless."
"Was the fall an accident?"
"Completely."
"Your witness."
Crawford gestured, declining to cross-examine.

Olive was called next, and testified that Boisy's death was an accident. Tansey, weeping and wailing, repeated what Olive had said. Birdie and Hercules testified that it was an accident.

Riel watched the jurors. Beau's fate was in their hands. All of them, Riel noted, had paid close attention. The judge gave them their instructions. Then they filed into the jury room to begin their deliberations.

The courtroom crowd waited for the verdict. Maybe it wouldn't take more than thirty minutes, it being nigras. Tansey wept constantly. Beau had never looked at her once when she was on the stand. Birdie sat close to her, murmuring. Hercules and Riel sat motionless, Riel's thoughts frozen on freedom. Beau must go free. Olive's back grew tired; she forced herself to sit straight, and prayed silently. Deedee wept, tears wetting her cheeks and running down her neck. The Rivard folk hoped for the best.

It was four hours before the jury filed back into their box again. The judge took his place on the bench. Crawford was at his table; Lester and Riel at theirs. The very air of the room seemed to tighten, to break under suspense.

The verdict was handed in and read. "We, the jury, find Beau Rivard guilty of accidental manslaughter. We recommend mercy in his sentencing."

All the Rivard women wept openly. Riel stiffened so he wouldn't shake. The sentence, he reminded himself, the sentence is yet to come. The sentence on which his own future, as well as Beau's, depended.

The judge didn't leave the bench. He considered briefly, then intoned, "Five years at hard labor. Sentence suspended."

Beau was expressionless. Deedee rushed to him, embraced him, shook hands with Lester. The other Rivard folk gathered round, shaking Beau's hand. Olive kissed him on the cheek. Tansey edged close, but Beau still didn't look at her. Deedee and Birdie, who hadn't spoken since the whipping, exchanged a long, cool look. Riel waited his turn, and then he embraced his son.

At Rivard, when Beau parted from the others, Tansey followed him into their house. There, tearing off her dress so that he might see the lash wounds circling her from shoulder to ankle, the forming scars which would never fade, she went on her knees to him.

"I swear," she wailed, "that it's you I love, only you! I sinned against you, and I repent. I'll nevah look at anothah man! Before the Lawd, I swear it, Beau! Don't punish me no more, Boisy was punishment enough, don't cast me off!" Her head tipped back; tears flowed over her lovely, unmarked face and into her mouth, and she swallowed them and wept on.

Beau's love for her, torn as her flesh from Boisy's rape and his mother's lash, filled him. He lifted her up and took her back into his bed.

Chapter XL

At first Tansey was content to be back with Beau. She didn't even mind working in the garden, where Deedee gave her still more to do, treating her coolly but with careful kindness.

Her monthly came, and everybody in the quarters as well as Riel and the rest of the family, knew. At least she'd escaped getting pregnant through rape.

But there was no excitement. No man to meet on the sly, and she was too young yet to really settle down. She decided that whatever she could do secretly and get away with, she had a right to do. Just so Beau never found out; he was her favorite man, her security.

The very first day in the garden, she found three red beads in the dirt and when she got home put them on a string and started a necklace. The necklace was a turning point.

Somehow, it set her mind free. She hated Boisy, who was dead, hated Deedee, who had whipped her, loved her mammy and pappy. And she loved Beau; he made her feel safe and warm.

She didn't forget her promises to Beau, but the lust for different men, especially René Leblanc, returned as she healed. She toyed with the idea of slipping away to the rose house. She just knew he'd go there from time to time, and if he did, he'd leave a mark—maybe some broken vines in a corner—to let her know. Besides, she had other men sliding looks at her again, and that was exciting.

She fingered her beads, thinking of different men. She'd like to have a necklace of lovers, a few beads from each one until the string was filled, and then she'd quit and there'd be only Beau.

Deedee made it harder now. She gave Tansey less time to feed Ben, but Tansey managed. She gave the baby his bottle, left him in his crib and ran like the wind to the rose house, and somebody really had broken the vine in one place. She broke it in another place as reply, sped back to the house, and Ben was asleep, so she picked him up and went back to work. Wednesday was the day René liked to meet, but before then she aimed to bed with that black David and maybe with the man from Mercer's.

It worked, in spite of Deedee. She met René at the rose house; David slipped into the overseer's house. The Mercer black found out the safe time, and he sneaked in too, no one the wiser.

And Tansey's necklace grew.

Beau noticed it and asked where she'd got it.

"I found some beads when I hoed in the corn," she said. "I keep watching."

Now Beau searched for beads in the fields, never finding any. Seeing Tansey's necklace grow, believing that she was still finding the beads, he promised her that when the cane was sold, he'd buy her a whole new string of beads.

"What color do you want?" he asked.

"I'll think on it," she said, not wanting his beads, but the one from her lovers.

One Wednesday when Deedee was picking beans, Tansey approached her. "I know I'm s'posed to stay in the garden," she began, then paused. It didn't bother Tansey a bit that she was meeting other men. What Beau never found out couldn't hurt him, and whatever she could put over on Deedee was a victory. Besides, in the end, when she had her beads, she was giving up all men but Beau. Which made everything she did in between all right.

"See that you do what you're supposed to do," Deedee said crisply in reply. "It's up to you." She wasn't going to keep following the girl. If Tansey sneaked away, sooner or later she'd be found out. And by that time, surely even Beau would want to be rid of her.

"What's up to me, ma'am?"

"Whether you have a good life. What sort of mistress you'll be for Rivard."

"I just want to go hunt fresh greens for Beau's suppah," Tansey said. "He likes 'em so with ham and grits."

"That means leaving the garden."

"For an houah or less. I can't get in no trouble findin' my husban' a basketful of greens. It won't take me an houah, even."

She knew a spot where she could fill her basket in a shake and have time for René, if he showed up. "And I'll take Ben," she added.

Grimly, Deedee gave consent. She couldn't make the girl a prisoner. Either she'd be fit to be Beau's wife, or she wouldn't.

Tansey, Ben on one hip, basket handle around her free arm, ran like the wind. At the patch of greens, she dumped Ben on the grass and let him cry while she filled her basket. Then she took him up, put the filled nursing bottle on top of the greens, ran for the rose house.

René was waiting.

"I didn't know if you'd come," he said. "I took a chance."

She flashed him a smile, dropped her basket, laid Ben in a corner with his bottle. She flipped her shift up and off, stood before him, turning, so that he could see how the scars wound round her body like a snake. The beads hung between her uptilted breasts.

"I heard she did that—your mother-in-law," René said. "But I never dreamed it would be so extensive."

"She tried to ruin my looks. But Beau don't mind." Naked, she switched her scarred hips, slanted him a look.

René was undressing fast, all his clothes, the first time

he'd ever done that. He saw her watching. "I want to feel those scars against my skin, all over me," he told her. "I find them exciting."

He held out his arms and she leapt into them. They fell to the grass, bodies entwined. The feel of him coming into her made such a wildness as she'd never known with him, and though she was still sore from the whipping, she took joy in their pumping and thrusting until fire ran from where they were coupled, clear into her head, down her back, and into the lower region again, ready to repeat itself. She gloried in seeing his white skin against her black. She lifted mightily so that her hips were in midair, and she held him there.

Hanging thus, borne up by Tansey, held by the flame which burned from him into her, René thought of the scars and flamed the hotter. Suddenly they slapped to the ground and she laughed, the notes drifting away into the trees.

While he tried to set their tryst for the following Wednesday, she scrambled into her shift. She straightened her beads, took the four new ones he gave her, shook her head.

"Week from Friday if I can," she said. "If I go to get greens same day ever' week, that Deedee get suspicious for sure. We got to keep changing the day—skip a week, even. Deedee one smart lady, but we smarter!"

She took her basket and her baby, went running homeward, fast as a bird could fly. She could fool Beau. She could fool Deedee. She could fool Riel Rivard.

Chapter XLI

When Tansey was pregnant again, though by what man she knew not, Beau was overjoyed at the news and called their parents in to visit and tell them. Proudly, his arm around Tansey, who was smiling uncertainly, he made the announcement.

Birdie rushed to her daughter, pulled her away from Beau, embraced her. Then she turned, hand on Tansey's scarred arm, and looked coldly at Deedee, the woman who had lashed her daughter. Hercules kissed Tansey, looked uncomfortably away from his glaring wife, muttered congratulations.

Riel, knowing of Tansey's monthly after the rape which meant this was not Boisy's child, and convinced for the moment of Tansey's fidelity, was deeply excited. He said at once that Tansey must do less work this time.

Deedee disagreed. "She worked hard while she carried Ben," she reminded them. "Her health was perfect, and Ben was perfect."

"He's only five months old," Riel pointed out. "It's bound to put a strain on her, two babies in fourteen months."

"She can start her training at Rivard now, instead of later when she'll have two children to look after," Deedee said. "She can also work in the garden for exercise."

"No!" Tansey cried. "You said I could wait! I'll start trainin' aftah the new baby, I promise! I'd rathah take Ben to the garden like I been doin' and work there!"

It wasn't that she wanted to keep on meeting men. It was that she didn't want to be mistress and run that big house. Pregnant, she was through with men now. All but René Leblanc. She wanted to keep up with him until the new baby was born, and from then on there'd never be anybody but Beau. She was smart, knew she couldn't keep up her secret life much longer.

It was agreed before the evening ended that Tansey could wait until after the new baby was born. Then she'd leave both babies in the Quarters with one of the younger girls while she was busy. She was purring inwardly when they all left.

"You'd better remember," Deedee told Riel as they undressed, "that Tansey hasn't been true to Beau. And Boisy did say there'd been a white man."

Riel went abruptly still. Then he put on his nightshirt. "Ben's Beau's son, looks exactly like him. Except he's black."

Deedee forced herself to continue. Riel must have some preparation, some warning. Fervently, she hoped it would prove nothing. "One day I followed her; I saw her with a white man."

He swung on her, his jaw like stone. "What man?" he grated. "Where?"

"I don't know him," she said, speaking a half-truth. "You don't know him. It was in the woods."

"But it wasn't very recent."

"N-no," she said, another half-truth.

"It was before the rape?"

"Yes."

"She did get raped. She got whipped. Those scars will never fade. Has she learned a lesson, or—Tell me, Deedee, have you seen her with the man again?"

"No, but I can't watch her every second. That's why I want her training here in the house."

"Beau tells me things are fine between them. He beds her every night."

"Then she's pregnant by him," Deedee said, relieved. "That's all that matters."

"And Beau wants her. He's to have her, but she's got to be kept straight. And we're the only ones to do it."

"When she wants to get wild greens for Beau, what then?"

"Give her a very short time."

Riel got into bed, seemingly calm, but Deedee knew he was roiling. For Tansey's betrayal of Beau threatened Riel's whole life plan. And he'd never let Tansey ruin it, no matter what he had to do to stop her.

Deedee settled into bed, lay against him. He was rigid. "This baby she's carrying," he said. "It's not to be born."

"The chances are that it's Beau's."

"Chances? I deal in realities!"

"You can't get one of those potions, Riel. Beau would turn against you, turn against breeding black. You can't use a potion!"

He lay silent. "Heavy work, then. In the fields. See to it she miscarries."

"And if she doesn't miscarry?"

"Then she'll have her baby."

"And if it isn't Beau's, how will you know?"

"I'll know. I'll decide." That was his last word on the subject.

Next day, Riel himself put Tansey to field work with her

mother, refused to let her go to the house for Ben's noon bottle. "You go, Birdie," he ordered. "Tansey can get more work done while you make the trip."

Day followed day and week followed week. Riel worked grimly with his flocks of chickens. Tansey did not miscarry; her muscles strengthened and her face shone with health. Only in the evenings, when she could leave a bit early to feed Ben before Beau came in from the fields, did she manage to see René, and then only for moments. They came together briefly, hotly, then she ran back, staggering, to her house where she left Ben in his crib, and he was always safe. And, miraculously, she was never caught.

Once Beau found her out of breath, and she said it was the field work; with her belly growing, it took her breath.

Beau sent straight to Riel and said he wanted Tansey out of the fields. "The garden's hard enough," he said. "I want her there."

Riel, figuring the time for miscarriage was past, grunted his consent. He was in the throes of his obsession now, willing and demanding of unseen powers that the child be black, breeding and crossbreeding his chickens.

Would this baby be as black as Ben? If he wasn't as black, could Beau be the father? Turning to his chickens for the answer, this idea went round in his head like a treadmill. Everything hinged on the new baby. Riel was curt with everyone but his wife and his grandson. He waited. The obsessive treadmill continued. He was so unapproachable that Olive was frightened of him, dared not ask what was wrong.

Tansey, worn out with scheming and running, her belly heavy, continued to meet René. Every time it was harder to get away. Each encounter was shorter than the last one. René, knowing their meetings were numbered, that Tansey could never manage them with two babies, partook of her like a starving man.

Deedee, frantic over Riel's obsession, followed Tansey one more time, saw her with René. After Tansey had left, running, Deedee returned slowly and went into the house.

All night she lay awake beside a tossing, dreaming, muttering, teeth-grinding Riel. What did she owe this beloved, tortured man—the truth about Tansey—or the right for him to clutch at hope? And if the baby, blessedly, was black, force Tansey to take her training as mistress, keep her so busy she could never betray the family again?

If she remained silent, Riel's obsession would deepen. But if she told what she knew, he'd be driven to some wild, unprecedented act. At last she decided to hold her tongue. She prayed that the baby would be black as coal.

Then, she thought, she'd have it out with Tansey, threaten exposure unless she settled down. And, if Tansey persisted in her deceitful ways, then she would tell Riel and he could deal with the matter.

As for Tansey, she still hadn't figured out whose baby it was. She'd been with Beau, with René, with David, with the Mercer field hand. When she let herself think about it, she was sure the baby would be black. Three chances against one for it to be black.

But then she'd think about Beau's pa, about how mean he spoke to her now, then would grab Ben and toss him in the air, catch him and kiss all over his laughing face. Once it seemed to her that Riel knew. And then she shrugged away the thought. If he knew, he'd act, and he did nothing at all.

After that she didn't worry very much. Just so the baby was black, that was all that mattered. Riel or no Riel. Chickens or no chickens.

Chapter XLII

René had changed. Ramona could smell it. She could feel it, in bed. The edge of his eagerness was dulled ever so slightly, but dulled. Which could mean only one thing—another woman.

She made no accusations; she watched, sensed. He didn't go off in his pirogue more often, in fact, it was less often. To Ramona, that meant the woman was nearby, and for some reason the assignations were less frequent. She waited, every nerve alert. She'd give him no warning, accuse him of nothing; she'd catch him in the act, and that was when she'd make her move.

Suddenly, as her time drew near, Tansey was scared. Scared that the new baby wouldn't be as black as Ben. She shivered so with René that he asked what was wrong, and she told him.

"Nobody can prove anything, even if it's mulatto," he said.

"Papa Riel can! He'll find a way!"

"How? It's impossible. You're too afraid of the man, Tansey!"

"That's what you think. But I wouldn't nevah tell on you, René. I'd claim it was a throw-back to Papa Riel himself!"

Uneasily, René made love to her. Next meeting would be the last. It was time to end it.

Ramona listened to René tell her how he was going downstream to inspect the levees. It was early morning, and she wasn't dressed yet and looked sultry and lovely.

"Why inspect them?" she asked, suspicion in full cry. "You did that last week!"

"So did pa. We agreed there were a few spots that'd bear watching."

She let him go without further comment, but René was uneasy as he went downstream to Tansey. He'd get it over with as gracefully as possible today, tell her they must part, never meet her again. He oared slowly, watching bayou traffic. He didn't want to be seen turning into the little bayou beyond which led to the rose house.

He'd taken but one stroke of the oar when Ramona jerked Sally, her buck-toothed maid, away from the bed which she was about to make. Sally, instantly terrified, cowered back.

"What Sally do now, Missy?" she quavered.

"Oh, you fool! Nothing, yet! But you're going to do something and do it well, or I'll make you sorry you were evah born!"

She backed the shrinking girl into a corner and, speaking fast, told her exactly what she was to do and why, and that she was to keep her mouth shut about it forever and ever.

Sally, face wet with instant tears, protested weakly but gave her promise, sobbing.

And then Sally went stumbling and crying for the mistress's own pirogue, got into it and followed the master up ahead. Stiff with fear that he look back and see her, she oared, sweating and sniffling. But when he turned into the little bayou he still hadn't looked back, and by the time she dared follow she saw his pirogue, empty, tied up, and him walking into the woods.

Drenched with fear, she trailed him, barely breathing, lest he turn and see her. He went on into the wilderness, Sally tiptoeing behind him, hiding behind one tree and then another, driven by her mistress's orders to find out where he went and what he did.

At last he stopped. Sally stood behind a big tree. She felt like her heart was climbing into her mouth.

Peering around the tree, she saw the rose arbor. In it were the master and that Tansey Rivard, and Tansey's belly was big with sucker. She saw the master put his arms around Tansey, and then she fled, trembling, back to the mistress's pirogue.

She tied up at L'Acadie landing, ran to Old House crying so hard. Sure enough, the mistress was waiting. She was holding a dagger set with green stones; her face looked as sharp as the dagger blade. She hit at Sally with her free hand, pushed her into the master suite, closed the door.

"What did you find out?" she hissed. "Stop that blubbering and talk!"

"The mastah he went to Rivard!"

"What did he do there?"

"M-met that Tansey. She m-married to—"

"I know who she married! Why did he meet her?"

"H-he put his arms 'round her an' they talk."

"Did he bed her? Did he?"

"I don' know. Her belly, it so big."

"You mean she's pregnant?" whispered Ramona, lips white. She began to stroke the dagger.

"She goin' to have a suckah."

"What did they do next?"

"I don' know. I too scairt to stay. He begun to kiss her an' feel her titties an' they goin' to take they time today, he said that. I rowed home, an' he nevah showed up behind me."

"They're still together!" whispered the mistress, eyes glittering. "This little bayou . . . is it the first one or the second one?"

"It the f-first, Missy." Then, as Ramona began to run for the stairs, Sally followed, wailing, "What you goin' do, Missy?"

Ramona didn't answer. She had the plan, full-born from the depths of her mind. The plan had lain dormant all these months until she should need it. And now she did.

She was going to catch René and Tansey in the act. And she was going to avenge herself.

She didn't know that after his session with Tansey, René had broken off with her, then gone to St. Martinville. Here he had bought a fine gold bracelet for Ramona, a coming-back-home gift, the significance of which she'd never know.

He'd felt relieved to be rid of Tansey; he'd tired of her. He hoped, for her sake, that her baby would be black, but if it was light-skinned no one would ever connect him with it.

At home, René couldn't find Ramona. Eventually he discovered Sally, face tear-swollen, cleaning the bedroom and doing everything wrong. The bedcovers hung awry, the window drapes didn't look as usual. Sally grabbed up the chamber pot, supposed to have been cleaned long ago, and tried to sidle past him.

"What's wrong?" he demanded. "Where's the mistress?"

The girl burst into sobs. Her shoulders jerked, and she hugged the chamber pot as if it were her only refuge.

René, staring at her, recalled vaguely that Ramona's pirogue hadn't been tied up at the landing. Surely she hadn't followed him! He turned on the blubbering, gulping Sally.

"Tell!" he gritted.

She shook her head, wailing, hugging the chamber pot.

Alarmed, angry, he carefully wrested the china pot from her, put it under the bed. He grabbed her shoulders and shook her until her head flopped. His alarm turned to apprehension as she continued to wail, and he gave her one last violent shake.

"Now, talk!" he roared, and pushed her so hard she landed on the bed.

Cowering, sobbing mightily, she stammered out what Ramona had demanded of her, how she'd followed him and what she'd seen, how she'd come rushing back, how Ramona had a green dagger when she ran to her pirogue and left.

Before Sally finished, René was on the run for his own pirogue. He had to overtake Ramona before she could get to Rivard, to Tansey.

Chapter XLIII

Tansey ran all the way back to the corn patch after René left. She was glad she'd been able to leave Ben with Old Granny today, because she had a stitch in her side from running and it'd hurt more if she'd had to carry him. The stitch gave a sudden, hard yank and she stopped and waited, holding her breath, until it was gone.

That was no stitch, she thought, running to get back into the corn before she was missed. Not a stitch, but a birthing pain. René must have brought it on, the way he'd pounded. It was a good thing she hadn't got caught in the rose house to birth. René would have left, of course, but she'd of had trouble explaining what she was doing there, away from the corn patch, having a baby.

Another pain took her; she doubled over but kept running as best she could. There was the corn patch just ahead where everybody thought she was. Another pain. She staggered on, crashed into the rows of yellowing stalks, found her hatchet, grabbed it. The pain gone, sweating from it, she swung at a stalk of corn, cutting it off near the ground, and it fell. She gripped the next stalk, cut it, heard it fall, cut the next, and the next.

Maybe the pains were just from sporting with René; maybe they'd stop. Maybe her time hadn't come, and when it did, she'd be safe in the house with Beau. If it happened like that, everything would be like before, with Ben. The baby would be black, Riel wouldn't do something horrible to punish her, and she'd never let any man but Beau touch her again.

She straightened, took a long breath, luxuriated in it.

Her hatchet-swinging went into a rhythm. She didn't feel exactly right, but that was from René. Those hadn't been birthing pains, they'd been René pains; she smiled at the idea. She felt her bead necklace, four new beads on it today. She put it away. She'd wear the new one that Beau was going to buy for her.

The new pain took her right in the belly. It felt like a huge needle stuck through her insides, pulling them together. She bent over, clutching the hatchet, unable to breathe, unable to call out to others at the far end of the patch, unable to scream. She wanted her mammy, her pappy, but Mammy was in field, Pappy was at his forge, and this really was a birthing pain, and she dared not go to the house for fear the baby be the wrong color.

When the pain let up, she straightened again, shakily cut another stalk. The sun beat down on her, making her sweat almost as much as the pain had done. She smelled the sun, smelled her body, the corn, the dirt. She cut another stalk, and another.

Her water broke. She stood trembling, water running down her legs, puddling at her feet. She didn't know, couldn't remember, if pain came first, then water, or the other way around. Or both at once.

When the water quit, a long pain knifed her the same instant she cut down another stalk. She moaned, but bit back her cries, for nobody must know. She was cutting this section alone, Deedee and the others at the far end, which was why she'd been able to get to René.

Arms shaking, she cut another stalk, another, another. She should go to the house, but she was terrified of Riel. She worked on, cutting stalks, enduring contractions, biting her lips and holding her breath as each one struck and passed. Surely it couldn't be long now. She'd have the baby here, alone, be sure it was black before she took it home. If it wasn't black, she'd have to leave it and run.

It was hard to stay on her feet. A long, terrible contraction cut its path through her, and she fell to the ground, clutching her belly, lips back, eyes stretched open. She swallowed her screams as this new pain cut and ravaged, swallowed her moans. She choked, and somehow managed to swallow her cough, and for an endless time she couldn't breathe.

The pain dwindled, slid out, away. Arms and legs dancing, she got to her hands and knees. She found her hatchet and began to cut stalks furiously. She had to keep working, had to destroy stalks; they drained her almost as much as the pain, but they built a kind of strength, one that let her endure each oncoming pain.

The world became a cornpatch, an agony of cutting stalks. It became a torment of staggering, of wildly slashing, of holding back moans, screams, which filled her along with the spasms.

Again the pains fought her to the ground; again, this time biting her lip through, she kept from screaming, from begging for help, from shrieking that somebody must get this baby out of her or she would die.

Once more she won the battle, got onto her feet, found the hatchet, whacked at the stalks and they fell. The terrible, continuous stabs which assailed her body made her fall, too, ovcr and over, but she always got up. The stalks couldn't get up. So she would win, had to win.

Reeling in a haze of anguish, she cut the stalks. She had to do it until the baby fell out of her, fell onto the cut stalks, fell so she could see what color it was. And it had to be soon, right away, or Deedee would come to check on her and all would be lost. On she staggered and plunged; on she sliced at the stalks.

Suddenly, without warning, a screaming woman crashed through the rows of corn and attacked, stabbing at her with a dagger which flashed in the sun. Tansey stumbled aside clumsily, hatchet instinctively up. The woman came at her again, screaming, and Tansey, one of those long, relentless stabs beginning, swung her hatchet at the twisted white face and missed.

Now, with birth-torture all through her, Tansey tried again with her cornstalk hatchet to hit the shrieking woman. The woman was mouthing vile words, stabbing for Tansey's belly, cutting Tansey's hip, drawing blood which soaked her shift.

Riven, Tansey reeled from side to side, away from the dagger, hatchet ready. A new, horrific convulsion joined onto the last and Tansey, herself screaming at long last, lunged at the woman and smashed down the hatchet, striking her broadside on the head. The woman fell.

Before Tansey could hit her again, the convulsions built, one upon another, and she continued to scream and almost fell. The woman sprang up, came at Tansey. With a desperate swing of the hatchet, Tansey caught the woman in the shoulder, cutting so deep the hatchet remained in the wound. At the same time, the woman slashed Tansey's nose away, then, as Tansey fell, cut her belly, drawing the dagger the length of it. A line of blood appeared, and the woman, shrieking in killer rage, raised the dagger to plunge it into Tansey's heart.

René, knowing that Tansey was going back to work in the corn, raced for Rivard at a dead run. As he pounded up to the cornpatch he saw people gathering, saw Ramona, arm upraised, dagger in hand, saw Tansey on the ground. He leapt, throwing himself onto his wife's back, gripping her dagger arm, and they both fell.

She tried to turn the dagger on him as they wrestled, but he twisted her arm until the bone snapped sharply, and she shrieked vile obscenities at him. He grabbed the dagger, threw it into the corn, grappled with her, brought them both to a standing position, and held her in iron grip.

She wept and screamed and swore. She struggled, but was no match for his strength. Her shoulder was bleeding, the hatchet fallen away, and he slapped his handkerchief onto the wound.

As René subdued Ramona, Tansey's screams continued, weaker now, Birdie at her side, Deedee there. The screams softened into moans. Beau, Riel, Olive, all of Rivard stood there now, drawn by the screams, staring, as the moans faded.

Silence fell, thickened. There was neither sound nor movement from Tansey.

Chapter XLIV

"She's dead!" Beau shouted. "The baby—get it out!"

But when Deedee moved, Beau pushed her aside and himself reached up into his dead wife, got a grip, slowly pulled the baby out, feet first.

Riel, his worst fears realized, stared in horror. The baby was light-skinned, a girl, and it wasn't breathing. He stood in the ashes of his life.

He swelled. He seemed to grow. He turned granitelike, for an instant, and then merciless rage filled him. All his life since he'd known he was Negro, he had striven to live truth, not to hide his black blood in white, but to use it to drown the white in the Rivards.

He'd been half-mad at times, getting Beau married black, waiting to see if Ben would be black. He was now, this moment, the man he'd been growing into all the years. He knew why he had led his life so. It sprang from his youthful love for Marie-Louise Leblanc, finding that she was his half-niece, finding that they were both partly black. That had motivated his Rivard dynasty, still motivated it.

He heard Deedee cry, "The baby! It must breathe!"

As in a fog, he saw Deedee take the baby by the heels, smack and smack it. He saw all the watchers beyond Tansey's bloody body, saw her stricken parents kneeling there.

He saw René Leblanc III, saw him look up from his wife's bleeding shoulder, heard her cursing him hoarsely, steadily, saying, "No court will convict me of murder! That black bitch died in childbirth! You can't make it any other way, René Leblanc!"

He noted that René didn't bother to tell her that Tansey had died from the dagger, that the Leblancs now had fresh scandal.

A thin wail rose from the newborn. Riel moved away from Olive, who had come to stand beside him, anxious, daring to put her hand on his arm.

He pulled free, took the crying infant from Deedee, clamped his great hand over its face, held it there. Some of the people moved to stop him, but he glared at them and they stopped, frozen. To Hercules and Birdie who moved toward him, he commanded fiercely, "Stay back!" And such was his cold, crazed authority that they did. In midstep they froze; horror stood on their faces.

When Riel lifted his hand, the child was dead. "This one was no Rivard," he grated. "There was no place for it here."

Silence filled the corn rows, the world. A bird trilled.

"Put the child with its mother, Birdie," Riel ordered in a terrible, quiet voice, and she did. "Cover them," he said, and some of the men who wore shirts took them off and did so. "Get up from there, Beau," he continued as his son, weeping, knelt beside the bodies. Slowly, Beau stood.

"You've got a son you know to be Rivard," Riel told him, that mad fierceness deepening, frightening all. He was like an avenging God. "Give him a stepmother, a virtuous black girl, within a year. It is your duty, your part in the Rivard dynasty."

Face wet, Beau gazed at his father, the master, terrifyingly changed now. At last, his eyes locked into Riel's, Beau answered, "I'll see to it, Pa."

"How can you do this, Riel?" Olive quavered. "You're white . . . the baby was part white . . . Felix . . . God help me, I'm white . . ."

Riel's eyes narrowed. Suddenly, tears filled his eyes. "Forgive me, Mama, but all white must go."

Riel stepped to Olive, chopped the side of his great hand down on her neck, caught her as she wilted and, tears streaming, laid her on the ground, dead.

It was Beau who found his voice. "Why did you do it, Pa? Why in the name of God did you do it? Your own mother!"

Riel, tears gone, pulled his calm, utterly sane look across all their faces, ending with Beau, Deedee, Ben. "To finish my work," he said. "Years ago, the madwoman of L'Acadie, Carita Leblanc, killed three blacks to purify her blood. Today I have removed three whites from the Rivard line. There is no white matriarch; there is no light-skinned baby; there will soon be no white master. Only Rivards are left. Black Rivards, truly black, pure black. As it was meant to be."

The frozen listeners waited, the last words of Riel, the master, seeping into them. And they knew that Riel, mad or not, had entrenched them. And that they must endure, according to his plan.

ABOUT THE AUTHOR

SALIEE O'BRIEN has been writing for as long as she can remember, and publishing stories since the age of fourteen. She was lured away, while in her twenties, by community theater and radio broadcasting; but they couldn't keep her from her first love—writing. Stories began appearing in a wide range of magazines: *Saturday Evening Post*, *Collier's* and *Blue Book*. Novels followed, and in abundance. They include *Farewell the Stranger*, *Too Swift the Tide*, *Heiress to Evil*, *Bayou*, *So Wild the Dream*, and *Black Ivory*. Cajun is her tenth novel. Ms. O'Brien is married and lives in Florida.